A HYMN BEFORE BATTLE

A HYMN BEFORE BATTLE

JOHN RINGO

A Baen Books Original

Baen Publishing Enterprises
P.O. Box 1403
Riverdale, NY 10471
www.baen.com

ISBN: 978-1-4814-8326-1

Cover art by Patrick Turner

First Baen trade paperback, May 2018

Distributed by Simon & Schuster
1230 Avenue of the Americas
New York, NY 10020

10 9 8 7 6 5 4 3 2 1

Pages by Joy Freeman (www.pagesbyjoy.com)
Printed in the United States of America

This book is dedicated to my loving wife, Karin,
and my wonderful daughters Jenny and Lindy,
for not leaving me while I wrote it.

Living with a writer is a lesser Circle of Hell.

PROLOGUE

"How many worlds does this make?" The dialogue took place before a wall-sized view-screen. The image was not one to make for happy conversation.

The aide knew the question was rhetorical. As the Ghin aged he was becoming soft, without direction. Yet powerful still.

"Seventy-two."

"Not including Barwhon or Diess."

"They have not yet fallen."

The answer was silence. Then,

"We will use the humans."

At last!

"Yes, your Ghin."

Silence, a glance at the view-screen.

"That makes you happy, does it not, Tir."

"I believe it to be a wise decision, as all of your decisions are wise, your Ghin."

"But slow to come, late. Without decisiveness, without, what is that human word? 'Élan.'"

The words of the aide's reply were carefully chosen. "Had the decision been reached sooner, there, perhaps, would have been greater profit. Certainly the loss would have been reduced."

A long minute later the answer: "The profit will be greater in the short run, surely. But at what loss in the long, Tir?"

"Surely the programs have taken effect. The humans are controllable."

"So thought the Rintar group."

1

"Those humans were half formed, brutish. They were unrefined and wild. The new races are much more malleable and well adjusted to technological controls. They are minimally dangerous and after the invasion the few that remain will be grateful for any bone we toss them."

Another long silence as the Ghin stared at the view-screen.

"Perhaps you are right, Tir. But I doubt it. Do you know why I am allowing the human project to go forward?"

"If you think the premise flawed, I wonder, yes."

Silence.

"Why?"

"Guess."

A pause, a breath, then a longer pause.

"Because we will lose many more worlds without their aid?"

"In small part. Tir, we will lose *all* the worlds without the humans."

"Your Ghin, our projections indicate that the Posleen will fail if slowed to their current rate, they will senesce. However, we stand to lose two hundred more worlds before that happens, surely an unacceptable loss."

"Those projections are flawed as our projections of the humans are flawed. At the end of this era the humans will be the masters and the Darhel will be an outcast race living on the edge of civilization scavenging the garbage. And your human project will be the cause."

The Tir carefully schooled his features. "I . . . question that projection, your Ghin."

"It isn't a projection, you young fool, it's a statement."

On the view-screen a world burned.

1

Norcross, GA Sol III
1447 EDT March 16, 2001 AD

Michael O'Neal was a junior associate web consultant with an Atlanta web-page design firm. What this meant in practice was that he worked eight to twelve hours a day with HTML, Java and Perl. When the associate account executives or the account executives needed somebody along who really understood what the system was doing, when, for example, the client group included an engineer or computer geek, he would be invited to the meeting to sit there and be quiet until they hit a snag. Then he opened his mouth to spit out a bare minimum of technobabble. This indicated to the customer that there was at least one guy working on their site who had more going for him than good hair and a low golf score. Then the sales consultant would take the client to lunch while Mike went back to his office.

While Mike had fine hair, he played neither golf nor tennis, was ugly as a troll and short as an elf. Despite these handicaps he was working himself steadily up the corporate ladder. He had recently gotten an unasked-for raise in lieu of promotion, which surprised the hell out of him, and other rattling noises had been heard that indicated the possibility of further upward mobility.

The office he moved into was not much; there was barely room to turn his swivel chair, it was right next to the break room so several times a day it was overwhelmed by the smell of popcorn, and he had to install a hanging book rack for his references. But it was an office, and in a time of cube farms that meant everything. Someone in the background was grooming

3

him for something and he just hoped it was not a guillotine. Unlikely—he was the kind of aggressive pain in the ass every company secretly needed.

He was currently in a mood to kill. The overblown applets on the newest client's site were slowing their page to a crawl. Unfortunately, the client insisted on the "little" pieces of code that were taking up so much of their bandwidth, so it was up to him to figure out how to reduce it.

He sat with his feet propped on his overloaded desk, gripping and releasing a torsional hand exerciser as he stared up at the *Tick* poster on his ceiling and thought about his next vacation. Two more weeks and then it would be blue surf, cold beer and coral reefs. *I should have gone SEAL,* he thought, his face fixed in a perpetual frown from weight lifting, *and become a surfing instructor. Sharon looks good in a bikini.*

He had just taken a sip of stale, cold coffee, thinking blue thoughts of Java surgery, when his phone rang.

"Michael O'Neal, Pre-Publish Design, how can I help you?" The phone snag and stock answer were performed before his forebrain kicked in. Then he nearly spit out his coffee when he recognized the voice.

"Hi, Mike, it's Jack."

His feet slammed to the floor with a crash and *XML for Dummies* followed it. "Good morning, sir, how are you?" He had not talked to his former boss in nearly two years.

"Good enough. Mike, I need you down at McPherson on Monday morning."

Whaaa? "Sir, it's been eight years. I'm not in the Army market anymore." By nearly Pavlovian response, he started to catalog everything he would need to take.

"I just got finished talking to your company's president. This is not, currently, an official recall..."

I like that little hidden threat, boss, Mike thought.

"But I pointed out that whether it was or not, you would be eligible to return under the Soldiers and Sailors Act..."

Yup, that's Jack. Thanks a million, ole boss o' mine.

"That didn't seem to be a problem. He seemed to be kind of upset at losing you right now. Apparently they just got a new contract he really wanted you to work on..."

Yes! Mike chortled silently. *We got the First Onion upgrade!*

The site was a plum job the company had been chasing for nearly a year. The account would guarantee at least a solid two years of lucrative business.

"But I convinced him it would be for the best," the general continued. Mike could hear other conversations in the background, some argumentative, some subdued. It seemed almost like the general was calling from a telephone solicitation company. Or several of his cohorts were making the same calls. Some of the muted voices in the background seemed almost desperate.

"What's this about, sir?"

The answer was met by silence. In the background a male voice started shouting, apparently displeased with the answer he was getting on his own call.

"Let me guess, OPSEC?" Any answer to the question would violate operational security directives. Mike scratched at a spot of ink on the varnished desktop then started working the gripper again. *Blood pressure . . .* It was security and dominance games like this that had partially driven him away from the military. He had no intention of being sucked back in.

"Be there, Mike. The SigInt building attached to FORCECOM."

"Airborne, General, sir." He paused for a moment, then continued dryly. "Sharon is going to go ballistic."

Mike was cleaning broccoli when he heard the car pull up. He wiped his hands and opened the door to the carport so the kids could get in, waved and went back to the sink.

Cally, the four-year-old, made it through the door first and got a big, wet hug from daddy.

"Daddy! You got me all wet!"

"Big, wet daddy hugs! Arrrh!" He gestured at her with soapy hands as she went shrieking towards her room.

In the meantime Michelle, the two-year-old, had toddled in and handed him her latest creation from preschool. She got a big, wet daddy hug, too.

"And what is this masterpiece?" He looked at the scrawl of green, blue and red and flashed a quick helpless glance at his wife, just coming through the door.

"Cow!" she mouthed.

"Well, Michelle, that's a very nice cow!"

"Mooo!"

"Yes, mooo!"

"Juice!"

"Okay, can my big girl say please?" Mike asked with a smile, already headed for the refrigerator.

"P'ease," she answered, mildly.

"Okay," he reached into the fridge and extracted the cup. "No spill."

"Mess!" she countered, clutching the no-spill cup to her chest.

"No mess."

She carried the cup into the living room for her afternoon video. "Pooh!"

"Cinderella!"

"'Rella!"

He heard the video player start, courtesy of the older girl as his wife walked back into the kitchen after a quick change. Slim and tall with long raven black hair and high, firm breasts, even after two pregnancies she still moved with the grace of the dancer she was when they first met. She'd joined the club he worked at to improve her muscle tone. He was the best in the club at muscle management schemes so he got assigned to her, naturally. One thing led to another and here they were eight years later. Sometimes Mike wondered what kept her around. On the other hand it would take a crowbar to separate him from her. Or, at least, the hand of duty.

"Your agent called me at work," she said, "he said you weren't in."

"Oh?" he said, noncommittally he hoped. His stomach had already started to churn. He pulled a bottle of domestic Chardonnay out of the refrigerator and began hunting for the corkscrew.

"He says he needs another rewrite, but Dunn may be interested." She leaned back against the counter, watching him carefully. He was giving off all the wrong vibes.

"Oh. Good."

"You're home early," she continued, crossing her arms. "What's wrong? You should be excited."

"Umm." He bought time by wrenching out the cork and pouring her a glass of wine.

"What?" She looked at the Chardonnay suspiciously, as if wondering if it were poisoned. After six years of marriage there was not much he could get past her. She might not know exactly what was coming, but she could tell it was nasty.

"Uh. It's not bad, really," he said, taking a pull of his own beer.

The mellow home-brewed concoction dropped to his stomach like lead and started doing dances with the butterflies. Sharon was really going to hit the roof.

"Oh, shit, just spit it out," she snapped. "What, did you get fired?"

"*No*, no, I got called back up. Sort of." He turned back to the stove, picking up the pot and dumping the al dente pasta into the colander.

"What? By the Army? You've been out, what? Eight years?" The words were low but angry. They tried to never argue in front of the kids.

"Almost nine," he agreed, head down and concentrating on getting the pasta just right. The smell of garlic permeated the air as he tossed the crushed cloves into the mix. "I'd been out nearly six months when we met."

"You're not reserve anymore!" She reached out and touched his arm to get him to turn around and look at her.

"I know, but Jack called Dave and twisted his arm into letting me go for a while." He looked up into her blue eyes and wondered why he could not tell Jack, "No." The hurt in her gaze was almost more than he could bear.

"Jack. You mean General Horner. The 'Jack' who wanted you to get a commission?" she asked with dark suspicion, setting the wine down. It was her way of clearing the decks and he took it for a bad sign.

"How many Jacks do you know?" he asked playfully, trying to lighten the mood.

"I don't know him—you know him." She had moved in close to him, crowding his space and more or less making him back up.

"You've talked to General Horner before." He turned back to the pasta, running from the argument and he knew it.

"Once, and it was until you got to the phone."

"Mmm."

"And why the hell do they want you?" she asked, still crowding in. He could faintly feel the heat from her body, raised by a combination of the wine and the argument.

"I don't know." The fettuccine ready, he added the Alfredo sauce, covered and warming on the stove top. The heady smell of parmesan and spices filled the air.

"Well, call General Horner and tell him you're not coming until we know why. And fettuccine Alfredo will not get you out of anything." She crossed her arms again, then relented and picked up the wine for a sip.

"Honey, you know the drill. When they call, you go." He portioned out the kids' supper, readying trays for them to eat in front of the TV. Normally they tried to eat together, but tonight seemed like a good night to create a little distance from them.

"No. Not with me," she retorted, gesturing sharply enough to slosh the Chardonnay. "Not that anybody has asked, but they'd get a little more argument if they tried to get me back in the Navy. The hell if I'm ever serving on another carrier." She tossed her head to move an imaginary hair out of the way and waited for a response.

"Well, I guess I don't know what to say," he said softly.

She looked at him for a long moment. "You want to go back." It was clearly an accusation. "You know, I'm going to have a hell of a time keeping up with both work and home if you're gone!"

"Well..." The pause after that looked to go on forever.

"God, Mike, it's been years! It's not like you're eighteen anymore." With her mouth pursed into a frown, she looked like a little girl "saving up spit."

"Honey," he said, rubbing his chin and looking at the ceiling, "generals don't recall you from civilian status, personally, to go run around in the boonies." He dropped his eyes to meet hers and shook his head.

"Whatever it is, they'll want me for my know-how, not my biceps. And sometimes, yeah, I wonder if being, maybe, by now, a company commander in the Eighty-Deuce wouldn't be a little more...important, useful, I don't know, something more than building a really boss web page for the country's fourth largest bank!" He garnished the generous helping of fettuccine with a chicken breast in garlic and herbs and extended it to her.

She shook her head, understanding the argument intellectually, but still not happy. "Do you have to leave this evening?"

She took the plate and looked at it with the same suspicion as the wine. A little alcohol and complex carbohydrates to calm the hysterical wifey. Unfortunately she knew that was exactly how she was acting. He knew all about her knee-jerk reaction to the military and was trying to compensate. Trying hard.

"No, I have to be at McPherson on Monday morning. And that's the other thing, I'm just going to McPherson. It's not like it's the back side of the moon." He picked up a rag and wiped away an imaginary smear on the gray countertop. He could see the light at the end of the tunnel, but with Sharon on the warpath it could just as well be a train.

"No, but if you think I'm taking the kids to south Atlanta you're out of your mind," she retorted, losing ground and knowing it. She sensed that this was a critical argument and wondered what would happen if she said it was her or the Army. She had thought about it a few times before, but it had never come up. Now she was afraid to ask. What really made her mad was that she understood her emotions and knew she was in the wrong. Her own experiences had poisoned her against the military as a career, but not against the basic call to duty. And it made her wonder what would happen if she faced the same question.

"Hey, I may be commuting. And it may not be for long," Mike said with a purely Gallic shrug and rubbed his chin. His dark, coarse hair had raised a respectable five-o'clock shadow.

"But you don't think so," she countered.

"No, I don't think so," he agreed, somberly.

"Why?" She sat down at the kitchen table and cut a bite of the chicken. It was perfectly done; delicious as usual. It tasted like sand in her mouth.

"Well...just say it's a gut call." Mike began to fill his own plate. He suspected *poulet avec herb* was going to be lacking in his diet in the near future.

"But we have the weekend?" she asked taking a sip of the oaky Chardonnay to wash down the wonderful meal in a mouth gone quite dry.

"Yes."

"Well, let's see what we can think of to do." The smile was weak, but at least it was a smile.

"Can I see some ID, sir? Driver's license?"

I got up pretty damn early for this crap. Three hours driving separated his home in the Georgia Piedmont from Fort McPherson, Georgia, home of the Army's Forces Command. Perched just off of Interstate 75-85, the green lawns and numerous brick structures hid a mass of secure buildings. Since it commanded all the combat forces in the Army its secure meeting facilities were top-notch but the press hardly noticed it. If a large number of military and civilian personnel suddenly congregated in Fort Myers, Virginia, or Nellis AFB it would be noticed; places like that were carefully watched but not Fort McPherson. Serviced by Hartsfield Airport, the largest in the United States, and covered by Atlanta's notorious traffic, the only people who noticed the gathering were the carefully selected soldiers acting as military police. But, while the soldiers had been carefully selected, they had not been selected from the ranks of MPs.

"Thank you, sir," said the somber gate guard after a thorough study of Mike's driver's license and face. "Take the main road to a 'T' intersection. Turn right. Follow that road to Forces Command; it is a gray concrete building with a sign. Go past the main building to the guard shack on the left. Turn in there and follow the MP's direction."

"Thank you," said Mike, dropping the Beetle into gear and taking the proffered ID.

"Not at all," the guard said to the already moving Beetle. "Have a nice day." The Delta Force commando in an MP uniform picked up a recently installed secure phone. "O'Neal, Michael A., 216-29-1145, 0657. Special attention Lieutenant General John Horner." For a moment the sergeant first class wondered what all the fuss was about, why he was wearing rank three grades inferior to his real one. Then he stopped wondering. The ability to quell curiosity was a desirable trait in a long-term Delta. *Damn*, he thought, *that guy looked just like a fireplug*, then dismissed him from memory as the next civilian car pulled up.

"I'd forgotten how much he looks like a fireplug." Lieutenant General John J. (Jumpin' Jack) Horner murmured to himself, standing at a comfortable parade rest as the Volkswagen puttered into a parking place. Over six feet tall and almost painfully handsome, the general's appearance was the epitome of a senior military officer.

Slim and hard looking, stern of mien, the only time he smiled was just before he pulled the rug out from under an incompetent junior officer. Erect of carriage, his Battle Dress Uniform fit as if, contrary to regulation, it was tailored. With closely cropped, silver hair and glacial blue eyes he appeared to be exactly what he was: an iron-clad modern scion of the Prussian warrior class. Were he wearing a greatcoat and jackboots he would slip unnoticed into the WWII Wehrmacht Oberkommando.

His twenty-seven-year career had been spent exclusively in airborne infantry and special operations. Despite having never attained a keystone desire, command of the Ranger regiment, he was undoubtedly *the* world class expert in infantry tactics and doctrine. Furthermore, besides being an excellent theoretician and staff officer, he was considered a superlative commander, a leader of men in the old mold. In his career he had come across many characters, but few matched the squat juggernaut rolling across the emerald grass towards him. Horner laughed internally, remembering the first time he met the former NCO.

December 1989. The weather conformed to official standards for a North Carolina winter and Fort Bragg, Home of the Airborne, had been under sullen rain and sleet-swollen clouds for a week. With the exception of the weather, and it had its good points, Lieutenant Colonel Horner was pleased with his first ARTEP as a battalion commander. The units he and his sergeant major had grilled mercilessly for three long months had just performed flawlessly despite the environment, whereas the year before, under the previous commander, they brutally flunked the same Armed Readiness Testing and Evaluation Program test. Even with the rain it appeared that God was in his heaven and all was right with the world right up until his jeep suffered a sudden and spectacular blowout.

Even this was no obstacle. Jeeps come with a spare tire; the driver's rucksack was hanging from it, containing tools to handle just such an eventuality. But when his driver confessed that he had neglected to pack those self-same tools, Lieutenant Colonel Horner instantly smiled. It was a very Russian smile; it did not reach the eyes.

"No tools?" asked the colonel tightly.

"No, sir." The specialist swallowed, his prominent Adam's-apple bobbing up and down.

"No jack."

"No, sir."

"Sarn't Major?" snapped the colonel.

The sergeant major, not having anywhere he was supposed to be and snug in his camouflage Gore-Tex rain-suit, was deriving some humor from the situation. "Shall I draw and quarter him, sir?" he asked, tucking his hands into his armpits and preparing for a long wait in the sleet. He hoped like hell it would start to snow; there would be less of a chance of hypothermia.

"Actually, I'm prepared to entertain suggestions," said the colonel, holding on to his temper by a thread.

"Other than the obvious, sir, call the CONTAC team?" A grin split his ebony face at the commander's discomfiture. Jack was the best battalion commander he had ever met, but it was always fun to watch him handle minor problems. The colonel hated dealing with little shit like this. It was like he was born a general and was just waiting until he had an aide-de-camp to handle drivers and their failings.

"Other than getting on the net and admitting that my driver is an idiot by calling a recovery team for a simple flat. Reynolds," he said, turning to the specialist fourth class, standing at attention in the drizzling sleet, "I would love to know what the hell you were thinking."

"Sir, we have the operational readiness survey coming up," said the specialist, desperately wishing his internal processes would just stop or a hole would open up and swallow him.

"Uh huh, go on. Feel free to use more than one sentence," said the colonel.

"I think I know where this is going," chuckled the sergeant major.

Taking a deep breath the quivering specialist continued. "Well, the PLL kit is only good for minor shit like changing a tire..."

"Like now!" the colonel snapped.

"Yes, sir," the specialist continued, doggedly, "and when the vehicle is good the tires rarely go bad. And this is a good jeep, that's a new damn tire! But at ORS the inspectors know that the commanders' vehicles get first dibs so they really go over 'em with a fine comb. And if they can't find something major they look for little shit like chipped paint on your jack and stuff. So, I got the maintenance chief to swap me for a new set of PLL and since I didn't want it to get fucked up..."

"Knew it!" laughed the NCO. "God, I hate that trick. Next time, Reynolds, get *two* sets of PLL and keep one in your locker!"

"Reynolds." The colonel forced himself to pause. Ripping the head off the idiot would solve nothing. One of the reasons he was so angry was his own sense of failure for not replacing this particular weak link before ARTEP.

"Yes, sir?"

"You are almost remarkably lacking in sense." Horner looked at the heavens, as if seeking guidance.

"Yes, sir."

"I ought to send you to the Post Protocol office as a permanent driver," said the colonel, returning to the situation.

"Yes, sir."

"It is not a compliment," said the officer, smiling like a tiger.

"No, sir. Airborne, sir." Reynolds knew that when the colonel smiled like that you were totally screwed. *Scouts,* he thought, *here I come.*

"Sergeant Major Eady?"

"Alpha weapons." While the discussion had gone on, the sergeant major had pulled out and consulted a tactical dispositions map. The sleet turning to rain pooled and dripped on the acetate cover, occasionally requiring a shake to clear the view. By evening it was sure to snow. The sergeant major decided he wanted to be back at the Tactical Operations Center by then; all his comfort gear was there.

"Where?" snapped the colonel, stalking over to his own seat.

"South to the next firebreak, which should be on the left about two hundred meters, around the bend, then about a hundred fifty, two hundred. Clearing on the right. If I remember correctly, there's a lightning-struck pine at the edge of the clearing along the road." The NCO had been driving these roads before the specialist was a gleam in his daddy's eye.

"Reynolds," growled the colonel, throwing himself into the seat of the open jeep and propping his foot on the mud-splashed shovel lashed to the side.

"Sir."

"I assume you can run four hundred meters in your field gear." The colonel assumed the same position as the sergeant major in the back, gloved hands thrust into armpits, body slightly crouched to reduce surface area. The position of an experienced and heartily pissed infantry officer preparing for a long wait in the cold rain and sleet.

"Airborne, sir!" The specialist snapped to attention, happy to have somewhere to go out of the glacial gaze of his commander.

"Go."

The embarrassed spec-four took off like a gazelle. The icy red mud splashed for yards in every direction with each stride.

"Sergeant Major," said the colonel, conversationally, as the figure disappeared around the first bend.

"Yes, sir!" snapped the sergeant major, coming to attention in his seat, but not removing his hands from his armpits.

"Sarcasm?" asked the colonel, tightly.

"Sarcasm? Me, sir? Never," he said, leaning back in his seat. Then he held up his right hand with forefinger and thumb slightly separated. A pea might have fit between the two. "Maybe, maybe, just a bit. A bit." As he said it, his fingers separated until they were at maximum extension. "A bit."

"I have been meaning to talk to you about getting a new driver..." said the colonel, letting some of his tension go. The situation was just too stupid and petty to get really angry about.

"Oh? Really?" The sergeant major chuckled.

"It's not so much the fact that he is so damn stupid," the colonel continued, resignedly. The Smaj would have his little laugh. "It's that when he's not arrogant, he's obsequious."

"Well, Colonel," said the NCO, taking off his Kevlar helmet and scratching his head. A flurry of dandruff drifted off in the cold wind. Basic personal hygiene complete, he took care settling the helmet on his head and getting all the straps back in place. The chinstrap was greasy against his chin, the well-worn canvas soaked with skin oils after the long field problem. "The sergeant major is only an enlisted man and we're not cleared to know what obsequious means. But if you mean he's a little ass-kisser, that's why he got the job in the first place. That and he's a hell of a runner; Colonel Wasserman was big on running." The ebony Buddha, a noted runner himself, smiled contentedly. From his point of view this was the last item that needed major repair in the whole battalion.

"Colonel Wasserman came within a hair's breadth of being relieved for cause and is currently headed for the street," snorted the colonel. He and the sergeant major had tried to bring the soldier up to the standard that they expected but it just had not happened. Reynolds just seemed to be one of those soldiers best suited for the "Old Guard." He looked great during inspections, but just could not get his head out of his ass when it came to combat training. Horner sighed in resignation, realizing that there were some situations that training would not solve.

"In general I use the following criteria," he continued. "If Colonel Wasserman thought it was a great idea, I try to go in the exact opposite direction. In a way it's too bad I can't follow him through the rest of my career, it's like a guiding light. Move

Reynolds out gracefully. Give him a nice letter, your signature, not mine, and send him back to Charlie company. Find a good replacement. God help us if we had to go to war with this bozo."

There was a period of silence as the two leaders listened to the falling precipitation. It seemed to have settled for sleet, but there were occasional flurries of snow and still a little freezing rain. In the distance there was a rumble of artillery from the Corp artillery having its bi-yearly live fire bash. Weather like this was good training for the cannon-cockers. Good training was an army euphemism for any situation that was miserable and, preferably, screwed up. Their present predicament met all the requirements for "good training."

"Where the hell is the jeep?" asked the colonel, resignation echoing in every tone.

Coming down the road was a sight that would have been comical in other circumstances. Reynolds was tall and slender. Walking with him, carrying a gigantic overstuffed rucksack, was a short—Horner later learned he was five feet two inches tall—incredibly wide soldier. He looked like some camouflage-covered troll or hobgoblin. His oversized "Fritz" helmet and, when he got near enough to see, equally oversized nose completed the picture. Under one arm he carried a large chunk of pine, easily weighing seventy or eighty pounds and his face bore a deep frown. He looked far more annoyed than the colonel or sergeant major.

"Specialist, hmm, O'Neal, one of the mortar squad leaders," the sergeant major whispered as they approached. He climbed out of the jeep and the colonel followed, getting ready to deliver a world-class ass chewing, Horner style.

"Sir," said Reynolds, continuing his saga of despair, "when I arrived at the weapons platoon, I found all the vehicles were gone to refuel…" As he spoke O'Neal walked to the rear of the jeep without a word or a greeting to the senior officer or NCO. There he dropped the log and his pack and grasped the bumper. He squatted, then straightened, lifting the corner of the thousand-pound jeep into the air with an exhalation.

"Yeah, we can do this," he said with a grunt and tossed the jeep back into the mud. It bounced on its springs and splattered Reynolds with more of the cold glutinous clay. O'Neal's actions had effectively shut off the flow from Reynolds. "Good afternoon, sir, sergeant major," O'Neal said. He did not salute.

Despite standing division orders to do so, the 82nd continued the tradition of considering a salute in the field a "sniper check" and thus a bad thing to train for.

The sergeant major stuck out his hand. "Howarya, O'Neal." He was astounded at the return grip strength. He had dealt with O'Neal peripherally but had never appreciated the specialist's almost preternatural condition. The baggy BDUs apparently hid a body made of pure muscle.

"Specialist," said the colonel, sternly, "that was not a good idea. Let's try to think safe, okay? Rupturing a gut would just make a bad situation worse." He cocked his head to the side like a blue-eyed falcon, pinning the soldier with his most arctic stare.

"Yes, sir, I guessed you would say that," said the specialist, the officer's stare bouncing off him like rain off steel. He worked a bit of dip over to one side and spit carefully. "Sir, with all due respect," he drawled, "I work out with this much weight every damn day. I've lifted the gun jeeps before for exercise, I even clean jerked one, once. I just wanted to make sure the extra radios didn't make it too heavy. We can do this. I lift it, the sergeant major slides the log underneath, we change the tire, reverse the procedure and you're outta here."

The colonel peered down at the specialist for a moment. The specialist looked back up with a matching scowl, the bit of dip bulging his lower lip. The colonel's scowl deepened for a moment, a sure sign of amusement. He carefully did not ask why the sergeant major was sliding the log under the jeep instead of the driver. Apparently O'Neal had the same opinion of Reynolds that he and the sergeant major did.

"You have a first name, O'Neal?" asked the colonel.

"Michael, sir," stated the specialist. He moved the dip to the other side. Other than that his expression of terminal annoyance did not flicker.

"Michael or Mike?" asked the colonel with a deepening scowl.

"Mike, sir."

"Nickname?"

Reluctantly, "Mighty Mite."

As the sergeant major chuckled the colonel scowled fiercely, "Well, Specialist O'Neal, I reluctantly approve this procedure."

"How're we gonna break the bolts?" asked the sergeant major. That had been wearing on his mind more than lifting the jeep.

There were plenty of things to use for levers if necessary but not a lug wrench to be seen.

Specialist O'Neal reached into his cargo pocket and with a flourish withdrew a crescent wrench all of eight inches long.

"Good luck," snorted Reynolds, "they got put on at Brigade with an impact wrench."

A smile violated the frown on O'Neal's face for a moment. He knelt in the mud, cold water seeping into the fabric of his BDUs, adjusted the wrench and applied it to the nut. He drew a deep breath and let it out with a "Saaa!" His arm drove forward like a mechanical press and, with a shriek of stressed steel, the nut loosened.

"Craftsman," he said, relaxing and letting the rest of the breath out slowly, "when you care enough to use the very best." He spit another bit of dip out, deftly spun the nut loose and started on the next.

The colonel scowled, but there was a twinkle in his normally cold azure eyes. He turned to be unobserved and gave the sergeant major a wink. They had found their new driver.

"Howarya, Mike?" General Horner asked, as the approaching figure brought him back from memory lane. He extended his hand.

Mike shifted the cedar box under his arm and took the outstretched hand. "Fine, sir, fine. How are the wife and kids?"

"Fine, just fine. You wouldn't believe how the kids have grown. How're Sharon and the girls?" he asked. He noticed in passing that the former soldier had lost none of his musculature. The handshake was like shaking a well-adjusted industrial vise. If anything the former NCO had put on bulk; he moved like a miniature tank. Horner wondered if the soldier would be able to retain that level of physique given the demands that would shortly be placed upon him.

"Well, the girls are okay," said O'Neal, then grimaced. "Sharon's not particularly happy."

"I knew this would be hard on both of you," said the general, smiling slightly, "and I thought about it before I called you. If it wasn't important I wouldn't have asked."

"I thought generals had aides to meet low-level flunkies like me," said Mike, deliberately changing the subject.

"Generals have aides to meet much higher level flunkies than you." Jack frowned, taking the opportunity to leave it behind.

"Well the heck with you then." Mike laughed, handing the officer the box of cigars. "See if I cough up any more Ramars."

Even while on active duty, Specialist O'Neal and then-Lieutenant Colonel Horner had developed a close relationship. The colonel often treated Mike more like an aide-de-camp than a driver. The specialist, and later sergeant, was invited to eat with the colonel's family and Horner explained many of the customs of the service and functions in the staff that would normally remain a mystery to a lowly enlisted man. Mike in turn increased the colonel's computer literacy and introduced him to science fiction. The colonel took to it surprisingly well, considering that he had never read it before. Mike took great care, however, in the subject matter, starting with the great modern combat science fiction writers to pique his interest.

After Mike left the service they continued to correspond and Mike followed Jack Horner's career. They had lost touch in the last three years, mainly because of a disagreement over Mike's career. After Mike completed college, Horner fully expected him to take a commission, and Mike wanted to work in web design and theory, while writing on the side. The colonel could not accept Mike's reasoning and Mike could not accept Jack's inability to take "no" for an answer.

Mike sometimes felt that a career in the Army might have made more sense than civvie street, but he had seen too many officers' lives strained to the breaking point by the demands of the service. When his time to reenlist came he got out instead and went to college. The pressure to take a commission, especially during the tough years when he was just getting started and after Cally came along had been hard on him and hard on his marriage. He had never told Jack but the implicit blackmail was what had caused Mike to sever their relationship.

Sharon had experienced the problems that he only witnessed. Her first marriage to a naval aviator had ended in divorce, so she had no intention of letting Mike go back into the service. His brooding on the severance from Jack, in many ways like that of a son from a father, had distracted him from a discordant note: Jack's rank.

"*Lieutenant* general?" asked Mike in surprise. The morning sun glittered on the five-pointed stars of the new rank. The last Mike had heard, Horner was on the list for major general. Three-star rank should not have come for another few years.

"Well, 'when you care enough...'"

O'Neal smiled at the reference. "What?" He retorted. "Given your well-known resemblance to Friedrich von Paulus, they decided major general wasn't good enough for you?"

"I was a major general until four days ago, Chief of Staff at the Eighteenth Airborne Corps—"

"ADC-O. Congratulations."

"—when I got yanked out for this."

"Isn't that kind of fast to get 'the advice and consent of the Senate'?"

"It's a brevet rank," said the officer, impatiently, "but I have it on excellent authority it will be confirmed." He frowned at some private joke.

"I didn't think you could frock—" Mike started to say.

"That'll have to wait, Mike." The general cut him off, smiling slightly. "We have to get you briefed in and that will take a secure room."

Mike suddenly saw a familiar face that made him sure the conference was about science fiction. Across the lawn, surrounded by a sea of Navy black, was a prominent writer who specialized in naval combat.

"Can you give me just a minute, sir? I want to talk to David," he said pointing.

General Horner looked over his shoulder, then turned back. "They're probably taking him in for the same conversation; you two can talk after the meeting. We have a lot of ground to cover before then, and it starts at nine." He put an arm around Mike's shoulders. "Come on, Mighty Mite, time to face the cannon."

The secure conference room was windowless but it was probably on the exterior of the building; there was noticeable heat radiating from one wall. Another wall sported a painting of an Abrams tank cresting a berm, cannon spouting fire; the title was "Seventy-Three Easting." Other than that the room was unadorned: not a plant, not a painting, not a scrap of paper. It smelled of dust and old secrets. Mike ended his perusal by grabbing one of the blue swivel chairs and relaxing as General Horner settled across from him. As the door swung shut, the general smiled, broadly. It gave him a strong resemblance to an angry tiger.

Mike's scowl deepened. "It's that bad?" Horner only smiled

like that when the fecal matter had well and truly hit the fan. The last time O'Neal had seen that smile was the beginning of a very unpleasant experience. It suddenly made him sorry he had given up tobacco.

"Worse," said the general. "Mike, this is not for dissemination, whether you choose to stay or not. I need your word on that right now." He leaned back in his swivel chair, affecting a relaxed posture but with tension screaming in every line.

"Okay," said Mike and leaned forward. It suddenly seemed like a perfect time to reacquire a habit. He opened his recent gift to the general and extracted a cigar without asking.

Horner leaned forward in his chair and lit the cigar at the former NCO's lifted eyebrow. Then he leaned back and continued the briefing.

"You and about every other son of a bitch who's ever worn a uniform is about to be recalled." The smile never left his face and there was now a hint of teeth to it.

Mike was so stunned he forgot to draw on the cigar. He felt his stomach lurch and broke out in a cold sweat. "What the hell's happening? Did we go to war with China or something?" He started to draw on the flame but the combination of surprise and trying to light a cigar caused him to choke. He put the cigar down in frustration and leaned forward.

"I can't get into why until the meeting," said the general, putting away his lighter. "But, right now, I've got a blank check. I can bring you in on a direct commission..."

"Is this about that again? I—" Mike leaned back and almost started to rise. The statement could not have been more inflammatory given their previous arguments.

"Hear me out, dammit. You can come back, now, as an officer, and make a difference working with me or in a few months you'll be called back anyway as just another mortar sergeant." The general extracted his own Honduran from the box and lit it expertly, in direct defiance of the building's no-smoking regulation. They had both learned the hard way, and in many ways together, when to pay attention to the niceties and when the little stuff went out the window.

"Jesus, sir, you just sprang this on me." Mike's normal frown had deepened to the point it seemed it would split his face as his jaw muscles clenched and released. "I've got a life, you know?

What about my family, my wife? Sharon is going to go absolutely ballistic!"

"I checked. Sharon's a former naval officer, she'll get called up, too." The silver-haired officer leaned back and watched his former and hopefully future subordinate's reaction through the fragrant smoke.

"Jesus Christ on a crutch, Jack!" Mike shouted, throwing up his hands in frustration. "What about Michelle and Cally? Who takes care of them?"

"That is what one of the teams at this conference will be working on," said Horner, waiting for the inevitable reaction to subside.

"Can Sharon and I get stationed together?" asked Mike. He motioned for and caught the tossed lighter and relit the Ramar. For the first time in three years he took a deep draw on a cigar and let the nicotine bleed some of the tension off. Then he blew out an angry stream of smoke.

"Probably not. . . . I don't know. None of that has been worked out, yet. Everything is on its ear right now and that's what this conference is about: straightening everything out." Horner looked around for a moment then made an ashtray out of a sheet of paper. He flicked his developing ash into it and set it in the middle of the conference table.

"What gives? I know, you can't tell me, right? OPSEC?" Mike studied the glowing end of his cigar then took another draw.

"I can't and I won't play twenty questions." General Horner stabbed the conference table with a finger and pinned his former subordinate with a glare. "Here's the deal," he continued, blowing out another fragrant cloud. The room had rapidly filled with cigar smoke. "This conference will last three days. I can hold you as a tech rep, for a really stupid amount of money, for the conference, maybe a week. But that is only if you agree to take a commission now. Further, we'll be locked in for quite a while afterwards, maybe a couple of months and any communications with home will be monitored and censored. . . ."

"Hold it, you also didn't say anything about a goddamn lock-in!" Mike snapped, his face stony.

"Debate is not allowed about the lock-in so don't even go there, it's been ordered by the President. Or you can go home and in a few months get orders to report to Benning as a sergeant."

Jack leaned back and softened his tone. "But if you come on board now Sharon will get the tech rep check in a week—I can disburse it out of Team funds—and after that you'll be making O-2's salary and benefits including medical and housing, and so on." Jack cocked his head and waited for an answer.

"Sir, look, I'm working on a career here...." Mike twiddled the cigar and contemplated the top of the conference table. He found himself unable to meet Horner's gaze.

"Mike, do not kick me in the teeth. I would not have requested you if you were stupid. I will make this as plain as I can within the limits of my orders: I need you on my team." He stabbed the table again. "Not to put too fine a point on it, your country needs you. Not writing science fiction or making web pages, but doing science fiction. Our kind."

"Doing...?" Then it hit him. The other writer specialized in naval sagas. *Space* naval sagas, not "wet" navy.

Mike closed his eyes. When he opened them he was staring into a set of blue eyes as cold as the deep between the stars.

> The earth is full of anger,
> The seas are dark with wrath,
> The nations in their harness
> Go up against our path:
> Ere yet we loose the legions—
> Ere yet we draw the blade,
> Jehovah of the Thunders,
> Lord God of Battles, aid!
> —Kipling

2

Ft. Bragg, NC Sol III
0911 EDT March 16th, 2001 AD

The secure phone on the broad wooden desk of the commander, Joint Special Operations Command, buzzed and he tossed the file he was annotating onto the pile of similar documents.

"JSOC—" pronounced Jay-Sock "—General Taylor." The room was tastefully decorated with an impressive "I love me" wall of battle decorations, paintings of notable battles and commission photographs. The carpeting was deep, rich blue and the wallpaper was matching but the view was pure walls. The room resided deep within a featureless concrete building, one of several, at Fort Bragg, North Carolina.

Joint Special Operations Command was founded out of disaster. During the Tehran Hostage Crisis, the inability of the services to coordinate was critical in the debacle at Desert One. Special operations require depths of coordination and training that the regular services could not supply. As just one example, the forecasters for Desert One were not told precisely where the flights would go and, therefore, could not warn the planners about the dust storms the helicopters encountered. The Marine pilots, while capable and valiant to a normal level, were under-trained for a mission of that intensity, leading to the "pilot error" crashes at the site and other failures.

These critical failures of communication, intelligence and training, the cornerstones of any military, crystallized a movement to centralize the various services' special operations groups under one umbrella organization. Joint Special Operations was

23

the child of that movement. It was from JSOC that such high-quality actions as the Special Forces and Ranger raids in Panama, the Force Recon insertion into Baghdad and the SEAL diversion during the assault in Desert Storm drew their planning and implementation.

Now, the Joint Special Operations Command was a mature unit, ready to provide the right forces at the right time for special operations anywhere on the globe. But they were about to be tasked for a mission outside those parameters.

"General Taylor, it's Trayner," said the cold voice on the phone.

"And what can JSOC do for the Vice Chief of Staff today?" asked General Taylor, leaning back and staring unseeing at the picture on the far wall: a line of blue-clad soldiers charging out of a mist against a similar line of soldiers clad in gray.

"It's an awkward tasking," said the VCA. "I need one of your people. I'm going to give you the specifications and you tell me who I need. Also, this should be obvious since I'm stepping all over procedure, this is as 'black' as it gets. Are we clear on that?" "Black" operations are so secret sometimes they never happened. There are no records and no reports, only results. Politicians, even presidents, hate black operations.

"*Capice*, sir," the commander replied, wondering what the fuss was. This was SOCOM's meat and drink. "What are the specifications for this oh-so-special individual?" he asked. He picked up a letter opener off his desk and started to balance it on the tip of his index finger.

"NCO or officer," continued the VCA, "to put together a team, mono-service or joint, for unspecified reconnaissance in hostile territory and environment outside the continental United States."

Taylor scratched the back of his neck and changed his stare to the picture of a tropical beach on his desk. A much younger, bronzed Taylor had his arm around the waist of a skinny laughing blonde. He appeared to be trying to cop a feel. "That's pretty damn vague General, except the 'hostile' part." He flipped the letter opener in the air. It landed point down in a cork target just to the left of his monitor, obviously placed there for that very reason. He paid it no attention, assuming the letter opener knew where it was going.

"Don't fish, Jim," snapped the VCA. "This is as black as midnight; that's straight from National Command Authority, the

President. It wasn't even from the SECDEF or SECARMY, they're out of the loop. I was given this tasking personally by the NCA."

"Jesus, this is deep shit," snorted Taylor. He thought for a moment then laughed, "Okay. Mosovich."

"Shit, I knew you'd say that," the other general growled. "The sergeant major'll shit a brick."

"He's your sergeant major, not mine," Taylor laughed again. "You want black reconnaissance in hostile territory, Mosovich is the Man. I notice you don't suggest Bobby-boy," General Taylor continued smugly.

"He hates to be called that," said the VCA, resignedly. It was an old and worn argument. "Okay, okay, put him TDY to my office. Tell 'im to sneak by the sergeant major if he's so damn stealthy." The phone clicked in Taylor's ear.

"You wanted to see me, General?"

At the quietly spoken words the report the Vice Chief of Staff had been reading flew upward in a blizzard of paper. In the three days since his call to the JSOC commander, Trayner had hardly left his office. When Command Sergeant Major Jacob "Jake the Snake" Mosovich had entered his office or how long he had been sitting quietly on the Vice Chief of Staff's couch was a mystery. The startle factor and long hours caused the VCA's temper to snap.

"God damn you, you, you, fucking juvenile delinquent! How long have you been sitting there?" he shouted, slapping his desk. All it did was hurt his hand; the implied reprimand slid off Moso-vich like rain off a roof. "And have you ever heard of reporting properly?" the officer snarled. He started to reassemble the file as if it were the shredded remains of his temper.

"I've been here since 0500, sir, about twenty minutes before you got here." Jake's scar-seamed face split in an uncharacteristic grin, "General Taylor told me to avoid Bobby-Boy."

Sergeant Major Mosovich was a thirty-year veteran of covert special operations. Five feet seven inches tall and a hundred fifty pounds soaking wet, his head was almost totally bald, one side of it scar tissue, but his dress green uniform was virtually unadorned. He sported few decorations for valor and his open military record, his 201 file, listed him with limited time in combat: a few actions in Grenada, Panama, Desert Storm and

Somalia. For all that, and the total lack of any official Purple Hearts, his face was pockmarked with black pits, indicative of unextracted shrapnel, and his body was covered in the ropy scars made by metal when it violates the human body. His medical file, as opposed to his 201, had so much data on trauma repair and recovery it could be used as a textbook. He had spent his whole career, except a first tour with the 82nd Airborne, in special operations, moving from Special Forces to Delta Force and eventually back. No matter where he was, officially, he always seemed to be somewhere else and he had a permanent tan from tropical suns. Over the years he had amassed quite a retirement fund from temporary duty pay and he never went anywhere, anymore, unless it was at max per diem.

The necessity to avoid the Sergeant Major of the Army stemmed from an unfortunate incident the year before at the Association of the United States Army annual convention at the Washington Sheraton.

Once a senior NCO reaches a certain rank, all the positions are technically equal. Obviously, however, there is a certain prestige to the Command Sergeant Major position of, say, Third Army as opposed to Third Brigade, Fourth Infantry Division, Fort Carson, Colorado. But the higher prestige positions do not necessarily go to the sergeant majors with the most time in grade or combat experience, but rather to the sergeant majors who are willing to expend the political energy or have the patronage and desire.

The current Sergeant Major of the Army was Command Sergeant Major Robert McCarmen. Sergeant Major McCarmen was a contemporary of Sergeant Major Mosovich and they had both come up through Special Forces. But, whereas Sergeant Major Mosovich was always somewhere overseas doing something odd or unmentionable, with few exceptions Sergeant Major McCarmen had been at Fort Bragg, North Carolina (5th and 7th Groups), Fort Lewis, Washington (1st Group) or Fort Carson, Colorado (10th Group) except for training missions. He had, however, deployed for Grenada, Panama and Desert Storm. Somehow, despite the fact that these operations had involved minimal real combat for special operations personnel, with a few glaring exceptions, Sergeant Major McCarmen had amassed an impressive set of medals. Silver Star, Bronze Star with V device for valor in combat, and even the Distinguished Service Cross, the second highest award

for courage in the military pantheon. Each medal was fully authorized and if the citations were a little vague, well, what could be
expected for a "Black Warrior." The fact that the citations were
all written by commanders with whom the sergeant major had
a close and warm relationship was beside the point: it had to be
your commander who made the commendation and McCarmen
always interacted well with his officers.

His many citations and his ability to interact smoothly with
senior officers and politicians had garnered him the most coveted
position of any Army NCO: Sergeant Major of the Army, Top
Dog of the whole Big Green Machine.

At the previous year's convention, Sergeant Major Mosovich,
Command Sergeant Major of Fifth Special Forces Group in a
virtually unadorned Dress Green Uniform and Sergeant Major
McCarmen, Command Sergeant Major of the Army, in a medal-
bedecked army-blue Dress Uniform, had happened to enter an
empty elevator together, both somewhat in their cups. When it
reached the ground floor, the Sergeant Major of the Army, some
eighty pounds heavier than Jake Mosovich, was unconscious and
bleeding on the floor and Sergeant Major Mosovich was seen to
exit the elevator shaking his right hand as if it hurt.

"Yeah, I guess I told him that, Jake," said General Trayner,
mollified, "but I told building security to inform me when you
arrived."

"Well, General, General Taylor indicated that it was pretty
important and the way he said it made it sound like maybe this
conversation never happened. So, since building security logs
entry and exit..." The scarred NCO shrugged.

"You slipped the Pentagon security net?" asked the Vice Chief
of Staff, storm clouds building in his eyes.

"Well, you did say it was black," said Mosovich, stretching out
the kinks. He had been sitting totally motionless for the last three
hours. If he had been a spy, it would have been tedious but fruit-
ful. It was amazing what generals would discuss, assuming their
words were not being overheard. Jake was not sure what the bottom line was, the general had not talked about that directly, but
the conversations clearly indicated that something large was afoot.

"Not that fucking black," the general growled. "God dammit
Jake, this is too fucking much. I covered for you last year, but
watch your fucking step."

"Roger, General, sir." The NCO continued to smile slightly, obviously unrepentant.

The general dropped his anger as ill-spent and laughed. "You always were impossible to discipline, you little fuck." He rubbed the tip of his nose and shook his head.

"Yeah, and you were impossible to train, even as a snot-nosed LT." The NCO smiled again and got up to make himself a cup of coffee. The general invariably had the best coffee in the Army, a result of having spent a year doing cross duty with the Navy. Jake poured himself a cup of the excellent concoction and took a deep and satisfying whiff of the aroma. A sip confirmed that it was the general's usual excellent brew.

"So, what's up?" he asked cocking an eyebrow and recapturing his seat on the couch.

"Well, the shit has well and truly hit the fan, Jake. Have you ever gotten wind of the ULF projects? They ever rope you in?" asked the general, taking a sip of his own java.

"Unidentified Life Forms? Yeah, they were nosing around for a special unit back in, what? '93 or '94? Some dumb fuck gave 'em my name and I went through the stupidest series of psychological evals in history. I get paid a hundred fifty bucks a month extra to jump out of airplanes so naturally one of the questions is 'would you jump from a high place.' Jesus." He sighed in exasperation. "Shrinks."

"Where do you stand? Do you think they're out there or not?" The general might have thought he had a poker face in place, but Jake had played too many poker games with him not to see the signs.

"You must know something, or we wouldn't be having this conversation," said the NCO, not rising to the bait.

"Yeah, well, we need a special team. You won't necessarily lead it; that will be decided later." Trayner pulled out a purple file folder, elaborately enwrapped in Top Secret tape. "About seven to ten, various specialties, to perform a covert insertion in a hostile environment with hostile indigenous forces to do order of battle and terrain assessments."

"You can't get that with overhead, boss? And where in the hell are we going to send a team against 'hostile forces'? We're currently at peace, miracle of miracles." He wiggled his finger, indicating that the general, sir, should stop being coy and hand

over the file. He could smell the mission and it smelled dangerous and interesting, two attributes that always caught him. For
all his bitching about running open-eyed towards danger, if he
could have walked away from an adrenaline rush he would have
gotten out of this business a long time ago.

"We . . . can't get overhead. There's coverage. And the where
is in this folder," Trayner said, waving it back and forth as if to
waft it under Jake's nose. Trayner knew Jake's weakness of old.

"Okay, drop the other shoe, General. What's it got to do with
ULFs?" Jake sometimes felt that he was the proverbial terminated
cat; curiosity was definitely going to kill him someday.

"Ahem, let's just say you're not the sneakiest son of a bitch
in town anymore." The normally somber general smiled. "Himmit
Rigas, now might be a good time." With those words, the wall
to the right of the general's desk unfolded into a four-limbed
being, its skin color rippling from the thin green stripes of
the wallpaper to a uniform purple gray. The arms that had
been stretched upward to the ceiling slowly slipped to the floor
until it was in a quadrupedal stance. It now appeared to be an
equi-limbed frog with four eyes, one set on either end, and two
mouths, one on either end. There was a complex honeycomb
formation above the mouths and between wide-set eyes; it could
have been an ear or a nose. The skin continued to ripple as
the being flowed forward and raised one of its paw/hands in
an obvious invitation to shake. A box strapped to the wrist/
ankle began to speak in a high tenor.

"You are remarkably still for a human. Do you know any
good stories?" it said.

This moment would come to many people over the next few
years. Each would deal with it in a defining way. For the first time
in the history of mankind, people would know without doubt that
man was not alone in the universe, that there was other intelligent life in the galaxy, and would look on the face of an alien
being. Some would react with fear, some with friendship, some
with love, each response as diverse as mankind. Sergeant Major
Mosovich simply stretched out his hand in return. At the touch
of the alien paw, his adrenaline gland shot a leemer, defined by
the military as a cold shot of urine to the heart, into his system.
The proffered appendage was cool and smooth, covered with a fine
coating of silken feathers. Jake carefully controlled his breathing

and voice. "Thanks. You're not half bad yourself. How long have you been there?"

"Since yesterday in the day. After the second meal you take, but before the general's afternoon briefing. I entered from the ceiling through the door while the guard directed a visitor. The lock was insignificant. It was, as you discovered, readily manipulated through a magnetic pick. The general has had fifteen visitors and seventy-eight phone calls in the last eighteen hours. He has been present for fifteen of those eighteen hours. His visitors were, in order, his aide, Lieutenant Colonel William Jackson, on the subject of his canceling a previously scheduled social engagement. The second visitor—"

"Excuse me, Himmit Rigas, but I need to hold an initial briefing for Sergeant Major Mosovich." The general smiled politely, having already become used to the Himmit's characteristic volubility. His smile carefully did not reveal teeth.

"Certainly, General. My tale can wait to fully unfold."

Jake slowly turned back to the general and collapsed onto the couch. He refused to watch as the Himmit flowed back into camouflage against the wall.

"The background brief is in here." Trayner finally tossed Jake the purple file. "Read it here; it doesn't leave this room. Then start thinking about a team to take off-planet for a reconnaissance mission. The world will be Earth-like, swampy and cool. You'll be preparing here and there extensively with the Himmit. When we get done with the initial operations order I'll send you back to Bragg. Set up a team, but you don't brief them until you've decided on the final group. After that they go on lockdown, that's from NCA too."

"How did the Pres. become involved?" asked Mosovich, not yet opening the file.

"They called him on the phone," answered the VCA.

"Really?"

"Really." The officer shook his head. "They just called him from orbit on his direct line, along with the heads of the G-7, China and Russia. That was three days ago."

"Fast work for Washington." Jake took another sip of his coffee, opening the file as he did so. As he did he noticed that the whole file was constructed of slick flash paper. This was being held awfully close to the vest if the VCA was handling a flash file. The file felt greasy and cold in his hands and he had a premonition that the mission was going to feel the same way. "Okay, but I'll need one other person to help recruit the team."

"Who?" asked the general, suspiciously.

"A sergeant first class named Ersin."

The general thought about it briefly then nodded. "Okay, you can brief him in on my authority. Understand, right now this is as closely held as anything I've ever heard; it's all on the old boy network. Do not reveal anything to anybody else."

"I don't even tell myself half the things I do." Jake said with a smile and, with one last glance at the Himmit retracting into camouflage, he began to read the file.

3

Ft. McPherson, GA Sol III
0931 EDT March 18th, 2001 AD

"Ladies and gentlemen, my name is Admiral Daniel Cleburne and for those of you who don't recognize me, I'm the Chief of Naval Operations." The secure auditorium was about half filled with a mixture of uniformed and civilian personnel, mostly male. Something about most of the civilians made Mike suspect they had once worn blue or green. Apparently others besides General Horner had dipped into former commands.

"I was chosen to deliver this address to communicate the gravity of the information and because I could disappear more easily than the other Joint Chiefs. For the record I am currently sailing in the Bahamas.

"As covered in your agreements, each of you should have already contacted next of kin and informed them that you agreed to be locked in for a period of two to four months. You are working with a former colleague on a secret project and you will be home soon. Please, in your future communications, downplay the severity of this situation as much as possible. That a project has shanghaied a number of civilians will, inevitably, come to the ears of the press, but the longer we can stonewall the core information, the better for the nation and the world. We prefer to release it timed with other countries and in such a way as to minimize . . . uncontrolled reactions.

"My wife hates the old 'good-news-bad-news' routine but here goes:

"The good news, for most of you science fiction buffs anyway, is that first contact has been made with a friendly alien species."

He waited for the muted reaction to die down. Most of the people had been playing the "what's-this-all-about" game and had reached at least that side of the answer. A few had guessed the rest. Now time for the other shoe.

"Bad news: they're in the midst of a multiplanet war."

This time the buzz of conversation went on for some time before he raised his hands.

"Please, we have a lot of ground to cover and not much time, so I'm going to make this fast and dirty. I want everyone to have a general feel for our goals and constraints. You will all be issued briefing papers," he gestured to a number of officers moving down the aisles and passing out files, "and there will be alien advisors," a stir started, "and technologies," and grew, "to draw on. *At ease!* We don't have *time* for this, people."

He referred to the papers before him. "First a little background. For the last hundred thousand years or so there has been a political entity, for purposes of translation we are referring to it as a federation, occupying the habitable planets surrounding Earth. They're all peaceful races, apparently, because all the war-like races had wiped themselves out before they discovered deep space flight. For those of you Sci-Fiers," he grimaced, "who have been pondering over the 'Drake Equation,' whatever that is, they're the reason we haven't been getting any mail. Until now, at least.

"About one hundred fifty to one hundred seventy-five years ago the periphery of the Federation experienced an invasion by a new race called the Posleen. This species is about as vile as anything you SF guys ever came up with. Basic information on them is included in the briefing papers and more detailed information will be on the planning team net. In general they are four-legged sort of centaur-looking omnivores that lay eggs. Their technology is about equivalent to the Federation's and generally similar in scope, but they don't seem to use it very effectively.

"However, being totally nonviolent, none of the Federation races have any history of conflict. In addition, they have some difficulties with engaging in or even discussing violence, even after having been in a war for nearly two centuries. They have only two races that are able to 'pull the trigger' so to speak and those races have some problems with it. Because of their problems, they have been unable to slow the advance of the enemy. They've tried to create artificial intelligence devices—self-willed combat robots—to handle the problem but after one disastrous experience when the robots tried to take over they outlawed that approach."

With the exception of the rustle of paper, the large room was now totally silent as hard-faced men and women started flipping though the explosive documents in their hands. Mike smiled grimly at the layout. The document was subdivided into categories: Introduction, Threat, Friendly Forces, Mission and Appendix. It was the most succinct document of its kind he had ever seen.

"The main friendly race involved in actual conflict, the Himmit, are cowards. That's not an insult, it's just the way they are as a species. If they think they've been detected, even suspect it, they break contact. The other race, the one we have had most contact with, the Darhel, are only able to fire once as individuals. Then they are turned into some sort of automaton by the very action of taking a life. The other two races, the Indowy and the Tchpth, are so totally nonviolent they have no capacity at all for violence." Mike flipped past the threat portion and looked over the information on the first alien races ever encountered. Whatever happened over the next few months, this conference was going to be interesting.

"So now, basically, the Galactics let AIs do the driving, push a button, automatically lose the button pusher and hope for the best.

"The best has not happened. They have lost over seventy worlds and the rate of loss is growing. They have some, really very little, success in space but are totally lost in ground warfare.

"There has apparently been a faction that has wanted to enlist the aid of humans for practically the whole war. The plan of this faction was to get the help of humans not only as fighters, but as weapons and tactics designers. Because of their lack of experience at war, the Federation has been copying the enemy when it comes to those areas, but the enemy is not exactly the most efficient group at either one.

"They, the Posleen that is, have one thinking leader to control around four hundred 'troops' that are not much more intelligent than chimpanzees. Their weapons do not have sights so they depend on mass fire, somewhat like a Napoleonic war broadside. And their ships are laughable, from a real war perspective.

"Since that is all the Federation had to work with for ideas, they use a tank that fires a sort of broad-area energy mine for ground combat. Their 'warships' are converted freighters." He snorted in disgust and looked over toward the mass of black uniforms. "I think we can come up with better, and so do the world's leaders. You'd damn well better, or I'll have your commissions." There was some grim laughter but most of the attendees were listening with half an ear and flipping rapidly through their briefing papers.

"The idea of this conference, therefore, is for each team to determine the sort of weapons and tactics that they envision their country using for this war.

"Now for more bad news. The upper level commanders, that is myself and some of the 'type' commanders, are going to have to hash out a few things. But there are some political and budgetary constraints that the Federation has on its military. Those constraints are going to cause most of the Navy, Air Force, Marines and elite Army to be absorbed by the Federation forces." At that a buzz of conversation filled the previously silent room. Cleburne motioned them to quiet down and kept talking.

"In some cases we will interact with other countries' militaries that are going through the same thing, especially allied militaries. And the final plans for spaceships, comsat shuttles and space fighters, things related to the Federation fleet, will have to be agreed upon through a joint committee. On the other hand, because America is such a predominant power in those areas, we will have primary position on the committee. Let me be clear about the bottom line here: the people who are coming up with the concepts for warships and infantry forces had better get it right. There won't be a hell of a lot of review and they're likely to be what we're fighting for our lives with. Because that is the last bad news.

"The reason the Federation avoided contact before this is obvious: they might be trading one devil for another. But, again obviously, this faction has gotten permission to enlist us.

"The reason is, they are losing, badly, and they finally had to fish or cut bait. We're the next planet in line. According to the Galactics four or five large invasion waves are headed for Earth. The first one will be here in only five years."

4

Ft. Bragg, NC Sol III
1824 March 19th, 2001 AD

"Mueller."

"Are you kidding?"

"No."

The most far-ranging reconnaissance mission in Terran military history was starting with two experienced NCOs and a sheet of lined paper. Over Mosovich's kitchen table, he and Ersin, a tall, slim, dark-haired master sergeant with faintly Eurasian features, were assembling a combined service team of the best people they could think of for the mission. Inevitably there were disagreements.

"You have to be," said Mosovich. "First, he's inexperienced as hell. Second, he's a goddamn loudmouth; the bastard can't figure out when to shut the hell up." He got up and went to the refrigerator and extracted a beer bottle. He held it up in question and Ersin nodded. Jake pulled out another for himself, popped the top on both, nailed the trash can and came back to the table.

"Except for that, he breezed Q course," continued Ersin, doggedly, "and he's got a great record before he joined special forces. But the real reason I want him is his terrain analysis background. We're going to need that know-how, since the whole damn planet is apparently one big swamp and I don't know a field soldier who can match it. It doesn't hurt that he's a goddamn pack mule, either."

"What about Simmons?" asked Mosovich, taking a pull on the beer.

Ersin pulled his head back and twisted it in a motion that

was faintly ratlike. "He moves like a fuckin' yak in the bush," he spat in distaste.

"You've worked with Mueller," said Mosovich. It was a statement.

"Yeah," admitted Ersin, swirling the beer around and taking a sip. He preferred a more cultured brew than the sergeant major had to offer, but free beer was free beer. "He used to hang with Harold. We did some pellet work and I ran him through the SOT course a couple of times. He's a good guy with his hands." In the Special Operations community the phrase carried a special panache. It meant a person who was weapons deadly.

"Well, God knows I've pissed enough people off in my time," admitted Mosovich, reluctantly.

"He's a know-it-all, but the real problem is he's usually right." Ersin dropped the argument as won.

"Well, that's Ops, Weapons, Commo, Demo and Medical. We need an Intel with a double up in medical. You."

"Okay. Mueller can double O and I and so can you."

"I'll double commo, Walters doubles demo and we can all double weapons in a pinch. Besides, it's a recon not a raid, who needs weapons?" smiled the scarred veteran.

Ersin snorted. "So, you're going unarmed?" It was not an unknown technique on a lone recon, but taking a team was another thing.

"Bet your ass I'm not. I hope we never fire a round, but I'm going to pack the heaviest hardware we can manage. I hope that Trayner comes through with those blanket requisitions. We're gonna need some special weapons. That reminds me, we need a couple of other slots."

"Let me guess. One wouldn't be Trapp, would it?" Ersin smiled at a memory and wiggled his fingers in front of the sergeant major's eyes, like someone doing magic.

"Yeah," smiled Mosovich. "We might need somebody to do close-in work. Speaking of which, we need better information on those things' physiology before we land. Who else?"

"I don't know. Another engineer?"

"What happens if we have to break contact?"

"Oh. Okay." Ersin thought for a moment over another malty sip of beer. His whole face twitched like a rodent flicking its whiskers. "Sniper?"

"Yeah. But who?" asked Jake raising an eyebrow. He obviously had someone in mind.

"Fordham," said Ersin, instantly.

"Nah. He's good but you ever heard of Ellsworthy?"

Ersin looked uncomfortable. "I don't know, Jake, a woman?"

"You ever seen that bitch shoot?" Jake smiled. His scars pulled the grin into something from a nightmare.

"No, I've heard about her though. Bannon met her at Quantico. They call her 'The Spook.'" Ersin's face twitched again. He did not like the idea.

"I can't think of anyone I'd less like after my butt. There's a bunch of people that seriously tried to take me that I've never lost sleep over, but if that chick ever got pissed at me, I'd just dig my own grave."

"You're the boss, boss," said the sergeant first class, with obvious reluctance.

"Betcher ass."

Seven men and one woman sat or stood in a small, poorly lit room located in the bowels of the John F. Kennedy First Special Warfare Command Headquarters, Fort Bragg, North Carolina. They wore four different uniforms and a multiplicity of unit patches. Each of them was experienced in their own specialty. Most of them had combat experience. None of them were currently married. They represented the Marines, Army and Navy. Only one of them had any inkling of the mission. Sergeant Major Mosovich wandered in a minute late and headed to the top of the conference table. As he sat, the rest began to pull out chairs around the old wooden conference table, several of them continuing conversations.

One of the talkers was a blond bear of a man wearing the uniform of a Special Forces staff sergeant from 7th group. Well over six and a half feet tall, he filled his BDU uniform like a human tank. He was debating knife fighting techniques, complete with gestures, with a short, wiry chief petty officer sporting a SEAL badge. The petty officer was laughing through snaggly teeth, obviously unimpressed. The PO's forearms looked like his role model was Popeye from their thickness, and his hands and wrists were heavily scarred.

A tall, soft-looking Special Forces sergeant first class with a

van Dyke beard was carrying on a one-sided conversation with
the sole female. She was good looking in a long-faced way with
thick, short auburn hair and dark green eyes. She wore the carefully tailored uniform of a Marine staff sergeant. Her unadorned
jacket was cut almost skintight and made of such a lightweight
fabric that every movement of her small but firm breasts was
clear. Likewise, the skirt had been cut to accentuate her figure
and, unless Jake was mistaken, was at least two inches short of
regulation. Her shoes, while a regulation black, were a nonregu-
lation patent leather and had a sharply spiked four-inch heel.
Between the uniform and the scent of heavily musked perfume
that hit him like a sledgehammer as he entered the room, the
staff sergeant was an incitement to riot. She also had the still-
est features that Mosovich had ever seen. Her hands and arms
remained motionless at her side throughout the entire conversation
and her head never swiveled. Her eyes were fixed on a point on
the wall, thousand-yard stare firmly in place. The bearded staff
sergeant continued his monologue, totally oblivious.

Besides those four there was Ersin, a gigantic ebony master
sergeant with a Special Operations Command patch, and a rotund
black staff sergeant from 1st Group.

"Okay, let's get this started," Mosovich said as the group settled
in and quiet fell. "First introductions. On my right is SFC Mark
Ersin, 7th Group. He will be the Intel sergeant for this little op."
He gestured to the ebony master sergeant. "And this is Master
Sergeant Tung. He's sort of an odd jobs man at JSOC."

Several of those present chuckled. The master sergeant, a
long-time instructor as well as field soldier, was as much a legend
in the special operations community as Mosovich. "Oh, some of
you know Master Sergeant Tung. Good, that will save no end of
problems. Master Sergeant Tung will be handling operations." He
gestured at the large blond staff sergeant. "Staff Sergeant Mueller comes to us from 7th Group also. Don't be confused by his
looks, he's not just big and dumb: he's big, dumb and mean. Petty
Officer Trapp," he gestured to the SEAL, who gave a friendly
snaggletooth smile and comic wave, "comes to us from SEAL Six.

"Sergeant Martine," Jake waved to the stocky black sergeant,
"from 1st Group is an excellent commo tech and general fixit man.
Sergeant First Class Richards," he gestured to the staff sergeant
with the van Dyke who had been chatting up the female marine,

"is an extremely experienced canker mechanic." The sergeant gave a grimace at the old-fashioned term.

"Sergeant Ellsworthy," Jake continued, gesturing at the female marine, "comes to us from Marine Sniper School. Gentlemen, and I do not jest this time, do not get on this young lady's bad side; she's even deadlier than she is pretty. Now, you all are probably wondering, 'Yeah, sure, why me and what the fuck?'..."

"'Scuse me, Sergeant Major," the female marine said in a little girl's voice, nearly a whisper, "but did you know there's some sort of thing perched on the wall behind your chair?" She had a thick southern accent; the words flowed like honey.

The talk stopped as six sets of trained eyes started scanning the indicated area; one by one they settled on the appropriate spot.

"Yeah," said the SEAL, "I see it now you mention it. Looks like a octopus."

"No," said Mueller. "More like a camouflaged frog. What the hell is it? It looks real." He leaned forward, curiosity written all over his face.

"It's real," said Ellsworthy. "It moved one of its eyes."

"So," Tung rumbled, "what the fuck is it, and how the hell'd it get in here?"

"I don' know," said Trapp, a knife mysteriously appearing in the SEAL's hand, "but iss' one frog's about to be gigged."

"Hold it," said Mosovich, "it's friendly. Himmit Rigas, you weren't supposed to attend this meeting."

"First meetings are always so revealing," said the Himmit, shifting from the color of the wall to its natural gray-purple then back. It appeared to be agitated.

The group of special operations personnel reacted with mixed but muted reactions. Only the black commo sergeant got up and stepped away.

"Siddown Sergeant Martine, it's harmless," snapped Mosovich.

"Da-da-da-hell! Wha-wha-isit?" Martine stammered. His stutter was as well known as his ability with code.

"ET sure as hell," stated Mueller, examining Rigas with interest, no sign of fear or horror on his face at all. He turned to Mosovich with a quizzical expression. "Alien, right?"

"It's part of the reason for this briefing. It was supposed to wait to be introduced, dammit!" Mosovich snapped.

"Where'd it go?" whispered Ellsworthy. "I only took my eyes

off it for a second." She began a centimeter by centimeter scan of the wall.

"I don't know," said Mueller, snapping his head back around, "it just disappeared."

"Shit-fire," said Trapp, knife flipping agitatedly, "where is the lil' toad?"

"Calm down," said Mosovich, "it won't reappear until it's comfortable. It's a Himmit. You want to know, shut the hell up and listen...." Slowly they regained their sense of discipline and turned their attention back to the sergeant major, not without some covert glances at the walls.

"We've been tasked by SOCOM to do a deep penetration of an enemy planet. Yeah, 'an enemy *what*?,' right? Okay, here's the background."

He covered the high points about the contact from the Federation and the approaching Posleen threat.

"The bottom line is that we don't have enough information about the Posleen. Intelligence is one of the keystones of military operations and it's one we ain't got. The Himmits are like ghosts, they've been all over the Posleen planets, snoopin' and poopin'. But the problem with them is that they won't go into places that they might come into contact, which means that they haven't been able to do close recon, and they don't look for the sort of things we do. Last but not least, sorry Rigas," he nodded towards where he supposed the camouflaged alien lurked, "higher, which in this case means the President, wants an independent evaluation. Right now all of our information is based on intelligence fed to us from the Darhel and Himmits. The Pres. wants human eyes on the problem, and we're the eyes."

Jake consulted his notes and hoped that his selected professionally paranoid individuals were listening; he could almost taste the unease in the air. They mostly seemed to be scoping out the walls trying to find the invisible Himmit. Having been through the same exercise several times, he was fairly sure they would fail. Ellsworthy had surprised him again by spotting the alien at all.

"Our mission is to proceed with Himmit Rigas to a Posleen-held continent on one of the planets that is about to get our close personal human attention in the form of the First MarDiv and sundry other units. There we will conduct order of battle and doctrine intelligence gathering on the Posleen. We will ramp up here on Earth, spend about four months on a ship and then perform a covert insertion.

"If we insert undetected we'll be able to use the Himmit ship for extraction and movement. If not, we can wait until another Himmit ship is scheduled for pickup four months after landing. If we miss that pickup we are SOL folks; the next boat is the expeditionary force and it ain't expected for a couple of years." He paused and considered the rough notes he and Ersin had sketched out. They were not in detail; with a team like this one you solicited input as the training and preparation proceeded.

"A couple of notes. We'll be loading heavy. The food on the planet will not be edible but we'll have personal processors to convert the plant and animal matter if we have to forage." He smiled at the various grimaces on the team members' faces. Every one of them at one time or another had dealt with "foraging" on the run, and it was not a pleasant experience. Ellsworthy wrinkled her nose as if she smelled something awful. "If we can work from the Himmit stealth ship as a base it won't come to that."

"Nonetheless, on each insertion we'll have to carry certain items that the science types tell us are unconvertible like vitamins and specific amino acid combinations along with our converters. And although those don't sound very heavy, they are when you're carrying a five months' supply. Second, we don't want to have any contact at all if possible, but we're not going to plan that way. You're all big boys and girls, so decide what you want to pack as we prepare. Think heavy: an M-16 will not cut the mustard with these things.

"That's it for now, we'll be meeting tomorrow morning to start training and issue. See Ersin for billeting and training schedule." With that he simply stood up and walked out of the room. They could stay and try to figure out if the frog was still watching.

High lust and froward bearing,
Proud heart, rebellious brow—
Deaf ear and soul uncaring,
We seek Thy mercy now!
The sinner that forswore Thee,
The fool that passed Thee by,
Our times are known before Thee—
Lord, grant us strength to die!
—Kipling

5

Ft. McPherson, GA Sol III
1115 EDT March 18th, 2001 AD

As the buzzing mass of uniforms and their civilian cohorts stood up to exit the auditorium, General Horner waved Mike back into his chair. He waited until the babbling crowd cleared out of the large room, and looked around.

Several other team chiefs had pigeonholed members of their teams for hasty conferences, and he grinned internally. The flag officers one and all, himself included, found themselves out of their depth to an unpleasant degree. Prepared as they were to battle humans, none of them had ever seriously contemplated fighting nonterrestrial forces. The very concept was absurd, or so they had thought, an outdated scenario sitting on a shelf in the Pentagon, dreamed up by a wild-eyed Cold War brain-trust weenie.

But now they had to learn, had to dust off that ludicrous scenario, and he was uncomfortably aware of the adage about an old dog. The science fiction nuts like the troglodyte he had called upon might be pie-in-the-sky dreamers, but they had at least thought about this type of emergency to some degree and were suddenly worth their weight in gold.

He only saw two team chiefs talking to military personnel— the others were talking with civilians, so at least most of them knew where the meat was going to come from.

When he was sure they had a comfortable privacy zone he turned to the former NCO. Mike had been flipping through the issued briefing papers. The clean white incandescent lights on the high ceiling glinted off the laminated pages' images, bringing out the TOP SECRET stamps liberally imprinted on the pages.

"Well?" The general gestured with his chin at the papers. "What do you think? I want to get a feel for your impressions before we meet the rest of the team."

"Off the top of my head?" asked Mike, examining the schematic of some type of vehicle.

"Yes."

"We're fucked." The former NCO slapped the notebook closed and met the general's humorless smile with a somber gaze. He looked slightly more upset than normal, which the general knew from past experience could mean nothing or everything.

"Would you care to be more specific?" Horner asked, smiling tightly and steepling his fingers.

Mike shifted sideways in his seat, the better to meet the general's eye, and tapped the briefing papers for emphasis. "According to this, we can expect five invasion waves spaced about six months apart with additional scattered landings before, during and after the main waves. The first full wave will arrive in about five years. Each wave will consist of between fifty and seventy large colonial combat globes, each of those comprised of about five or six hundred combat landing craft. Each of these landing craft will have the Posleen equivalent of a division of troops, although we are calling it a brigade. Am I right? Five or six *hundred* divisions?"

"Correct. Very short, maybe pocket, divisions. I prefer the brigade designation." Horner had opened his own briefing papers and was checking the numbers.

"But each globe will have approximately four million troops of all types. Correct?" Mike pursued.

"Correct."

"That means each wave will drop *two hundred and forty million* heavily armed alien soldiers." The accusation was quiet but fierce.

"Right."

"Five times. Each drop, apropos of nothing whatsoever, exceeds the last estimate I had of total personnel under arms worldwide. And each of the Posleen is an actual fighter, not the one in ten ratio in modern armies."

"Unfortunately." Horner gave Mike the benefit of another of his humorless smiles.

"Do you see a problem with this?" asked Mike quietly, his hands clenching and unclenching rhythmically.

"I'm waiting for you to get it off your chest," Horner admitted.

"Fair enough. Now, these... Posleen use companies of about four hundred. Each company has one 'God King' leader-type in command with a vehicle-mounted heavy weapon." He paused and thought for a moment about the force structure. Something about it was nagging at him but he could not for the life of him bring it to the fore. Then he thought of it and smiled quirkily.

"What?" asked Horner, watching him closely.

"You know what this reminds me of?"

"What?"

"The force structure in Sun Tzu's day." He looked up and noticed the general's puzzled expression. "One heavy chariot to ten infantry," he prompted.

Jack thought about it for a moment and nodded. "So what does that tell us?"

"'When the enemy is strong, retreat, when the enemy is weak, attack.'"

"Yeah, and 'devise stratagems.' But as to the weapons to be used?"

"A Posleen company will have about eight heavy rocket launchers," Mike continued, looking back to the briefing papers. "As far as anyone can guess, they are capable of going through an Abrams the long way. Several more three millimeter Gauss guns that will probably do a soft kill on an Abrams and will definitely screw up a Bradley."

"They're unaimed," the general pointed out.

"With all due respect, no, sir, they're not," Mike disagreed. "The weapons are sightless, that does not mean that there is no aiming. For all we know the Posleen are naturals for shooting from the hip."

"Good point," Horner admitted. "But firing from the hip is only a short-range answer. Are we going somewhere with this?"

"Yes, and that's the point. If we get in close they'll screw us using any modern system." Mike cocked an eyebrow.

"I had actually gotten that far myself," Horner noted. He gifted Mike with another cold smile and folded his hands in his lap. He had tired of complaints, it was time for ideas.

O'Neal nodded and reopened the briefing packet. "To stop them will require infantry. We can degrade them with artillery;

air is out; we might be able to come up with a wonder tank, but if it's too big the production end will kill us. But we have to have something that can take the fight to them, not just fight in fortifications, stop them in place and survive even when being swarmed, call for fire..."

"I had two thoughts," Jack added.

"Hmm," Mike was back looking at the design of the God King's vehicle, a saucer-shaped anti-gravity sled with a center-mounted heavy weapon. The pictured system mounted a multi-barreled heavy laser.

"I was thinking that walkers would be the way to go," said the general, leaning slightly sideways to see if the former NCO was listening. The slight contemptuous snort was sign enough. "What?"

"See this?" Mike asked, pointing to the laser.

"Yes."

"Says here the God Kings mount heavy lasers, heavy Gauss guns or multiple repeating Hyper Velocity Missile launchers. Now, unless you're talking about enough walkers for target overload, I wouldn't want to be in anything that stands out like a walker." Mike gestured again at the picture. "Five or six of these things would eat a walker for lunch and there are between fourteen and twenty per 'brigade.' Not to mention that it would be some walker to survive these Hyper Velocity Missiles. Last, but not least, I think that cav would consider the walkers their system."

"I'll worry about turf fights," the general corrected, "you worry about systems. So, what about killing them before they get the chance to kill us? We should be able to engage at long range and take out the God Kings."

"Sure, under the best of circumstances, Jack, but what happens to you when they finally close? Or you suddenly find yourself in their midst? Come on! You taught me that one. I won't ask if you remember the Grenada jump."

"Well, then, combat suits, which was my other idea, would be out, too," said the general with a grimace. Facing these forces with unarmored infantry would make a butcher's bill beyond belief.

"Not necessarily," interjected Mike. He flipped to another page of the briefing packet. "Think of it this way. The Posleen fight in phalanx, right? Large blocks of normals with God Kings at irregular intervals, usually well back from the front."

"Right." The general's eyes narrowed as he watched Mike, working through the logic.

"And they basically can't be routed. You can't frighten them or hammer them into retreat." Mike scratched his chin in thought.

"The Galactics never have been able to," Horner pointed out. The possibility that humans might be able to was inherent in the correction.

"So you have to kill them, each and every one." Mike shook his head at the thought, tapping his cheek and scratching the slight stubble already arising. "But, even if you're at a terrain obstacle, and they're on a limited front, if you kill the first million, there's only two million behind them."

"Right," concurred Horner. "So you have to have something that is robust enough to kill them in the millions and survive getting hit by millions of them simultaneously." He thought about what he just said in terms of anything remotely "infantry-like." "You're right, it's impossible, we're fucked." The general shook his head, lips pursed, eyes focused in the distance on the problem.

Mike's eyes flashed wide and he snapped his fingers. "Right on the first constraint; wrong on the second. They don't have to survive being hit by millions of attackers simultaneously." He stabbed his finger at each point for emphasis. "If you have a classic walker, it will stand out above their formation and be a target for virtually every Posleen in range. But, if you have a suit of combat armor, it can be at their level, notionally, if the terrain is fairly flat, and only hit by the forces in the front rank. If a unit of suits is putting out enough hell on its own, it will suppress the fire directed against it, especially if it is heavily supported by artillery.

"In addition a unit will be able to pass through choking terrain, terrain that will be impassable to the Posleen and damn difficult for tanks or walkers, move faster than Posleen can and bring a world of hurt down on them at every contact. With the right Command Communication and Control systems a suit will be able to call for fire with pinpoint accuracy while simultaneously laying down close direct and distant indirect fire." Mike nodded in finality. "I was emotionally in favor of the suits from the beginning, I just wanted to ensure that my instinct met reality." He sat back and smiled, a feeling of relief flooding through him. The coming storm would be costly, but if the Galactics could supply powered combat armor humanity might yet survive.

"Okay," said Horner, thinking about the concept and nodding to himself. He began to frown, a sure sign that he was pleased. "I can buy that. If the Galactics can build it."

"And if we can afford it; they're gonna be expensive. Speaking of which, do you have anything on the budget and force structure discrepancy? It's not very well explained in the packet." Mike flipped to the back and searched the index but the only entry referred to a single uninformative line.

"Well," said Horner, his face turning even more grim, "this is what I was told. The Federation has been fighting this war since before our Civil War. At first they would contest each planet as a Federation, but after they lost planet after planet, they couldn't handle the mounting cost. So now each planet is on its own when it comes to planetary defense, while the Fleet is supported by the Federation. Planets that are under assault can normally raise funds through their corporate networks for defense. Since we have no corporate allies, where we are going to get the funding for our planetary defense is a major question."

"Well, if the Fleet is in gear, they'll never reach the ground," Mike pointed out.

"Right," agreed Horner, nodding, "but the Fleet right now is composed of fairly poor quality ships. That is what the Navy and Air Force guys are supposed to correct." He gestured at another flag officer, an admiral in this case, deep in conversation with another civilian.

"And guess who gets the Navy contract," snorted Mike, noticing who the civilian was. "So, we are going to be left here to rot on the ground," finished Mike sourly. "I hope we can at least get a hop in a combat shuttle out of it."

"Not entirely. The units that we envision here at this conference, the ones that are based around Galactic technologies, will first go to the Fleet. Some of them will be slated to 'home' defense, but most will be deployed off planet." Horner's face was blank, waiting for the inevitable reaction to that statement.

"Oh, joy," said Mike, angrily. "So we dream up this stuff, then send all the forces off planet and lose Earth behind them? What are we, a modern Australia?" he asked, referring to the role that country had played in WWII. With the vast majority of its forces battling the Germans in North Africa, Australia was nearly invaded by the Japanese. Only American intervention and a stroke of luck in the Coral Sea prevented the inevitable loss of the continent to the Japanese.

"Like I said," said Horner, patiently, "a fair proportion of it will be slated to home defense. But the point is, the equipment and R and D costs will be picked up by the Galactics. Also, we won't just be dreaming it up. We really need to have all our ducks in a row, because what is dreamed up at this conference is, more or less, what we're going to take into combat. We will not only dreamland the weapons systems, we'll also be the full authorizers; these weapons will not go through the usual procurement ritual."

"What? Why?" asked Mike, surprised. Development and procurement was normally a long-term process involving a cast of millions. While it was more than himself and the general on the team, a group like this would usually just start the design process rolling.

"Think about it, Mike," the general snapped. "We've only got five years, less if you think about fielding forces for planets already under assault and the attacks that will probably occur before the main landing. We have to get these systems designed, simmed, tested out, the manuals written and fielded in time for units to do a total conversion before the landings." Horner smiled ferally. "And that also means that every swinging dick of a military contractor with a four billion dollar piece of crap does *not* get to bid. Our team and some Indowy and Tchpth are going to be designing it from the ground up."

"Yeah!" said Mike with a smile. "But where are we going to get the bodies?" he continued. "Even if we do a general call-up and recall everybody like me, who's still young enough they can be half-ass effective, we're not going to have enough bodies. Not for the Fleet and the ground forces."

"First of all," said Horner with a glittering smile, "our job is to concentrate on the systems and let personnel worry about the bodies. But, to give you a little peace of mind, there's no problem with bodies. When I said every swinging dick who ever wore a uniform, I was serious.

"The Galactics have been generally reluctant to discuss medical technology because of some of their bioethics laws, but they are supplying a rejuvenation and life prolongation technology. We're going to recall people who haven't worn a uniform since Vietnam if necessary. Maybe even earlier."

Mike thought about that for a moment, opened his mouth, then closed it and thought some more. He furrowed his brow and shook his head. "Has anyone really thought that through?"

"Yes," said Horner, with another tight smile.

"I mean," Mike paused trying to process the enormous thought. "Hell, turn over any rock and you find a vet. Vets might only make up ten or twenty percent of the population but they are everywhere..."

"And quite often it seems that the guy who is the glue holding something together is a vet."

"Yeah," Mike breathed in agreement. "This is going to body slam everything. Manufacturing, transportation, food production, legal...well, maybe not legal services or marketing."

Horner smiled at the slight joke. "It will. On the other hand, we're not actually going to call back everyone. The current plan is to use a matrix of current age, ending rank and a score based upon the 'quality' of their service."

"'Quality'?" chimed Mike. He could just see a group of civilian bureaucrats deciding who was to be recalled and who was not on the basis of evaluation reports. Since ERs often reflected how well leaders parroted their commander, they were sometimes not the best method to use in judging combat officers and NCOs.

"'Quality.' Maybe I should say 'Combat Quality.' By weird luck I was in that meeting." Horner frowned hard. "And I managed to point out that what we are going to need are combat qualified officers and NCOs. Real veterans in other words. So each medal for valor acts as a multiplier, as does a CIB or time spent in a combat zone..."

"Oh, shit," Mike whispered again and gave a little laugh.

"...so no 'rear-echelon-chair-warmers' need apply," finished Horner with a rare chuckle of his own.

"Damn," said Mike, surprised once again. "Okay, so there's no problem with bodies that have military training and experience."

Mike rubbed the developing stubble on his chin and studied the section on Galactic technologies. "The Federation has a high degree of control on gravity and all the other inertial affiliated phenomena, which includes energy systems." He turned a page and wrinkled his brow in thought. "And apparently some really good materials science. No psi or other 'magic' stuff, good nanotech, but not combat nano that can be related to combat conditions. Yet. It's all 'vat' nano or biotic. I think I can hazard a few guesses from this stuff, but how do we get actual technical questions answered? And how good is their IT?"

Horner slid a black box the size of a pack of cigarettes out of his brief case and handed it to Mike. "This is an artificial intelligence device, voice activated and very interactive. It is in contact with a network of similar devices and all the extraterrestrial databases they have available to them." He slid his own AID out and queried it. "AID, this is General Horner."

"Yes, sir." The voice was an accentless, fluid tenor, totally androgynous.

"Please initiate the other AID for the use of Michael A. O'Neal. In all areas relating to GalTech information he is to have all my clearances and information overrides, on my orders. Is that clear?" asked Horner.

"Yes it is, General. Welcome to the GalTech Infantry Design Team, Sergeant O'Neal."

"I haven't been reactivated, yet." O'Neal smiled. It was the first piece of Galactic technology he had encountered and it met all the criteria for good science fiction. On the other hand, the first thing it did was get a fact wrong.

"The President signed emergency reactivation papers on all members of the GalTech conference with prior service at seven twenty-three AM this morning. Paperwork to discharge you for the purpose of accepting a commission and acceptance of a commission are prepared for your signature."

The NCO's stone-hard face tracked to the general like an armored turret.

"Not my doing, Mike." The general shrugged. "I guess somebody figured better safe than sorry. I'll admit to having the papers on accepting a commission prepared."

Mike scratched his chin and looked at the ceiling, taking note of the black domes of security cameras. He had a sudden premonition of a future filled with uniforms and security cameras, his life blown on the winds of fate. He closed his eyes, head still tipped back and said a quiet, sad prayer for the end of a golden age, an end of innocence, an ending still known to few.

"Well, General, sir," he said quietly, eyes still shut, "I suppose we ought to go earn our munificent pay."

6

Orbit, Barwhon V
1530 GMT, June 25th, 2001 AD

As the ship dropped from trans-light, Barwhon opened up before them, a planet of purple vegetation and mists.

"We're going in through an unsecured belt, an area that we think is still free of Posleen." Sergeant Major Mosovich went over the mission profile one last time. The personnel of Eyeball 1, as the team was now officially designated, were gathered around a small table in the cramped Himmit ship eating breakfast and sipping their last real coffee for a while as the planet swelled in the view-screen. The atmosphere was stressed; a smell of tension hung in the air like a fog. Even though they were seasoned soldiers, they were very much aware they were going to be among the first humans ever to set foot on an alien planet, and their surroundings hammered that point home. Since they had taken their Hiberzine injections before the ship even lifted from Kwajalein Atoll there had barely been time to get over a simple feeling of alienation before the shots took them and they faded into sleep. Now, every item in view gave off a subtle aura of wrongness.

The lighting was deceptive. Indirect, it was neither incandescent nor fluorescent and seemed poorly designed for human eyes. There was a subtle hint that it was not dim, but that most of the light was in a spectrum invisible to them. Objects and markings wavered on the edge of vision, seen and yet unseen. The team's woodland camouflage turned to odd flares of blackness and shimmering green under the strange illumination.

The colors of the decks and bulkheads were wrong, mostly

muddy blues and browns. Again there was a hint that there were bright colors, simply not those that could be viewed by humans.

There were faint acrid odors, odd and having that same sense of alienness, neither discernibly organic nor mechanical, just other. Occasional chittering sounds echoed at the edge of hearing, nagging at their subconscious, possibly shipwide announcements, maybe subsystems kicking in, maybe ghosts of dead Himmit. Adding to the discomfort, the furniture was all wrong. The table was too high, the benches too low, the seats too short. The furniture was obviously made for humans, but not by anything that had to use it.

Everything around them screamed "alien" and they packed together all the tighter in the uncomfortable environment, shoveling down their food and, secretly, each to themselves, wishing just once more for honest greens and yellows.

Himmit Rigas was in attendance, but if there were other Himmit crewmembers present they were not making themselves visible. To the Himmit a predator was a predator was a predator, and Rigas had to be crazy to interact with them.

"The planet doesn't have continents or oceans to speak of, just one continuous blend of jungle and swamp. We'll be coming in through a region that is more swamp and less jungle, since the acoustic and thermal signature of a decelerating spacecraft are impossible to mask. Then we'll swing over into this region." Mosovich pointed at a spot on the view-screen for a change, just to drive the point home that, yes, it was almost show time! "This is the region the Posleen first invaded and where the assimilation should be well in hand. We will initially perform a simple sweep of the area, trying to get a feel for what the general activities of the threat are. If all goes well, and it seldom does, we will bounce to other sectors to check on different periods after conquest."

As he talked, Ellsworthy carefully picked out all the meat in her stew and pushed it to one side, then separated out the potatoes, then the vegetables. The vegetables were further subdivided into green, yellow and orange colors. With a childlike grimace, she then separated out anything that was not clearly one of the major food groups. By the time she was done, everyone on the team had finished eating and sat back to watch the usual ritual. For nearly a month before lifting off in the stealth ship the team had trained together. They had time to discover each other's strengths and weaknesses, pet peeves and idiosyncrasies. They had gone from being a superb collection of individual warriors into a well-coordinated team. Along the way they had become accustomed to each member's little habits.

Now, bets were whispered on whether she would determine one or another bit as being real food or, in her terms, "icky stuff." When she was done, she carefully scraped as much of the sauce off the meat as possible and ate it. She examined the other piles minutely, turning her head from side to side and lowering to sniff at them before finally pushing the rest of the plate aside. To Sandra Ellsworthy there were carnivores and herbivores and she knew which one she was.

At a waggling of his bushy blond eyebrows, she silently slid the remains of the meal across the table to Mueller. The huge NCO picked up the plate and shoveled into his open mouth all the leftover piles of individual components, including, and here she had to close her eyes, the "icky stuff." When he was done his cheeks were stuffed like a chipmunk. He wiped a bit of sauce off his chin and waggled his eyebrows again.

"If you're quite done." Mosovich chuckled. The little ritual always served as an icebreaker when the tension got too high and in the alien environment of the Himmit ship it was more welcome than ever. He never worried about Ellsworthy knowing her part of the mission. If he asked she could have spit back the entire spiel word for word.

"Contingency extraction is by a second Himmit ship due in four months. Martine has the long-range communications equipment; if need be he can reach the courier standing by the jump-point. We have five months of supplies in mobile form and the ship stores when we're in contact with the ship. Are there any questions?"

There were none; they had heard the same briefing at least a million times before.

"Okay, insertion is in one hour. Let's get suited up, people."

They shoved back from the table and started down the narrow hall to the Number One pressure hold as Rigas headed to control. Mueller picked up the last three slices of fresh bread and stuffed them into his mouth, bulging out his cheeks even further.

"I can't believe how you eat," said Trapp, the gold of a SEAL badge glinting from his beret.

"I goff a lotta maff. Nah lak you runfy guyf!" the huge NCO muttered around the mass of protein and starches.

In the cramped pressure hold of the diminutive ship the lockers of equipment and weapons were being opened by Sergeant Martine, whose stutter did not slow his actions at all. He began assembling his commo kit as Ellsworthy slipped past him to lay out the weapons. Mueller packed himself into the space, not much bigger than a closet, to open up his cases of survey equipment and explosives as Ersin and Richards began a final check of medical stores. In some cases the equipment was enhanced by Galactic technologies. The communications equipment used a subspace field that was supposedly detectable but untraceable. About the only major Federation technology that was not represented was AIDs, to the chagrin of the Darhel. They had been apologetic, but there were simply none available that had not already been bonded to another user.

As the rest of the team made some last adjustments to their rucksacks and combat harnesses, Mosovich slipped in the earpiece of the communications system and gestured for everyone else to slip theirs on. When everyone had complied he applied the throat mike to his Adam's apple.

"Testing, commo check," he subvocalized without opening his mouth or making more than a softly inaudible hum.

"Operations." "Intel." "Sniper." "Point." "Medical." "Commo." "Demo." Mueller pulled out a couple of bricks of C-9 blasting explosive and did a quick juggle. Mosovich quelled him with a look.

"Command, good check. From here on out you only open your mouth to eat." The system transmitted microbursts at low radiation levels that would be far less detectable than voices. If the Posleen were using detection equipment at all, the encrypted microbursts would appear as nothing more than the sort of subspace anomalies usually found on planetary surfaces.

Packs were rechecked, equipment reshuffled and finally everything was settled. Moments later, Himmit Rigas' voice came over the system.

"We'll be entering the atmosphere momentarily. Please assume landing positions."

The team strapped on their packs and weapons then moved to the last hold area and clambered awkwardly into specially designed crash couches. Their packs, fitted into contours designed for them in the crash couches, remained on their backs. As each settled into place, a plasticlike substance extruded and filled in all the open areas between them and the couches then extended to cover their bodies, creeping up their heads and down their arms and over their strapped-on weapons, finally leaving them cocooned except for their faces. Once the smart-plastic shock cocoon felt it had a good fit, it shrank and applied pressure along the extremities. That way if there were a severe inertial event, the team had some chance of survival. Each of them had practiced the maneuver in simulators at Kwajalein, but there was still a moment of panic as the strange substance began to creep across the face before settling alongside the eyes, nose and mouth. Just as the shock cocoons snapped into place the stealthed spaceship hit the outer fringes of the atmosphere and bucked like a bronco.

"Hey, Sarn't Major," Mueller grunted over the commo circuit. "Why the buffet? If they've got inertial dampers, we shouldn't be feelin' a thing."

"Hell if I know, Mueller," snapped Mosovich, "just shut up and hang on." At the same moment the craft took another sharp downward lurch, combined with a hard bank and the sergeant major's face went green.

Ellsworthy, the member with the least experience in rides like this one, suddenly belched vomit, an experience made all the worse for not being able to double over. The stink of regurgitated stew set off a chain reaction. Presser beams swept the cabin, catching the globules of muck and drawing them into the walls as nannites swarmed over crash couches and the team's faces, cleaning every square inch. One unexpected benefit of the design was that the equipment and uniforms were protected from the ejecta.

"Sergeant Mueller," the intercom chimed as spiderlike nannites swept his twitching face for debris, "this is Himmit Rigas. You are not experiencing the full effect of the maneuvers this craft is performing. We are following a path where the probability of detection is the lowest. The last bank was a real effect of two hundred of your Earth's gravities. At the same time, since we cannot mask our thermal characteristics, we are attempting to mimic the flight path of a highly eccentric meteor. Now, as the sergeant major said, shut up and hold on." Some of the team gave a grim laugh as the craft performed an erratic barrel roll followed by a tremendous downward surge.

"Thirty seconds." The crash couches rotated upward on command then flipped, placing the team in a face-down position. Sections of the floor pulled back, leaving them staring through force screens at the purple trees of Barwhon. The primeval forest flashing by faster than a freight train seemed bare inches from their noses. The multicanopy jungle was the most dense in the known universe; suddenly the idea of making a combat jump into it did not seem like a good idea.

"Ten seconds."

Mosovich drew a deep breath as the smart-plastic suddenly receded into the couch. He clutched his twelve-gauge Street Sweeper to his chest, preparing to place more faith in alien equipment than he had in himself. Suddenly the cabin was filled with a roar of air, the voice of JC well known to all Airborne units, and almost immediately Mosovich felt himself hurled downward. Dropping under the combined effect of the ejection system and gravity, there seemed no way the team would avoid being spitted on the Promethean forest giants. As the mantislike trees reached for them Mosovich heard a whine from his pack, and the rate of closure dropped. Without any sensation of slowing other than the testimony of his eyes he came to a halt in midair. Looking around he saw the rest of the team dangling from their harnesses as he was. With a gesture he cut in the drop circuit on the Galactic antigravity device and the Special Operations team began falling toward the alien forest.

7

Washington, DC Sol III
2012 EDT August 16th, 2001 AD

The President stood behind the podium of the Speaker of the House, hands placed firmly to either side and swept his gaze from the members to the teleprompters and back. There had been none of the usual applause at his entry. The announcement of a speech to be delivered before the combined House and Senate was too sudden, too ominous, for any sign of pleasure. In the scant days between the announcement and the speech, the country and world had reached towards panic as rumors raged like wildfire. Units throughout the world had been placed on alert without any indication of what the emergency might be. Increasing numbers of scientists and technicians had disappeared, major projects shutting down right and left as key personnel disappeared into an informational black hole. Everyone knew, now, that there was a secret and that it had world-shattering implications, but the secret had held. Held until this fateful night.

"Members of Congress, Justices, my fellow Americans," he began, expression as somber as any that the country had ever seen, "this is such a night as will live in history, such a night as will burn in the memory of mankind should we exist for a million years." His gaze swept the room again and he could almost smell the unease rising from the assembled politicians. It was the first time he had ever seen the usually distracted group actually concentrating on someone else's words; this was one speech they did not know the text of and were not going to be doing instant commentary on.

"There have been many rumors in the media about recent events, secret meetings, military movements and sudden changes in the budget. I am here tonight to lay to rest all the rumors and bring to you the truth of the matter, in all its wonder and all its terror.

"My fellow Terrans," he continued, using a phrase that keyed many who were listening to the coming words, a phrase never used before in such a setting, "five months ago, I and other world leaders were contacted by emissaries of an extraterrestrial government." He raised his hands to quell the buzz of conversation that erupted on the floor. "They brought greetings, a plea and a bitter warning...."

Not bad, thought Mike as he watched the C-SPAN coverage in the cafeteria. He could have watched from his room but, somehow, after all the time the teams had spent together it just seemed natural to watch as a group. The GalTech teams were gathered in their groups, sipping whatever was their chosen potable. While they watched the most viewed speech in television history; unlike most they were able to take the terrible news in stride and even comment on the delivery. They waited as the President worked slowly through the description of the threat and the situation. Mike smiled at the ironies. In the first week after the disappearances began, a noted off-beat Internet columnist had looked at the list of missing personnel, realized that better than thirty percent were science fiction authors, and combat SF writers at that, with the remainder being military, and had come to the correct conclusion. He was generally and summarily dismissed by the majority of the media. "Martian Menace?" was the kindest headline. Mike could see the journalist in his mind's eye, bottle of whiskey in hand, shouting a loud "yee haw!" at being right.

"... The delay was agreed upon by all the contacted leaders to ensure the truth of the situation. What if, despite their apparent friendliness, they were lying to us?

"Validation arrived only three days ago. The team sent out with these emissaries included a multinational assortment of scientists, military officers, government officials and press. I will come back to that in a moment.

"In the meantime, in secret, teams of military and industrial personnel have worked round the clock with their Galactic counterparts to develop new weapons combining Earth, Terran, know-how

with Galactic technology. In that time these teams, locked away on
military bases, unable to see friends and family, unable even to tell
them why they were separated, have made great breakthroughs. In
spite of their many sacrifices, they have worked miracles."

"Ah, it wasn't a sacrifice," quipped a fighter jock behind Mike.
"The bastard was going to leave me anyway."

Mike glanced at General Horner. The officer was staring at
the screen, stone-faced, his expression suddenly lined and old.
Only the day before the final determinations had been made on
what forces were going to be equipped in what order and who
was going to lead them. Despite his obvious qualifications for the
slot of Commander Fleet Strike, the position was going to another
and General Horner was to return to the "regular" forces, there
being no other lieutenant general slots in the Fleet. If he had not
been promoted to lieutenant general he might have been given
command of one of the divisions, but as it was, his fate was up
to the Army personnel placement program. Furthermore, since
he was not going to Fleet, he had been placed on the regular
roster for rejuvenation. With his relative youth it might be years
or even decades before he would be up for therapy. All in all
the news that day had not been good. The capper of receiving
divorce papers had only been frosting on his cake.

"Designed and ready for evaluation and production are the
fighters, dreadnoughts, carriers and missiles that will destroy the
enemy in space. Also designed are new rifles, armor and tanks
to protect our nation and world on the ground...."

Mike shrugged almost unnoticeably and detached his AID
from his wrist; he definitely knew the rest of this story. The teams
had been working twenty hours a day for the past two months
and there had been a lot more interaction with the international
teams than expected at the beginning. There were still disagreements among the primary partners, the G-8, about tactical details,
but with very few exceptions, the designs for everything from
superdreadnoughts to the suits that were his particular baby
had been finalized. It was a validation, production and fielding
problem now, and he suspected that he was going to be on the
sharp end of that, too.

He lifted the AID to his ear and whispered, "Home." The AID,
released only a moment before to contact outside lines, tapped
into the regular telephone system, dialed Mike's home phone and

billed it to his phone card account. Around him, others did the same and a babble of relieved conversation filled the air.

"Hello?" said a wary female voice.

"Hi, honey, guess who." He found it hard to choke the words out and his eyes misted over at the familiar tone. His mouth tasted of salt.

"Mike? Cally, it's daddy! Come here. I guess that was you?" asked Sharon.

"Yeah, me and about a hundred fifty others in the States. Thanks for not up and leaving me." He winced as he realized what he said, but General Horner seemed to be on another plane.

"You mean throwing your clothes out the door? I've got most of the grass stains out." The throaty chuckle held a note of tears.

"Well, everybody wasn't so lucky," he said quietly, glancing at the general.

"That's the way the President made it sound."

"...I must, unfortunately, report that the loss of human life has already begun..."

"What? Sorry, honey, I'll call you back." He squeezed the AID, breaking the connection, and slapped it back around his wrist. He hoped Sharon would understand.

"...in the press pool was the internationally famous reporter, Shari Mahasti. She, her cameraman Marc Renard, soundman Jean Carron and producer Sharon Levy, along with Marshals Sergey Levorst of Russia and Chu Feng of China, Generals Erton of France, Trayner of the United States and a French paratrooper security detail were all lost on Barwhon 5..."

"Good God," said the fighter jock. "How the hell did that happen?" The various personnel in the room, one and all cleared for any information related to the coming war, reacted with shock to the surprise announcement. The buzzing got loud enough that a senior officer finally had to shout for quiet.

"...explain what happened and show you the face of the enemy in my office, the senior editors at CNN and the DOD press office have prepared the following tape. It serves as the final work of that fine journalist and shows, as no words can, the true face of the devil. This transmission was the last set picked up by the supporting Federation stealth ships. Parents should ask small children to leave the room."

❖   ❖   ❖

"General Trayner, I'd like to thank you for this opportunity…" The dark-haired female reporter speaking had serious eyes, deeply troubled. She was in a clearing in apparently unbroken forests of looming purple. Twisty blue and green edifices could be seen on the edge of the camera view, thin and sinuous; they seemed too delicate to withstand normal gravity. A low crab shape scuttled across the background, a Tchpth on some unknown errand, forever impressed into immortality. "What is your impression so far of the Posleen forces and the security of our position here? We seem to be more or less surrounded by fighting." There was a distant crackling, like a thousand lightnings and the sky in the background lit in actinic fire.

The general smiled confidently. "Well, Shari, as you know, the Posleen are generally unable to cross rivers and mountains if they are under fire. Although the Galactics have a lot of problems fighting the Posleen effectively, they are holding this area with a fair degree of confidence. The region is bounded on two sides by large rivers that stretch for some distance away from the primary Posleen infestation. As long as the enemy doesn't flank the rivers upstream, and with the support of our Legionnaire forces," he gestured at the French Legionnaires on security, "we should be fine."

"General Erton," she swung the microphone to the American's counterpart, "do you agree?"

"Oh, *oui*." The tall aristocratic Frenchman wore dark gray camouflage that somehow blended well with the overall purples of the background. He also gave the reporter a blinding smile as the Chinese and Russian marshals waited for their opportunity to reassure the nervous reporter. What none of them considered was that the reporter had more time in combat zones than all of them combined, and had developed a certain nose for trouble. "The Posleen so far have shown no ability to force a crossing of these rivers. In addition, according to the intelligence we have been given, they do not seem to use their landing craft after the initial invasion as would humans for 'airmobile' purposes—"

"*Mon Général!*" shouted a voice in the background, "*Le ciel!*"

The camera swung wildly then settled down with a wonderful view of the soaring Tchpth towers against a setting violet sun. Looming over the purple forest giants and the towers of the town was a monolithic block of darkness, silver lightnings stabbing downward at the defiant Darhel and human defenders. In response to a lazy lift of tracers toward the distant Posleen lander, a silver bar of steel lightning slammed down, picked up the camera on a shock wave of air exploding away from the beam of plasma and tossed it into the air like a child's toy.

Now, the camera view was sideways. Something, a button or a scrap of cloth from the body it leaned against, blocked the lower part of the screen. An American jump boot was propped limply on a gray set of rags, the torn body of a former enemy. The single living human in view, a French paratrooper, removed his empty magazine and stared at the feed in stupefaction. Tossing it over his shoulder he reached down to his belt and drew his bayonet. Fixing it he leapt out of view with a cry of *"Camerone!"*

Moments later leprous yellow-scaled legs with eaglelike talons entered the view. The camera tumbled for a moment, losing focus, and the screen exploded in a cloud of red. There had never been a clear view of the enemy.

"My fellow Americans," said the President as the view returned to the podium, "we face a storm unlike any in our history. But, like the majestic oaks of our land, our roots are deep, our Union strong. Before this storm we will lose leaves, we will lose branches. But this Union under God will weather the storm and in the spring we shall bloom anew." There was a moment of silence, a hush, then a single member began to clap. The applause spread and caught until there was a thunderous roar, an affirmation. For one brief moment the nominal leaders of the strongest republic on earth were joined in a single vision, a vision of survival and a future beyond the darkness. For that one brief moment there was unity against the storm.

8

Ft. Bragg, NC Sol III
1648 November 19th, 2001 AD

Staff Sergeant Bob Duncan, Chief Fire Direction Controller for the 2nd Battalion 325th Infantry Heavy Mortar section, was occasionally a problem for his chain of command, what is euphemistically called a leadership challenge. For his entire career in the Army he never quite fit in. He had all the merit badges expected of a ten-year veteran of the 82nd Airborne, the Ranger tab, the jump-master's wings, staff sergeant's stripes, but despite these he was never quite trusted by his first sergeants and platoon sergeants. Part of this was the nature of his career. For whatever reasons, and they had varied, he had never been cycled to another unit. He'd arrived fresh from Infantry Individual Training and Airborne school as a private, was promptly assigned to D company (then CSC Company) of the 2nd Battalion 325th PIR and there he stayed. Not for him the rotations to Korea, or Germany. No tours to the Airborne units in Italy, Alaska and Panama. Instead, during his term it seemed he had done every job in the company. Need a scout to round out the platoon? Sergeant Duncan's been a scout. Need a TOW HUMVEE commander? Sergeant Duncan. Need a head for your Fire Direction Center? A mortar squad leader? Call Sergeant Duncan. Operations sergeant? He was a fixture of D company more immutable than the barracks, far more fixed than the command groups, the constantly cycling first sergeants, lieutenants and commanders. Whenever the new first sergeants, lieutenants and commanders had a question, the finger was inevitably pointed at Sergeant Duncan.

It would seem that, in any fair world, such omnipotence about the function of the company, from the supply room (supply clerk, nine months, year three) to the function of the antitank platoon (acting platoon sergeant, nearly a year, gunner, jeep commander, motor pool sergeant) would lead to steady acclaim and rapid promotion. Any job dangerous and dirty, any job difficult, dusty and dry give it to Sergeant Duncan.

But that led to another problem with Sergeant Duncan. How could anyone give the same lecture, teach the same lessons over and over, not to subordinates but to superiors, and not develop a faint aura of scorn? When the company commander constantly had to ask you questions, it inevitably led to invidious comparisons. When twice in your career you ended up leading the (notional) remnants of the company in graded field maneuvers, once getting a far higher grade than the current commander, when the most trying task became routine, when you were always chosen first for any difficult and tedious job because you were just so blamed good at it and coincidentally it got you out of the first sergeant's remaining hair, an ennui exceeding all normal course begins to wear away at the soul. This ennui, in the case of the Sergeant Duncans of the world, leads to tinkering. Would it be better if the wires went this way? What would happen if we did it that way? Could we use these civilian fireworks for booby traps? The repercussions from that particular experiment were still occurring.

It would have been far better for Sergeant Duncan, for the Army, if not for D company, were he cycled out to fresh pastures and new challenges. But, nonetheless, for many reasons he stayed a fixture of the company, of the battalion, and, in an exceedingly Airborne way, festered.

As fate would have it, the change came to him instead of the other way around. He twisted the black box around as he sat on his bunk across from his current detested roommate. He had noted the phenomenon that he apparently had three roommates he detested for every one he got along with. This one was about due for a refund; a scout sergeant, he thought scouts shit gold. Well, Duncan had been a scout when this little turd was in middle school and had already outshot him on the Known Distance range, so as far as Bob Duncan was concerned this scout could just pack his ego back in his fuckin' duffel bag and march on out any time. The stupid bastard was carefully stropping a dagger about as long as his forearm on a diamond sharpener, as if he was going to be using it on Posleen the next day. As far as Sergeant Duncan had been able to ascertain, the Posleen had, like, nowhere you could plant a knife and do vital damage. Furthermore, how did he think he was going to use it in a combat suit? The constant stropping was beginning to be more irritating than the scratch of the wool blanket on his bed. *Jeez Louise! For godsakes Top get this guy out of my room!*

To take his mind off of the stupid bastard as he waited for last formation to be called, Duncan studied the latest black box they had been issued. It was about the size of the pack of Marlboros in his left breast pocket and flat, absorbent black, very similar in appearance to their AIDs. Black as an ace of spades. And, somehow, it projected a field you could *not* put a .308 round through. He'd already tried. Several times, just to be sure. And it didn't even move the box when the shells ricocheted off; that was freaky. Mind you, the guys around him moved *prrrretty* damned fast when those .308 rounds came back up range at the Fort Bragg Rod and Gun club. Fortunately there weren't any jerks around. The other shooters just laughed and went back to jacking rounds downrange from an amazing variety of weapons.

Okay, so it stopped bullets. But the field only extended out about seven feet in either direction and it stopped when it touched an obstacle. Stopped. It didn't wrap around the obstacle. Just stopped, which sucked if you thought about it. And you should be able to brace it into something, not just depend on whatever it was that kept it in place. He'd had a little talk with his AID and it turned out the damn thing had some sort of safety lock. So he'd talked with his AID a little more and convinced it that since they were an experimental battalion, with experimental equipment, they had the responsibility to experiment. The AID checked its protocols and apparently agreed because it had just released the safety interlocks on the device. Ensuring that it was at arm's length, Duncan activated the unit.

The Personal Force Field unit functioned by generating a focused reversal plane of weak force energy as analogous to a laser beam as a line is to a plane, meaning not. The unit was designed to produce a circle 12 meters in area for 45 minutes. Given the option of maximum generation, it generated a circle 1250 meters square for 3 milliseconds before failing. The plane was effectively two-dimensional. It extended outwards 20 meters in every direction, sliding through the interstices between atoms and occasionally disrupting the odd proton or electron.

The plane sliced as effectively as a katana in air through all the surrounding material, severing I-beams, bed structures, wall lockers and, in the unfortunate case of Sergeant Duncan's roommate, limbs. The slice, thinner than a hair, reached from the basement supply room, where it, among other things, sliced through an entire box of Bic pens causing a tremendous mess, to the roof, where it created a leak that was never completely fixed. However, once the entire base was overrun by the Posleen the leak became moot. In addition, the throughput on the unit exceeded the parameters of the superconductive circuitry, and waste heat raised the case temperature to over two hundred degrees Celsius.

"Jesus!" screamed Sergeant Duncan and dropped the suddenly red-hot case as his bunk dropped to the floor. As the floor began to settle, he slid forward as did his roommate on the other bunk. His roommate let out a bloodcurdling scream as his legs, from just below the knees, suddenly slid sideways away from his descending body and arterial blood spurted bright red to blacken the army blanket.

In his time Sergeant Duncan had seen more than any man's share of ugly accidents and he reacted without thought. He rapidly wound parachute cord around the stumps. The knife made an effective tightener for the first tourniquet; placed right it did not even cut the cord. The second tourniquet slowed the blood loss through the simple expedient of using a self-tightening hitch, very common when preparing vehicles for heavy drop or certain kinds of girls for bed. The unfortunate roommate screamed imprecations and began to cry; to such a man the loss of his legs might as well be death.

"Forget it," Sergeant Duncan snarled as he slid a screwdriver under the second tourniquet and tightened it until the blood flow stopped. "They can regrow them now." The soon-to-be ex-roommate was going glassy eyed as the blood loss began to affect him, but he caught the central idea and nodded as he passed out. "I'm the one who's fucked," Duncan whispered at last and cradled his burned hand to his chest as he crawled up the incline to the door. "*Medic!*" He yelled into the hallway and slumped back against the doorframe staring blank-eyed at the floor sloping towards the mirror-bright cut.

✧   ✧   ✧

Sergeant First Class Black entered the battalion commander's office, did a precise right-face and rendered a hand salute. Staff Sergeant Duncan followed him in lock step and stood at attention.

"Sergeant First Class Black, reporting as ordered with a party of one," said Sergeant Black crisply, but with a hush to his voice.

"Stand at ease, Sergeant Black," Lieutenant Colonel Youngman said. He stared at Sergeant Duncan for a full minute. Sergeant Duncan stood at attention and sweated, reading the officer's commissioning document on the opposite wall; his mind had otherwise retreated to a safe place that did not include the probability of a court-martial. He had the intense feeling that the recent events had to be a dream, a nightmare. Nothing this awful could be real.

"Sergeant Duncan, and this question is purely rhetorical, what am I to do with you? You are tremendously competent, except when you fuck up, and you apparently do that by the numbers. I have had a chat with the sergeant major, your company commander, your platoon sergeant and, ignoring protocol, your former first sergeant. I have already officially heard several opinions of you from your current first sergeant."

Youngman paused and his face worked. "I will admit to being at a loss. We are certainly expecting combat in the very near future, and we need every damn trained NCO we can put our hands on, so a trip to Leavenworth," at that word both NCOs flinched, "which is the least you damn well deserve, is nearly out of the question. However, if I put you before a court, that's where you're going. Do you realize that?"

"Yes, sir," Sergeant Duncan answered quietly.

"You caused fifty-three thousand dollars worth of structural damage and cut your roommate's legs off. If it weren't for this new Galactic," the term was practically spit, "medical technology he would be a cripple for the rest of his life and as it is I'm out a superior NCO. He is being detached to patient's status and then to general replacement. They tell me it will take at least ninety days to grow him new legs which means we likely as not will not get him back. So, as I said, what am I to do with you? This is an official question, do you wish administrative or judicial punishment? That is, do you want to take whatever I order as your punishment or do you want to face a court-martial?"

"Administrative, sir." Duncan breathed an internal sigh of relief at being given the opportunity.

"Very smart of you, Sergeant, but it's well known that you're smart. Very well, sixty days' restriction, forty-five days' extra duty, one month's pay over sixty days and one stripe." The colonel had effectively thrown the book at him. "Oh, and Sergeant, I understand you were up for sergeant first class." The officer paused. "It will be a cold day in hell. Dismissed."

Sergeant Black snapped to attention, barked "Right face!" and marched Sergeant Duncan out of the office.

"Sergeant Major!"

The sergeant major entered the office after escorting the NCOs from the building. "Yes, sir."

"Get with the first sergeants and the S-4. We don't understand this equipment and we don't have time to mess with the booby traps in it right now. With Expert Infantry Boards coming up we need to concentrate on basic infantry skills; the scores on the latest round of core training processes were abysmal.

"I want every bit of GalTech equipment locked down, right now. Put all that will fit in the armories and the rest under lock and key in the supply rooms, especially those damn helmets and AIDs. And as for Duncan, I think he's been in the battalion too long, but we're critically short on NCOs so I can't rotate him out. What do you think?"

The stocky blond sergeant major worked his protuberant lips in and out as he thought. "Bravo could use a good squad leader in their third platoon. The platoon sergeant is experienced but he's spent most of his career in leg units. I think Duncan would be a real asset and Sergeant Green should know how to handle problem children."

"Do it. Do it today," the officer snapped, washing his hands of the matter.

"Yes, sir."

"And get that crap under lock and key."

"Yes, sir. Sir, when do you anticipate an ACS training cycle? I'll be asked." He had been asked already and repeatedly by the company first sergeants. Bravo company's first sergeant, in particular, was crawling all over his ass on a daily basis.

"We've got ninety days after EIB before we're scheduled to lift for Diess," Youngman said, sharply. "We'll do an intensive training cycle then. I've already submitted for the budget."

"Yes, sir."

"Dismissed." The colonel picked up a report and started to annotate it as the senior NCO in the battalion marched out.

9

New York, NY Sol III
1430 November 20th, 2001 AD

"My name is Worth, I have an appointment."

The office was on the 35th floor of a fifty-story building in Manhattan, a totally unobtrusive location were it not for the occupants. The sign on the door stated simply "Terra Trade Holdings." However, it occupied the entire floor and was the de jure trade consulate of the Galactic Federation.

The startlingly beautiful receptionist gestured wordlessly at the couch and chairs set to one side of the large and airy anteroom and returned to puzzling out her new computer.

Mr. Worth, instead of sitting, wandered around the reception area admiring the artwork. He considered himself a connoisseur, of sorts, of fine art, and quickly recognized several of the works for originals, or at least forgeries of extraordinary quality. There were two Rubens, a Rembrandt and, unless he missed his guess, the original "Starry, Starry Night" which was last seen firmly clutched to the bosom of the Matsushita Corporation.

As he passed among these trophies he began to notice that the furniture might also be originals; each piece appeared to be a genuine Louis XIV antique. Which made his mind return to the receptionist. If everything else in the room was original, a sincere possibility, a true collector would require some extraordinary level of originality for the receptionist. It only followed. He glanced surreptitiously her way, but was, frankly, stumped. As her console chimed she looked up and noticed the covert glance; it obviously affected her less than a puff of wind.

"The Ghin will see you now, Mr. Worth."

He stepped through the slowly opening doors and into shadow. Across a cavernous office was a desk the size of a small car. Behind the desk, silhouetted by the limited light from the curtained windows, sat a figure that could be mistaken for a human.

"Come in, Mr. Worth. Be seated," said the Darhel in its sibilant tones, gesturing languidly at the seat across from it.

Mr. Worth walked slowly across the office, trying to focus on the silhouetted figure. Since First Contact, the Darhel had been everywhere and nowhere. They were, apparently, either in person or represented at all important governmental meetings and functions. They seemed to understand that more business is decided over canapés than in all the meetings in the world, but usually they were either swathed in robes for protection against the strong Earthly sun, or represented by paid consultants. Mr. Worth realized that he was about to be one of the fortunate few who saw one face-to-face.

Still unable to get more than a hint of saturnine head shape, Mr. Worth sat in the offered chair.

"You might, as the saying goes, be wondering why I asked you to come here today."

The tones were so mellifluous, Worth felt himself caught in a sort of spell. He shook his head. "Actually, I was wondering how you got my number at all. Very few people have it and as far as I know it is not recorded anywhere." He steeled himself against the sound of the Ghir's voice, waiting for a response.

"It is, in fact, recorded in at least three databases, two of which we have ready access to." The figure shook slightly in what might have been laughter in a human. There was a faint acrid smell, sharp and ozonelike; it might have been breath or a Darhel version of cologne.

"Oh. Would you care to illuminate?"

"Your number, and a general, shall we say, job description, is recorded in CIA files, Interpol files and a database belonging to the Corleone family."

"That is most unfortunate." He made a mental note to discuss his data security with Tony Corleone.

"Actually, I should say they did record that datum. There are now certain inaccuracies." There was a pause. "You have no comment?"

"No." Worth had noted that there were times to keep one's mouth firmly shut. He suddenly decided that this was one of those times.

"The Darhel are a business concern, Mr. Worth. As in any business concern, there are issues which are soluble and those which are insoluble. There are also issues which, while soluble, require a certain subtlety of approach." The Ghir paused, as if choosing his words very carefully.

"And you would be interested in retaining my services to... deal with these subtleties?"

"We would be interested in retaining services," the Darhel said, very carefully. There was another quiver from the figure.

"My services?"

"Were you to submit invoices for reasonable expenditures," another shudder and a pause. The Darhel seemed to shake itself and took a long, deep breath. Then he continued. "If someone were to submit invoices for reasonable expenditures, in the interests of resolving issues related to Darhel interests which might come to light, either through casual conversation with Darhel or through your own intelligence," there was another pause. After a moment the Darhel continued, his cultured voice now strained and squeaky. "There would be fair remuneration." The sentence ended on a high strangled note. The Darhel turned its head to the side and shook it hard, breath shuddering.

Mr. Worth realized that his new, employer? client? control? was not just unwilling, but virtually unable to be specific.

"And these would be submitted how? And paid how?" Being circumspect was one thing, but business was business.

"Such details are for others to determine," the Darhel responded, breath shuddering. "I take it that is agreement," it continued, sharply. There was a note of anger in its voice.

"To what?" asked Worth. "When did we meet? I don't think I've ever talked to a Darhel. Have I?"

"Ah, just so." The figure drifted forward and there was a sudden gleam of teeth. Worth shuddered at their resemblance to a shark's. "So glad not to do business with you, Mr. Worth."

Worth's eyes widened as the figure was revealed.

The Chief of Procurement, Army of the People's Republic of China, Shantung Province, tapped a pen on his documents as he related to his superior, Commander of Forces, Shantung Province, the facts that had just come to light. One of his junior officers, during preliminary discussions related to production and procurement, had hit a stumbling block. Believing that it was a problem with the AID's translation—such things had happened before—he questioned his Darhel opposite number closely and at length. The elfin Darhel had an almost amazing ability to steer conversations away from problem areas but finally, after referring to both an Indowy technician and a Tchpth science-philosopher, the junior officer broke off negotiations and composed a long report. This report and an expansion composed by the major's superior were now in the marshal's lap as he reported the bad news.

"I am, perhaps, remiss in my understanding. How can they have no industrial capacity? I have seen their ships. Where do these AIDs come from?"

"It is a question of translating the word 'industry.' They produce phenomenal products, wondrous spacecraft and these attractive helpers, but each item is *hand* crafted; they have no concept of assembly line manufacture. Do not think of assembly lines as a technology; they are a philosophical choice not a strictly mechanistic development. Furthermore, production by assembly line creates a fundamental need for planned obsolescence or else the assembly line, by its own efficiency, would fill the needs of everyone in the market and be forced to shut down. So, our industries here on Terra continually create new products to fill the production capacity and, to an extent intentionally, produce products that use less expensive materials and do not last as long.

"Yet the flip side to industrial, and by that I mean assembly line, production is that individual items can be produced quickly and at relatively little cost. That is why everyone is forced to use it." He stopped and considered his choice of words.

"There is, however, another way. We are sure now that the Federation is both highly structured and largely stagnant. I can refer you to the appropriate papers...."

"I've seen them," said the marshal, picking up a pen in turn and beginning to twirl it between his fingers. He gazed out the window at the towering sky scrapers of China's fourth-largest city and wondered how they could possibly defend it if the Galactics could not build a fleet in time.

The chief of procurement nodded his head. "There is a strong degree of specialization in this Galactic ant colony." He again stopped and considered how to say the next item.

"Our place, it would seem, is to be soldier ants. The Indowy, those greenish dwarf-looking bipeds, are the worker ants. They create high technology at an almost instinctive level. Their tolerances are so exact that the products look as if they were made in a factory. And each product is made to last a lifetime. Since each product is handcrafted and is designed to last for two or three *hundred* years, each one is incredibly expensive. It may take a single Indowy a year to produce the Galactic equivalent of a television. The cost is comparable to a year's pay of an electronic technician or electrical engineer. The sole exception seems to be AIDs, which are manufactured using mass processes by the Darhel. There is apparently also a shortage of rejuvenation nannites developing for the same reason."

"How does anyone purchase anything?" asked the commander, perplexed.

"The Darhel," responded the procurement officer, dryly. "There was a term associated with everything that we took to be price and that was how the AIDs were translating it. A more precise translation would be 'mortgage' or 'debt.' Unless you are massively wealthy, to buy the simplest items you have to take out a loan from the Darhel." He smiled thinly. In every procurement officer there is a slight love affair with a really good scam.

"Federation wide?" asked the commander, thinking about the numbers involved. It was a staggering concept.

"Yes. And the loan is payable for up to one and a half centuries. At interest." The procurement officer gave a very Gallic shrug. "On the other hand the products never break and are warranted for the life of the loan."

"The ships?" asked the commander, returning to the most important subject.

"That was what brought about the understanding. The Indowy must have a hierarchy more complex than the Mandarin Court. An Indowy chooses a field, has one chosen for him, at a young age, the equivalent of four or five years old in human terms. The most complex hierarchy, and the highest paid, are the ship builders. Every piece of a ship, from hull plates to the molycircs, are made by the construction team, usually an extended family. Raw material comes in, finished ship comes out. Every part is signed and cleared by the master of the subsystem and the master builder. Every part. Thus, Indowy ships have a useful lifetime in the thousands of years and virtually no maintenance. No spare parts required; if anything breaks the component is remanufactured by hand. It is as if every ship is one of those skyscrapers," he waved out the window at the towers beyond, "with every part made on site. All of their systems, equipment, weapons, etceteras are built the same way.

"An apprentice starts as a 'bolt' or 'fitting' maker then progresses through subsystems—plumbing, electrical, structural—learning how to make each and every component of the system. If they are lucky, in a couple of centuries they can be a master, in charge of construction of an actual ship. Because of this process, and the fact that there are very few masters available to make ships, there are rarely more than five ships completed each year in the entire Federation."

"But...we need hundreds, thousands of ships within a few years, not centuries," said the commander sharply, tossing the pen onto the desk. "And there are plans to produce *millions* of space fighters."

"Yes. That particular bottleneck is why their ships are all converted freighters. They apparently did produce some actual warships, but very few, and losses against the Posleen have wiped them out. There is a Federation-wide shipping shortage because they are losing these converted freighters much faster than they can be replaced."

"You would not have brought this to me if there wasn't an answer," the commander said. Sometimes the chief of procurement could be intensely pedantic, but his answers were usually worth the wait.

"There are only about two hundred master ship builders in existence..."

The commander was startled by the number. "Out of how many Indowy?" he asked.

"About fourteen trillion." The chief smiled faintly at the number.

"Fourteen *trillion*?" the commander gasped.

"Yes. Interesting figure, don't you think?" smirked the procurement officer.

"I should think so! For one thing, the pricing ratio on our troops was based upon Indowy craftsmen wages. There are, at most, one billion potential human soldiers," the commander growled. "Putting their worth as equivalent to an Indowy now seems ludicrous."

"Yes, our personnel are a comparatively finite resource. We seem to have been 'taken,' as the Americans would say, by the Darhel. But that is apparently normal. The Indowy make up eighty percent of the Federation population but their power is quite limited. The Darhel appear to skillfully control their interplanetary media and hold virtual control of the money supply. Since the Darhel control the money, they control the 'chutee,' the mortgages.

"Each Indowy has to purchase tools for his trade. If an Indowy steps out of line his 'chutee' is called and he becomes bereft of income and an untouchable. There is no social support for such; they either commit suicide or die of starvation. Even their family will not help them from a combination of associated shame, similar to the Japanese Giri and Gimu, and fear of retribution. The Indowy also are the servants of the Galactics and fill all servile and menial positions. That is why they are so common in the videos from Barwhon. Although technically a Tchpth planet, eighty percent of the population is Indowy."

"Solution." The commander stood up and paced to the window. He stood with his hands clasped behind him and thought about his longtime friend Chu Feng, lost due to faulty intelligence from these Darhel bastards. And now this.

"We should look for profit to ourselves for our nation specifically in this, but it will be necessary to develop a concerted front with other countries. We should convey this information to the other agreement parties, then begin using the Darhel's strategy against them. Problems should occur in preparing the expeditionary forces; questions unrelated to the central issues should be raised. Finally, the central issues should be quietly raised and some agreements renegotiated. The soldiers and their governments should be paid at a rate conforming to their scarcity; a private should probably make as much as one of the Tir negotiators, for example. And the Darhel must use their power to induce changes among the Indowy." He consulted his notes and tapped the pen on the papers.

"Although there are few accredited master ship builders, there are a vast number of component makers that can work from specifications. The Indowy must be induced to become component producers for assembly plants to be built in various locations. They will be unwilling—it goes against what could be called their religion—but they must be persuaded or forced.

"Then assembly plants can be built in the Terran System. . . ."

"We don't know that we can hold this planet," pointed out the commander. In the distance a flight of pigeons wheeled through the light blue sky. He wondered if such as they might survive a defeat of the humans, or if only the rats and cockroaches would.

"Not on the planet," corrected the junior officer, pedantically. "In orbit around other planets, Mars for example, or in the asteroid belt. Our current information is that, despite the resources available there, the Posleen do not explore or exploit the spatial regions of the planets they attack. Nor, for some strange reason, do the Galactics. Therefore placing production plants in our system is a limited risk. The Posleen will be virtually certain to overlook them; they have bypassed numerous spatial installations in other Galactic systems.

"To continue, there is sufficient excess capacity among the Indowy craftsmen to produce the necessary components for the war effort, but point-by-point assembly will not work in the time allotted. What we must do is produce a navy that assembles like the American 'Liberty' ships of WWII. If we can reach agreement on a few limited designs, components can be made throughout the Federation and shipped to this system. In the meantime we can be constructing assembly plants in various hidden locations in the system. Even if we lose control of the surface, most of our war-production capacity and a sizable gene pool will survive. Maybe enough to retake Earth."

"Funding?" Retaking Earth was not something worth discussing since it meant the loss of China as an extant body. The Middle Kingdom had a culture five thousand years old. The Posleen would destroy it, literally, over his dead body.

"That should be no problem. First, all the orbital facilities can be paid for through Navy funds while being leased on a long term by Terran companies. Special grants were authorized early in the war for Indowy craftsmen to purchase new tools and supplies to produce war goods.

"We, and by that I mean Terra, shall experience technical difficulties in supplying forces until grants for the facilities are made. We use Galactic training systems to train Indowy and humans for work on and in the plants. The Galactics have a multisensory training system that can quickly train personnel in complex skills. We build the facilities, using prefabricated materials, all the way up until the first wave. These facilities produce the weapons, systems, and ships we need to defend Terra. We sell the systems to the Darhel to equip *our* forces and to acquire planetary defense equipment. We get weapons, the Indowy get work and the Darhel pay for it. Furthermore, since the plants will be in our system and controlled by us we will reap the long-term benefits."

"Why would they do all that?" The commander turned back around and pierced the procurement officer with a stare.

"The question of production forced many pieces of the Galactics' puzzle to the surface. Our staff anthropologist now believes that the 'home sector' of the Darhel is the one hundred or two hundred planets inward from Earth. All five of the planets currently being assimilated or about to be attacked are Darhel. The others lost over the last hundred fifty years, the 'more than seventy planets' they always complain about, are all Indowy colonies, Galactic sweatshops. With the exception of Diess, they were poor and considered unimportant. Now the Posleen are striking at the core worlds of the Federation. Do not let the Darhel fool us again; they are desperate and will pay anything to stop the Posleen.

"And there is one other thing to consider."

"Yes?"

"With humans that are like these Darhel, there is rarely one layer of deception. It is more often a complex web."

"Brad, what do you think?" The President had his back turned to his advisor, staring out through the green-tinted armored glass windows of the most famous small room in the world.

"Well, Mr. President, I say we go with most of the Chinese plan, but hit a little lighter on the negotiations." The secretary of state consulted his notes. "They want the Darhel to foot the whole bill for planetary defense and I don't think they'll do it. And even if they do, the negotiations will be really drawn out and meanwhile we're not producing zip. I think we can get salaries upped pretty easily and the facility grants but let's not get greedy. With progressive taxes on Federation-paid troops, the expeditionary force troops and the space facility corporations, we'll be much better set financially anyway."

"Finance is Ralph's call, Brad, yours is international negotiations," snapped the President. He had been getting uncomfortable with some of the decisions the secretary of state had been making lately. "And I would like you to keep in mind that you work for the United States, not the Darhel. It's our country we stand to lose, Brad, our planet, our children."

"Yes Mr. President, but if we negotiate too long we stand to lose it also. Let's start at full funding but settle for the production equipment grants and, maybe, full funding for planetary defense equipment. As it is we're looking at some pretty tough terms on the loans for the equipment. It would help out a lot."

"Fine Brad, but that's the minimum. If they don't take it, no expeditionary forces, no technical support for their fleet. We'll fight in our boxer shorts before we'll fight as slaves."

"Yes, Mr. President."

"I got him to hold at grants for the production facilities and the expeditionary force equipment." The secretary of state carefully did not watch as the Darhel attempted to eat something very much like a carrot. Bits fell to the table and onto the Darhel's fine robes as the razorlike teeth shredded the vegetable into slivers.

"That is good. Those are judicious expenditures. We will not stint in our payment." The wide cat-pupil eyes dilated in an emotion unreadable by the human as six-fingered hands picked bits of vegetation out of the being's throat crest. "But, full funding for local defense... far too generous."

"Don't get stingy," said the secretary, picking at his steak. Something about eating with the Darhel always took his appetite away. "Humans can be stubborn to the point of spite. If you get the image of a Scrooge, nobody will fight for you; at least, nobody who is any good."

"We are aware of this." Again the pupils dilated and the long foxlike ears twitched. The secretary decided he would pay just about anything for a primer on Darhel body language. "It was my contention that the terms were unreasonable from the start but I was overruled. No matter, all will be resolved with time. A favor is owed."

"I trust the payment will be circumspect." The secretary knew that the boss was suspicious of his contacts as it was.

"Assuredly. Your granddaughter is very bright. Perhaps an invitation in about four years to study at an off-planet university?"

"You read my mind." There were some things that money couldn't buy.

> For those who kneel beside us,
> At altars not Thine own,
> Who lack the lights that guide us,
> Lord, let their faith atone.
> If wrong we did to call them,
> By honour bound they came;
> Let not Thy Wrath befall them,
> But deal to us the blame!
> —Kipling

10

Ft. Benning, GA Sol III
2321 December 23rd, 2001 AD

Mike looked up as General Horner entered his tiny office.

The space was barren without any personal items, workstation, or any other objects that indicated it was in use except a
combination-locked filing cabinet. The lieutenant had spent so
little time in the office in the last few months that he felt it
was more of a convenient place to call an office than an actual
workspace. Instead of a conventional computer he had his AID,
which was capable of any form of input but direct neural and
had more processor capacity than the entire Intel Corporation.
As for family pictures, every video of the girls from before he
had the AID, along with every contact he had had with them
since, was in permanent storage, available for retrieval.

And as for an "I-love-me" wall, he did, and he could care
less who knew it.

"Yes, sir?" he asked. He could see the general's new senior
aide hovering in the background.

The sight that greeted the general might have been comic
before the advent of the Galactics, but now it was as common-
place as a mouse. The lieutenant was tapping at the top of an
empty desktop, eyes fixed on a spot in midair. The wraparound
glasses he was wearing interacted with the AID on his desk to
create the illusion of a keyboard and monitor. Horner could not
see the items, projected directly onto the lieutenant's retina by
a microscopic laser projector in the glasses, but—since he used
the same system—he was well aware of the reality.

"Are you finished with the upgrade proposals?" he asked Mike, ignoring the new aide.

Although Mike was officially his junior aide, the general had made it abundantly clear to the newly assigned lieutenant colonel that Lieutenant O'Neal was his day-to-day alter ego. Once the colonel had his feet on the ground he might be half as helpful as Mike, but in the meantime the colonel could just pass the canapés and stay out of their way.

The way the non-Airborne officer had been shoved down his throat was unpleasant and ominous. It meant that the Ground Forces' personnel department felt it was gaining enough of an upper hand on GalTech to begin dictating personnel policies, even traditionally "personal" ones like the choice of an aide. Once the ACS units were detached to Fleet the problem would subside, but in the meantime it was another political battle and one Horner did not choose to fight at this time. However, since he wrote the evaluation review for the officer in question, the colonel had better be able to swallow the implied insult and pass the damn canapés.

"Yes, sir," Mike answered. "Since they definitely will not permit the use of AM as an energy source, the only remaining suggestion is incorporation of enhanced cloaking mechanisms. My prototype has shown a four percent higher survivability in every reasonable simulation that we have run. I think that pouring a little more money into tactical deception systems just makes sense."

"What about the officer and enlisted training time issue?"

"I say a thousand hours; personnel wants a hundred and fifty. I say in the field or simulated in the field; they say book learned is okay. Impasse," Mike concluded.

"All right, time to wave my stars in somebody's face. Time or type?"

"Type," replied O'Neal, meaning to try for realistic training. "Try for longer than one-fifty, but not at the expense of type. Good training over short periods is probably better than long bad training."

"Good training, huh?" Horner frowned in amusement.

"Yes, sir," Mike smiled, remembering how they first met.

"And that's the GalTech promise," continued Horner. "'If it ain't good training, it ain't GalTech.'" He paused and smiled humorlessly.

"The Expeditionary Force evaluations also fall under GalTech. The NATO units of the AEF will comprise, for now, one corp using current generation weaponry. The main force components will be 2nd Armor, 7th Cav, and 8th Infantry.

"There will also be a battalion of ACS drawn from the 82nd Airborne Division, the 2nd Battalion 325th Infantry. They've got most of their equipment and—having passed an ORS"—Operational Readiness Survey—"and an inspection by the IG—are designated as ready for combat."

"What about an ARTEP?" Mike asked. The Army Readiness Testing and Evaluation Program was the final exam of all units in the area of combat readiness. "We specified an ARTEP before a unit could be designated as combat ready."

"We got overruled. The rest of the EF is ready for deployment and the ACS batt goes with them, ready or not."

"Do they have Banshees?" The anti-grav armored fighting vehicles were critical for strategic mobility in the ACS.

"Very few and the artillery support is 105, 155 and MLRS. The HOW-2000 is being held back."

"Jesus," Mike shook his head and picked up his gripper. "Are they going to Barwhon or Diess?"

"Diess."

"How are we going to do the eval?"

"Well, Lieutenant, you know that prototype ACS command suit you have stashed somewhere?"

"Pack my bags?"

"You're scheduled to be at Pope Air Force base a week from next Tuesday, by 2400 hours. At least you'll be able to spend Christmas with Sharon and the kids."

"Then Diess?"

"There's going to be a briefer at Pope from USGF TRA-DOC"—United States Ground Forces Training and Doctrine Command—"to go over the details. Your orbital lift is scheduled for seventy-two hours afterwards.

"Now, besides the evaluation, you have another mission. The unit is woefully undertrained and they don't have any in-house experts; for all practical purposes only the members of the design team and the infantry board can be called such. So, your other mission will be training and advisement of the battalion on employment and tactics. The problem is that you are a lieutenant.

I happen to have the acquaintance of the battalion commander, Lieutenant Colonel Youngman. Remember my predecessor in the battalion?"

"Yes, sir. I hope you don't mean what I think you mean."

"Lieutenant Colonel Youngman has an excellent record and previous combat command experience. He is also a good leader. But, he's just a little bit arrogant about his abilities and knowledge for my taste. I also suspect he may be phobic about the new technologies. That may cause some problems."

"Then why did he get the first ACS battalion?"

"They knew that it was going in harm's way so they assigned a good solid combat commander; there aren't that many choices. And, as always, there are political considerations. The Marines got to decide what unit got the first ACS on Barwhon and Airborne got to decide who got it on Diess. I would have preferred someone who was a little more flexible, but older and wiser heads decided, for whatever reason, that the first group should be the two/three twenty-fifth and the commander should be Youngman. Lieutenant Colonel Paul T. Youngman wouldn't like another lieutenant colonel 'advising' him, much less a lieutenant, so you're just going to have to use as much tact as possible. I can't get free right now and you're the next best choice."

"What about Gunny Thompson?" The senior NCO of the GalTech infantry team had been pulled out of Fleet Marines for the program. Initially pessimistic about the armored combat suit program he had become one of its major proponents.

"He's taking the same position with the Marine detachment on Barwhon, so, Tag! you're it. And you won't have much support here or there; since the design phase is over and production is in gear, our star is on the wane."

"So after the eval what happens?"

"What I hope happens is that we both get combat commands. You deserve a company. But running rough shod over the design and procurement process has had a negative effect on my career. I expect I'll get something like 'J-3, Mid West Guard Command.'"

"That's stupid, with all the old war-horses they're rejuving, that should go to somebody who last heard a shot fired in anger in 'Nam."

"Don't worry about it, Mike. You and I are warriors. If there is anything that history teaches us, it's that at the beginnings of wars the career officers are divided into two camps, the managers and the warriors, and the managers rule. It's happened in every war; Halsey was a captain at the beginning of WWII and Kusov was a colonel. As the war goes on the managers go back to personnel and logistics and the warriors take command. Our stars will rise again when the shit hits the fan. Bet on it."

11

Ernie Pappas was a United States citizen born in the Territory of American Samoa. In 1961 at eighteen years of age, he enlisted in the United States Marine Corp as a private. Samoans are an odd and desired commodity in the United States military. Odd because along with generally Herculean physique they have distinctive Polynesian features that stand out among a sea of medium-sized black and white. They are desired because along with the afore-mentioned Herculean physiques come sharp intellects and unflappable personalities. Samoans attain rank fast and commanders with Samoan NCOs argue strenuously for their unit stabilization beyond normal periods. Their reenlistment rate is high.

In 1964, Lance Corporal Pappas married sixteen-year-old Priscilla Walls of Yemassee, South Carolina. This marriage violated several taboos in the eyes of Mr. and Mrs. Walls. First, although not Negro, Lance Corporal Pappas was of "color." In 1964 in Yemassee, South Carolina, white girls, even lower income white girls, did not marry people of color. Second, Missy Priscilla, their Baby Prissy, was underage for such things; although marriage among her peers, and her parents' peers, had occurred as early as fifteen. Third, the young man was an enlisted marine. Although Priscilla considered this a step up in life—her peers could be most kindly referred to as "lower income rural"—her parents were of the opposite opinion. Lower income rural had been good enough for her grandfather, a share cropper, and great-grandfather, a share cropper, and it was better than a "chink jarhead." (Mr. Walls' knowledge of the Territory of American Samoa rivaled his knowledge of nuclear physics.)

Despite these facts, the Walls signed the obligatory papers and stood before the justice of the peace with Prissy's sister acting as matron of honor and Lance Corporal Pappas' gunnery sergeant as best man, because Prissy had missed two periods and appeared to be in a family way.

It was now November 5, 2001 AD and retired Master Gunnery Sergeant Earnest Pappas sipped hot, black Kona coffee in his own kitchen and appeared to contemplate his Saturday *San Diego Times*. Intermittently he would blow his cheeks out and puff the resultant air with a gentle motoring sound.

Mrs. Earnest Pappas was clearing the breakfast dishes and from thirty-seven years experience correctly judged his mood as black. She even knew the reasons for his mood.

The reasons were twofold. Despite the fact that he had given them three good-looking grandchildren, all college graduates, had never raised a hand to their daughter, had been faithful to her and had attained for her a standard of living the envy of her siblings, he was still intensely disliked by his in-laws. The fact was unstated but obvious that the feelings were mutual. He therefore regarded her parents' upcoming visit both with annoyance and the resignation he applied to all situations that were unavoidable. Change the things you can, don't worry about the things you can't. Which brought him to the other thing he couldn't change. Age.

For thirty years Earnest Pappas had trained for a defining moment: the defense of the United States. But the war bearing down on his country would be borne upon the backs of the young men, the hale. He was just a broken down war-horse, too old to be of any use.

His, he thought, carefully concealed dank mood was shattered by his wife handing him a mailgram. It had his name and social security number in the address window and the return address of a well-known Department of Defense bureau located in St. Louis, Missouri. With a feeling of utter disbelief, under the shuttered eyes of his wife he carefully wiped off a knife, most recently used to section a grapefruit, and applied it to the envelope. Within was a multifolded document which read:

Dear Sir:

Pursuant to Presidential Directive 19-00, you are ordered to report to <u>CAMP PENDLETON, CA MARINE BASE,</u> no later than <u>2400 HOURS, 20 NOVEMBER, 2001,</u> for duty. Failure to report will be prosecuted under Section 15 of the Uniform Code of Military Justice: Failure to report for hazardous duty. All requests for waivers on the basis of age, civilian position, health or compassion shall be considered after reporting.

Public transportation may be compensated using the attached vouchers. These are good for air, train, bus or taxi, but may not be used to reimburse travel by personal vehicle.

DO NOT BRING: personally operated vehicles, personal weapons, radios with attached speakers, large musical instruments or ANY communication devices to include cellular phones or pagers.

Do bring: 1 (One) week's civilian clothing, uniforms, toiletry items, small entertainment devices, radios or music players with headphones, small musical instruments and/or reading material.

He first checked to see that it was indeed addressed to him and referred to his social security number. Then he carefully reread it as he scratched his head with the butt of the knife, a habit which drove his wife to distraction.

He blew a small quantity of dandruff off the letter, looked up at his wife and stated the obvious: "I'm fifty-seven years old!" Then he thought, re-reading the letter, *Damn, I'm still going to be here when those white trash assholes visit!*

12

Ft. Bragg, NC Sol III
0907 December 15th, 2001 AD

The barracks 2nd Battalion 325th Airborne Infantry Regiment occupied were temporary buildings from World War II. They were wooden fire traps and the double-decker bunks were relics of an earlier day as well, but they continued to adequately serve the purpose of temporary shelter for units preparing to embark from Pope Air Force Base. Well over the age of the senior member of Congress, until some local official pushed through a bill to replace them they would have to do.

The 325th was preparing to embark for Diess, a planet that until the previous week no one in the regiment had ever heard of. The powers that be had decided that until their departure they should be "locked down," placed incommunicado, and thus they lingered here in "C-LOC," an acronym that none of them could decipher.

Those with loved ones were completely cut off from communication, for no reason anyone could determine. The barracks were damp, cold and uncomfortable and they had no opportunity to train, since their equipment, including their suits, had been palletized for ease of loading. The food was miserable, tray rations morning and night with MREs for lunch. The skies had been cold, gray and sodden with rain since they left their battalion area. They faced an unknown enemy, reputed to be unstoppable, on a distant planet. And in the case of Bravo Company, Third Platoon, Second Squad, with a squad leader sunk in black depression.

Sergeant Duncan pushed the door open and slumped into

the nearest bunk. His troops, grouped at their end of the barracks, looked up from a variety of tasks, some make-work, mostly recreational. There was an endless spades game between four of the squad. Two more of the squad were playing handheld computer games, one was reading and the rest were either sleeping or cleaning equipment. They waited a moment to see if Duncan was going to pass on any information, then all of them went back to the serious business of ignoring their current existence.

Duncan stared at his boots for a moment and then straightened. "The shuttles are landing this afternoon," he said and yawned, "but we're not loading yet."

"Why?" asked one of the card players.

"Who the fuck knows," said Duncan, tonelessly. "Probably for the same reason we're in this fuckin' icebox with our thumbs up our ass."

"It's like somebody wants us to fuck up!" snarled Specialist Arlo Schrenker and hurled his book across the room.

"Wadda ya mean?" said Private Second Class Roy Bittan, trumping with a four.

"Cheep, cheep, cheep," chirped Specialist Dave Sanborn, the Bravo team leader, scooping in the trick. "He means that if we don't get some fuckin' practice with those suits we're gonna be fucked."

"F-U-C...K-E-D...A-G-A-I-N!" sang Sergeant Michael Brecker, the Alpha Team leader, covering Bittan's queen with an ace on the next trick. "We might have done something with the equipment we're trained with, cherry, but we're gonna get corncobbed by the fuckin' Posleen 'cause we don' know shit about how to use those fuckin' suits."

"Yeah," said Schrenker lurching to his feet and pacing between the steel-framed bunk beds. "That's what I mean. I mean, we can't train here, we didn't get to train 'cause we had to get ready for EIB, we didn't get a fuckin' ARTEP, to show 'em we're fucked and there's no way we're gonna be able to train on the ships, right? So it's like somebody wants us to fuck up! Why the fuck are they sending us, huh? Why not send the fuckin' armor or the goddamn cav? Why fuckin' Airborne? We're like, lightweight assault troops not plodders. I mean, what? They gonna drop us from orbit?"

"The Airborne and Marines are all getting the suits," said Bittan, studying the sergeant's king at length.

"Come on, any day now. Get up or go home. Where'd you hear that?"

"My buddy in S-4. They're gonna group us together as some new group. An' he said we're gonna get some hotshot from GalTech Infantry to help us train up." He finally tossed a low trump on the king. "I think I'm startin' to get the hang of this game."

"Thank fucking God," said his partner.

"Yeah," said Duncan, pulling out the recently issued field manual and flipping to the second page. "O'Neal, Michael L., First Lieu...nah."

"What?" said Schrenker.

"There used to be an O'Neal with the One Five-O-Five. Come to think of it he was Horner's driver and Horner is the head of GalTech. I wonder if it's the same guy?"

"What's he like?" asked Schrenker.

"Short, hasn't got much of a short guy's attitude though, 'cause he's built like a fuckin' tank, big-time lifter. Ugly as sin. Quiet, but kinda wise guy when he opens his mouth. Doesn't give 'no-brainers' much slack. Gotta punch like a mule."

"When'd you meet him?" asked Schrenker.

"'97? '98?"

"Where'd you find out about his punch?" asked Bittan, fascinated.

"Rick's." Duncan answered shortly, naming off an infamous topless bar in Fayetteville. "There's some interesting shit in this," he continued flipping through the field manual.

"Like what? How to play tiddlywinks while wearing a suit?" asked Brecker, taking the last trick with a ten of diamonds. "Shit, gotta sandbag."

"No, shithead, how to fuckin' survive," snapped Duncan.

"Hey, asshole!" snarled Brecker, tossing aside the trick and surging to his feet, pointing his finger like a knife. "If I wanna hear shit from you, I'll squeeze your head 'til it pops!"

"You'd better at the fuck ease, Sergeant," snarled Duncan in turn, his teeth drawn back in a rictus. The rest of the squad was frozen watching the arguing NCOs. The long-awaited clash had taken everyone, including the principals, by surprise. Duncan slammed the field manual to the floor when the other sergeant refused to back down. "And you better at ease right fuckin' now," he continued. "If you have something to say, we need to take it outside," he ended, sounding nearly normal, but the hard lines of his face were unchanged.

Brecker's face worked, his anger and pride driving him into a corner, but the discipline that had enabled him to reach his current rank forced the words out, "Okay, let's take it outside, Sergeant." The last word was a spat epithet.

The two NCOs stalked outside with the hard eyes of the squad trailing after.

"Okay," snapped Duncan, stopping and spinning to face the shorter NCO as they turned the corner of the barracks, "what the fuck is eating your ass?"

"You, you fucked up son of a bitch!" growled the junior NCO, restraining a shout with difficulty. They were standing just off the company street and both recognized the danger they were in. Overt conflict would mean instant punishment from the present chain of command. "This was my goddamn squad before you got shoved down our throat and it's fallin' fuckin' apart! Get your shit together, dammit!"

Duncan's face was as cold and gray as the skies but he could not find an immediate rebuttal. Given the silence, Brecker continued his attack.

"I could give a fuck how we got you. If you got off your ass. But I can't order the fuckin' squad around while you pout, they won't listen. So quit your cryin' you shit and lead! Lead, follow or get out of my fuckin' way!"

"Oh, so you know all there is about bein' a squad leader?" whispered Duncan, clenching his fists convulsively. He was on the defensive, knowing the truth of the accusation.

"I know I gotta do more than sit on my ass and mope!"

"Oh, yeah?..." Duncan suddenly turned away from the hot eyes on him and looked at the blank wall of the barracks. He felt tears welling up and abruptly changed the subject. "Ten fuckin' years Brecker. Ten fuckin' years in this shit-hole. I can't get away from it. I put myself on levee to Panama or Korea or any other shit-hole just to get out and get graded as vital or talked into staying by the CO. Then the fuckin' chain-of-command changes and the new CO thinks I'm uselesser than dirt. But then there's no levees. I re-up for something else and get classified as critical so I can't change my MOS. The only fuckin' way out of Bragg would be to terminate my airborne status, but that's just another word for quittin'. Finally, finally I get my fuckin' staff stripes, like four years after I should have gotten 'em and now this. I just cannot fuckin' face it, I can't."

"You gotta. At least they left you some rank. I would've sent you to Leavenworth."

"They couldn't have."

"You cut Reed's legs off, you bastard! Of course they could have!"

"Yeah, you knew him, didn't you?"

"We were in the same Basic fuckin' platoon, yeah I knew him."

"They couldn't have court-martialed me and won," Duncan muttered. "I mean, it wouldn't have even gotten past the JAG. I didn't know that at the time. I should have let 'em. It was experimental equipment, all of it is. It would be the same as court-martialing a test pilot for punching out of plane or us for not jumping. I should not have been *able* to do what that thing did. You just don't issue equipment like that, you *don't*. If it was anybody's fault, it was GalTech's for issuing that piece of crap."

"We've still got 'em!"

"They re-issued 'em, remember? You can't get them to generate the same field; I tried."

"*What?*"

"I was *careful* this time. It won't do it, anyway. But the point is, you can court-martial someone for not following proper regs, but when an accident is not covered by training or experience there are clear regulations that state that an individual cannot be prosecuted for it, no matter what the consequences. So should I be a sergeant now? You tell me?"

"You should be a fuckin' civilian," snapped Brecker, but it was without heat. He could see the logic of the argument, whatever his personal dislike. "But this isn't about whether you should be a sergeant, it's about whether you should be a squad leader. Are you gonna get it together or not?"

"I don' know," admitted Duncan wearily. He slumped to a squatting position and leaned against the sodden barracks wall as the runoff soaked into his beret. "Every other time I felt crapped on I was able to shake it off, but this time it's so hard."

"You didn't get crapped on, you idiot, they gave you a walk."

"No, I got some pretty good scuttlebutt that the colonel was aware of the reg. He could have let me walk on the basis of it, and I could request a review, probably, and get my stripes back, that's what I'm trying to work out. But while I'm thinkin' about that, I'm not thinkin' about the squad."

"Yeah, well you better start thinkin' about your responsibilities or Top's gonna certify you as unfit and bust you to specialist."

"'Slippin' down the ladder rung by rung,'" whispered Duncan.

"Yeah, you are," agreed Brecker, tightly, not recognizing the quote. "But you don't gotta. All you need to do is wake up a little, maybe do some extra training and they can't do it."

"Yeah," said Duncan, as a thought hit him like a brick. He paused for a moment and considered it. He felt as if a black cloth had been taken off of his eyes. "You read that FM?"

"No, what's the point, we don't have suits to train in."

"No, but we got PT uniforms."

"Yeah," agreed Brecker, bitterly, not yet noticing the sudden change. "Like we're gonna do any running on Diess. The only fuckin' running we're gonna do is away."

"There's the field here," muttered Duncan, continuing a different conversation. His mind was starting to turn furiously.

"Yeah, let's go run around the track. It works for the colonel, night and day. Come rain, come shine, there's the colonel, motivating us to run on a muddy track by his own example. I'm sure the squad would love to go running all day and night in the rain. Not."

"'In the absence of available suits, suit drills can and should be conducted in lightweight physical training uniforms, using either standard issue or field expedient simulations of standard suit weapons and equipment.'"

"What?"

"It's in the FM. That's the new training schedule. I'll go talk to Sergeant Green. Get the guys pulling out their PT uniforms."

"It is pissing down out here, you know," said Brecker, gesturing at the sodden skies.

"Big whoop, they're infantry, they can handle a little rain. And get 'em thinkin' about what to simulate their weapons with."

"You're crazy."

"You're the one who wants to survive, right?"

"Yeah, but..."

"So we gotta train, 'in the absence of suits...'"

"Yeah, so we run around a muddy field in fuckin' sweats? Why not BDUs?"

"You wanna run in boots? Get shin splints? I mean, we are gonna be runnin', not joggin', that's the essence of suit drills."

"But..."

"Get moving, Sergeant Brecker. I'll go see the platoon sergeant."

"Okay..."

"Duncan, what have you been smoking?"

The senior NCO's room was simply a closed-off corner of the barracks. Across from it was another enclosure to be used as an office; unfortunately the Army in its infinite wisdom had not seen fit to furnish that room at all. The furniture in the platoon sergeant's bedroom was virtually identical to the platoon's: a steel bed frame with an uncovered mattress. The platoon sergeant's bed was made as neatly as possible with a poncho liner and Gore-Tex sleeping bag. Sergeant Green had been hunched over the new field manual, fighting off incipient flu, when Duncan entered. One of the other squad leaders had already told him of the harsh words between Duncan and Brecker and their abrupt exit, so he was expecting a report that the fight the other NCOs in the company had been expecting had finally occurred. Duncan's rapidly delivered request had caught him completely off guard.

"Nothing, Sergeant," Duncan replied, shocked. It was not that drug use was unknown in the Army, it was just that it was as relentlessly sought out and as rigorously persecuted as homosexuality or communism in the forties and fifties. It was extremely unlikely that he had smoked, dipped, popped, shot or snorted anything not prescribed since his entry ten years before or he would not have lasted ten years. "I just think we're missing a golden opportunity."

"So, what is it you want to do?"

"I want to take the squad out to do suit drills, on the parade field. I mean, those movement methods are completely different than what we're used to. I want to get out there and start working on coordination and timing. I really like the systems they've worked out, the way the units move and coordinate. And it would get the squad off its ass, an', hell, it'd get me off my ass, too."

"Yeah," said Sergeant Green after a moment's consideration. He had been looking at the same sections and wondering when they could start training on it. But the suggestion in the manual about training without suits had not caught his eye. "Okay, I want to get with Top about the rest of it, but here's what I want you to do. Take your squad out and start them training. Get them as picture perfect as you can. If we stay here three more days, I'll try to get the rest of the company out there also, and your squad will demonstrate. How's that?"

"Great!" The first grin Sergeant Green had seen on Duncan since his Article 15 flashed across his face. "We'll get right on it!"

"Keep the faith, Sergeant," Green said with a nod. As Duncan bounded out of the room, one of the crushing weights on his shoulders lifted.

The squad was lined up in a wedge formation, with Sergeant Duncan at the apex. He turned to face the eight unhappy looking troops in gray PT sweat suits.

"Right," he said as the skies began to drizzle again. "The difference between ACS and normal infantry tactics is that ACS calls for much more in the way of shock and speed tactics. Airborne infantry is deliberate compared to ACS; ACS is more like armored cav. We're going to train on a few simple maneuvers at first. Think of them like football plays: wedge, echelon right, echelon left, lean right, lean left and bounding line. And the only way to train for open field ACS combat is at the run. We're going to start off slow then work up to speed. Don't worry, you won't be noticing the rain a'tall in just a bit."

"Captain Brandon, sir, it's the S-3," called the company clerk through the open door of the commander's office.

Bob Brandon had been more than halfway expecting the call since his company began intense ACS drills in the parade field two days before. He picked up the extension phone reluctantly. "Captain Brandon."

"Bob, it's Major Norton."

"Yes, sir."

"Why are your troops training in ACS drills?"

"It seemed the thing to do, sir. We are an ACS unit."

If Major Norton noted the sarcasm, he declined to comment. "The problem is, too many of these ACS tactics need review. The colonel and I have been studying the manuals and when we're ready, and by that I mean Operations, we'll publish a training schedule of what we want trained on. There's too much armor and not enough infantry in their damned tactics, they'll get us all killed if we use half that stuff! In the meantime you are to stick to the prescribed training schedule, do you understand that, Captain?"

"Yes, sir. Might I point out that the training schedule calls for equipment maintenance. Our equipment is stored with the S-4."

"I know what the training schedule calls for, dammit, I wrote it, remember? Next week's is being revised for some of that ACS work, work that the colonel and I have reviewed and agree with, and until then you are to continue with the published schedule! Am I making myself perfectly clear, Captain, or do I have to have the colonel call you and explain it in greater detail?"

"No, sir, that won't be necessary. I'll be speaking to the colonel about this at length in the near future."

"And this is...?" asked Sergeant Duncan, holding up a flash card. "Sanborn?"

"Umm, a Lamprey?"

"Right, and a Lamprey is...?" he asked, referring to the information on the back of the card.

"A landing craft. Umm, space weaponry, like...uh, plasma cannons and shit. Some antipersonnel stuff, really nasty shit. Oh, sweeps for artillery, so, like, no call for fire if you're around one."

"Yawhol. Anything else, like, how many troops it carries? Shit like that?"

"Oh, about four, five hundred? Yeah, like, one of their companies. And one or two God Kings."

"Right. Okay, how do you identify one?"

"If it looks like a skyscraper but it fuckin' moves, it's a fuckin' Lamprey," said Sergeant Brecker, laconically.

"Ek-fuckin'-zactly," noted Duncan, neatly flipping the flash card into the trash. "If you are unable to identify a Lamprey, you desperately need your eyes examined. Next on our daily prescribed training of Posleen equipment identification, is this big motherfucker," he held up the flash card. "Bittan?"

"C-Dec, Command Dodecahedron. Core unit of a B-Dec or Battle Dodecahedron. Twelve-faceted cube. Random mix of interstellar weaponry on eleven facets. Antipersonnel secondaries. Interstellar drive. Umm, about 1600 personnel nominal, buncha God Kings, some light armor. Locks on twelve Lampreys to form a B-Dec which is the central fighting unit of the Posleen."

"Very good. Excellent, even. How do you identify one?"

"It looks like a B-Dec, except smaller and the B-Decs have noticeable gaps between the attached Lampreys."

"Close. The correct answer is: if you want to piss your shorts and run it's either a B-Dec or a C-Dec and it don't really matter much which."

"How much longer we gotta put up with this shit?" asked Sergeant Brecker, rhetorically. The training schedule, by order of the battalion commander, had been read to each company during morning formation. Authorized ACS training, a total of thirty-five hours for this week alone, was currently "Identification of Known Posleen Vehicles and Equipment." There were twenty-five items. The following week there was "Know Your Combat Suit," an in-depth list of all the items on the suits. That, too, would have to be out of a book; there weren't any suits to study.

Bittan fished the Lamprey flash card out of the trash. "I'd really like to keep this," he said diffidently.

Duncan looked chagrined. "I'm sorry, man, I shouldn't let my attitude fuck the rest of you up."

"Don' mean nothin'," said Sergeant Brecker. "I mean, as bad as those fuckin' grass drills were, at least we felt like we were learnin' somethin'. It ain't your fault battalion's got it stuck so far up their fourth point of contact they couldn't find light with a nuke."

"F-U-C...K-E-D..." Stewart began to intone.

"Attention on deck!" snapped a specialist halfway down the barracks.

"At ease, rest even," called Captain Brandon. "Get the troops from next door and wake everybody up, I got newwws!"

"Whass happ'nin' sir?" asked one of the mortar troops.

"Wait'll we're all here. I don't want to have to go over this twice." He grinned. "How are you liking the training?"

Feet shuffled for a moment, then the mortar specialist answered. "It fuckin' sucks, sir."

"Glad to hear that the first sergeant and I aren't the only ones with that opinion." The gathered troopers got a real chuckle from that.

Troops were trickling into both ends of the barracks. As the trickle fell off and the group pressed forward, Captain Brandon hopped up and sat on one of the upper bunks. He looked around at the sea of black, white and brown faces to make sure that most of the troops were present.

"Okay, here's the deal. We've been scheduled to lift day after tomorrow." There was a muttered and confused chorus. "Yeah, is that good or bad? Well, we'll be out of C-LOC, but we'll be even more imprisoned. However, battalion has indicated that we might get access to our equipment once we're on board ship. In the meantime I want you guys to bone up on all the ACS lore you can. We're not going to get much work with the equipment before we're engaged, so I want you guys to read the fuckin' book! I understand that there's only one per squad, so read aloud or share the reading. Read it in your spare time, read from it between deals! It's the only damn card we've got to play! So study like you never did in school. Williams," he pointed at a Second Platoon NCO, "maximum effective range of the M-403 suit grenade launcher?"

"Uh, a klick, sir?"

"Twelve hundred meters, close but no cigar, Sarn't. If you don't know it, I know your troops don't. Duncan, maximum effective range of the M-300 grav rifle?"

"Maximum effective range of the targeting system, sir."

"Explain."

"The grav rifle has the ability to leave Earth's orbit, sir. It will hit something as far away as you can aim."

"Right. Private Bittan, what is a Lamprey and how do you identify it?"

Bittan glanced at Sergeant Brecker and got a nod. "Umm, it's the lander portion of the B-Dec, the outer layer that surrounds the Command Dec. An'...if it looks like a skyscraper, but it's flyin', it's a Lamprey, sir."

Captain Brandon laughed. "Good answer, troop..."

"Complement of four hundred normals, nominal, with one to two God Kings. Single random anti-ship weapon on its vertical axis. Normal space lift and drives..."

"Thanks, Bittan, that's the idea. You all need to get up to snuff on this stuff. Weapons, tactics, enemy equipment. Let's hope we get to use the equipment once we're on board, but in the meantime, study, study, study. We move to embarkation at 1030 hours day after tomorrow. That's all."

"Sir," said Schrenker, "are we gonna get to call our families?"

"No." Captain Brandon did not look happy to pass on that news. "We've been ordered locked down and that's the way it's gonna stay. Once we're on board we'll have the ability to send mail to our families, but not until we're in space."

There was a disgruntled mutter at that, but no more. "Yes, sir."

"All right men, get back to it. And?"

"Study," they chorused.

He waved and walked out as the company broke up into buzzing groups.

13

Ttckpt Province, Barwhon V
0205 GMT, June 27th, 2001 AD

"Man," growled Richards over the team net, "does it ever stop raining here?"

"Well," answered Mueller, subvocally, "if you consider this admittedly heavy mist to be rain, no."

"Can it," snapped Mosovich as he slithered over a fallen Griffin tree, "we don't know what's around."

Barwhon, like the Pacific Northwest, was a land of incessant mists and rain. And, as soldier after soldier has discovered, although Gore-Tex deals well with rain, mist slices right to the bone. The constant cold and damp would have sapped the energy of a normal group of soldiers, would be a major handicap to the expeditionary force, but Mosovich and Ersin had chosen well. The team of special operations veterans had long before become totally inured to cold and wet; but that never stopped a soldier from bitching. The air currently had the texture of cold, wet velvet and the mist was slowly turning to rain. Their footfalls on the sodden purple humus were muffled; between the slightly reduced air pressure and the mist the sound barely carried to their own ears. Unfortunately, since they knew there was a Posleen outpost somewhere out there, it also meant they would be less likely to hear the Posleen.

They had been traveling for two days through the damp forest without incident and Mueller and Trapp had made up a game of naming the different kinds of trees. They were up to three hundred and eighty-five different species and almost all of them were larger than terrestrial rain-forest giants. The most common, nominated as a Griffin tree by Trapp, averaged over a hundred seventy-five meters high, more than three times as high as the tallest terrestrial rain-forest king. The "wood" was incredibly tough, as it had to be to support such a structure even under Barwhon's slightly reduced gravity, and degraded slowly under the influence of Barwhonian saprophytes and the ubiquitous beetles. Massive limbs, lianas and ferns snarled the forest floor and the triple canopy devoured the light.

Through the amethyst mire the team moved like ghosts. The insectoid animal life would stop as they passed, analyze them in their animal fashion, then get on with the serious business of survival. The team could have been the only sentients on the planet until Trapp suddenly froze and held up a clenched left fist.

The team slowly sank down into the bog on their haunches as Trapp extended his hand twice, then held up two fingers. He made the sign for random movement and enemy. Just out of sight a dozen Posleen were doing something not in the hand signal lexicon. Considering that the team was there to figure out what the Posleen did on a day-to-day basis, that wasn't very surprising.

Mosovich crept forward and slid his head slowly around the liana shielding Trapp from view. An even dozen Posleen, normals from what he had learned of their anatomy, were slowly moving across the clearing, picking feathery leaves and purple berries.

The aliens were Arabian-horse-sized centauroids. Long arms ending in four-digit talons, three "fingers" and a broad, clawed thumb, protruded from a complex double shoulder. The legs, ending in elongated talons, were longer than a horse's, and sprung on a reverse double knee that seemed arachnoid. The design of the knees caused them to move with an oddly sinuous bouncing gate, like oversized jumping spiders. Their long necks were topped with a blunt crocodilian snout. The necks of the squad wove a complex pavane, sauroid mouths opening and closing in a constant low atonal hiss that was almost a chant. The neck movement was hypnotic and sinister, speaking to the lizard brain of fanged hunters in the dark.

Ten of the Posleen were in a line, with two more following. Each of them wore a harness to which was attached their primary weapon. Four carried 1mm railguns, long gray rifles that looked misshapen to humans, six carried shotguns with bulbous ammunition storage; one of the trailers toted a hypervelocity missile launcher and the other sported a 3mm railgun. The missile launcher was a small weapon, not much more than a yard long, but the bulbous rear housing carried six missiles with onboard grav-drives that could accelerate them to a large fraction of the speed of light in less than twenty meters. The damage when one hit a solid object was catastrophic.

Occasionally one of the pickers would take a sample back to the trailers and give it to the one with the HVM. It, in turn, would slip the sample into a complex construction carried over one shoulder. There were no significant vocalizations until a beetle the size of a rabbit was startled out of cover by the skirmish line.

The skirmisher that startled it let out an odd warbling cry and darted in pursuit. When the Posleen caught the unfortunate hemipteroid it popped the beetle into its maw. The trailer with the 3mm let out a high-pitched bellow, whipped up its 3mm and butt stroked the skirmisher on the back of the head. The beetle popped out relatively unscathed and tried to crawl away, but the chastened Posleen picked it up and handed it to the technician.

Mosovich tapped Trapp on the arm and pointed for him to stay in place. He motioned for Ersin and, after a moment's hesitation almost too faint to notice, Mueller. Master Sergeant Tung, in the meantime, had gotten the team cautiously dispersed. Mosovich suddenly realized that Ellsworthy had disappeared, which was just fine by him. It meant that if it dropped in the pot, the wrath of God would suddenly descend on the Posleen.

With a silence that Mosovich found completely acceptable, Mueller moved into a position to overlook the Posleen and began filming them with a microcam. Ersin just looked, getting a feel for the enemy. As they watched, another small beetle was driven up and the Posleen went through the same little skit of attempted consumption. Despite being on a recently conquered planet, the Posleen did not have any security out; the Posleen with the 3mm seemed to be more of a subleader than security. They would have been remarkably easy to ambush.

After his two intel NCOs had gotten a good look, Mosovich motioned them backwards. He signed for Trapp to lead the team wide around the foragers to the left and pulled back. The team pulled out, and swung wide. Ellsworthy appeared as silently as she had disappeared, pulling a small piece of rotting vegetation off of her ghilly suit as she reentered the perimeter. She held it at arm's length by two sculptured fingernails for inspection then tossed it aside with a grimace. Mueller snorted quietly and shook his head as Tung rolled his eyes toward the heavens. After the little by-play she hefted her "Tennessee 5-0" .50 caliber sniper rifle and silently moved out. The ease with which she handled the massive weapon belied its thirty-pound weight.

Throughout the rest of the day they continued to bump into rummaging Posleen with greater and greater frequency. Their objective was an "upland" area where a Tchpth colony city had formerly resided, but as they neared the objective the density of Posleen had increased to the point that Mosovich pulled them back as darkness fell and called a council of war.

At the stop Ellsworthy finally demonstrated where she had been hiding each time by slinging her thirty-pound rifle, slipping on fingerless, spiked "tiger" gloves and swarming thirty meters up a Griffin tree. The movement was so fast and silent that it was surreal, like something from a horror movie, the petite marine moving more like a spider than a human. The highly trained and physically fit special operations NCOs watched the action and, with the exception of Trapp, knew that there was no way they could replicate it. Trapp just nodded his head, noting a few things about the eccentric little marine falling into place. In the velvet darkness above, her ghilly suit blended her into invisibility.

"Okay," Mosovich subvocalized over the team net as the other NCOs sat down to munch MREs, "we're running into more and more Posleen. We might be able to sneak through them, but we will probably run afoul of at least one party. I am accepting input, junior first. Martine."

"P-p-p-pull back. Iss-iss-iss a recon, na a raid."

"Mueller?"

"This is our first penetration. Let's hold back and observe the parties for a while then pull out to the second area. This area is getting established; it only got overrun about five weeks ago. Maybe a more established area will have fewer skirmishers."

"Trapp?"

The SEAL just nodded his head.

"Does anybody want to go deeper?"

"Ah' always lahk it deeper, Sergeant Major," whispered Ellsworthy from her perch.

There was muted laughter as Mosovich shook his head. "Ersin, dammit, I told you she'd be trouble!"

"Me? It was your idea!" the intel sergeant protested.

"Yeah, but I still told you she'd be trouble."

"That's mah middle name, Sarn't Major. And speakin' a trouble, there's some Posleen headed this way right now." She bent over her scope. "Another of them rat packs, about fifteen."

"Okay, fall back to pickup. Trapp, take it slow and cautious. Martine, signal for pickup two days from now, site A."

"R-r-r...You know."

14

Habersham County, GA Sol III
2025 December 24th, 2001 AD

By mutual agreement Mike and Sharon had decided not to move
from their house in the Piedmont. The kids had gotten used to
regular visits with his father up in Towns county and Sharon had
her job as an engineer. Despite the recent call-ups the majority
of the conscription would not begin for another year when the
equipment construction really got on line. Mike was in a position
to pull a few strings and they had that to talk over. The drive
home gave him time to put his thoughts in order; it was going
to be an odd week.

Pulling into the driveway of the old farmhouse he stopped and
looked across the field at the sunset. One of the recent reports
generated by some Beltway Bandit, one of the numerous con-
sulting firms on Washington's Beltway that provided specialized
studies for the United States government, dealt with climatological changes. Mike knew just enough climatology to doubt that
anyone could accurately predict what the climatological changes
might be when the activities of the enemy were still unknown,
but the least that was sure to happen was some kinetic or nuclear
bombardment. How much the weather changed depended on the
severity of the bombardment.

If there was a minimal spatial bombardment there would
be a minimal drop in worldwide temperature. The converse
was of course true. A minimal bombardment, sixty to seventy
weapons scattered across Earth's surface, targeted solely on the
projected Planetary Defense Centers, would have the approximate

113

climatological effect of the Mount Pinatubo eruption. That had caused a global temperature drop of nearly a degree and some spectacular sunsets, but otherwise weather was hardly changed.

However, as the number of weapons increased so did the relative severity. Two hundred kinetic energy weapons in the five to ten kiloton range would have the equivalent effect of the Mount Krakatoa explosion, which had plunged the world into a mini-ice age, causing year-round frosts in the late eighteen hundreds. At over four hundred weapons it was projected that a real ice age would ensue, especially as the rate of carbon dioxide emission was projected to drop to nearly nothing over the next twelve years.

That particular datum called for the largest caveat in the entire report. The report tossed a bone to a theory that Earth was currently in the midst of an ice age and that the only thing holding it off was the current rate of CO_2 emission; in essence that the current scheduled ice age was held at bay by "greenhouse effect." If the theory were true, and some climatologists were willing to admit it might be, ending the era of fossil fuels could coincidentally cause an ice age in and of itself.

If an ice age ensued from the war, win or lose, some of the most civilized regions of the world would become untenable. And the conditions projected for the war itself? Mike had seen the raw reports, the ones that so far had not leaked to the press. That knowledge and calling in a few favors owed him had created an awareness of a situation that no parent should ever have to face. With his mind on those thoughts he got out in the deepening twilight and walked into the kitchen of the holiday-festive house. There was a scent of the cedar Christmas tree cut from the family farm, and Sharon had been baking cookies.

"Hi, honey, I'm home!" The expression was trite, but the emotion behind it was heartfelt.

Sharon came into the room leading the youngest. Mike's heart lurched when he realized Michelle was almost too large for her pink footie pajamas.

For the past long months Mike had spent between sixty and eighty hours a week at GalInf headquarters in Fort Benning or hopping from one military base to another. As one of the few experts on the new infantry systems, every time there was a snag he had to go troubleshoot. In most cases there were honest difficulties with assimilating new technology but on several occasions he had run into the technophobia mentioned in regards to the new ACS commander.

Eight months with almost no contact with his family and darn near no social contacts at all had left him drained. It was time, however short, for a break.

"Merry Christmas, sweetie," he said to his daughter, opening his arms for a hug. "Do you have a hug for Daddy?"

"No!" She hugged her mother's leg and buried her face in its protective warmth.

"Why not?"

"Not Daddy."

"Am too!"

"Not!"

"Meanie! Pooh!" He blew on her hair and she giggled.

"'Top!"

"Meanie! Pooh!"

Giggle. "'Top!"

"Meanie!..."

"Pooh!" Giggle.

"Aggh! Got me! Hug?"

She wrapped her arms around him and, just for a moment, all was right with the world.

"Do you have the holiday off?" asked Sharon. End of moment.

"Actually I have the week and a bit. But there's bad news to go with the good."

"What?" There was another surprise here and she was getting tired of surprises. Coping as a single mother for the last eight months had not helped.

"I'm getting attached to the ACS unit deploying to Diess with the expeditionary force as an advisor," he said, standing up with the pink bundle of his daughter in his arms. "You sure are getting heavy!"

"You're going off planet?" Sharon asked, stunned.

"And how." Mike nodded, dreading the coming argument.

"When?"

"Next week. This is the pre-deployment leave."

"How come everyone else gets a couple of months' warning?" Sharon demanded.

"Probably because everyone else has a normal job," said Mike, reasonably.

"Well, dammit!"

"Honey," Mike gestured that he was still holding Michelle. "Can we save this for a bit?"

"Sure. Since you're home you can give Cally a bath."

"Okay. Did I miss supper?"

"Yes, and if you hadn't I'd have thrown it outside anyway."

"Honey."

"I know, but this is just a little bit hard to take, okay?" Sharon had tears in her eyes. "It's kind of hard being a single mom all the time, okay? And it's kind of hard knowing what's coming. And I've just about had as much as I can take. The projects are piling up and I feel like every time I take time off for the family I'm letting our side down!"

Mike stood silent. This was one of those times when no words would help.

"Why is Mommy crying?" asked Michelle

"Because Daddy has to go away for a while."

"Why?"

"Because it's Daddy's job."

"I don't want you to go away!"

"I know, sweetie pie, but I have to go."

"I don't want you to!" In sympathetic reaction Michelle started to cry.

Shit. "I didn't want to get into this, honey, but maybe we could go down to Florida for the week. Mom would love to see the kids, I'm sure."

"Granma?"

"Yes, pumpkin, Granma."

"We're going to Granma's house!"

"We're going to Granma's house?" asked Cally, arriving late from a potty break.

"Honey, I don't know if I can get the time," said Sharon, automatically. "We're knee deep in modifying the F-22s."

"If Lockheed won't let you go under the circumstances, quit. It's not like we'll need the money and you could spend more time with the kids."

"Let's not talk about this now," she said, shaking her head. "Let's get Michelle and Cally to bed and then we'll talk."

"Okay."

✧   ✧   ✧

After the children were tucked away Mike and Sharon pulled out a bottle of "the good stuff" and talked; it was a good way to wait up for Santa. Sharon, curled on the couch, brandy snifter in hand, tried as best she could to bring him up-to-date on the children's lives, all the little things that he had missed over the previous months. Mike, sitting on the floor, watching the lights of the Christmas tree blink, told her in greater detail about his work and about the overall preparation for the upcoming war. And, violating security, he finally told her about the full nature of the threat and what it meant.

"Everything?" asked Sharon, setting down her snifter.

"All the coastal plains. We just will not have the equipment to fight the Posleen by then. And that's just in the United States. Don't ask me about Third World countries."

"Then why are we sending a suit unit to Diess and Barwhon?" asked Sharon in bewilderment, picking the snifter up and taking a deep slug. The warm burn of the cognac helped reestablish her hard-won calm.

"A battalion of ACS will not be a deciding factor, at least that is what the High Command thinks and I agree."

"You mean the Joint Chiefs."

"No, I mean the High Command. How they're going to sell it, I don't know, but that's what the upper command echelon of the United States Defense Forces are going to be officially called. New service, new names. Like Line and Fleet and Strike Commands; out with the old, in with the new. The remainder of the Navy and Air Force that aren't being transferred to Fleet are going to be rolled into the whole, with the High Commander being an Army general. The part that no one is talking about is that it takes a layer of civilian control out of the military. There are some constitutional issues that I don't think are being fully explored.

"Anyway, we had hoped to earn enough funds from the units on Diess and Barwhon to equip multiple ACS units. But, because of procurement issues, the first equipment will go to the ACS units for the deployments to Barwhon and Diess. Only after their needs are satisfied will dedicated Terran Fleet Strike be supplied. But those Galactic-funded units are going to be parceled out to all the invaded planets, not just Earth. We need dedicated Ground Force ACS units, lots of them, and we probably won't have any when the first wave arrives.

"Some forces might get *un*-powered suits just before the invasion. Might. We've been fighting for training time but I don't think we'll get much." Mike sipped pale cognac and considered how to go on. There was so much he felt she should know, both as his partner and as a soon-to-be-recalled naval officer.

"We need a navy even more, but most naval units will still be under construction when the Posleen arrive. The battle wagons, the big guns that can go toe-to-toe with the globes, won't be available until about a year after the first wave hits, but before the second wave, thank God." Mike took a pause and looked particularly unhappy. "Which brings us to you."

"Why?"

"A little-known caveat of all these activities won't be little known for long. Fleet and Fleet Ground Strike personnel stationed off Terra will be given the option to have one relative per serviceman relocated to a non-threatened planet. I checked and you were going to be stationed stateside. Before the regulation becomes widely known I can pull a couple of strings and get you stationed off planet. That means that either Cally or Michelle could be relocated to a safe planet."

"Who would raise them?" asked Sharon, eyes widening. Mike realized that he probably should have spread the shocks out, but they had just run out of time.

"Probably an upper-class Indowy family."

"Would it be the planet I was stationed on?"

"Probably not. The guy who owes me a favor can get you off planet but not to a location of choice. It may be to the Terran Defense Task Force, or Titan Base, who knows. All I know is that I can get you off planet and I can't do the same thing for myself right now."

"Why?"

"That's not my mission. I'm slated for the Diess force, but only as an advisor on temporary duty, not as a permanent change of station, so it doesn't count as off planet. And, for that matter, the AEF personnel are not counted as being off-Terra since they're only there temporarily. How temporarily is a good question, but it is not considered a change of station."

"How long are they going to be there?" asked Sharon.

"Nobody knows, but you have to be in Fleet or Fleet Strike to be considered for off-planet duty and the AEF units are not considered Fleet Strike, yet. Effectively, your salary has to come straight from the Federation, rather than through a planetary or national formation."

"So, I have to decide whether to have one of our children safe but separated from us both." Her face twisted into an expression he couldn't read.

"Not really. If you wish to blame me for arm twisting, feel free, but you had better take the position. I cannot guarantee that I will be back by the time of the invasion and I virtually guarantee that neither of us will be able to be with our children during the combat. That means that they will be without our protection and I've already told you how bad it will probably get. Let me be clear. We are going to lose the East and West Coast, all of it, all the way to the Appalachians in the east and the Rockies or Cascades in the west. We may lose the Great Plains, although I think we can contain or delay that loss significantly. Urban areas inside the defensive ring are going to take a pasting.

"Nowhere on Earth will be completely safe. There are going to be shelters for less than ten percent of the population unless a miracle happens and I don't think, and this is a professional estimate, that the defenses for the shelters are going to work. Digging them underground is a waste of resources and, possibly, criminally stupid. If we leave the girls with family, we can leave them in Florida, which is going to be one vast abattoir, in northern California or in the Georgia mountains, on the back side of the continental divide. That's the safest by far but it's still too close to Atlanta."

"I can't believe that they would force me back into uniform given those conditions," Sharon said, furiously.

"Believe it. No one is avoiding service this time, not if they are even marginally qualified. We will both have responsibilities to meet. Family hardship will not be considered a recognized reason for discharge."

"Then I can't believe you want to leave them with your father," argued Sharon. She hated Mike when he was like this, he set up these logic juggernauts and just drove over everything in his path. Her own experience with lifer military, especially officers, had been less than pleasant.

"Dad's a kook, but the right kind of kook for the conditions," said Mike, trying to tack back towards a normal tone.

"Your father is not a kook, he is flat bughouse nuts. Round the bend. Bats in his belfry." Sharon twisted her finger by the side of her head.

"Yeah, but what kind of bats? All his bats carry AKs. He's just the kind of nut that might keep one of the kids alive."

"Honey, he's dangerous!" complained Sharon, losing the argument and knowing it.

"Not to kin."

"Most murders involve relatives!" she rebutted.

"My father is far too professional to murder family. All of his murders are quick, discreet and untraceable to him."

Mike shook his head in bafflement. "He is the perfect person to leave one of the kids with given the situation. What? You want to put them up with your parents? Mr. and Mrs. 'White-Carpets, Don't-Run-In-The-House, I-Can't-Believe-This-It's-All-Just-A-Government-Scare'? Or perhaps my mother? Who, while a wonderful person, has no capacity to defend herself much less one of our children? And who lives in California, home of a thousand and one great places for a Posleen to land. Or, put them with an ex-Ranger, ex-Green Beret, and ex-mercenary? Who stays in shape, maintains a wonderful and completely illegal weapons collection and has a farm in the mountains? Come on!"

"I don't like his stories. I won't have him feeding the children all that hogwash." She was starting to be petulant and knew it. If Mike would just back off she might have time to consider, time to adjust. Instead he had to keep pushing.

"What hogwash? He's got citations to go with most of his stories. And they all have some sort of moral to them. 'Never pull a pin on a grenade unless you have somewhere to throw it.' 'Always remember to booby trap your ally's positions. You can trust your enemy, but never trust a partner.' It's not like he was a heartless assassin; he insists he never killed somebody he liked." Mike smiled. He agreed that his father was bughouse nuts. But he was perfectly adapted for the coming storm.

"Oh, Michael!" Sharon snapped.

"Oh, Sharon!" Mike replied.

"So, which one do we leave? Oh, God dammit honey! How do you make a choice like that?" Her face in the lamplight was pinched and suddenly very old.

"Fortunately that is one decision we don't have to make. When the program was designed they decided that that was one decision not worth leaving to the affected personnel. Fleet will decide for us and the choice is not open for discussion. It shouldn't affect either of our kids but if one of them had a genetic defect, no matter how the parents felt, that one would not be the one to go. Part of the purpose is to move a good quality human gene pool off Earth and to do so without there being real cause for argument. On the other hand—since the fleet is being drawn from the ranks of navies—it is heavily skewing the gene pool to northern Europeans. That was an item for discussion and still is. I don't think that it is going to change, though, no matter how much the Chinese call it racist."

"Is it?" Sharon was willing to digress. It was better than thinking about the situation.

"I don't think so, although don't ask me to analyze Darhel psychology. They are remarkably labyrinthine and I am altogether too blunt; I can't even start to get a handle on them. I wish I could, because I think it's the most important thing anyone could be doing right now, even more important than preparing for the Posleen."

"Why is understanding the Darhel important, and how could it be more important than preparing for the Posleen? I mean, they've been pretty up front, letting us send delegations off world and giving material help, now even offering off-planet evacuation for dependents. I think they've been fairly nice. You can't expect them to spend all their energy defending us."

"Oh yes I can. We are, basically, the Darhel's only option for pulling their irons out of the fire and they know it. So they should put Earth first in line for everything, to preserve the soldier pool if for no other reason, but they haven't. Why? At the end of this war, by the best case scenarios I have seen, our available fighting force is going to be reduced by seventy to ninety percent. Those are the humans that the Darhel really depend on and they have not made every effort to preserve them."

"Well, there's more to the Federation than the Darhel. Politics can mess things up; maybe some of the Federation doesn't agree with that analysis."

"The Darhel, I am convinced, control everything in the Federation. Every time there is a discussion of intent, the Darhel send a representative. You can gauge whether a meeting is worth attending on the basis of whether the Darhel will be there or not. And, often, they subtly guide the meetings I've attended.

"So, if you have one group that is probably working off a game plan at all the meetings where decisions are made subtly guiding the meetings to the decisions that they want? You'd better know what their purpose is.

"And I question some of the basic premises that are used to arrive at the question of funding our defense. The Darhel keep talking about a free and equal federation among the stars, but it is always the Darhel talking, or occasionally a carefully chosen Tchpth. The Darhel control all the monetary transfers, all the loans. Among the Galactics there is no charity; if the Darhel call your loan, you're doomed, and the Darhel are absolutely hierarchical. If you piss off one Darhel they pass it through the chain and you never get the chance to piss off another. These are the people we've been getting ninety percent of our information from, including the information about planetary defense funding, required allocation of Fleet resources and availability of off-planet manufacturing capacity."

"I think you're getting a little paranoid. The Galactics seem fine from my perspective," Sharon disagreed.

"Maybe. Maybe my paranoia is hereditary. But Jack wanted me because I was a science fiction writer. Any good science fiction buff knows the story 'To Serve Man.'"

"I don't."

"For shame. Real fifties story. Aliens land and start to help the human race. Better nutrition, end war, population control. They all carry this little book, they say the title is *To Serve Man*. One of the characters is a linguist trying to translate their language. All he has to work with is one copy of the book. End of the story a fortunate few are invited to go to the aliens' planet. Linguist finally translates the book. It's a cookbook."

"Uck. Besides, what's the point? I thought the Darhel were vegetarians."

"All our translations are through the AIDs, programmed by the Darhel. All the information we have from off planet is through the Darhel. All the important decisions I have been witness to are influenced by the Darhel. I suspect they are involved in virtually all decisions relating to how to fight the war, and some extremely poor decisions are being reached. I know, the way they avoid being photographed you've probably never gotten a good look at one. Trust me, they may only eat vegetables, but they are not designed as herbivores. The Darhel are intelligent and pragmatic, so, why the bad decisions?"

"What kind of bad decisions?"

"All sorts. Hell, the current choice for Joint Chiefs, the future 'High Commander,' is a weasel!"

"Mike, gimme a break! The Darhel don't choose the Chairman of the Joint Chiefs."

"You would be amazed what the Darhel have influence over."

"Isn't anyone, I don't know, cross-checking the assumptions? Looking at the Darhel?"

"Yeah, there's a supposedly black project doing just that, but that's another thing: with very few exceptions the guys I've met who are on that project couldn't find their ass with both hands. Now a project that is arguably the most fundamental intelligence requirement we have should have the best and brightest, not the incompetent nincompoops that have been assigned."

"Are you being... well, you can be kind of over-critical... occasionally."

"I can be a class-A son of a bitch is what you mean. Honey, one of the guys asked whether we could just perform an amphibious invasion of Diess, I shit you not. He did not quite seem to grasp, among other things, that space is a vacuum, that lasers travel in a more or less straight line and that Earth is curved. Either David Hume, who is the project manager, is a great actor, or he is one of the most remarkably stupid persons on Earth."

Lieutenant Commander David Hume twisted his Annapolis ring twice and scratched the back of his head. His chief linguist, Mark Jervic, arguing a minor note of Tchpth declension with his assistant, paid absolutely no attention. After a moment Jervic nodded his head vigorously to some point or another and waved his arms wildly as if including the whole universe in a unanimity of linguistic holism.

After lunch at a local delicatessen, Commander Hume walked to the Washington Mall and turned towards the Capitol along Independence Avenue. A bitter north wind was blowing down the mall, whipping the skeletal branches of the cherry trees back and forth in a way that was frankly ominous. He watched them for a moment wondering why they bothered him so. Finally, he realized that they reminded him of a line from Dante's *Inferno*. The shiver that swept over him then had little to do with the bitter Christmas cold.

When he was opposite the reflecting pool he turned into the mall and walked over. A moment later he was joined by Doctor Jervic, and the two ambled along the path to the Vietnam Memorial, just two more lunchtime strollers walking off their pastrami.

Commander Hume pulled a bulky package from his briefcase and punched a crudely affixed button on the roughly formed plastic case. A passing jogger cursed all things Japanese as the powerful electromagnetic pulse shut down his Walkman for all time.

"What about laser?" asked Jervic when the deed was done.

"Difficult at best under these circumstances, same with shotgun mikes, and the background noise is the same frequency as human voice."

"Lip reading."

"Keep moving your head around," Hume said, turning to look across the pool as he sat. "Well?"

Although eighty percent of the personnel in "Operation Deep Look" were, in fact, high-grade morons, neither the project leader, who was a very, very good actor, nor his actual chief assistant fell into that category.

"Shouldn't you have asked that before you crossed the Rubicon, so to speak?" Mark asked, gesturing languidly at the EMP generator. "They are watching us, you know." The Mystic river accent flowed like its namesake.

"Of course I know; with my information we were across the Rubicon anyway. What do you have to add?" Hume asked sharply. He was willing to act the fool for the mission, but sometimes Dr. Jervic seemed to forget it was an act. After the two of them had battled it out in Boston for six long years, Mark should know by now who the brains of the outfit was.

"Well, the AID's translation programs have some interesting subprotocols in them. Very interesting." Jervic, the former Harvard professor, paused and cracked his knuckles.

"Skip the damn dramatics," Hume snarled, "there is precisely *no* time."

"Very well," Jervic sighed, "the protocols are deliberately deceptive, primarily in areas related to genetics, biotechnics, programming and, strangely, socio-political analysis. The deception is more than mere switching of words, it has a thematic base. The programming side of it is out of my depth, but there is no question that the Darhel are deliberately causing us to move towards dead ends in those fields. I find the thematic approach in sociology to be both the strangest and the strongest. There are constant deliberate translation errors and modifications of data related to human sociology, prehistory and archetypes."

"Archetypes," mused Commander Hume. He glanced at Washington's monument and wondered what George would have made of all of this. Probably not much; he would have foisted such underhanded shenanigans off on Benjamin Franklin.

"Any of several apparently innate images in the psyche, found throughout human..."

"I know what a damn archetype is, Mark," David interrupted, angrily, drawn from his reverie. "That was 'Archetypes,' with an unspoken 'Damn' attached in the subjunctive case. Not 'Archetypes? What the hell are archetypes?' It happened to fit in with my data. Okay, it's time to see if we really do have presidential access," he continued, standing up. "You would not believe what I found in a Sanskrit translation..."

"Hey, man, you got a light?" One of the ubiquitous street people of the Washington Mall stumbled blearily towards them, fumbling a dog-end.

"Sorry, soldier," said Commander Hume, noting the field jacket and scars, respectful to even this fallen soldier at the last. "Don't smoke."

"It don' matter, man," the unshaven bum muttered, "Don' matter." Four rapid huffs from a silenced .45 caliber Colt followed and the pair of scientists slumped into the reflecting pool staining the pure waters red. "Don' matter," the bum muttered again, as the screams began.

15

Camp McCall, NC Sol III
1123 May 6th, 2002 AD

"Move it! Move it! Get out! *Off the bus! Move it!*"

The young men in gray piled off the Greyhound bus, some in their haste tumbling to the ground. These unfortunates were unceremoniously yanked to their feet and hurled towards the group now milling into a half-assed formation. The three brawny young men and one brawny young woman doing the shouting had, four months before, gotten off the same kind of bus. Despite the corporal's chevrons on their sleeves they were recently graduated privates chosen for their size, strength or fierceness as much as their motivated attitude. They broke the formation into four ragged groups and moved them, overloaded with duffel bags, to their respective assembly areas. The new recruits were chivvied into rough lines comprising three sides of a quad and then they got their first experience of a real drill sergeant. In second platoon's unfortunate case it was Gunnery Sergeant Pappas. He was standing at parade rest in the center of the formation, apparently doing nothing but rocking backwards and forwards contemplating the pleasant spring day. What he was actually doing was applying his personal philosophy of life to a situation he found totally out of control.

He and the group recalled with him had been told that, thank you, we have all the senior NCOs we need for the Line and Strike formations. They were instead parceled out to Guard and training units as a leavening of experienced personnel. This was intended to "stiffen up" the units to which they were assigned. Gunny Pappas often considered the old adage that you cannot stiffen a bucket of spit with a handful of buckshot.

But he was a Marine (or whatever they wanted to call him this week) and when given an order said "aye, aye, sir," or "yes, sir," or whatever, and performed it to the best of his ability. So when told he was going to be a DI, he naturally requested Pendleton, since that was right by his home of record. Ground Force Personnel naturally sent him to Camp McCall, North Carolina, three thousand miles away.

Being in McCall might have been for the best. The Galactics had started to come through on one of their promises and he was one of the first group offered rejuvenation. The rejuv program was being run on a matrix of age, rank and seniority. Since the military ran on a framework of both an officer Corp and an equivalent NCO Corp, senior NCOs were prioritized with "equivalent" officers. As one of the oldest NCOs in the second layer of enlisted rank, he had received rejuvenation ahead of many sergeant majors that were younger. Thus, after a month of truly unpleasant reaction and growth, he found himself a physical twenty-year-old with a sixty-year-old's mind. He had forgotten what it was really like, the physical feeling of invincibility and energy, a coursing drive to do something, anything, all the time. Regular heavy-duty workouts were returning the musculature of his prime. They also served to occupy his other energies.

He had been a Marine for thirty years, twenty-seven of those married. During those twenty-seven years he had never strayed from the marriage bed. Not for him the phrase "I'm not divorced, just TDY." He never thought less of the other NCOs, or officers, who took advantage of deployments to pick up some action; as long as it did not affect their performance he could care less. But he had made a wedding vow to "cleave unto no other" and he believed in keeping a promise. It was the same as "'til death do us part." Now, however, he had a twenty-year-old's body, and drives, and was married to a fifty-something wife. He was experiencing some difficulties with the situation. Fortunately or unfortunately, the pace of training the recalls and then using the recalls to train the new enlistees was so fierce he had not been able to get back to San Diego. The rejuv program was eventually supposed to be distributed to dependents of the military but he would believe it when he saw it. There were already rumors that the rejuv materials were running low, so who knew what to expect long term. He was really sweating his first meeting with Prissy.

Heaping insult on injury, since the most senior NCOs, like himself, were recalled first, there was currently a glut of E-8s and E-9s, the two most senior enlisted ranks. In the Navy they were referring to it as "too many Chiefs." In addition, because the emphasis was on training, most of the senior NCOs and officers were being assigned to basic and advanced training facilities. Therefore, instead of being assigned as the senior NCO in a company, he was assigned a mere platoon of recruits.

Thus he was not in the best of moods when he greeted the group of forty-five young men he was to make into Marines (or Strike troopers or soldiers or hoplites or whatever the FUCK you wanted to call them). Characteristically this made him smile at them. The less perceptive, seeing that the drill sergeant was not the sadistic cretin they had been warned of but a kindly smiling fellow, tentatively smiled back. The more perceptive suspected, correctly, that they were in serious trouble.

"Good morning, ladies," he said in a low, friendly tone. "My name is Gunnery Sergeant Pappas." The tone forced them to strain to hear. "For the next four months I will, I am sorry to say, be your drill sergeant. This fine, fit young fellow," he gestured at the attending drill corporal, "is Drill Corporal Adams. Think of us as your personal Marquis de Sade. Sort of an aerobics instructor gone horribly wrong.

"To begin learning that thing called military courtesy you will refer to me as if I were an officer. You will call me 'sir' and salute when greeting me. Is that clear?"

"Yeah." "Okay." "No problem." "Yes, sir!"

"Oh, I am sorry. I didn't hear that. The correct response is 'Clear, sir.'"

"Clear, sir."

He inserted a finger in one ear and dug around. "Sorry. I'm a bit hard of hearing. All the screams of dying recruits. A bit louder if you please."

"*Clear, sir!*" they yelled.

"I am apparently not making myself clear," he said very slowly and distinctly. "Front leaning rest position, move. For those cretins, meaning all of you of course that are unfamiliar with the term, that command means turn slightly to the right and assume the pushup position." A few of the recruits quickly dropped, some began, hesitantly, to follow the quietly given order but most continued to stand uncomprehending.

"*Get down! On your face! Move it! Move it!*" he boomed, much louder and more forcefully than the corporal, louder than their whole group. "*Bend your elbows! You! Off the ground! Get yer butts down you pansies! Hold that!* Look directly forward, heads up, eyes focused in the distance. Now, when I give an instruction that you understand the response is 'Clear, sir.' I expect it to be readily audible on *Mars! Clear?*"

"*Clear, sir!*"

"Now, I have found this position to be remarkably centering of attention. But, I can see that at least one of you is a body builder." He walked over to this unfortunate, a hulking youth with a build like Hercules and lank black hair and squatted down so that he could look him in the eye. "I suspect that this is little strain for you, big boy. Is it?"

"*No, sir!*"

"Ah, truth, very good." Sergeant Pappas stood up and then stepped carefully on the recruit's back, centered on the shoulder blades. The burly youth grunted when the two hundred fifty pound drill instructor stepped on, but he held. "In the next sixteen weeks, *Get yer head up asshole!* it will be my duty to turn you *pussies* into Strike troopers. *Get yer butts down, faggots!* Strike units will be deployed from their home bases as formed units *Get yer butts up! You pussies! If this asshole can hold me up, you can stay up yourselves!* as formed units to engage the Posleen whenever and wherever they are badly needed. That means that while Guard and Line units *may* see combat, *You! I said get up off your belly, cocksucker! Corporal Adams!*"

"*Yessir!*"

"*That fat cocksucker in the second row! See how far he can run before he throws up and passes out!*"

"*Yessir! On yer feet, asshole! Move it!*" The drill corporal yanked the unfortunate recruit to his feet and trotted him off into the distance.

"Where was I, oh yes . . . While Guard units may see combat, you *will* see combat. My mission is to make you pussies hard enough and fast enough that some of you may survive." He stepped off the recruit. "*On your feet!* I am about to fall you out into the barracks. There is no bunk assignment or shakedown. Inside the barracks there are two red boxes. If you have any contraband, drugs, personal weapons, knives, anything you suspect you shouldn't have, put them in the box. If you keep them I *will* find them. Then I will send you to a place that makes boot camp seem friendly and homelike. Everybody but this asshole," he indicated his erstwhile soapbox, "*Fallout!*"

As the recruits grabbed their gear and pounded into the barracks he looked the remaining recruit up and down, noting the high wide cheekbones.

"What's yer name, asshole?"

"*Private Michael Ampele, sir!*"

"Hawaiian?"

"*Yes, sir!*"

"Daddy a marine, howlee?"

The recruit blanched at that insult, where the expected "asshole" had little effect. "*Sir, yes, sir!*"

"Think that's gonna make me easier on you, howlee?"

"*Sir, no, sir!*"

"Why not?"

"*Sir, the strongest steel comes from the hottest fire, sir!*"

"Horse shit. The strongest steel comes from a precise combination of temperature, materials and conditions including a nitrogen fuckin' atmosphere. I'm gonna kick yer ass for two reasons. One, nobody's gonna accuse me of favoritism and two, these mainland wahines need an example."

"Yes, sir!"

"Okay, yer the platoon guide," he decided. "You know what that means."

"Yes, sir," said the private, his face slightly green. "They fuck up, I get my ass kicked, sir."

"Yerright," said Pappas with a smile. He puffed his lips out and grinned. "We got no time to fuck around with training, you little yardbirds are gonna be driven harder and faster than any group in history. *Comprende?* You think you can handle that and the responsibility of a platoon guide?"

"*Si*, sir," agreed the private

"I'll take it on faith, howlee. I think you're full of shit. Fall out."

Pappas shook his head in resignation as the private followed the others into the barracks. They kept dropping the training time, pushing the pipeline to deliver the recruits no matter what. Well, he would train them, as well as anyone could expect in the time allowed. But he was glad he was not going to war with them. It was too chancy a business.

16

Ttckpt Province, Barwhon V
0409 GMT, September 28th, 2001 AD

The second objective of the Special Operations recon was a two-week hike through a killer swamp; more than half the time they were up to their necks in frigid water. Their brief halts at night were broken by involuntary shivering, and by the time they reached the objective area even Master Sergeant Tung was looking wan. The previous area's foragers did not seem to be in evidence, but the team increased their caution as they neared the Tchpth town. Soon the regular buzz of an encampment could be heard through the sound-devouring mists, and Mosovich sent Trapp and Ellsworthy forward to investigate. The wait seemed interminable until the irrepressible SEAL suddenly appeared out of the muck in their midst. With a muddy grin he gestured them forward and led the way to the edge of the wetland.

Peering through the curtaining lianas at the edge of the hummock, the team was greeted with a view of determined activity. In most places the fragile towers described in their briefing were scattered on the ground, being demolished to mine the base materials. In a few places, ziggurats or pyramids of metal and stone were rising. They were well spaced and in between were low barracks of stone and mud. In the distance a causeway through the swamp was being constructed and what looked like defensive works were under construction near them. By the nearest ziggurat was a series of pens but what the pens held could not be seen from the team's angle.

"Ellsworthy," murmured Mosovich, "what's in the pens?"

133

"Little posies in most," she whispered from her accustomed over-watch. "A few Crabs in one."

As she was talking, a Posleen walked over and dumped a double handful of squirming Posleen nestlings into one of the pens then trotted away.

"Mega gross," whispered Ellsworthy.

"What?" asked Mueller.

"The other ones are eating new ones, mostly. I think some of 'em survived."

"Yuck," muttered Richards.

"Get it on tape," ordered Ersin. The video would in fact load onto a Flash BIOS memory chip.

"I've got a feed going off my scope, don't worry."

"Okay, we're gonna pull back a little and get up and dry," whispered Mosovich. "We'll trade off observers until it seems like we've got it all and then pull back to the pickup." He began moving back into the swamp. "Ellsworthy, you've got first watch."

"Yessa, massa. I keep a good watch."

Two days later they were mostly dried out and badly confused.

"You're sure of what you saw?" asked Mosovich for the fifth time.

"Y-y-y-es, dangit!" Martine was by turns angry, disgusted and horrified.

"No species could survive that way!" exclaimed Mueller, the subvocalization going vocal for a moment.

"Pipe the fuck down," snarled Mosovich, "If he says he saw it, he saw it. I just wish you'd gotten it on the microcam."

"B-b-b-by the t-t-t-time I-I-I-I . . ."

"Yeah, I know, it was already over. Okay, we have data on their building rate and materials use. We've gotten a look at their fixed defenses. We have an idea what they forage for and some idea of what they eat. We have one unconfirmed report, sorry Sergeant Martine, on some specialized feeding habits. Anything else."

"Why the pyramids?" asked Mueller. When completed they would resemble Central American pyramids to an uncomfortable degree. At the base of each was a large hut and the beginnings of a parade or playing field. The God Kings had been observed to spend most of their time in and around the huts. The one nearing completion had a small house or palace at the apex.

"Worship?" wondered Richards.

"Of who? The God Kings?" asked Ersin.

"I wonder if that's why they call them that?" asked Trapp, stroking his Bushmaster quietly on a diamond stone.

"Seven pyramids, seven God Kings?" mused Mosovich.

"We've counted at least ten, maybe more. They're hard to tell apart," noted Mueller.

"So, not one pyramid per God King. Over thirteen hundred normals, right?"

"Right," agreed Mueller, pulling out a palmtop computer. "Thirteen hundred normals, 10 or so God Kings and 123 Crabs, down from a high of 220. Total of 500 . . . shuttled through."

As the pyramids neared completion, the pens of nestlings had been moved nearer. And the reason for the penned Tchpth became clear. The team had watched helplessly as Tchpth after Tchpth was taken from the pens and slaughtered. They were well aware that they were watching intelligent, in many cases extraordinarily intelligent, beings being killed and eaten but there was no way to affect the outcome without compromising their mission. It was one of those unfortunate cases where the importance of the mission outweighed the death of any single individual or even group of individuals. It didn't mean they had to like it. Nor did they like it when the occasional group of new Tchpth would be herded out of the jungle and into the pens.

"But what about this report of Martine's?" asked Richards. "Why would any species do that?"

"I-I s-s-saw what I-I-I-I s-saw," said the commo NCO, firmly.

"Might be a response to limited resources," suggested Trapp.

"What limited resources?" scoffed Mueller. "They just conquered a food-rich planet."

"Might be they like the taste," said Tung.

They all turned to look at him; he was notoriously chary of words, so when Tung spoke people listened.

"Sure, they've probably been designed to be able to eat anything, but that's the only home food they got. Maybe they like the taste." Everyone just stared at him in amazement. It was the most anyone had ever heard him say in one sitting. It also made perfect sense; it would explain why the God Kings ate their clan's nestlings, as Sergeant Martine had witnessed only an hour before.

"Okay," stated Mosovich, "we'll take that as a possibility until a better one presents itself. I think we've covered about all there is to cover here. Time to go look at another site. We'll start our extraction tomorrow morning. Get dry tonight people, it's the last chance you'll get for a few weeks."

17

Planetary Transport Class *Maruk*,
N-Space Transit Terra-Diess
0927 January 28th, 2002 AD

"Lieutenant Michael O'Neal, reporting as ordered, sir!" Mike held a rigid salute, eyes fixed six inches over the battalion commander's head.

"At ease, Lieutenant." The tall, spare officer went back to studying the hardcopy report in front of him, making annotations at irregular intervals.

Mike took the opportunity to study the room and its occupant, as "at ease" permitted, his feet shoulder width apart, hands clasped behind his back. Lieutenant Colonel Youngman was slightly balding and very lean. His wiry frame bespoke a high degree of physical fitness but he looked almost fragile compared to O'Neal. He was definitely a runner; from the starved greyhound look, probably a weekend marathoner.

The room was a barren almost Spartan ellipsoid, less, Mike suspected, as an extension of the occupant than due to cultural conflict. The blank gray plasteel walls were impervious to all normal attachment systems—glues would not stick and nails would bend—while the organic-looking tubes overhead, indicative of Indowy construction, were impossible to hang anything from. There were no mirrors, lockers or shelves, only a desk, two chairs and the floor. The light was the odd greenish blue favored by the Indowy. It gave the rooms a cold dark look, reminiscent of a horror movie.

On the floor were several boxes, undoubtedly filled with all the items this battalion commander considered *de rigeur* for office decorations. Mike began to list the probable contents starting with "national colors, one each." When he reached "wife and children, picture of, five by seven, photo of mistress artfully concealed beneath" he realized that his good intentions of remaining calm were slipping. After ten minutes the colonel put down his second report and looked up.

"You look upset, Lieutenant."

"I do, sir?" Mike asked. Despite this jerk showing his importance by having Mike cool his heels for ten minutes, Mike was sure his expression had not changed.

"You have looked pissed off since you came in the door. Actually, you look like you could bite the ass out of a lion." The colonel's face had assumed a disapproving pucker.

"Oh, that, sir," said Mike, no longer surprised. The mistake was made all the time. "That expression's a fixture. It's from lifting weights."

"A 'lifter,' hmm? I find that lifters are generally poor runners. How are your APRT scores, Lieutenant?" asked the colonel with a lifted eyebrow.

"I pass, sir." *I usually about max it, sir,* he thought with a note of wry humor. *And if you think "lifters" are poor runners, you ought to see a marathoner on the bench.* Being able to press twice your body weight made pushups and sit-ups a cinch. The running was a pain, but he usually made the runs in nearly max time for his age group.

"Passing is not enough! I expect maximum physical performance out of my officers and, while you are not actually assigned to this unit, I expect you to be an example as well. There are absolutely no fit areas on this ship to run, but when we reach the planetary objective I expect to see you 'leading the way' in daily fitness. Do I make myself clear?" The colonel attempted to wither him with a glare. After years of experiencing icy Jack Horner dressing downs at the slightest mistake, the glare slid off Mike like water off diamond.

"Airborne, sir," Mike snapped, with apparent perfect seriousness.

"Hmm. That brings us to your mission. As I understand it, you are to 'advise' me and my staff on the functions and uses of these combat suits. Is that correct?"

"Sir," Mike paused and launched into his carefully prepared spiel. "As part of the GalTech Infantry Team, I have an intimate knowledge of the strengths and weaknesses of armored combat suits. The team also specified the requirements for operational readiness. The pressure of circumstances have made it imperative to deploy your battalion before it met all training parameters and before anyone, the GalTech team, GF TRADOC or Fleet Strike Forces, felt it was fully ready. So I was assigned to help. Sir, you know all about light infantry tactics, probably heavy infantry too, but I know suits and suit tactics. I've got more time in them than anybody in the Fleet," he concluded, not without pride. Mike paused, not sure how to go on.

"Are you saying, Lieutenant, that you don't think we're fully trained, fully prepared to fight?" asked the colonel, quietly.

Mike looked shocked. "No, sir, not even close. You're no more prepared than the Marines were to invade Guadalcanal but you're being deployed for much the same reason."

"Well, Lieutenant," said the colonel, smiling like a cat with a canary, "I hate to disagree, but your vaunted suits are not that hard to use. I got used to mine very quickly. They'll be a real bonus on the Air-Land Battlefield but I don't see how they'll change tactics significantly. And learning how to use one is a cinch, so, as far as I can see your main purpose is to look over my shoulder."

What "Air-Land Battlefield"? Taking to the air around Posleen is a short ride to carbondom. "Sir, part of my function *is* to evaluate the performance of this battalion, but, sir, with all due respect, my main function is advisory. A standard suit has two hundred thirty-eight discrete functions that can be combined in a near infinite number of permutations. For full ability, a soldier has to be able to multitask at least three in a combat environment. I mean, you can get by with just one or two, but three to five is 'run, jump and shoot' infantry. A command suit has four hundred eighty-two discrete functions. Its primary problems, almost faults, are information overload and function difficulty," Mike paused and looked up, remaining at a Parade Rest position. He wished he could light up a cigar, but this officer was obviously not a smoker.

"Unless you have an AID that is really attuned to your needs you risk overload of C3I"—command, communication, control and intelligence—"flow. You either overload on information or filter out too much, either of which is dangerous. As to purely suit functions, a command suit has so many special functions designed to permit the commander to keep up with multiple highly mobile units and keep him alive, that you again risk either overload or suit drain.

"Sir, the TRADOC requirement is a minimum of two hundred hours training time for the standard suits and three hundred hours for the command suits. Records show that only E-4s and below have in excess of one hundred hours. Sir, I have three *thousand* hours and I feel like a novice. Among other difficulties with limited suit time, the autonomic systems grow with the user and go through periods of instability. They've never been tested in actual battle and their instability is marked below a hundred hours." Mike paused, wondering if the commander understood his total horror at the nearly inexcusable lack of preparation of the battalion. He knew from the tenor of his briefing that Fleet TRADOC had the same reservations.

"Son, I understand what you mean about overload, I ran into it early on. I did what any good commander would do, I delegated and set up a communications net. As to using the suits, you're right, they're too complicated and that autonomic nervous system is a piece of shit. That's in my report. You see," he lifted one of the papers, "I make reports too. And I kind of expect that the reports of a battalion commander with over twenty years in this man's Army will carry a little bit more weight than a damn lieutenant's.

"Now, I don't care what you think your mission is, or who you think you are. What I want you to do is go to your cabin and stay there for the rest of the trip. You're not confined to quarters or anything but I decide how *my* battalion is run, how it trains, what its tactics are. Not any former E-5 with a shiny silver bar that thinks he's hot shit. If I find you in the battalion area without my direct permission, in the training areas, or talking to my officers about tactics or training I will personally hang you up, shake you out and strip you of commission, rank, honor and possibly life. Do I make myself clear?" concluded the battalion commander, the words dropping into the quiet like iron ingots.

"Yes, sir," said Mike, eyes fixed on a point six inches above the commander's head.

"And when we get home, if you've been a good little boy, I'll send along a nice neutral report instead of one that uses 'arrogant' and 'insolent' as adjectives. Clear?" The officer smiled thinly.

"Yes, sir."

"Dismissed."

Lieutenant O'Neal came to the position of attention, did a precise about-face and marched out the door.

When the cabin door opened, Mike was lying on his bunk wearing battle silks and a set of issue Virtual Reality sunglasses nicknamed Milspecs. Battle silks—officially, Uniform, Utility, Ground Forces—was the uniform developed for day to day use by CES and ACS infantry. It was not designed for combat and since it was developed by a GalTech team, they had rammed through a uniform based on comfort and style. Light gray in color, it looked something like a hooded kimono. The material, cotton treated through an Indowy process to "improve" it, was smooth as silk, lightweight, and temperature reactive. With a few twists to close or open throat and cuffs it was comfortable from one hundred to zero degrees Fahrenheit. Mike was conspicuous in them because, despite the fact that they had been issued to the ACS unit, everyone besides him wore BDU camouflage.

It had been a month since his abortive meeting with the battalion commander and he occasionally reflected that he was in the best shape of his life. Since he could not perform his secondary missions, training and advisement, he spent his time in evaluating the battalion's readiness (low), working out, and improving his own readiness. Despite the colonel's pronouncement that there were no areas large enough for running, Mike had discovered desolate corridors stretching for miles. With difficulty he tracked down an Indowy crew member; most of the Indowy were staying far away from the unpredictable predators in their midst. After circumspect courting of the skittish boggle he gained access to gravitational controls in most of the unused sections.

The hallways were primarily maintenance corridors for cavernous holds now filled with ammunition, spare parts, tanks, rations and the myriad other things civilized man takes to war. Normally they contained machinery, tools, food, seeds, nannites and the myriad other things Indowy take to colonize, for it was an Indowy colony ship. The expansive cylinder, five kilometers long and a kilometer across, now carried the NATO contingent of the Terran expeditionary force on its four-month voyage to Diess.

For the past month the corridors had rung to the sound

of plasteel on plasteel as Mike ran, jumped, dodged, shot and maneuvered units in full Virtual Reality mode under gravities ranging from none to two. When the door opened, he was refining one of the VR scenarios: "The Asheville Pass."

America found itself in a situation unprecedented in its history. The last significant conflict in the contiguous U.S. was the Civil War and, with a few notable exceptions, neither side in that conflict had had any interest in causing civilian casualties. The Posleen had every interest in causing casualties; they saw the population as a mobile larder. There would be times, especially for ACS forces, when an un-American concept, the desperate last stand, would be required. Given that fact, it was a situation to be trained for like any other.

The Asheville scenario required an ACS unit to hold a pass against a superior Posleen force to buy time for the city to be evacuated. It tailored the Posleen force to the defending unit and its supports, but in every case they were outnumbered at least a thousand to one. In the original scenario at a certain point another unit broke and the Posleen advanced through that pass and the city driving the refugees into the rear of the defending unit with devastating results.

Originally designed as a no-win scenario, Mike was changing it so that one time in ten, if the defending unit did everything right, they would "win." In the new scenario the other force held, permitting the evacuation to proceed until the destruction of the attacking force.

Mike was considering a memo for record that the assault force needed to be increased or statistically enhanced. Despite the fact that it was designed as a "no-win" scenario, using the standard battalion task force Mike had started to defeat the Posleen two times out of three, other force breaking or not. This should not have been possible with seven hundred troops defending against 1.5 million Posleen; a ratio of more than two thousand to one. It turned out to be a matter of artillery employment more than anything. Admittedly the battalion ended up as a short platoon and it required the battalion commander to survive and rally the troops to the end. But still.

When the door opened he was down to a reinforced company, he had "scratched his back," called fire on his own position, three times and was getting that detached feeling just before the rope tightens in a hanging. He was, therefore, badly disoriented when his glasses automatically cleared and the visions of Posleen, violet fire, blood and shattered combat suits cleared to reveal a mild-looking medium-height captain with short cropped blond hair standing in his doorway. Behind the captain, virtually towering over him, was a skeletally thin, extremely tall staff sergeant.

Mike yanked off his shades and tried to come to attention but the VR effect caused a sudden wave of dizziness and nausea as he stumbled sideways into the bulkhead.

The captain's eyes sharpened. "Have you been using drugs or something?"

"No, sir!" gasped Mike, dropping glasses and ceremony as he pawed for a drop sickness bag. "VRrrr sick, hnuff, hnuff, put, pah, shit! 'Scuse me, sir." He dumped the bag in the disposer slot, kicked up the ventilation, pulled a Pepsi out of a cooler and pawed through his desk until he found two ampoules. He pressed them each in turn against the inside of his forearm, right through the clothing.

"Now I'm doing drugs, but they're fully authorized, sir. Sudden cessation of VR training systems, such as when you're killed or when a senior officer walks into your room, causes such severe physiological reactions that we rammed two GalTech meds through the authorization process. One is a really super analgesic that is stopping the blazing headache I would otherwise have right now and the other is an anti-nauseate I didn't get to in time. This concludes lecture number one hundred fifty-seven: side effects of sudden VR termination, Chapter 32-5 of the Armored Combat Suit Field Manual."

The captain began to clap as the NCO behind him shook his head. "Bravo, bravo. Really wonderful, considering you started it in the middle of a regurgitative event. Are questions now accepted?"

"Certainly." Mike responded with a wince, the analgesic was fighting the incipient migraine but it was down to best two falls out of three. "Questions, comments, concerns?"

"Why not just lock the damn door?" asked the captain.

"You can't, sir, it's an Indowy ship. Hadn't you noticed?" Mike answered.

"Mine damn well locks."

"Then you haven't had a personal visit from Colonel Young-man or Major Pauley." Mike smiled solemnly. The NCO behind the captain winked.

"No, I haven't." There was something in that bald statement that set off an alarm in Mike's head.

"Would you like to come in, sir?" asked Mike, stepping back into the small space. The ventilation had washed away the residual smells of ejecta, but the cramped "room" was the size of a walk-in closet. The bed Mike had been sitting on helpfully retracted into the wall then reformatted as a set of small station chairs, while a tabletop extruded from the farther wall. Even with the well-designed locations of the furniture it would be cramped for three, especially with someone of Mike's breadth and the NCO's height. Nonetheless, the captain immediately stepped into the room, with the sergeant following. The captain took a chair and, at that sign, Mike and the sergeant followed suit. The NCO ended up with his knees pulled nearly to his chest.

"I suppose Major Norton could open your door also, sir," Mike said, continuing the conversation. "The Indowy are extremely hierarchical. Any higher caste Indowy can walk in unannounced. Those who are of equal rank cannot. The ship's AI is programmed for that protocol and frankly it's a real bitch."

"Huh. I've been on this tub a month and didn't know that," mused the captain. "What else don't I know?"

"Well, I would guess that your company has not been doing VR training and I know I'm the only human who has found lebensraum on this ship. Any other rhetorical questions, sir?" Mike ended bitterly.

"You know," said the captain, with a slight smile, "you really need to learn to control that tongue of yours."

"Yes, sir, no excuse, sir."

"No, you have an excuse. You've been treated like a pariah and not allowed to do your job. Nonetheless, learn to keep a lid on."

"Yes, sir."

"Now, I've come here because I am on the horns of a dilemma. By the way, I'm Captain Brandon of Bravo company."

"Yes, sir." Mike nodded. "I recognize you."

"I was under the impression you hadn't been allowed to communicate with anyone in the battalion," said the commander, cryptically.

"I haven't, sir. I brought up the information on my AID."

"You're pretty good with these AIDs, aren't you?" asked the commander.

"I would hope so, sir."

"And you are suit expert."

"I am a suit master, sir," said O'Neal, with a slight smile.

"Well," said the commander, with a smile in return, "that's good because we need some help."

"Sir," said Mike, uncomfortably. "I've been given certain orders..."

"Lieutenant," said the captain, sternly. "I realize the importance of orders. I'm a professional officer on my second hitch in command of a company. I truly recognize that violation of an order is not something to be taken lightly. So, I don't think that you should violate your orders."

"You don't?" said Mike, startled.

"You don't?" said the NCO, if anything more startled.

Mike smiled at the tall enlisted man. The NCO smiled back.

"I understand that you have met Sergeant Wiznowski?" said the captain. "The sergeant is head of the company scout/sniper squad."

"Yes, sir, of course," said Mike, stretching out his hand. "How do you do, Sergeant."

"Oh, one below the other, Mighty Mite, like usual. How's 'bout you?" Wiznowski's hand wrapped around Mike's to the extent that he was more or less holding on with his thumb.

Mike snorted.

"Actually," said the captain, "I was given to understand that you were in prior service together."

"Hey, Stork," said Mike, "long time."

"Now that we're all friends..." said the captain, with a smile that quickly faded. He started to speak then stopped and looked around the cabin. "I was going to continue with my reason for coming here, but I have to ask a few questions. How the hell did you get this lighting?"

It took Mike a moment to realize what the commander was talking about. Then he laughed. The illumination of his quarters was not the sort of blue-green lighting found throughout the rest of the ship. It was more or less "Terran normal" but rather than looking like lighting from an incandescent bulb or fluorescents, it was the sort of pellucid light found only in the morning right after a snowfall. "Oh, well..." Mike started only to be interrupted.

"It's not funny, Lieutenant. This lighting thing is driving people nuts. And your chairs are the right height, and your bed was the right size. Dammit, I've been traveling for two months on a bed built for an Indowy half my size!"

"I've been sleeping on the floor," said Wiznowski, sounding less than resigned.

Mike stared at the commander with amazement. "You're kidding, right?" he asked in horror.

"No, Lieutenant," said the upset commander. "I am assuredly not kidding."

Mike thought for a moment of the troops stuck in lighting from a bad sci-fi horror flick for the last month, living with accoutrements that were completely misdesigned for them, and felt physically ill.

"Jesus, sir," he whispered, scrubbing his face with his hands. "God dammit. I'm sorry." He shook his head. "Didn't anybody talk to the goddamn Darhel coordinators?"

"I have no idea, Lieutenant. As far as I know there are no Darhel on the ship."

"Michelle," Mike queried his AID, turning away from the commander abruptly, "where are the Darhel coordinators?"

"The Darhel liaisons cross-boarded to a Flantax class courier vessel at the Dasparda emergence. They are going to rendezvous with the Expeditionary Force on Diess."

"What!" he exclaimed. The liaisons, according to his briefing, had been explicitly directed to accompany the EF all the way to Diess. There was an advance party already on Diess to handle anything they might be needed for. The fact that a Flantax-class courier would get them there in half the time and much greater comfort should have been beside the point. He scrubbed his face again in rage and took a deep breath.

"Did the Darhel give any instructions regarding adjustment of quarters and training areas to Earth norms?"

"There is no record of such orders in my database," stated the AID with uncharacteristic bluntness.

Mike thought for a moment then nodded. "Are there any records of such requests between humans and the Darhel?" he asked carefully. He knew there had been virtually no Human-Indowy interaction.

"That information is proprietary to the parties involved or

restricted by classification." Again the tone and response were abrupt. Mike had started to recognize that there were stock answers that were in some way "hardwired" into the AIDs and bypassed their "personalities." He probably had the overrides to gain records of the conversations in question, a function of his position on the Board, but that would send a record of the request to the parties involved. He was not yet ready to kick that particular dragon in the snout.

"Curiouser and curiouser," Mike murmured.

"What?" asked Wiznowski, quietly. The captain started to ask something but Wiznowski respectfully held up his hand for silence. O'Neal was, meanwhile, on another plane. He shook himself and seemed about to say something then settled into silence. After nearly a minute, Wiznowski prompted him again.

"Mike?" he said, "where are you?"

O'Neal shook himself again and looked up. "This is really fucked up," he proclaimed.

"Explain," said the captain.

"Well," O'Neal temporized, trying to figure out where to start. "Well," he said again. "First thing..." He looked at the lighting and started there.

"Everything on this ship is controlled by the Indowy crew," he said, fixing the captain's eye. "You understand that?"

"Yes," said the commander.

"Okay, everything, the water, the air, the food. Where have you been getting your food?" he suddenly digressed, puzzled.

"Well," said the captain, surprised, "we brought a mess section..."

"Oh, Jesus!" snapped Mike. "Sorry, sir."

"Well, I would prefer that you refrain from taking the name of God's only begotten son in vain in front of me," said the captain with a tolerant smile, "but I generally agree with the sentiment. What is wrong with using a mess section?"

"What are they using to heat the food?" asked Mike, dreading the answer.

"Field mess equipment," answered Wiznowski. "Propane stoves, immersion heaters. We've been eating a lot of T-rations."

"That has not been good for morale," noted the captain, dryly.

"Oh, man, sir, how fucked up can this get?" Mike asked then thought about what he said. "Sorry for the French."

The captain nodded tolerantly. "Perhaps you should tell me how this is supposed to go," he said.

"Okay," said Mike, focused back on track. "The Indowy control everything. The original plan—remember I was just peripheral to this so it's as I recall—but the original plan called for the Darhel coordinators to arrange everything for the units through the Indowy. The Indowy can selectively or generally adjust lighting, gravitation, air mix, what have you." He checked to make sure the two soldiers were comprehending his words and went on when the captain nodded his head.

"The entire human area of the ship should have been adjusted for humans long ago. Right after we boarded, as a matter of fact. The Indowy also control the primary food stores. Are you getting fresh fruits, vegetables, meat?" he asked.

"No," said Captain Brandon, shaking his head. He suddenly realized the implication of the question. "You mean there's fresh food on this tub?" he continued, starting to get angry.

"The mess sections should have been able to order stuff, just like they were back at Bragg. Jesus, if we're this fucked up, I wonder what the damn Chinese are like?" Mike mused.

"Can you get this corrected?" asked the captain, patiently bringing the distracted lieutenant back on point.

"I don't know," said Mike, scratching his chin again. "Maybe. What I don't understand is why Oberst Kiel isn't already on top of this."

"Who?" asked Wiznowski.

"Colonel Kiel, the head of the German unit of ACS," Mike explained. "He's a smart Kraut. I wonder why he hasn't jumped on this? Michelle?"

"Yes, sir?"

"Has Oberst Kiel been making inquiries in regards to Indowy support for human forces?" asked Mike.

"I am not..."

"Supervisory override, voice and general sensory recognition. Whatever priority you have to assign," he snapped.

"Yes, he has, Lieutenant," said the AID in a now waspish voice. It had recently decided to be bitchy about overrides.

"And survey says...?" asked Mike.

"If by that colloquialism you mean 'what has the outcome been,' the answer is 'none,'" snapped the AID.

"Why?" asked Mike.

"Because," answered the AID. If a black box could sulk, this one had its lip pouted.

Mike closed his eyes and counted to three. "Michelle, are we going to have to be debugged?" he said, mock sweetly.

"No," said the AID, in a more normal voice. "Oberst Kiel has communicated with the Indowy through the AID network. However, the Indowy captain has refused to provide more than he was specifically ordered to by the Darhel before they left. Furthermore, he has refused to meet directly with Oberst Kiel. As you know..."

"The Indowy have a real thing about face-to-face," Mike continued, nodding his head and meeting the captain's eyes again. "Okay, now I know what the problem is."

"Can you fix it?" asked the captain, puzzled.

"Yeah," said Mike. "Probably, sir," he qualified.

"I told you he was Mr. Fixit, sir," said Wiznowski.

"Why can you?" asked the captain, "when the German colonel and, presumably, the Corp commander cannot?"

"Size partially, sir," Mike grinned in deprecation. "And body language. To an Indowy I don't look that over-muscled; most of them are pretty stocky. And I'm just tall, not huge. Also, they respond really well to the sort of body language you do 'gentling' horses. That was how we broke them on the farm," he explained parenthetically. "So, I can get along with them where a lot of humans have problems.

"Probably the Corp commander has been communicating through Oberst Kiel, sir. I don't know why, but the Indowy will rarely do anything without at least one physical liaison. If I can secure a meeting with the ship's captain I can carry the message directly. So, if I meet with the captain, point out the planned process, get him to accept Oberst Kiel's requests as valid, that should take care of it."

"Hmm," ruminated the commander. "And if it doesn't?"

"Then, sir, I go around getting all the areas adjusted one by one," answered Mike.

"Okay," said Brandon. Then, plaintively, "There's really fresh fruit on this ship?"

"And vegetables," Mike confirmed, "in stasis, so they'll keep fresh indefinitely. Would you like a salad?"

"No," said the commander. He glanced at Wiznowski, who was looking quizzical. "No. If we can't get it to the troops..."

"Yes, sir," said the NCO. "See, Mike, all the fruit we've had since the pogie bait ran out is the dried stuff in MREs. And can peas, can corn, can green beans. It's really getting to the troops."

"But not you, right Stork?" Mike smiled. "Scurvy?" he asked turning back to the commander.

"No." Brandon shook his head. "We're okay there. Everyone is taking vitamins and the food is loaded. Not to mention some of the drinks. But there is a hell of a morale problem. There have been riots among other contingents, even American." He shook his head again, this time in resignation.

"Well, we'll get it licked, sir," said the lieutenant, confidently.

The captain smiled. "Good to hear. But that brings me to the real reason I was here. Training."

It was Mike's turn to frown again. "I'm under orders, sir."

"And can you divulge the nature of the orders?"

"I am not to mingle for training. I'm not to discuss training with officers. I'm not to enter the battalion area or the training areas." Mike had brooded on those words for quite some time.

"Hmm," said the officer and smiled. "Good, I'm glad that my source had the wording right. As I said, I don't want you to disobey your orders..."

"Well, sir," said O'Neal, "since the orders were invalid on the face..."

"But you must remember, Lieutenant," said the captain, sternly, shaking his finger at the junior officer, "that the last order from a superior officer is to be obeyed."

Brandon dropped the humorous pose. "Besides, disobeying the colonel is bad for discipline and would destroy your career." The captain fixed him with a glance to ensure that his point was made.

"Yes, sir," said Mike. He could tell that the commander was headed somewhere but was not sure where.

The captain looked up and thought about what he was about to say. He closed one eye and wrinkled his forehead. The eyebrow of the open eye bounced up and down.

"Let me just be sure of something. Have we discussed training with combat suits or any other galactic equipment?" he asked. "At all," he emphasized.

"No, sir," said Mike after a moment's thought. Wiznowski just shook his head.

"Okay," the captain nodded his head in agreement. "And we're not going to discuss training. But let me ask you a hypothetical question. If the company was to have a company party, and you were 'directing' it, would you have to be there? In person?" asked the commander with a leading tone.

Mike frowned more deeply in puzzlement then his eyes widened. He flashed a look at the Virtual Reality glasses on the table then started to say something. He thought about it for a moment then realized why the crafty old company commander had brought an NCO to the discussion.

"Hey, Wiz, you guys got any of these?" he asked, holding up the Milspecs.

Wiznowski's eyes narrowed in thought. "Yeah," he whispered with a slight smile. Then he grinned. "Yeah!"

"*Well*, gentlemen," said the captain, quickly standing up and placing his hands on his hips. "I'm sure you have a lot of catching up to do." He smiled beatifically at them, the image of bonhomie. "However, although I will permit Sergeant Wiznowski to visit with you briefly, since you are old friends, I hope that you will remain circumspect about your conversations. Don't ask, don't tell, doncha know." He winked, turned and whisked out of the cramped cabin.

18

Washington, DC Sol III
1424 EDT November 12th, 2002 AD

The group of military officers and civilians around the conference table stood up as the President entered the Situation Room. Since Tchpth never seemed to sit, but always bounced on their stumpy spider legs, it was difficult to tell whether the ten-limbed pseudo-arthropod was rendering proper respect to the leader of Earth's only remaining superpower. On the other hand, it was a senior philosopher-scientist among a race of superscientists and could be permitted a certain amount of indiscretion. It was now being indiscreet by dancing on the black glass table.

"Tchpth Tctchpah," aspirated the President, rather well everyone thought, "thank you for coming. You wanted to address us about our projected nuclear, biological and chemical policy for the upcoming conflict." He took his seat and waved for everyone else to join him.

The senior Tchpth waited for the group of advisors and military personnel to take their seats; the group included all the senior members of the National Security Council as well as the High Commander and his primary staff. Their various aides lined the walls, human tape recorders for the event. Once the expected rustling died down the Tchpth made an exaggerated bob and waggled his eyestalks at the President.

"Yes, Senior Leader of this Archaic Group of Vicious Omnivores. And I thank you for the limited forum." At the form of address, everyone surreptitiously looked at the President. The light blue Tchpth used an AID for translation, just as everyone

153

in the room. Whether the series of insults were overtranslation by the AID or a realistic translation of an intentional insult was unclear. The President decided to take it like a man and everyone else took their lead from him.

"Specifically, I wished to address your biological and chemical doctrine." The arthropoid danced sideways as a hologram formed.

"Your present doctrine is for a reestablishment of a biological and chemical warfare assault department, a group of chemical and biological weapons experts who work on weapons to be used offensively against the Posleen." The hologram started to show unedited scenes of chemical weapons tests: goats shivering and vomiting under the effect of Sarin, and movie footage from the First World War of soldiers coughing out their lungs from mustard gas.

"While the Tchpth are philosophically opposed to conflict in any form, I understand the logic. Effective use of chemical or biological agents would be a significant force multiplier and you need a force multiplier given the difficulties you will encounter fighting the Posleen." The hologram shifted to scenes of Posleen incursions. Tchpth towers tumbled under the hammer of Posleen heavy weapons and charnel pits of slaughtered Indowy were buried by heavy earth movers.

"Unfortunately, that does not give the Posleen sufficient credit. To build a frame of reference for you backward alien vicious omnivores: are you aware, O High Leader of the Unenlightened, that if your cook were to mistake me for a terrestrial crab and boil me for your dinner, you would die were you to eat me?" The hologram shifted through scenes of various environments. More worlds than the group could count flickered in front of their eyes, from worlds of oxygen and water, through heavy hydrogen giants to scenes that might have been from a different dimension.

"That had been mentioned," answered the President, smiling at what he had decided was an overly accurate translation by the AID, and reeling from the impact of the images. "Something about incompatible body chemistries."

"Correct. Amazing, even the ill-mannered can learn. There are billions upon billions of worlds, none of the biologies perfectly compatible. However, the Posleen can dine on either of us with positive relish. Upon the denizens of any oxygen-water world they have invaded."

"You just did a pun in English, by the way. Yes, that . . . dichotomy had come to the attention of some of my science advisors," the President said, making a note. "Do you know why?"

"Not specifically. You realize that we have never had a Posleen corpse to examine?" The hologram shifted to a diagram of a human body, data streaming by in a cascade, then Darhel, Tchpth, Indowy, Himmit.

"Don't worry, we'll fix that problem, doc," chimed in the Vice Commander, the former Marine Commandant, to the accompaniment of grim chuckles. The comment relieved some of the tension occasioned by the less than diplomatic translations and imagery. Even the President smiled momentarily. General McCloy, the new High Commander, looked momentarily thoughtful and turned to whisper to his aide.

"Yes, I'm sure you vicious omnivores will do an excellent job. However, until then, we can only speculate." An image of a Posleen began to rotate in the hologram. The hologram exploded, showing areas known and unknown. The data scrolling down the rim was mostly question marks.

"The Posleen show every symptom of being genetically manipulated, so that is part of the answer. The full answer waits on available corpses, which your senior violent carnivore has so graciously offered for our sacrifice." The philosopher-scientist seemed totally unaware of the consternation his translation was causing in his audience. Still unable to determine if it was simply a matter of over-precise translation or intentional irony, the group vacillated between anger and laughter. The secretary of defense was holding his hand over his mouth while the secretary of state had simply buttoned down a poker face. The national security advisor had his head down, face hidden behind his hand, as he made furious notes. Occasionally his body shook as if he were coughing.

"There is, however, one bit of data specific to the subject. We, too, have weapons of mass destruction. We also have even more stringent regulations about their use. However, in at least one instance, desperation caused a population to attempt biological *and* chemical warfare against the Posleen. Despite the aid of renegade Tchpth, none of their solutions had the slightest effect." At that pronouncement most of the senior officials sat back in their chairs.

The High Commander traded a look with the SECDEF that combined uncertainty with resignation. The Tchpth had apparently penetrated the whole Weapons of Mass Destruction program. Although the weapons were outlawed by both the Federation and numerous pre-Contact treaties, the old designs and notes had already been dusted off and lab work started. Most of the production would be simplicity itself for any competent chemical firm, of which the United States had legions. The assumption of being able to use WMD—weapons of mass destruction like gas, nukes or biologicals—was central to the entire war plan. Without them, without chemicals particularly, most of the plans to date were out the window.

"I find that hard to believe," said General Harmon, Ground Forces Chief of Staff. "I mean, surely VX would have some effect."

"Actually, General, your VX gas would not even affect me; I could fill this room with it and walk out unscathed. Your vicious and disgusting mustard gas would make me quite ill at lethal concentrations, but nerve gases would be completely ineffective. Despite my oft-noted resemblance to a cockroach or a crab you are much more closely related to your order crustacea or arthropoda than I." The Tchpth bobbed up and down, its eyestalks waving in agitation. It briefly flushed turquoise.

"Your scientists and military commanders are well ahead of you," he continued, gesturing at the hologram. Scenes of personnel in full coverage and lab coats were interspersed with more scenes of a variety of terrestrial species choking, shaking and dying. The scenes were obviously recent, as ultramodern computers littered the area. There were even some Galactic devices, notable by the sinuous grace of Indowy manufacture. At the first scene the High Commander's face went paper white.

"They are already prepared for the first sample of Posleen tissues to experiment on and develop effective gases. However, the problem still remains: excellent and far superior Tchpth philosopher/scientists have failed in that very endeavor, with far greater technology and experience than humans. The Posleen are simply designed to be catastrophically resistant to all possible agents; I feel it would be a waste of your time as well as being immoral. And just plain wrong. The Ldd!ttnt! would not approve." The king-crab-sized arthropoid suddenly spun in place twice, bouncing up and down as it did so. "So say the Ldd!ttnt!"

"Very well, Tchpth Tctchpah," said the President, with a glance at the senior officers. "I understand your position and respect it. I also believe you. We will experiment, fully and openly, with chemical and biological agents when specimens become available, but if there is no initial success we will discontinue our efforts in favor of more lucrative opportunities. And more moral ones. Good enough?"

"Yes, O Munificent and Gorged Leader of the Unenlightened and I thank you for your time. For a ruthless carnivore you are not too unintelligent."

19

"Well," said Sergeant Major Mosovich after he read the e-mail from Special Operations Command, "I thought this mission was going too easy."

The team sat around the tiny table in the Himmit ship's lounge drinking hot liquids and waiting for the shower. The team had been on Barwhon for nearly a year, resupplied twice by the Himmit, and it showed. The initial quick in and out had been expanded and expanded again until the hard, hand-chosen warriors of yore became a group of near automatons. Gone were the jokes, the kidding, the asides. Every member of the team had lost weight, become pared down to the point that each looked anorexic. The constant cold and damp, and the anxiety of the penetrations were dragging down even the hardest members of the team. Tempers were frayed. Mosovich thought about that as he read the flimsy Rigas had handed him.

Not even the Galactics could drive a message through the maelstrom of hyperspace, so ships would carry burst packets of electronic mail from warp point to warp point. At most of the major warp nexi, deep space satellites would receive the compressed bursts of data, sort them and store them for transfer. As other ships happened by, the bursts of mail would be routed to those going in the right direction. Finally the mail would reach its destination, slowly or fast depending on the vagaries of the intervening ships. In the case of this missive, it had been burst transmitted to a dedicated Himmit ship shuttling between the nearest surviving beacon and the Barwhon system. The Himmit courier picked up data bursts like it from Earth and returned the team's data. That way whether the team survived or not the data would make it back to Earth. Rigas had received the most recent transmission shortly before the team made it back from Objective 24, a fully functioning Posleen city.

Mosovich thought about it for a moment more as Mueller stepped out of the shower stall.

"Next!"

"Hold it, Richards. Park it." With a frown Richards sat back down again in the uncomfortable chair. It had to be bad news; every time they received orders the situation just got worse.

"Okay, first the brass is muchem happy with the take from the entire mission. We're really here to confirm Galactic intelligence and to see if there's anything other carnivores can figure out about the Posleen that the Galactics can't. But they've also come up with another tasking. We need to get a Posleen, dead or alive, to be returned to Earth for study. They actually say a group of Posleen."

"Oh, joy!" exclaimed Ersin. "How the hell are we supposed to collect Posleen covertly? What the fuck happened to a reconnaissance? For that matter, what the fuck happened to a recall order?"

"This clearly states that a snatch is now the primary mission, reconnaissance is secondary," said Mosovich. It was just another wonderful example of how Washington considered special operations troops expendable. He was beginning to wonder if the brass had decided to just leave them on this ball until they rotted. And if he was thinking it, he knew the others were. So far they had not been detected and had not lost anyone. That was bound to change.

"Who's the signature?" asked Mueller, toweling his head.

"General Baird, COS-JSOC—Chief of Staff, Joint Special Operations Command—he's apparently filling in for General Taylor," answered Mosovich, glancing at the bottom of the flimsy. Tung held out his hand and Mosovich passed it over. After a moment's perusal Tung handed it back expressionlessly.

"Baird's Air Force. See any para-jumpers doing this shit?" snorted Trapp.

"Doesn't matter," said Mosovich, "it's an order. Fortunately they don't say how to do it, or what kind of Posleen. Himmit Rigas?" he asked in a raised voice.

"Yes, Sergeant Major," the Himmit responded from the intercom.

"Can the backup ship land here?" asked Mosovich. There was plenty of room in the clearing.

"They could but they won't. They are here purely for support and would not experience this particular event for all the stories in the Galaxy," responded the Himmit.

"Okay, the rest of the mission is off. We are going to perform our snatch and get the hell out of Dodge. Himmit, how many Tchpth can we cram in this tub, and can we cross shift after the first transfer point? For that matter will Hiberzine work on a Tchpth?"

"I see your objective, but your orders do not mention Tchpth. I read them."

"Fuck my orders," snapped the pissed off NCO. He was as tired as the rest of the team and even more unhappy about the orders. He personally thought those orders were a death warrant. "We're supposed to collect Posleen; do you see room for adult Posleen? I don't. So we collect nestlings. And since the nestlings are right there by the Tchpth..."

"We pull out as many Tchpth as we can," finished Ersin.

"Right."

"Tactically wrong. Morally right. Can we do it?" asked Tung. His midnight face was as still as stone. With nearly as much experience as Mosovich, he was just as aware of the impossibility of their current orders.

"Getting back's gonna be a stone bitch," said Trapp. "They're gonna be all over our ass." He pulled out his Bushmaster and started sharpening it.

"Lambs to the slaughter," murmured Ellsworthy, taking a quick buff at a nail.

"Lotta damn lambs," pointed out Mueller, "with a lot of damn weapons."

"So, we gotta get in and out without being noticed," said Richards, shrugging his shoulders.

"Diversion," stated Tung.

"Oh, now I know why you brought me!" laughed Mueller, "I'm supposed to die heroically planting the explosives! I saw the movie. Now, it was a good movie, don't get me wrong, but I'm not sure I want the part."

"Nail the God Kings," said Richards.

"That would be me," smiled Ellsworthy, dreamily. She held her hand out at arm's length and examined what was left of her nails. "Damn, I wish there was a nail shop on this ball." She buffed another rough edge.

"Mine the far approach, and the buildings," stated Tung with a shake of his head at the marine. Ellsworthy seemed to spend most of her time on another plane, but it only seemed to make her more effective when it dropped in the pot. "Come in in the dark, set the charges, hit them from the flank at BMNT."—Before Morning Nautical Twilight—"Most of the team pulls out the nestlings and the Tchpth while a group draws the Posleen on a wild goose chase."

"We don't know that they don't have vehicles other than the God Kings' capable of negotiating this muck," Mosovich pointed out. "Mostly good, but we need to avoid being chased at all. If we are chased, then we split off a team to lead them away. Let me work this over. Tung, Ersin, my cabin. The rest of you get a shower and some rest, I'm going to commune with higher and come up with an op-order."

Sandra Ellsworthy was in her element. Wrapped in rags of burlap, she nestled into the lower branches of a Griffin tree and plotted targets. As the first faint purple light of Barwhon dawn began to shade the horizon, it degraded the light enhancements built into her scope. However, since the Posleen had a higher body temperature than humans, and far higher than the semi-isothermal Tchpth, the thermal imagery enhancements picked them out like beacons against the cooler backdrop.

There had been changes since the team was last here. There were now seven complete pyramids, each surrounded by several pens. The causeway on the west side had been completed and the bunkers to either side, nearly a kilometer from Ellsworthy's hide, were complete. On the north and south sides trees were being cleared and it looked like a drainage project was under way. Fortunately clearing had not started on the west side, where the team waited, but the unexpected open area had slowed the diversion team's entry and would make its retreat less survivable. There were also nearly twice as many Posleen moving around as there had been at the time of the first recon. If anything went wrong with the snatch it looked like it would be a short, sharp shower of shit.

"Deese leettle pig went to market," she whispered, targeting the Posleen sentry most likely to engage the diversion force first.

Her task was to slow the pursuit without lowering the effectiveness of the diversion and without revealing her position. The nursery rhymes, set to a reggae beat, were a mnemonic to remember the order of fire. She had eleven rounds before reload and every round was plotted. "You know deese leettle piggy stayed home," the first guard's backup, "deese leettle piggy had roast beef," a superior normal bent over its 3mm, "an deese leettle piggy had none," its companion. The Posleen never seemed to be alone; they always moved in groups of two or more. "An deese leettle piggy went..." a Posleen crouched by the entrance to one of the now-completed pyramids near the nestling pens. About then she expected the God Kings to start making their appearance. She figured on taking out at least two of the seven to ten before reloading.

"Game," the demo team was pulling back.

"Set," as Trapp reached contact position. She was glad it was him and not her. The quick little bastard was a master, whatever his technical ranking.

"Match," she whispered taking up slack on the trigger.

"Initiate," growled Master Sergeant Tung.

She had barely seen Mueller and Ersin as they moved around the compound. Now their handiwork was evident. The two half-formed bunkers at the causeway were devoured in actinic silver fire as the C-9 atomic catalyst explosive did its job. Simultaneously the further line of bunkers was devoured in flames. Jets of plasma gouted from the palace on top of the farthest pyramid as a small antimatter charge detonated. Posleen began to pour from the huts like hornets from a hive as Ellsworthy serviced her targets and explosions continued to rock the compound.

One little piggy did indeed go to market and one went home. With each shot the fifty caliber slammed into her shoulder like the kick of a horse, nearly unseating her from her perch in the tree. But when the two-ounce rounds punched through the Posleen's centauroid chests the horse-sized creatures were hurled sideways, plate-sized exit holes and fountains of yellow ichor marking their end. Just as she reloaded, right on time, the first God King rushed into view, harness half slung. The leader caste was as easy meat as the rest and went up to the great smorgasbord in the sky, flattened across the deceased guard at its door.

While the master sniper serviced her targets, Trapp had another job. As the Posleen sentry nearest the nestling pens turned to look at the violent silver flashes, an unnoticed black shadow detached itself from the ground. Not trusting the power of the silenced 9mm rounds against something with the mass of a small horse, Trapp put seven rounds into the sentry's chest and three into its head in four seconds. The Posleen's head exploded like a yellow melon and it joined its brethren in repose. Trapp cautiously tracked it to the ground then moved west to cover the left flank of the entry team.

Richards moved directly into the compound and set up an M-60 light machine gun just beyond the pens as Master Sergeant Tung moved to the left with a medium laser. This left Mosovich and Martine to secure the objective.

One problem with the Tchpth was that the team had no translation devices. Human-adapted AIDs had not been available before they left and the Himmit had been exceedingly reluctant to give up any of theirs. Thus Mosovich was forced to try pidgin Tchpth on the prisoners who looked for all the world to him like blue Alaskan King crabs. Martine had, so to speak, drawn the short straw and he had three sacks to fill up with nestling Posleen.

Jake raced to the fence of the Tchpth compound and aspirated "TcKpth! !Klik! Tit! Tit!" which the Himmit had solemnly assured him meant "Friends here to help, move back, move back."

He was certain it would never work, but the instant the first word left his mouth, the remaining Tchpth jerked to the far side of the pen. He placed a sheet charge against the plastic slats and darted around the corner. The C-4 flashed white and a section of fence three feet across simply vanished. "Ikdee! Ikdee!" he shouted, gesturing for them to follow and ran for the jungle. He looked back and saw that none of them had moved. Each and every one remained in the pen. Cursing everything Galactic he ran back.

In the meantime Staff Sergeant Martine had his own extraterrestrial problems. He had had the foresight to wear gloves, since the carnivorous Posleen had teeth like razors even as nestlings, but standard issue leather work gloves were never meant to deal with carnivore jaws and raptor talons. When he bent over the fence and reached in for the first specimen, as he had seen the God King reach in months before, he immediately discovered that there was a knack to grabbing nestlings.

Like a snake, or a pissed-off cat, they were best grasped behind the neck. The blast of Mosovich's charge drowned Martino's bellow of pain and rage as the nestling snapped its tooth-filled maw onto his hand and whipped up to sink all six talons into his arm. But his imprecations could be heard clearly over the beginning sounds of battle in the distance.

"F-f-f-f-co-co-cocksucker!" he managed to say in an intense stage whisper. He pounded the tenacious whelp against the fence several times until he could stun it enough to lever its saurian jaws apart and detach its talons.

"Shit, shit, shit," he cursed as he stuffed the unconscious pullet into the sack. He surveyed the remaining throng while shaking the blood from his hand. They in turn watched him. They obviously hoped he was supper. He thrust his hand in again and this time managed to snag the floppy skin on the back of one of the nestlings' elongated necks. It let out a shriek and twisted in his grip, but he thrust the cat-sized extraterrestrial willy-nilly into the second sack.

Mueller and Ersin had laid a series of trip-wire and command-detonated mines along the path the Posleen would take in pursuit and their flashes served to maintain the distraction, but one God King, at least, noticed the commotion by the pens and began to rally a counterattack. That notion was effectively quashed by a .50 caliber high velocity round, but the normals of that God King, and the others whose bonds had been released, were in a hyper-aggressive mood with the death of their masters. A group of them moved toward the disturbance at the pens and it was time to rock and roll.

Richards opened the ball with direct fire from his M-60. The 7.62mm rounds tumbled Posleen to the ground, but the senseless carnivores totally ignored their losses and charged towards the source of the drifting tracers, few of them firing in return. Trapp and Ellsworthy added the weight of their fire, but until Tung added the power of his man-pack laser the tide was unstoppable. The combination managed to stop the first wave but the battle on the south side had drawn the attention of the main body away from the distraction, effectively negating its purpose.

Mosovich gave up coaxing the crabs when the firing started. He leapt into the pen, through a forest of pincers, to the far side and began kicking them out through the opening. The Tchpth first turned towards their former homes, but seeing the raging battle to the north, they scattered southward towards the jungle, chittering in fear. By tracking back and forth waving his weapon, which had better uses at the moment in his opinion, he managed to drive them in the right general direction. He heard silvery laughter on the team net and looked up towards the trees.

"Fuck you, Ellsworthy," he snarled.

She laughed again, preparing to meet the second wave. "Sorry, honey, but you look like a crab farmer with his flock." Her laughter broke off in a flurry of directed fire at the trees and a gurgle. He saw a black shape detach itself from a branch and fall thirty meters to bone crushing stillness.

"*Incoming!*" screamed Richards, as a God King saucer launched itself upwards. It swooped randomly up and left, as its heavy rail-gun tracked back and forth. Martine screamed and dropped as his legs were severed by the sheet of fire, and Master Sergeant Tung grunted and fell like a forest giant, blood pouring from his mouth.

Jake turned away from his animal husbandry and charged towards the spot where the remains of Sandra Ellsworthy sprawled. Sweeping up her massive rifle he tracked onto the God King saucer and gave it a little lead. The recoil of the powerful weapon rocked him backwards as he fired "off hand." The Posleen used an energy storage system similar to the Federation's. A solid state module buried deep in the "battery" generated a field that permitted molecular bonds to be twisted far out of alignment. As energy was released, the bonds twisted back into their correct position, releasing their stored power. It was a mature technology that, while inherently dangerous, worked just fine as long as the stabilization module maintained integrity.

The .50 caliber bullet punched through the light metal of the saucer and into its energy bottle. The round actually missed the stabilization module, but the dynamic shock wave of its passage transferred thousands of joules of energy through the matrix. Before the bullet had passed fully through the crystalline matrix the bonds had begun to shatter and release their massive energy in an uncontrolled explosion rivaling an antimatter charge.

The blast flipped the saucer into the air and the mass of the God King saucer disappeared in the bright white flash. The shock wave slapped the sergeant major and Trapp to the ground, tossed Richards through the air like a flapjack and stunned or killed most of the front rank Posleen. It was followed by a searing wave of heat.

After a moment Trapp and Mosovich stumbled to their feet, but Richards lay with his head flopped oddly to one side. Jake took one look at him, picked up Martine's sacks and his Street Sweeper then ran for the jungle.

20

Planetary Transport Class *Maruk*,
N-Space Transit Terra-Diess
1147 GMT March 14th, 2002 AD

Mike was lifting weights in a tiny gym tucked away between the number eighteen cargo hold and the gamma zone environmental spaces when his AID chirped, "You're requested to report to General Houseman at your earliest convenience."

This request involved a number of problems. The first was their relative location. There were four troopships in the Expeditionary Force flotilla. One was occupied entirely by the Chinese divisions. Two had Allied Expeditionary Force, NATO units, U.S. III Corp, German, English, Dutch, Japanese and French. The last was filled with a mixed bag of Russian and Third World troops, southeast Asian, African and South American. With the exception of the NATO troops, the contingents were kept strictly segregated. Besides avoiding the cultural conflicts that would inevitably arise, this permitted the use of other nations' forces when riots broke out within a force.

For two months troops, mostly ill-prepared and trained, had been left in an interstellar limbo. There was ample horizontal room, but the low ceilings designed for Indowy and lack of wind, sun and space caused the troops to become stir-crazy even once the air, food and light problems were fixed. With no communication in or out while in fold space the units brooded into explosion. Once in the NATO ships and four times on the mixed ship, local arguments had gotten out of hand.

The problem was that General Houseman, the III Corp and

American contingent commander, spent time on both the *Maruk,* the ship Lieutenant O'Neal was on and the *Sorduk,* the other ship with NATO forces, as the ships dropped in and out of hyperspatial anomalies. His office and the bulk of III Corp were on the *Maruk,* but his commander, General Sir Walter Arnold, British Army, was on the *Sorduk.*

"Where is the general?" he asked his AID, toweling off while stumping ponderously to the manual gravity controls.

"General Houseman is in his office, Alpha Quad, ring five, deck A, right abaft NATO Senior Officers' Quarters."

Made sense, the general wouldn't expect him to come to the *Sorduk* without any warning. Second problem: when a Lieutenant General tells a First Lieutenant "at your earliest convenience" he means "right damn now." But showing up in sweat-soaked PT uniform is Unacceptable Attire. Oh, well. He'd have to take time to change, but he was also about four kilometers away. This was going to be interesting.

"Please send a message to the general that I am unavoidably detained and will not be able to reach his location for a minimum of... thirty minutes."

Third and insurmountable problem: He didn't have the right uniform. All he brought were Fleet Strike uniforms and all the U.S. units were wearing regular Army uniforms: BDUs or Greens as appropriate. Therefore, he could show up in silks, daily work uniform, or blues, dress uniform.

"What's the uniform of the day for III Corp headquarters personnel?"

"BDUs." Battle dress uniform, regular camouflage. It would be replaced, had been in Mike's case, by silks, but the two uniforms could not be more different. Therefore, blues might even be less conspicuous; it might be mistaken for some other country's dress uniform.

The Fleet Strike uniform design team had really thrown caution to the wind with the dress uniform. The color was a deep cobalt blue with, in officer's case, thin piping at the seams in the color of the officer's branch, in O'Neal's case light blue for infantry. The piping was thermally activated and swirled with movement as the leg contacted the edge. The tunic was collarless without lapels and pressure sealed on the left side. It was a damn showy and conspicuous uniform, which militated against it. Silks it was.

Twenty-seven minutes later First Lieutenant Michael O'Neal in gray silks and Terra blue beret, entered the outer office of the Commander, United States Ground Forces, Diess Expeditionary Force. Installed in the outer office, Cerberus at the gates, was a thick-set command sergeant major who looked as if he last smiled in 1968. Mike could have sworn he was fighting off a grin at Mike's attire.

Lieutenant O'Neal had traveled four kilometers, washed, shaved and changed in those twenty-seven minutes. It was only possible because he brought his suit to the gym. Instead of using normal hallways he had passed through a series of zero gee and unpressurized holds at speeds that still had him shaking. The suit's semibiotic liner had scavenged his sweat and dirt and consumed the stubble on his face.

When he got into his cabin it was only necessary to pop out of the suit and change. Unfortunately this last was severely inhibited by the suit. Although the suit was no more bulky than a fat man, and a short one at that, it had to be leaned against the wall and was immobile until he put it back on. To put on his trousers in the cramped cubicle it was necessary to straddle the suit's leg and more or less bounce up and down. Once the process was done it left only an undignified rush through the junior officers' quarters "up-country" to the senior levels.

The sergeant major expressionlessly inspected the uniform then stood and walked to the inner door. He opened it without knocking. "Lieutenant O'Neal, sir."

"Send him in, Sergeant Major, by all means," said an affable voice. O'Neal heard the distinct sound of a sheaf of papers hitting others, as when a folder is tossed onto an overloaded desk.

The sergeant major stood aside, gestured for the lieutenant to enter and closed the door after him. Only with the door safely closed did he, without a change in expression, snort several times in laughter.

The general had much in common, physically, with his sergeant major. Both had stocky builds of medium height, round florid faces and thinning gray-blond hair. All in all they looked not unlike a matched set of champion bulldogs. But, whereas the sergeant major wore a perpetual frown, the general's face was creased in a smile and his mild blue eyes twinkled as Lieutenant O'Neal saluted.

"Lieutenant O'Neal, reporting as ordered," said Mike. Like all junior officers he was categorizing his sins and trying to decide which one had come to the general's attention. However, unlike most he had ample experience with flag officers so he was less intimidated than many would have been.

The general waved a hand at his forehead and said, "At ease, Lieutenant, as a matter of fact, grab a chair. Coffee?" The general grabbed his own mug and reached for a Westbend coffee maker hardwired into the wall.

"Yes, sir, thank you." Mike paused. "Did the Indowy wire that for you, sir?"

"Indowy, hell." The general snorted. "I had to get somebody from Corp maintenance to set up a portable generator a couple of compartments over then drill through the damned wall. We've got mostly standard office equipment and we're having a shitload of problems getting them integrated. Cream and sugar?" he continued graciously.

"Much of both, thank you, sir. I could look into that for you, sir. I get along with Indowy pretty well, I think it's because I'm their size."

"I understand that we already have you to thank for getting the damn lighting fixed. Not to mention finding the food we were supposed to be getting all along. Lots of time on your hands, Lieutenant?" The general handed Mike his coffee and took a sip of his own, peering at the lieutenant over the rim.

"Sir?"

"I had an interesting conversation with Oberst Kiel of the Bundeswehr the other day. I believe you know the Herr Oberst?"

"Yes, sir. He was one of the GalTech Infantry Design team leaders for the NATO committee."

"He came through General Arnold, who asked me to talk to him on the subject of my ACS battalion. Do you have any idea what he said?"

"Yes, sir."

"I understood that you were to advise the battalion on ACS techniques, is that correct?" asked the general, mildly.

"Yes, sir," said Mike. Now he knew where this was going. He was mildly surprised that the general was underinformed. The flag officer was in for a shock.

"And how would you rate the battalion as an ACS unit?"

"Low, sir," said Mike, taking a sip of the coffee. He suppressed a grimace. Apparently the general was a Texan; you could have floated a horseshoe in the brew.

"Thank you. Can I ask where you have been the last two months? Where you were today?" asked the general, anger building in his voice.

"Under direct orders, until we made planet-fall, to keep to myself," said Mike, forcing down another sip. Fortunately the way the conversation was going he was going to be able to put the cup down and avoid it soon.

"From whom?" asked the general, surprised.

"Lieutenant Colonel Youngman, sir."

"Direct orders?" asked the astounded officer.

"Michelle?" Mike prompted.

"Yes, Lieutenant O'Neal," she said. The experienced machine knew when to be on her best behavior.

"Run the applicable conversation."

"*Now, I don't care what you think your mission is, or who you think you are. What I want you to do is go to your cabin and stay there for the rest of the trip. You're not confined to quarters or anything but I decide how my battalion is run, how it trains, what its tactics are. Not any former E-5 with a shiny silver bar that thinks he's hot shit. If I find you in the battalion area without my direct permission, in the training areas, or talking to my officers about tactics or training I will personally hang you up, shake you out and strip you of commission, rank, honor and possibly life. Do I make myself clear?*" the AID played back.

"I confess, sir, that I did not handle the conversation very well on my side," Mike allowed, to stunned silence. "I let the colonel get my goat, to be frank and I was already upset with the posted training schedule when I arrived."

"Did you tell the AID to record that conversation?" the general asked, with a neutral expression once he had gotten over his shock.

"You didn't know, sir?" asked Mike, with an uneasy voice and a glance at the general's AID, sitting conspicuously on top of his desk. This was a turn he was not particularly happy about.

"Know what?"

"They record everything, sir."

"*What?*"

"We found out at GalTech, sir. Sight, sound, everything. It can be played back at any time in the future."

"By whom?"

"Currently they are designed solely for user-authorized playback, sir, with some caveats. Some of the countries wanted to make it anyone of a higher rank, but we, the Americans, and a few others, the British and Germans notably, refused. If our soldiers found out that their AIDs would rat on them at any opportunity, they'd 'lose' them all the time. However, the records are generally accessible in times of combat or by anyone interacting with the owning individual during the applicable moment."

"Okay. Damn, maybe you should be my ACS advisor. So, the colonel told you to remain in your cabin. Effectively under arrest. Have you?"

"No, sir. I've been keeping in training, physical and tactical. I also construed that I should not develop social contact with the members of the ACS battalion, so I've avoided the club, etc."

"So, you've been working out in a gym for the past month?"

"And with my suit, yes, sir."

"Have you been working with any units of the 325?"

"Sir?"

"Do you realize that you always respond the same way when avoiding a question? Among other interesting anomalies, it appears that Bravo company of the battalion is the only company in the ACS battalion that is hitting the expected milestones for suit training time. And, according to the Herr Oberst, Bravo has made a remarkable advancement in the last month. The Oberst seems to feel that the only part of my ACS unit that is worth wiping a nose with is Bravo company. Not actually up to where they should be, but not completely useless.

"Then it came to my attention that Lieutenant Colonel Youngman wrote an Officer Evaluation Report for his Bravo company commander that accused him of everything but sleeping with my daughter. According to the OER it seems that Bravo company is 'wholly unprepared for combat.' In a recent internal battalion EIB evaluation none of the company's personnel managed to pass," said the general with a thin smile.

"Sir, one of the EIB standards is a thousand-meter land navigation course. Where'd they do it?" For the first time in the conversation the general was beginning to remind Mike of General Horner.

"Good question. More to the point, since the EIB hasn't been upgraded for ACS standards, what's the point of training for it?" asked the general. The affable expression had turned to something very like a snarl.

"Ummh, his people...need to maintain proficiency for when they transfer to non-ACS units, sir?"

"Very good," smiled the general with a rueful shake of his head. "You make a wonderful devil's advocate, Lieutenant. Unfortunately, regulations currently call for permanent retention of ACS qualified personnel in ACS units. There goes that argument right out the window. Actually, the only line commander he's satisfied with is Charlie. Alpha also performed abysmally. However I also happened to notice that although the majority of the battalion is less than ten percent ACS proficient, Alpha and Bravo are at twenty and thirty percent, respectively. Comments, Lieutenant?"

"I suspect that Alpha and Bravo's brass is unshined and they haven't met their PT norms, sir."

"Sarcasm, Lieutenant?"

"Sorry, sir. Maybe a little."

"As a matter of fact, when I asked Lieutenant Colonel Youngman about Bravo company, he commented that he was considering relieving his Bravo company commander."

"Jesus!"

"Do you normally interrupt generals, Lieutenant?" the general asked, dryly.

"No, sir. No excuse, sir," said Mike. He took a deep breath and tried to get hold of his temper. Relieving Captain Brandon would cut the entire pipeline he had been using to get the battalion any decent training.

Infantrymen were past masters at disappearing. Partially it was a matter of their mission; being "ghosts" was half of what being infantry was all about. Another part of it was that without a war or heavy-duty training schedule, they were always first to be handed the worst details. So experienced individuals in infantry units learned to become functionally invisible outside of real training times.

Mike and Wiznowski had used this ability to the fullest. The companies were holding regular morning, early afternoon and recall formations, per battalion orders. However, some of the empty holds were practically right next door to the battalion area. Every day NCOs from Bravo and later Alpha company had slipped out of the battalion area and into the abandoned holds. There they had begun to master the myriad facets of their new specialty, the better to pass it on to their juniors. One of the ironic items was the fact that they bitched and moaned about not having the "GalTech expert" available to help them. Mike meanwhile was monitoring the entire process through his Mil-specs or armor, down to listening to the bitching. Whenever he felt that the situation needed something pointed out he filtered it through Wiznowski. As far as anyone knew, Wiz was running the whole training program.

If Captain Brandon were relieved, the entire masquerade would go down the tubes.

"I was informed of your habitual frown," General Houseman continued quietly, "but you are currently turning red and smoking at the ears. And would you kindly avoid drilling holes through the wall with your stare?"

"Bulkhead, sir. On a ship it's a bulkhead."

"Whatever. Now to return to my original question, did you in fact violate direct and indirect orders by interfering in the tactical training of one of Lieutenant Colonel Youngman's subunits?"

"Partially, sir," Mike equivocated. He was thinking furiously.

"By helping Captains Brandon and Wright with ACS training?"

"Sir, I have not discussed training or Galactic technologies with any officer of the battalion."

"Would you care to explain that?" asked the general with a raised eyebrow.

"I have not spoken directly to any officer about training, sir. That was in fact my order. Nor have I entered the battalion area, nor have I entered any training area. I have, in fact, obeyed the letter of the order."

"I see." The general smiled. "I suppose there is a reason that the NCOs and enlisted in the companies are doing better, overall, than the officers?"

"Possibly, sir."

"Related to your influence?"

"Possibly, sir. Then again, to be honest, it might have something to do with the officers spending more time in the 'club' than they do in suits."

"But you have influenced training," the general pointed out.

"Yes, sir."

"Despite the training schedule authorized by the Battalion S-3?"

"Yes, sir."

"Were you aware of the published training schedule?"

"Yes, sir."

"Good. I'm glad you didn't turn a blind eye to your misdeeds." The general shook his head, looking suddenly harried.

"Son, I'm going to tell you this by way of an apology. The battalion is an attachment as opposed to one of 'my' units, a III Corp unit that is. Therefore, it would be damned difficult for me to relieve Lieutenant Colonel Youngman, much as I would currently like to." He raised an eyebrow inviting comment, but Mike remained silent. He shook his head again and went on.

"It's a hell of a fix to take a unit into battle where I distrust the entire command team. So I've done what I can. Disregarding my long-standing rule against micromanaging my subordinate units, a rule the colonel has apparently never heard of, I gave Lieutenant Colonel Youngman a written order to initiate a *vigorous* training program in ACS combat. It states that, given his failure to date to train in vital areas, if the battalion fails to score eighty percent or better in ACS training norms by the date of our landing it will give me no choice but to relieve him for cause. He did not take it well at all. He seems to feel that since there is no way to prepare adequately because of 'grossly inadequate preparation time' on Earth, the battalion should be reissued standard weaponry and deployed as regular airborne infantry."

"Good God," Mike whispered. The upcoming battle was sure to be a bloodbath for ACS, going in as lightly weaponed airborne infantry would be suicide.

The general smiled coldly again. "I cannot tell you how much I agree. Trust me: I had disabused the colonel of that concept by the time I was done.

"Before some of this came up I sent a personal e-mail to Jack Horner. He said that your only problem was that you needed someone holding your leash. If there is a problem that requires a juggernaut all I should do is release the leash. That is why we are having this conversation.

"Now, I've given Colonel Youngman all the guidance I think he needs; I did not order him to use you as a training asset. So, if he doesn't contact you within a week, leave a message with my AID. I'll make an unannounced visit and drop a question about 'that GalTech expert, whatsisname?' Clear?"

"As crystal, sir."

"If I feel it necessary, I will tell you that you have carte blanche. At that point I will have to relieve the colonel. I don't have a replacement for him I trust that has *any* ACS time. You do understand the implications of having to place a captain like, for example, Brandon, in command of a battalion."

"Yes, sir," Mike was feeling weak in the knees. The personnel and policy wonkers in Washington would go ballistic. The repercussions for GalTech, which already had a bad reputation for ramming through conventions, might be worse than losing the battalion. The entrenched bureaucracy could throw up the damnedest obstacles when they felt threatened and did not seem to give a damn that there was a war on.

"Thank you for coming, Lieutenant. We did not have this conversation. This compartment will self-destruct in thirty seconds. Get lost."

"Yes, sir. Where am I?"

21

Camp McCall, NC Sol III
0917 July 25th, 2002 AD

"Afternoon, Gunny, siddown." Like many of the buildings spring-
ing up to support the expanding war effort, the company commander's combined office and quarters was a sixty-six-foot trailer.
The office occupied one end, with the living quarters on the other.
Among other things, this arrangement meant one less piece of
housing that had to be allocated for the burgeoning officer corps.
The company commander was a recycled second lieutenant and
the only officer in the training company.

With the new-old disciplinary techniques and the paucity
of officers on the training base, the gaps that had been closing between officer and enlisted corps in the past decade were
beginning to widen again. Despite the fact that their CO was
a basically nice if stupid second john, the recruits looked upon
him as sitting at the right hand of God; the battalion commander
was, of course, God.

Gunnery Sergeant Pappas and the other NCOs encouraged
this attitude; keeping the trainees in line was becoming more and
more difficult. Not only was it necessary to learn radically new
technologies, but the threat bearing down on Earth was causing
ripples of disruption at every level. Although the prestige of being
Strike Troopers was high, the stress of not knowing your eventual
duty assignment, not knowing, as the Guard troops did, that you
would be directly defending home and family, was causing a rise
in desertions among the Strike training companies.

Desertions were a problem that the United States military

had not had to deal with in years. Pappas had heard rumor that it was even worse among the formed units. Soldiers there would desert, taking their weapons and equipment, and return home to defend their families. The families would in turn hide them and their stolen equipment from the authorities. What the long-term solution would be no one knew.

Thus, creating a solemn figurehead out of this amiable cretin became a necessity. Sometimes, as a miracle of that strange art called leadership, a simple pat on the back or stern look from the briefly glimpsed company commander would keep a recruit from bolting. Once they graduated they became somebody else's responsibility.

"Gunny," the lieutenant continued as the gigantic Pappas settled carefully into the rickety swivel chair, "there's been another change in midstream. Now all the units, as they complete basic training, are to be shipped as units to their permanent posting. They will complete individual training and unit training there. And that is where the suits will be going."

"Okay, sir. I'll tell the troops." Pappas waited patiently. Sometimes the commander would have to think for some time to remember what the next item was. This time he seemed to have made notes.

"Yes, well, further," the lieutenant continued, looking at his notes with a sniff, "we are being levied to provide cadre. You are, personally, being levied as a first sergeant to a former Airborne unit that is to be converted to an Armored Combat Suit unit.

"You will be taking your platoon to Indiantown Gap to ramp up to readiness. That will be your permanent post, of course. I guess you'll be joined by other troops there."

Shit. This platoon? thought Pappas, mentally categorizing the characters he had just become "Top" to. "Yes, sir. Are you continuing as CO?" *No, no, no, no, no, no!*

"No, I've been designated as critical here, dammit. God knows when I'll get a combat command," said the portly officer, tugging at his uniform nervously.

Never if the battalion commander has his way. "Will that be all?"

"Not quite. Ground Forces training command has decided to cut short the training cycle, so the cycle will be ending in two weeks instead of four and final testing has been canceled. The unit will start clearing post next week and you will join them. Transportation is being arranged but they don't know when you'll receive the rest of your NCO cadre. Of course, your officers should be waiting for you."

"Yes, sir, I understand," Pappas said, thinking ominously of the phrases "should" and "of course." "Will there be movement orders soon?"

"Well, right now I'm passing on verbal orders to prepare your platoon and the company as a whole to ship out. Get with the first sergeant to arrange the details."

"Yes, sir."

"Dismissed."

22

Diess was a hot dry world, proof to Lieutenant O'Neal that the Galactics had an overpopulation problem. It had three extremely large continents; about sixty percent of its surface was land, with coastlines that received a limited amount of rain, about as much as the Sahara, and vast mountainous inlands drier than Death Valley.

Although the ecology of the seas was extremely complex, the dominant family was vaguely polychaetan with a complex structurally resilient polymer replacing chitin. There was virtually no terrestrial ecology. Instead the shores were packed with Indowy and Darhel megalopoli, their fingers jutting inland from the life-giving sea. Galactic technology easily extracted pure water and edible food from the plankton-rich seawater. It was obvious that a little food, a little water and raw materials were all the Indowy needed for life.

Worlds like this were the factories of the peaceful, loving Galactic Federation. Billions of Indowy slaving away day in and out with the fraction of Darhel skimming the cream. The peaceful worlds of the democratic Galactic Federation filled with peaceful little boggles whose only need was to serve. Dem dakkies a singin' in the field and the Darhel masters they's a lubbin' evy one of 'em. Galactic politics made Mike want to puke; but not as hard as what the Posleen were doing.

Galactic technology, high reproductive rates and the minuscule wants of the Indowy had permitted a population of twelve billion and booming before the Posleen arrived. The population was now five billion and dropping. One continent was wholly lost; one continent was still unscathed. The third had been lost except for a pie-piece shaped wedge in the northwest corner; the Posleen were as uninterested in the interior as the Galactics.

Mike stood on a virtual ridge inland of that pie-piece watching the floor of the valley hump and ripple like wind-wracked canvas. The Posleen were coming and 2nd Battalion 325th Mobile Infantry Regiment was preparing to meet them.

The first unit to engage was the battalion scout platoon, popping up from a conveniently perpendicular gully and opening fire with grav rifles. As lines of silver lightning connected them with the Posleen mass the front ranks began to explode. The teardrops burned through the air followed by lines of silver plasma. When they impacted they began to impart their kinetic energy to the flesh and liquid of the Posleen. The impact caused the bodies of the Posleen front rank to become their own bombs as blood flashed to steam and hydrostatic shock flashed the surroundings to ions. The fractional c depleted-uranium rounds impacted like hypervelocity grenades.

The scouts were difficult for Mike to see. By order of the battalion commander the armor had been spray painted a mottled brown to match the landscape. However, when Mike dialed his sensors to wavelengths visible to the Posleen, the chemicals in the off-the-shelf paint caused it to fluoresce under the energetic output of Diess' F-2 primary. He slugged this sensor adjustment to some of the other observers just as the Posleen returned fire.

Since the scouts had waited until the Posleen were under five hundred meters to engage, since they stood out like light bulbs in a dark room under UV-C, since they bounded completely into the open instead of firing from cover and since there were four thousand Posleen in the front rank firing at thirty targets it was a miracle of armor design that only nine scouts were killed in the first volley. The rest were thrown bodily backwards by the sheer mass of hypervelocity flechettes and flipped head over heels into the gully.

The fire thus suppressed, the Posleen rushed forward, as fast as lions for that short sprint, and were within two hundred meters before unconcerted fire resumed. At that range, despite full output from the few remaining functional scouts, the fire was beaten down and the position overrun in seconds.

Farther up the valley, Charlie company began long rifle and machine gun fire from over a thousand meters. Suit grenades and company 100mm mortars started to fall on the Posleen mass. The grenades and mortars would open wide holes like rainfall in a pond then the press of other Posleen would close over the fallen and the whole mass would press on. The lines of silver fire would drive two or three deep into the mass, but the pressure of the whole horde drove the horde forward against the fans of fire and spread it out to flank the extended company line. As the fire was redirected to engage the flankers it reduced the overall fire pressure and the horde drove forward at a swifter pace over windrows of its own dead. But the Posleen firmly believed in "waste not want not"; these bodies disappeared as the following ranks dismembered and processed them, rations for today and days to come.

Without a pause or waver the indefatigable enemy trotted towards the beleaguered company. Occasionally a mortar or grenade would, by chance, kill a God King. The mass around him would falter, momentarily, in its advance, then, as the individual normals of the fief shifted allegiance to other local God Kings, it would drive forward again.

Eventually the reduced mass, originally about three hundred thousand individuals, reached a range where their inaccurate fire began to affect the company. According to plan the company began to leapfrog back by platoon sections, two platoons maintaining cover fire as one withdrew. At this point another problem arose.

First, as a platoon stopped firing to withdraw, the retreat and reduced fire pressure caused the remaining mass to rush forward; the sight of the retreating platoon created a chase reaction in the normals and Posleen had apparently never heard of taking cover from fire. Second, the stop and bound nature of the maneuver was slow and difficult to coordinate. The combination caused 3rd platoon to be overrun in the second withdrawal as it made an out of position halt trying to cover 1st platoon.

At this point the original plan, a Cannae-like envelopment, went straight out the old air lock and Alpha and Bravo were ordered to leave their positions on the ridge, get down in the valley and prepare a defense for Charlie to pass through. Battalion weapons company was ordered to ascend the ridge and get plunging fire with their terawatt lasers.

A bright rear-rank God King, noticing the struggling troopers dragging the bulky lasers up the ridge slope, had his fief take the group under mass fire, destroying the battalion laser platoon. When Captain Wright of Alpha company was killed, the momentary confusion let a group of pursuing Posleen slip through with Charlie company. The flanking fire from this group, about two hundred and a God King, destroyed the Alpha second platoon and the whole Posleen mass poured through the breach, rolling up the battalion from its center. The centaurs poured over the troopers, stripping them out of their refractory suits and butchering them for a celebratory barbecue. Their hoots and cries of victory could be clearly heard on the ridge.

"Well," said General Houseman, on the observer channel, "that was... words fail me."

"A really quick way to lose a billion credits, sir?" Mike quipped.

"The worst defeat since Cumberland College versus Georgia Tech?" asked his chief of staff, General Bridges.

"Huh?" said two or three voices, General Houseman's among them.

"222 to 0, Tech," said the Rambling Wreck.

"*Clear VR*," they heard Lieutenant Colonel Youngman say on the command channel.

The visions of drifting uranium residue, smoke, dust and feasting Posleen cleared to reveal a large cargo bay scattered with fully intact combat suits in various states of immobility.

"AID, cut Lieutenant Colonel Youngman and Major Norton into this channel," ordered General Houseman. "Colonel Youngman, Major Norton, listen up. I want first reports on the G-3's desk at 1200 hours tomorrow. Hot wash on the exercise will be at 1630. Okay, you got your asses kicked, but you're improving. We'll do it again day after tomorrow, urban scenario. Get to work. Clear circuit.

"Christ," he continued on the local circuit, "I hope they're doing better on Barwhon."

23

Ttckpt Province, Barwhon V
1228 GMT February 25th, 2002 AD

"Sarge, you got any nine millimeter?" asked Trapp, taking a careful bead on a shotgun-toting Posleen slogging through the swamp. A massive forest giant had fallen and been consumed save for the root ball; in its lee the two human warriors crouched awaiting the centaurs.

"Sorry," grunted Mosovich, tying a bandage on his upper arm with his teeth. The shotgun flechettes had come within a hair of taking his left arm off and had torn away the transceiver on his hip, but close only counts with horseshoes and hand grenades.

The MP-5 *phut*ed and the Posleen point slumped into the purple muck. "Well, guess it's time to get down to hand-to-hand."

"I hope not, I've only got one. Here," Jake said, tossing Trapp his .45. "It's not much..." The .50 caliber ammunition was long gone, but it had been put to good use. The Five-O was the only weapon they had that could stop the God King's saucers. After the first week the God Kings had discovered not to follow too close to the chase.

Trapp and Mosovich had left a trail of Posleen bodies in their wake. The two master killers had used every bit of resource they possessed over the past month as they fled the vengeful residents of Site B but it was starting to look like the last morning at the Alamo.

"Fuck it, it's bullets," the SEAL said philosophically. "Can you handle that Street Sweeper with one hand?"

"I can kinda use the left, and it's only for steadying." Jake

185

studied the back trail for a moment and rested the shotgun on a gnarled root. He did a quick check to ensure the barrel was clear.

"I'll pop the next one that comes through, then when they spread out we'll move back. Got any demo left?"

"Only grenades," said Trapp. "And I wanna keep 'em."

"Fer what? Okay, get ready." There was movement in the bushes across the open area.

"With what?" muttered Trapp, slinging the MP-5 and pulling out a set of concussion grenades. Although there was minimal shrapnel effect because of the mud, the liquid transmitted the shock wave with great effectiveness. "Oh, well."

A group of five Posleen burst out of the concealing ferns and charged across the clearing. Mosovich's fire tumbled four of them, but another small group charged out slightly to the side. Neither group fired back, content to close to steel range in the teeth of the fire. As Mosovich tracked on the new group, Trapp hurled his grenades. One landed perfectly in the midst of the second group but the second was a slice and fell out of effective range. Just as both detonated, one taking down the second group wholly, a platoon-sized band charged out of the side of the clearing.

Mosovich switched from carefully controlled blasts to continuous fire as the centaurs closed. Trapp flipped three more grenades but the handful of remaining Posleen closed to steel range in moments.

Trapp flipped around his MP-5 and expended his last three rounds on three head shots as the Posleen got absolutely too close for a SEAL to miss. He threw the now-useless weapon at a closing Posleen as he drew his combat knife. He had studied the physiology of the Posleen the pair had killed. The Posleen chest turned out to be well armored by bone so if it came to hand to hand he had planned on being behind them, but this time lady luck was all over playing favorites.

Mosovich's shotgun locked back and he knew he was done. There were at least six Posleen still moving and he regretted giving up his .45 to Trapp. He drew his Gerber and stepped out from behind the root ball as the centaurs drew their own yard-long blades.

As the centaurs charged, Trapp grasped an out-thrust root and flipped himself into the muck. As the remaining Posleen closed with the injured sergeant major, a steel-filled hand swept out of the muck and disemboweled the trailer. A mud-covered figure erupted from the swamp and slithered across the back of the next Posleen before it could even buck, with a flash of steel faster than the eye could follow. As the nearly decapitated centaur slumped into the mud the group turned towards their slithering attacker but he had disappeared again into the bog.

As the leaderless Posleen milled, fumbling in the mud for the eel-like SEAL, Mosovich leapt on the back of another and quickly slit his throat. While not the match of the SEAL, he wanted to prove that he was no slouch with a knife.

At the same moment, ten yards from the huddle of fumbling Posleen, Trapp erupted once more from the water, his hand filled with Colt. He flicked the barrel downwards to clear it, adopted a two-handed grip and fired three rapid shots for three kills. As he tracked to the fourth Posleen, a shotgun blast threw him backward in a welter of blood and intestines.

The .45 spun from the SEAL's grasp and Mosovich knew he had only one chance. He launched himself in a shallow dive from the back of the deceased Posleen and followed the pistol into the muck.

The last two Posleen charged for the spot and began rummaging in the violet mucilage. One of them gurgled in delight as it snagged a combat harness and lifted the camouflage-clad survivor from the watery grave. Mosovich fought the grip like an eel, hooking his boot into its harness and bending like a contortionist to bring his arm around. The Posleen's last surprised sight was of a .45 caliber bore.

24

Orbit, Diess IV
2125 GMT May 15th, 2002 AD

The final conference on whether the ACS battalion would be deployed as planned was a hurried meeting on D-Day minus 1. Most units were already down and moving to their jump-off point, so the mood was somber as the meeting was drawing to a close. The small room had been hastily fitted with a rickety easel and a table large enough for all the people who thought they should have a say in deployment.

The battalion staff had put on a dog and pony show complete with a staff officer in armor. Mike knew to the minute the time the officer had in the suit and recognized various subtle signs of poor assimilation. Despite that fact, the suit and various multimedia demonstrations of the weaponry available to the ACS were effective arguments.

Mike was the last person giving a presentation and he concluded solemnly. He had listened carefully to the other presentations and he felt he knew where the decision was going to go. Despite the briefings that he had given to a vast number of audiences, he knew it all came down to this group. And they were simply not paying attention. Aides and officers scurried in and out of the room constantly, bringing information, carrying away orders. The meeting members were distracted and all and sundry had made up their minds in advance. It made him feel like Cassandra.

"Although the battalion currently meets the minimum eighty percent standards for operational deployment, high readiness and training in some areas, such as the noted performance levels among junior NCOs and officers, mask critical failures in other areas. The lack of comprehension of the technology by senior battalion officers and NCOs with the concomitant weakness in communications and control, leads to a situation ripe for point failure.

"Considering this from either a testing viability or a mission success viewpoint, the Design Team representative cannot recommend deployment at this time. Senior officers require a minimum of one hundred fifty more hours of tactical exercises without troops before they *may* be considered prepared. Thank you." He dropped the laser pointer into the sleeve of his silks, walked over to his spot and sat down. Since he was the Design Team representative, he at least had a spot at the table.

"Okay," said General Houseman, "let's be straight. Recommendations, deploy or don't deploy? I am accepting input from G-3, the Chief of Staff and the Design Team representative." Excluding the battalion representatives was a deliberate slap in the face to the airborne colonel. The battalion commander knew that if the battalion was not deployed his career was finished. "General Stafford, G-3 says go?"

"Yes, sir," said the lanky general, tapping the table with his fingers. "I take the lieutenant's point about the communications and coordination problems but, no offense, Lieutenant, he sees everything from the uncluttered viewpoint of a junior officer. Those sims are awfully realistic, real enough to create a 'fog of war.' In those situations, communications and coordination difficulties occur. Lieutenants, by and large, expect things to be straightforward; they're not. I think they're ready, let's let them off the leash."

"Okay, General Bridges?"

"It is a difficult decision," stated the fussy little chief of staff, "I think that with the way we intend to employ them, the respective units are going to receive heavy casualties irregardless of their preparedness level. However, it is my opinion that the suits and the communications package will act as a combat multiplier and we need the concomitant capabilities. These cities are a difficult tactical problem and the suits can maneuver in terrain closed to effective use by other combat systems. I recommend implementation despite patently insufficient preparation." At that description, the battalion commander and operations officer winced.

"Lieutenant O'Neal?"

"I agree that the suits will act as a combat multiplier, but I disagree strongly with the 'fog of war' argument. My favorite relevant quote is from a battalion commander in Desert Storm, 'Heroes happen because somebody made a mistake.' I think if we deploy the battalion, we're going to have a lot of heroes. The senior battalion command and staff are using the communications and intelligence systems exactly backward of how they are designed and complaining because they don't work right.

"The communications were designed to allow ease of communication, but the commander and S-3 are immuring themselves behind layers of underlings and this is causing a communication snag." He totally ignored the fact that the officers in question were present.

"Twice in sims this snag caused a critical failure because the people who were managing the whole picture and knew what to do were unable to effectively communicate that need. Furthermore, the battalion command and staff have systematically stripped the company commanders of any authority to react without direct orders. Were one or the other not the case, the battalion might have a chance. As it is there is none.

"They have trained like they are going to fight and it *will* happen in combat. Lieutenant Colonel Youngman and Major Norton are approaching this from a 'light infantry' direction but have left out every good light infantry technique and kept every outmoded one. If you deploy the battalion in its current condition it will be Little Big Horn all over again. I strongly urge you to hold them to training." By the time he was done the battalion commander was white-faced with rage and the operations officer was spluttering.

"Well Lieutenant O'Neal," said General Houseman, with a quelling glance at the furious field officers who had been forced to listen to the scathing diatribe, "it's two generals in favor to one lieutenant against. I'm going to have to go with the more experienced officers, but it is my decision. They're getting deployed, Lieutenant." He did not look particularly happy with his decision. Unfortunately, it was a situation where he agreed with the lieutenant on abstract. While the battalion showed an over eighty percent readiness, the unit had yet to survive a single simulated engagement. The hash of cavalry and infantry tactics that worked for O'Neal and that were specified in the ACS doctrine seemed to massively confuse most of the battalion command and staff. It was not a happy prospect.

"It is, of course, your decision, sir." From the look on the lieutenant's face the general suspected he was reading his mind. "Actually, sir, I doubt you could have gotten away with holding them back. Given the cost of fielding them and that they did make minimum specs, Congress would have you for lunch if you didn't deploy them." He shrugged the resignation of soldiers throughout history who were pawns to the political process.

"Lieutenant, if I thought we were going to lose the battalion I'd hold them in training despite all the bureaucrats in Washington."

After the drab interior of the colony ship and the megascraper's plain exterior, Mike was unprepared for the lavish decoration of the interiors. Despite the fact that the room was utilitarian, possibly the Indowy equivalent of a machine shop, the walls, floors and ceiling were covered with intricate paintings, friezes and bas reliefs. All of the corridors he had traveled and the rooms he had poked his head into were equally baroque. The Indowy love of craftsmanship apparently extended to interior decoration. Unlike similar decorations by humans, there were no scenes or portraits. All the decorations were intricate abstract curves and geometrics. Despite their alien nature they were pleasing to the human eye and surprisingly similar to patterns on Celtic brooches.

There were about sixty people milling around in the large room that was to be used for the battalion's tactical operations center. The machinery and tanks of mysterious liquid had been moved against the walls and a set of folding chairs erected facing a low dais; the front row included an upholstered easy chair. On the back of the chair was a sign depicting a silver oak leaf and the words "2 Falcon 6." A rooster in a cage clucked on one side of the dais. As Mike inspected it balefully, it crowed.

Also on the dais were several junior NCOs and enlisted men referring to clipboards and updating easeled maps. They were being supervised—Mike was reminded of the rooster with his hens—by the battalion S-3, Major Norton. A tall, distinguished-looking man, Norton, Mike had quickly come to realize, was not nearly as intelligent as he looked. Extremely energetic and able to parrot doctrine well, he responded poorly to novel situations and ideas. He and Mike had come to verbal blows several times during the battalion's work-up.

Mike dialed up the zoom on his glasses and looked at the battle plan being drawn on the board. "Christ," he whispered, "has anyone talked to the fire support officer?" Just then Captain Jackson, the FSO, got a good look at the board and walked over to Major Norton. When Captain Jackson tried to draw him aside, the S-3 brushed him off. He was, after all, Artillery, there for the battalion's support, and a captain; thus, he could be ignored.

Mike looked around the room filled with camouflage-clad officers and NCOs. There were the commanders of the five companies, with their executive officers, the staff with their assistants and senior NCOs, the attachment leaders, engineering, fire support, medical and artillery. They were all pointedly ignoring him; in the case of a few of them he knew it was for mutual good. Consorting with the company commanders would have drawn fire for both of them from the S-3. Then he started counting chairs.

"Michelle," he queried, "how many personnel first lieutenant and above in the room?"

"Fifty-three."

"And how many chairs?" he asked.

"Fifty."

"Michelle, who was in charge of setting up the seating?"

"The Battalion Operations section."

"Bloody hell." His relations with the battalion commander and his staff had not improved; if anything they had worsened. His, he thought, tactful and constructive critiques of communications and control were viewed as inappropriate to his experience, despite the fact that he limited his comments to subjects directly affected by the combat suits. He did not, for example, comment on the commander's proclivity to place the battalion in a movement to contact formation after the enemy's axis of advance had already been determined. Despite the enormous casualties caused by the resultant open field fighting, the colonel had apparently decided that the suits were invulnerable to the Posleen's weapons and preferred to meet them *mano y monstruo*. The training scenarios were, after all, "theoretical"; no data on Posleen behavior in combat had yet been gathered by human units. His disdain for the research involved in developing the scenarios had only heightened since Mike's abortive attempt to have the battalion held out of battle.

Mike had felt it necessary, however tactless it might have been, to comment on the communications structure. Lieutenant Colonel Youngman's lack of practice with the suits and general technophobia caused him to fall back on a communications section and RTOs for communications control instead of training his AID to communications tasking. The RTOs were designated for specific nets and the only personnel permitted direct contact with the commander were certain members of the staff and the battalion executive officer, Major Pauley. Further, Youngman had designated the battalion as the sole source to authorize all requests for support except medical and logistics. Company commanders were to contact him to request fire support, for example, and he would determine if the request was valid. The commanders, in fact, had to practically contact him for permission to pass gas. The colonel had discovered that the suit systems gave him an Olympian view of the battlefield, and the ability to control the movement of every platoon if he so chose. He chose. Thus he controlled all aspects of the operation. Perfect micromanagement.

Unfortunately, the resulting managerial and information overload he had chosen to blame on the suit instead of the process. He had responded by placing more layers between himself and the company commanders while continuing to deny them their normal initiative. Thus, in every single combat scenario run to date the battalion had bogged down around its inability to maneuver or respond effectively. And now they were going into battle.

At a few moments before 0900 the groups started to break up and find seats. Surprising him not at all, when everyone was done, Second Lieutenant Eamons, the engineer platoon leader, Second Lieutenant Smith, the scout platoon leader, two of the company XOs and himself along with all the enlisted from the sergeant major to the privates with red pencils were sans chairs. The sergeant major looked really pissed.

A few moments later Major Norton called attention and Lieutenant Colonel Youngman entered and strode down the aisle to his spot. Reaching his seat 2 Falcon 6 sat, accepted a cup of coffee from a hovering mess private and called "As you were," permitting everyone to resume their seats.

"Good afternoon, gentlemen," said Major Norton. "Our mission is as follows: Task Force 2nd 3-2-5 Infantry has been tasked with defense of the III Corp flank in the area of the Deushi megalopolis where it is contiguous with the Nomzedi massif. The S-2 will brief on the threat situation."

The S-2 was First Lieutenant Phil Corley. Dark of hair and slightly below average height, he was highly intelligent but lacked in great order common sense. He stepped up to an easel and threw back its canvas cover dramatically. The canvas cover had been thrown on moments before the colonel's entrance. It was liberally covered with large red TOP SECRET stamps. Mike was not sure who the map was supposed to be kept secret from since the Posleen did not, as far as anyone could tell, use operational intelligence.

"In the big picture, to the southeast the 'Bordoli Line,' comprised of Chinese, Russian, southeast Asian and African troops has withdrawn to strategic positions near the Bordoli massif in the Aumoro megalopolis. They are anchored by the massif and the sea. This is their second strategic withdrawal in the week since they landed but the line is now less than sixty kilometers wide. Since it is now held by nearly three quarters of a million troops, further withdrawals are not anticipated.

"The NATO associated Allied Expeditionary Force with attached Chinese and Japanese troops is currently completing its movement to jump-off positions. Delays in landing will force the units to prepare in two phases. The main line of resistance is intended to be in an area similar to the Bordoli Line in the Deushi megalopolis. At that point the Deushi massif stretches to within forty-five kilometers of the sea. NATO forces are to establish a line at that location and hold it. However, the Posleen speed of advance is such that they must be slowed in order to prepare the defenses. Mobile combat units of the Allied forces will, therefore, take up positions in the area of the Nomzedi massif along Avenue Qual.

"The line will be held by the 3rd Armored Division, 2nd Infantry Mechanized, 10th *Panzergrenadiere*, 7th Cavalry Regiment, *Deuxième Division Blindée*, 2nd Lancers Regiment and the 126th Armored Regiment, PRC. The 1st of the 26th German Armored Combat Suit battalion will act as a mobile reserve. The defense plan requires that the line hold, or withdraw no more than six kilometers for twenty-four hours. The Posleen are expected to reach Avenue Qual in twelve hours. Are there any questions?"

Captain Brandon's hand snapped up. "What are the numbers and location of the Posleen along the line?"

"Right now we don't know. As you know, the Posleen landing craft keep up a constant energy weapon sweep of the overhead into deep space. So far we can't get any overhead imagery. The information we are getting is from the Darhel administrators' reports of evacuating megascrapers and a little information from Himmit deep recon scouts. The information from the Darhel do not list any enemy numbers and the Indowy run if they get a sniff of the Posleen in the neighborhood. The Himmit give excellent reports, but their view is limited."

The S-2 answered a few other questions and stepped down.

Major Norton stepped back up to the dais, picked up a pointer and directed attention to the map board.

"The mission of Task Force 2/325 is to establish defensive positions along the Qual Line and coordinate with flanking units to hold a defensive line for a minimum of six, maximum of twelve hours. Our battalion has been tasked with a sector that normally would be held by a regiment, the same area as the entire 7th Cav for example. With our new weapons and equipment it is our belief that holding the sector will be relatively easy. Therefore:

"Task Force 2/325 will take up positions as follows. Alpha 2/325 will take up positions on the northeast corner of the Qualtrev megascraper with zones of fire covering the approach vector along the Sisalav Boulevard. Charlie company will take up positions in the northwest corner of the Qualtren megascraper coordinating overlapping fire on the Sisalav Boulevard with Alpha.

"Alpha Company will hold responsibility for integrating support with Bravo Troop, 7th Cavalry holding positions to seaward in the Qualtrek and Saltrek megascrapers. Charlie will provide fire support for flank interdiction. As you can see on the map, Qualtren is anchored in the massif, which will secure our flank. Battalion lasers will disperse themselves to Charlie and Alpha to provide fire support. Battalion scouts will take up hide positions in Naltrev megascraper to give approach warning and initiate the battle. Battalion mortars will locate to the rear of the Qualtren megascraper to provide fire support, company mortars to collocate.

"Upon positive location, as determined by battalion scouts,

Multiple Launch Rocket Systems from Corp and 105mm artillery from our task force battery will fire artillery support missions on call to the slot between Daltren and Daltrev. There, final protective fire will start. Fire plans are in the briefing packets. Bravo company will remain in reserve, split between Qualtren and Qualtrev. The reserve will be deployed only on direct orders from the battalion commander.

"Direct fire may be ordered by the company commanders when the enemy is within one thousand meters or when they are in view, whichever is less. No direct fire over a thousand meters; we want a maximum punch on the initial volley. Indirect fire once the Posleen are in view of the battalion will be under direct control of the battalion commander and the FSO. There are to be no visible fortifications erected, no barb wire, concertina or visible bunkers. The idea is to strike with shock and surprise, not give away our MLR. Are there any questions?"

Mike turned to Lieutenant Eamons and whispered, "How 'bout 'Did yo' momma drop you on your head?'" Lieutenant Eamons snorted without changing expression. Major Norton glanced angrily his way and Mike schooled his features like a child misbehaving in class. Every simulation he had run and every story he had read about fighting the Posleen told him that the battle was a prescription for defeat. Deploying the battalion vertically, as the plan called for, opened your forces up to being fired upon by the entire advancing force without any countervailing improvement in the battalion's effectiveness.

The basic tactic recommended for battling "swarming" Posleen was two dimensional. Get a heavy position, get packed in fairly tight—how tight depended upon how resistant your position was to HVM fire—and set up a wall of fire between your position and the Posleen. One of the Scottish GalTech officers had called it "sloshing them with Martinis," a reference so old that everyone but Mike had had to look it up. Fighting Posleen had also been likened to fighting a wildfire, and with good reason. And then there was the other problem.

Captain Jackson, the fire support officer, stood up. "This is not a question, *Major*, it's a comment. No-Can-Do."

"What do you mean, 'No Can Do,' Captain?" the major responded, snappily.

"Well, the Multiple Launch Rocket System is fully dedicated

to 10th Panzer Division. Corp intelligence, at least, thinks the Posleen will strike with the greatest weight on their location. We might, would, be able to get them for FPF, except for one thing: the damn megascrapers. There's only seventy-five meters between them and they're nearly a mile damn high. That presents an angularity problem that artillery cannot overcome. The artillery firing support for the other units is just backing up a few klicks and firing right down the avenues. We can't do that because of the dogleg that Sisalav takes from the mountain. So, basically, forget arty."

Major Norton looked stunned for a moment then rallied. "Okay, we'll forget artillery. Any other questions or comments?"

"No," whispered Mike, "'Who thought up this abortion?' would be tactless."

25

Fredericksburg, VA Sol III
1342 August 4th, 2002 AD

The first part of the trip from Fort Benning, Georgia to Indiantown Gap, Pennsylvania was a nightmare. Without a second drill sergeant, Pappas had run himself ragged keeping track of the recruits. PFC Ampele and Drill Corporal Adams became his right arms, chivvying the distracted recruits, who were seeing "real life" again for the first time in fourteen weeks, back into line. He felt less like a platoon sergeant during those two days than a cowboy, and he swore that when he had the troops back under his thumb in barracks they were going to pay dearly.

The entire trip was by bus, and it seemed that the driver insisted on a break every fifty miles. Since the bus had an onboard latrine, for most of the first day Pappas kept the platoon on the bus, but at last they had to debark for dinner. Since Line and Fleet Strike troops were entirely volunteer, the military propaganda machine had let itself go quite thoroughly and the recruits in their gray and silver battle silks drew the locals like honey. Pappas found himself deluged with questions, most of which he felt compelled to answer. Suddenly he realized that he could only count twenty or so of his forty troopers and swore when he realized that most of the missing troops were from the notorious second squad.

He had thought about breaking up second squad three or four times but each time he talked himself out of it. The problem with second squad was that they were about as good as they thought they were. In every training class the members learned the lessons spot on first time. Second squad members never fell asleep, their equipment was always perfect, their details were always done on time or early. They scored higher as an average than any but two or three other individuals in the company. It was one of those unfortunately rare occasions when a group in the military was uniformly competent and capable. Unfortunately the squad leader, PFC James Stewart, as charming a rogue as ever a young maiden could hope to meet, was quite possibly the Antichrist.

Shortly after the basic training group arrived inspections of the company and several companies around revealed increasing amounts of hard alcohol in the possession of recruits. While it was impossible to completely cut off the flow of illicit liquor in basic training usually a bottle would turn up once every few weeks in a training battalion. Suddenly several were being uncovered every week. Intensive interrogation of the frightened recruits could not reveal the source; the bootleggers were using dead drops.

A recruit would place an order at any one of innumerable locations. Small slips of paper along with the payment were slipped into a crevice in the barracks wall or in the bathroom or in the bleachers. The next day the bottle would appear in the recruit's equipment locker or he would find instructions on where to pick it up. CID, the Ground Force Criminal Investigation Division, was called in and tried for weeks to catch the smugglers in the act but was always just a little off in timing. Once investigators covertly watched a dead drop for three days only to find out that the hole in the wall went all the way through.

Alcohol, cigarettes, candy, pornography, but, strangely, no drugs. In the twelfth week the training for Alpha company included a two-week field exercise. By the second week there were no full bottles found in the company or the battalion. Obviously the bootleggers were centered in Alpha company.

The agents of CID descended in force on Alpha company but Gunnery Sergeant Pappas had known in his heart all along who the ringleader was. In the last week of training over an imaginary fault during Saturday inspection he threw the sort of raging fit usually associated with the first few weeks in basic. Ordering the platoon out of the barracks, physically hurling a few out the door, he and the company's first sergeant, a doggie Special Forces veteran with a longer and even more varied career than his, tore the barracks apart.

Beds were hurled out the windows to be followed by wall lockers, equipment lockers, clothes, equipment and anything else moveable they could find. As each item was ejected it was subjected to a brief but intense inspection. Nearly stumped, they finally found what they were looking for hidden in a hollow in the cinder block wall itself, concealed behind the wall locker of none other than the second squad leader.

It was a leadership challenge for the veteran NCOs. On the one hand, the violations of regulations were innumerable, but on the other hand the individuals were otherwise as good as any NCO could dream. The worst part was that being a military leader depends, strongly, upon respect. To order troops into a situation quite probably resulting in their deaths requires that those troops respect, love, fear you more than practically anything in the world. Sending a group of recruits off to battle believing that they could pull off a caper like this would be worse than giving them no training at all. But they were so good at the business of soldiering—Stewart particularly—they had such a knack that sending them all off to the stockade would be a waste of training and talent.

They had a few moments to discuss it. The drill corporals were running the recruits ragged with grass drills and Sergeant Pappas was fairly certain that they did not expect a search. He had not found the material before during his occasional fits nor would he be expected to now. They quickly finalized and implemented their plan, then left to torment the recruits. The reconstruction of the squad areas would be carefully supervised by the drill corporals. By the time Stewart had a chance to check the hidey-hole he would be forced to wonder whether it was the NCOs who raided the stash or a trainee.

Two days later there was an unscheduled field exercise. At two A.M. the recruits were hounded out of their beds, into field gear and out into the darkness.

The platoon was broken down into squads and put through hours of murderous squad drills. This is the sprint and dash technique of the infantry, dropping to the prone to take the enemy under fire as another squad moves then leaping to their feet and running forward to the next firing position. Deceptively beautiful to watch when well performed it is brutally physical work: a tremendous aerobic exercise. Run twenty or thirty yards throw yourself to the ground, fire a few blank rounds, push yourself to your feet with fifty pounds of equipment on your back then do it over and over again for hours on end.

The squads were supervised by the drill corporals as Gunny Pappas moved quietly through the darkness from squad to squad, observing them all, yet unobserved. All the fluff was gone now, the "civvie fat" that was so evident on their arrival, even on those who were in shape. Each of them was a hard, tough little bundle of killing energy, as dangerous as so many baby rattlers. Just the way they were supposed to be.

Towards dawn the squads were well scattered and, per instructions, the drill corporals gathered each of them in and in a complete violation of doctrine built a fire. Fire was anathema to the modern infantry, revealing of your position, potentially dangerous in the form of a forest fire and, yes, environmentally harmful. But Pappas knew the infantry man is in many ways atavistic. He revels in the dirt and the mud even as he curses it and fire strikes a special cord in the human breast. Fire opens up the soul in a way that few things can, to those who are open to it, and there are times when nothing but a fire will do.

As second squad settled back against its packs relaxing in the warmth and light Pappas stepped silently out of the darkness and gestured for the drill corporal to leave.

The squad sat up and shot covert glances at Stewart. He in turn fixed Sergeant Pappas with a basilisk stare; one of his many attributes was that he had a stare to give a bull pause. He had learned the first week not to direct it at Pappas but now it seemed time to do so.

Pappas reached into his thigh bellows pockets and drew out twelve wads of bills. "I suspect you might be looking for these," he said and tossed one to each of the recruits.

"Sir," started one of the recruits, "this isn't what it looks like!"

"Shut up," said Stewart in a voice he would use to order French fries. The recruit shut up.

"I want to tell you a secret, soldiers," said Pappas in a quiet, neutral voice. It was the first time he had used that appellation for them and they were universally startled. Technically they should not be referred to as soldiers until they completed their final tests. It was a goal they had all been striving for, whether they had realized it or not, a mark of approval more important than life in many ways.

"It's one of the big secrets," Pappas continued. "You know, the

Sergeant Secrets. It's one of the secrets you really believe exists even when you deny it. Recruits always believe that the sergeants have special secrets you never learn until you're a sergeant. Like we get told the secrets on our last day at 'Sergeant's School.'" He smiled at the weak joke and puffed out his cheeks.

"Well, you don't. You learn it just by being in a unit, by being in the military, whether it's in the Army, Marines, Line or Strike or whatever. You learn it usually in your first few months. But it isn't the big secret. It's a little secret.

"Here it is in three words," he continued, seriously. "'Contraband is everywhere.' There's always drugs, or personal firearms, or military demolitions somewhere in any barracks. And there's always a black market in the stuff. You guys weren't the first or the second or the two hundred and fifty-ninth. Contraband in barracks is as old as armies.

"And the stuff that we are going to be issued is a black marketer's dream. Everybody in the fuckin' country wants the Galactic weapons, the combat drugs, the Hiberzine. Hell, even the littlest GalTech shit, pens, Eterna batteries, everything, is worth big bucks. So, where we're going is the jackpot; you can get a piddly little twelve grand for one hit of regen. And that leads to another thing." He picked up a stick and stirred the dying fire, puffing his cheeks in and out in silence for a moment.

"There's a bigger secret," he said in a near whisper. "One little sentence. 'As long as it does not affect the unit's effectiveness, no big deal.'"

He smiled again and looked up at the circle of recruits. As he did his eyes turned frosty and his grin turned to a snarl. "But none of you cocksuckers were a gleam in your daddy's eye when I was in the fuckin' Marines. Back then the fuckin' officers in the Army had to have armed guards to go into the fuckin' barracks because the fuckin' drug problem was so bad, and it wasn't much better in the fuckin' Corp.

"If we had to fight a war during the seventies, warn't nobody coming. There wasn't a unit in the whole fuckin' Army, not the infantry, not the artillery, not the armor, not the airborne, that was combat ready because the criminals *owned* the Army. And the Corp would have been hard pressed to carry a war on its own, especially with our own drug problems.

"If you guys go up there thinking that you're being handed

the keys to the candy shop the unit that receives you will be fucked. When they really need the shit, when lives are going down the drain and your buddies are dyin' all around you, the shit they need won't be there.

"The ammunition and weapons and every little bit of equipment that we depend on will be sold out from under us. And then we are fucked. It's happened. And I'm damned if it will happen on my watch." He looked back at the fire and poked at the flames, his rage subsiding. He made a faint motorboat sound.

"We fought long and hard to erase that," he continued briskly. "We had to, 'cause a military like that just can't function.

"It's about respect. If you think you can pull one over on me, you haven't got any respect for me and you won't obey my orders, or the orders of your officers, when it's time to lay it on the line." He paused and looked at the fire for a moment, hoping that some of them were getting it. But he was really talking to Stewart and they all knew it.

"Now, you guys are good, really good, on paper. But if you think money is what it's all about you can't be Strike troopers 'cause you won't be there when I need you." He really did not want to lose the investment that he had made in them but he was deadly serious and both emotions showed. Sincerity usually does.

"So now you begin to learn the big secret, the biggest secret, maybe. I won't tell you what it is, you have to learn it on your own. I will tell you that it ain't 'money isn't everything' or anything trite like that. But this is a start. So, here's the bottom line: if you want to wear a combat suit, if you want to be what you've trained to be for fourteen weeks, you have to throw those bundles of money in the fire."

The squad had been listening intently to him, pulling it all in. Now they clutched at the bundles, gulping spasmodically as they looked at each other. They each held several thousand dollars and they had worked hard for it. They definitely did not want to give it up.

"Or, you can stand up and walk back to camp and after graduation you'll be cycled to your local guard forces, no pack drill, no court-martial, just a little paper shuffle.

"Statistically, you have a better chance of survival in the Guard. Unless the Posleen land directly on you, Guard is going to be holding fixed positions and won't be moved from battle to battle like

Line and Strike. As Strike troops, you are going to be fed into the blender over and over again, and no matter how good you are, a lot of you are going to die. All you have to do to join the Guard, is hold onto the money. That ought to be easy. Right?" Having said his peace, he leaned back against the pine tree behind him and waited for a reaction. He scratched his head with a short stick, automatically brushing the resulting dandruff off his shoulder.

Stewart still had him fixed with the basilisk stare. Now he finally spoke.

"We could cut you in."

The offer did not offend Pappas, it was fully expected and he had hoped for it to drive the point home. Also, he could tell that Stewart was offering it pro forma, without any expectation that it would be accepted.

"No, I don't think so. You see, I already know the big, big secret."

"Yeah," whispered Stewart, for the first time looking down to the wad in his hand. He slowly pulled the rubber bands off and fanned the bills out. Then he stacked them again and riffled them just under his nose, smelling them. He fanned them out one more time and without a word, or change in expression, tossed them into the fire. One of the squad, it was unclear who, gave a small gasp.

"Money can never be important enough, can it?" asked Stewart.

"No, but that's not the whole secret, either," answered Pappas. Then he watched as the squad, one by one, some with a visible struggle, but most, strangely, with hardly a sigh, tossed the money in the fire.

"Okay," said Pappas tiredly, "get some sleep. An' I hope you never learn what the rest is." Then he got up and ghosted into the night.

Now Pappas wished he had terminated their asses. Somewhere in the immediate area of the McDonald's the squad was loose and, if history served, getting in some sort of trouble. He spotted Ampele being led around a corner by a nice-looking, if slightly plump, young lady and ran him down.

"Where's Stewart?" he asked, pulling Ampele back around the corner.

"Wha...? I don't know, sir. I was just talking to Rikki here. He was over by the bathrooms with his squad just a minute ago." He started to step back inside the restaurant, then seemed to pull back as if connected to a bungee cord. The young lady's hand was out of sight behind his bulk and Pappas was tempted to shout "Hand check!" just to see their expressions.

"Miss," Pappas said gently, "if you'd just excuse us for a moment?"

Her hand reluctantly drifted back into sight and the sergeant dragged Ampele firmly away by one thick bicep.

"Focus. Worry about the wahines when we get to Indiantown Gap." He walked into the restaurant and caught a glimpse of a second squad member ducking through the employees' door. He caught the door before it could close then stopped, looked around and turned towards the bathrooms.

"Gunny, Wilson went that way," Ampele pointed out, rather superfluously.

"Yeah, and this is Stewart we're dealing with. The only thing I'm wondering is if it's a double bluff." He yanked open the men's room door, or tried to at least. Something had it stuck fast.

"*Stewart! Open this damn door or face the consequences!*" he snarled, dragging at the door with all his might. "*Hwone! Htwo!*" There was the sound of something being forcibly removed from the door and it opened just in time. Nine members of second squad were crowded into the not terribly large bathroom. One and all they were looking at him as if he had gone insane.

"What's wrong, Gunny?" asked Stewart, stepping back from the urinal so that the next squad member could move up. "That door does stick something awful for a Mickey Dee's, doesn't it?"

"Okay, where is she?" asked Pappas, meeting him stare for stare. The bathroom smelled like most, a little cleaner with a smell of dilute urine and other matters best left unnoticed. But underlying them all was a faint whiff of cheap perfume.

"Where's who, Sergeant?"

"The other half of the pair. The one you didn't sic on Ampele." At the reference the broad platoon leader looked chagrined; again the sergeant had proven he was two jumps ahead.

"I have not a clue what you are talking about Sergeant," said Stewart, an absolute picture of innocence. "There are no women in this bathroom," he continued gesturing around at the braced squad, "and you came in the only door." He shrugged his shoulders and shook his head as if wondering at the sergeant's strange aberrations.

"Ampele, stay here. Stewart," he said, sinking a meaty hand

into the slight PFC's shoulder, "we need to have another little chat." Pappas dragged him out of the bathroom and then outside into the autumn mists.

"If I have told you oncet," said Pappas mildly as he slammed the private into the outside wall of the burger joint, "I have told you twicet," he continued, driving the brim of his campaign hat into the bridge of Stewart's nose and his finger into the private's breastbone, "do not fuck with me. I think you may be officer material, but you're more likely to end up in Leavenworth. The stupid bitch is above the third acoustic tile from the left starting from the urinal, undoubtedly scared out of her life. There was a smell of perfume and a scattering of bits from the tile you were trying to hide behind the squad.

"Now, *get* your squad back out in line to eat, *get* her down and on her way, without any fucking around, and report to me when you're done, is that clear?"

"As crystal, Gunny." The hint of smugness enraged Pappas and a suddenly realized solution came as a bolt from the blue. He smiled evilly. At that sight a hint of wariness crept into the private's eyes.

"From now on I am off duty," Pappas said and smiled inwardly at the sudden confusion Stewart revealed. "If anything goes wrong," he continued, "it is your responsibility," a rock-hard forefinger drove into a breastbone again. "I am totally hands off, got it? When *you* fuck up," finger, "I am taking a stripe. You're a PFC, so you've got two to lose. When *they* fuck up, you," finger, "are losing a stripe. You are in charge of *all* activities as of when we reach the hotel, I'll announce it on the bus when we leave. *That* should keep you out of trouble. Is that clear?"

"Clear, Gunny," Stewart agreed, his face turning gray.

"Me and Ampele we're going to relax the rest of the trip 'cause you have all the responsibility. If anything goes wrong, public drunkenness, public lewdness, irate fathers, shopkeepers ripped off, vomiting in public, it is your," finger in the chest, "ass. All night and all day tomorrow. I intend to sleep like a baby. Is that absolutely, perfectly, crystal clear?"

"Yes, Gunny."

"Good." The NCO smiled broadly, his white teeth bright against his wide brown face. "Have a nice day."

And the rest of the trip was a picnic.

26

Andata Province, Diess IV
2059 GMT May 18th, 2002 AD

Lieutenant O'Neal stripped the box magazine from his M-200 grav rifle and stared unseeing at the thousands of teardrop-shaped pellets within. Then he reinserted the magazine and did the same with his grav pistol.

"Would you please quit doing that?" asked Lieutenant Eamons. Both of them waited by windows on the northwest corner of Qualtren. The angle was even greater than the FSO indicated and they had a clear view of the 1.145 miles to the next intersection. There the Naltrev megascraper cut back and blocked the view. Naltrev and its sister megascraper Naltren held the battalion scout platoon and the upper part of O'Neal's vision systems were slaved to the view from the scout platoon leader's.

"Where are your people, Tom?" Mike asked.

"Downstairs."

"Are they tasked?" O'Neal continued to watch the view from the scout leader. It was unsettling because of the flicker of a personal area force-screen—the PAF set up in the anticipated direction of attack—and because Lieutenant Smith had a nasty tendency to occasionally toss his head like a horse throwing a fly. The movement would swing the viewpoint right and up. *I doubt he even notices that he's doing it*, thought Mike, stripping out the magazine and reinserting it, *but I wish he'd quit.*

"Would you *please* quit doing that, Mike! And why do you want to know? No, they're sitting around with their thumbs up their butts."

"Quit what?" Mike asked, his attention focused like a medical laser on the view from his helmet. "Start having them emplace cratering charges across Anosimo and Sisalav at the Sal Line and then start placing C-9 charges at the locations I'll slave to their AIDs."

"Whoa, Mike. You're a nice guy and outrank me by a whole grade, but the hell if I'll piss my career away for you. The colonel will have my bar if I do that." The lieutenant tried to shake his head and stopped when he had to force it against the biotic gel filling the helmet.

The Jell-O-like material completely filled the helmet and the interior of the suit. It was responsible for more than a third of the cost of the armor and the only major part that was not, at bottom, O'Neal's concept.

Putting on the helmet of a combat suit was something like putting your head in a bucket full of jam. However, the material completely cushioned the wearer against the most extreme shocks and had a series of other important functions. It read the user's movement intentions through their own neural net and drove the suit accordingly. It recycled waste into potable water, edible food and breathable air. And it had enough medical technology and ability to keep its "ProtoPlasmic Intelligence System" alive as long as they did not take a direct hit to the heart, brain or upper spine.

All that did not make troopers any happier about donning the helmet. One third of all washouts in the first month of training were from troops who could not handle first putting on the helmet, then holding their breath as the underlayer humped and rippled creating pockets for breathing and vision. The wait until the suit was in position could feel like an eternity.

The underlayer also acted as an ersatz sensory deprivation device, another negative that led to occasional mishaps. The weapons and equipment of the units had to be specially modified all around. With no feedback from contacts, the suits had a tendency to destroy anything they touched.

Since there was no way to actually see through the underlayer, the helmet was totally opaque. What the user saw was a high-quality representation cast by tiny laser diodes that threaded out of the helmet wall. Instead of turning his head, when a trooper made a movement to look from side to side the viewpoint shifted. It was somewhat like controlling a point of view with a joystick.

Again, it took getting used to. There was no feeling of motion, so it could induce motion sickness, and a trooper could suddenly find himself looking backwards by overdriving the viewpoint controls. Similar leads tapped the mastoid bone for sound conduction.

For comfort, the suit would let the users move their heads side to side, but only slowly. However, since the diodes could do all sorts of neat tricks with vision, the peripheral vision was actually superior to normal and far and near sighting were enhanced. That was before any special requests like "heads up" displays, weaponry displays, distant viewing, split-screen viewing or sixty-seven other abilities.

"Lieutenant Colonel Youngman is currently busy and he won't notice unless we detonate them. When we detonate them, you will be a hero for taking the initiative because it will be the only thing that saves the right flank of the Corp from being rolled up."

"Is it that bad?" asked the engineer, wondering how much his friend's moroseness was justified. Although he would have preferred to lay out a full reception for the Posleen, the firepower of the battalion was massive.

"Tom, we're about to be corncobbed and there ain't a fuckin' thing I can do about it. After this day the name Youngman will be right up there with Custer, except George Armstrong had a brilliant career before he pissed it away. Now get rigging the charges. Make the cratering charges big ones. I want them to tear the faces right off the megascrapers; they've got forty minutes max."

"Fuck it," said the officer with an attempted shrug. "You're right, nobody will notice unless we have to blow 'em. You want both Boulevards mined? What about 7th Cav?"

"Yeah, if Cav falls back they'll want the cover," he paused. "There's the gust front."

"Huh?" asked the lieutenant, looking out the window toward where the enemy could be expected to appear.

"A bunch, a real shit pot full of Indowy are headed this way," said Mike, slaved to the distant view of the scout leader. "Get your guys to work, Tom. Now!"

Lieutenant Eamons gave his friend an unseen nod of farewell and casually blasted a hole in the wall with his M-200. Stepping into thin air, his command suit floated him, gentle as a feather, the ten stories to ground level. With the fusion bottles of the megascrapers to draw on there was no lack of energy and it was the quickest and most fun way down. Because it was "untactical" it was forbidden by the battalion but the unit was going to open up the minute they saw the Posleen, so what was one more hole? It made as much sense as not having his people prepare hard defenses because they would "reveal the MLR." Like the whole battalion opening up on them wouldn't reveal the MLR to the Posleen? Mike was right, they were going to get corncobbed.

Tom looked around as he drifted down, again marveling at the mixture of alien and familiar. Take New York City, *please!* Simplify the glass facades. Choose one style, similar to the twin towers. Make it .914 miles high and 1.145 miles square. The deep, dim canyons were similar to those found in any major Terran city, but deeper, darker. As he grounded he was reminded of the other differences. The gravity was slightly lower and the sunlight had a greenish tinge like fluorescent lighting. It was also brighter, bright as an acetylene torch when it shone on the hard-packed clay that replaced asphalt; the grav drives needed no special surface for support. And no plants, not even a blade of grass or the green of a window box. He entered a cavernous portal in the ground floor, one of several for vehicle entry and exit, and began bounding down the long, echoing corridor. "AID, give me a route to my platoon's assembly area and connect me to the platoon sergeant." It was time to do some work.

Mike continued to watch the thickening spray of Indowy refugees on Sisalav Boulevard. Cutting the view to one quarter of his visor, he saw them in real-time entering the battalion's sector. He heard "Hold fire" calls on the company nets he was monitoring and smiled; the little Indowy could hardly have looked less like the enemy. The hairy little bipeds were on foot, covered in a layer of yellowish dust from the roads and fleeing unencumbered. They seemed not to have the human urge to maintain possessions.

"AID, where's their transportation?" asked Mike, puzzled. There were none of the cars, trucks or even manhandled carts that would be expected with a similar group of humans.

"They have no need for it, so virtually no Indowy have transports. Few of them leave the megascrapers in their entire lives; indeed, few leave a single area, a floor or a sector. A few never leave a series of rooms. All they need is in the building, their quarters, food workshops and baths."

"Where are they going? Do they know?"

"No, there is no support for refugees. If they are nonproductive they are of no consequence. Some will find menial positions, a few with special skills may find employment, but the vast majority will eventually die of exposure or starvation."

Mike shivered in his plastic womb; the more he learned about Galactic ethos, the less he liked.

"Show me a schematic of primary water and sewer pipes connecting to Qualtren and Qualtrev with diameter and access notations." It bothered him that the plan was so one dimensional. A few of the upper stories were being used but the vast subbasements and sewers were being ignored. In WWII the Russians and Germans both used sewers to good effect. At least the entire Posleen mass would not be able to fire at them if they were underground. He studied the schematic and frowned in puzzlement.

"Michelle, those supply systems—I don't care how minimalist the Indowy are, there are not enough and large enough water supply lines or sewage disposal lines. What gives?"

"Most water and sewage are recycled in the megascraper."

"Hmm." The water pipes were still big enough to move around in. "Michelle, instruct all AIDs to begin a plot for every individual and small unit to the nearest water pipe access. Prepare a retreat plan to Saltrev/Saltren via underground connections and update a defense plan. Continuously update Kobe and Jericho on the basis of engineering platoon advancements. Prepare to coordinate demolition plan with Alpha and Bravo companies. And we'll have to find a way to shut down the flow." *Expect victory, plan for defeat.*

The flood of Indowy was starting to choke the boulevard, their gray-green bodies pressed together, packing the wide road from side to side. He could see more flooding out of Waltren from the point of view of the scout platoon leader, those tributaries adding to the flood. The street was as packed as Wall Street at lunch time, as packed as a papal mass with the lemminglike flood of Indowy. Their sturdy little bodies were being smashed against the unyielding metal faces of the buildings, crushing the young, old and weak alike underfoot. Lesser streams wound into and through Naltren and Naltrev, across the avenue and into Qualtrev/Qualtren, every individual contributing to both the pressure and the panic.

As the major force of Indowy refugees reached Qualtren/Qualtrev, the back pressure and the turn combined to drive thousands of the small humanoids into the northwest quadrant of Qualtren's lower floors. There they encountered 1st platoon of Charlie company and the effect was shattering.

Individually the Indowy had the manners and aggressiveness of a rabbit but in that vast panicked horde they acted like stampeding buffalo. When the wave front hit 1st platoon the Indowy entering the many ground floor openings at first went around the armored humans arrayed within. Then, as the pressure mounted, they started jostling the soldiers and climbing on and over them. As the weight mounted of first a handful, then a dozen then hundreds of panicked extraterrestrials, the suited troopers were toppled and began to thrash under the stampede. As they thrashed and kicked, trying to clear them away, the servo-assisted armor smashed and splattered the inoffensive little creatures painting their green ichor across the pastel walls. The ichor only added to the problem, making the floor slippery with body fluids.

The Charlie company commander and first sergeant rushed to the scene in a futile attempt to regain the platoon position but they, in turn, were swept under by the flood. Two of the battalion's terawatt lasers were in the mass, set to fire "right into the throats" of the Posleen, and they were lost as well. Thus, before the battle was joined, the crucial platoon and company commander of the battalion's defense along with thirty percent of its heavy firepower was neutralized. All without one Posleen in sight.

Mike switched onto the Charlie net as it became jammed with screaming and cursing. He attempted to contact the Charlie Company CO, Captain Vero, since the platoon's AIDs could be instructed to filter outgoing transmissions but the commander was stepping all over the net by shouting and cursing as loudly as his troopers. When Mike switched to the battalion command net, the RTO was overwhelmed with calls from Alpha, Weapons, Support and even Headquarters' company commanders requesting orders or guidance. Alpha's ground floor platoon, Third Herd was in danger of being overwhelmed as well. Mike heard Captain Wright request permission to move them to upper floors and be immediately denied by the RTO; it was obvious that he had not consulted Lieutenant Colonel Youngman.

Lieutenant Colonel Youngman and Major Norton were, meanwhile, conferring on the staff net. Major Norton's AID had been ordered to hold all incoming calls. This was a technique that worked with RTOs but only worked with the very literal AIDs after they had been "broken in." With an RTO, if he thought the call was really important, he'd pass it on. That was how you knew you had a good RTO. But an inexperienced AID was like a bad RTO. It took every order literally and had no sense of discretion. Until Major Norton countermanded the setting, if in the heat of battle he remembered, the company commanders could not contact their remaining link to the battalion commander when they were blocked by his RTO.

Captain Wright withdrew 3rd platoon without orders and placed them ready to resume their positions. Captain Vero finally calmed down and started to get those of his troops that he could withdrawn. About half of the Charlie platoon and most of Alpha had been withdrawn when the first Posleen Report came in. However, the lasers were left behind. The colonel and the S-3 were not even aware of the situation; they were totally cut off from communication outside their little world.

"Enemy in view" came the call on all command nets, the priority stepping on all other communications. Instantly every commander switched to feeds from the scouts.

Behind the flood of Indowy, like a hawk eating a snake, was an equally solid if more disciplined flood of leprous yellow centaurs. The front rank was trotting to keep up with the running Indowy, wielding their long palmate blades in either hand. They would hack down an Indowy and run to catch the next as the following rank lifted the body and passed it to the outside. Along the way the corpse would be gutted and dismembered until the rendered portions were stacked neatly against a wall. The force was a gigantic moving abattoir with the occasional snack nibbled along the way.

Behind this first block of about twelve thousand Posleen the remainder were broken into three streams. The center stream continued to follow the front group as backup, while the outside streams poured into the megascrapers.

The leaders, the God Kings, were clearly evident. They rode in their open saucer-shaped vehicles about two meters across with lasers or HVM launchers mounted on powered gimbals. According to orders the scout/snipers, one member of each three-man scout team, lifted their M-209 sniper rifles and, as a group, fired a low-velocity sniper round at a designated God King. Like a single string-cut marionette, ten God Kings fell. The whole mass checked for a split second and then responded.

The low-velocity rounds of the snipers left no more signature than a high-velocity rifle bullet; there should have been nothing to betray the position of the scouts. But previously unsuspected targeting systems automatically swiveled the vehicle-mounted weapons of the remaining God Kings and, as they locked on target, a storm of lasers and hypervelocity missiles swept back up range. In addition the subjects of the deceased reacted with hyperaggression, flailing the target points designated by the leader's fire with a sleet of needle and rocket fire. In a series of eye-blinking detonations and searing laser strikes the locations of the scout teams were swept away in the storm of fire. Huge holes were blasted deep into the building under the concentrated fire of twenty vehicle-mounted weapons and twelve thousand hand weapons, and if the force-screens had any positive effect it was unappreciable. The scout platoon disappeared in an unnoticeable haze of blood.

There was a sound of retching on the staff circuit and Captain Vero was muttering "Hail Mary, full of grace, the Lord is with thee," over and over on the command net. Other than that the nets were silent for a moment as the Posleen swept on unchecked. Their coordination suffered however; fewer of the Indowy bodies made it to the side and some of the front forces began trickling away into the buildings.

"Well," said Lieutenant Colonel Youngman on the staff net, stepping on whoever was retching, "I stand corrected. The threat analysis was understated. Major Norton?"

"Yes, sir."

"Get over to Saltren/Saltrev. Begin preparing fallback positions. I suspect we are not going to be in these positions for long. Ah, Lieutenant Eamons?" Unnoticed by the battalion commander, his AID switched him to the proper frequency.

"Yes, sir? Lieutenant Colonel Youngman?" the lieutenant was panting.

"Yes. I need you to set up cratering charges on Sisalav immediately."

"I already did, sir and we're mining the buildings now," said the engineer officer in a sharp tone.

"Good initiative. It may save our butts. After that pull back to Saltren and start putting in all the concertina and mines you can lay your hands on."

"Yes, sir." *Thank god he didn't ask what kinds of mines. Like O'Neal thinks I can't read a demolition program.*

"Captain Brandon."

"Lieutenant Colonel Youngman?" asked the company commander with a note of surprise.

"Yes. Prepare to cover the battalion's withdrawal to Saltren and Saltrev. I intend to take the Posleen in a running ambush. Your unit is to dispose itself along the boulevard on both buildings and slow their advance. Then extract through the buildings and cross the avenues away from Sisalav."

"Yes, sir. Sir, with all due respect, *where the hell have you been*? And where is Major Norton?"

"We're both at the Forward TOC. Or we were, Major Norton is headed to Saltren to prepare the secondary positions."

"Do you know that 1st of Charlie and Alpha 3rd were both overrun by the Indowy?" asked the company commander. The tone was one of fatigue and near despair.

"What?" asked the startled battalion commander.

"We haven't been able to reach you for the last fifteen minutes. There is no one on the ground floors and we've lost three lasers so far. We are totally open on the ground on Qualtren."

"Hold on." The colonel left the net for a moment. "My RTO says he couldn't get through to me either because he kept getting stepped on by Major Norton and myself." The officer cursed quietly for a moment. "I hate these fucking suits," he ended.

"Too late, sir. You need to contact Vero and Wright, ASAP. They've got some serious problems."

"Too right. Uh, suit, connect me with all the company commanders. Are we live? Alpha Six, Charlie Six, Bravo Six. Stand by to engage the enemy. The building is being mined by the engineering platoon, you are authorized to provide assets as available. If necessary and on my command we will begin a fighting retreat to the same relative positions on the Sal Line. Bravo is to cover the retreat. Attempt to retake the heavy weapons positions as assets are available. There's no time for questions just hit 'em low and hit 'em hard, that's what we're here for, Falcon Six, out."

"Tom, this is Mike."

"Yeah, Mike."

Lieutenant O'Neal was four stories lower and deep in the structure. He was mainly using support corridors; they were higher and wider and that way he avoided the majority of the fleeing

Indowy. There were still hundreds of them underfoot blocking the intersections and group areas. All of them were trying to leave simultaneously having ignored orders to do it before and hampering the combat operations. Mike stopped, temporarily stymied by a blocked stairwell and stared speculatively at a large tank of liquid connected to a fractional distiller.

"How's it coming?" he asked.

"We've finished the roads and the building is about twenty-five percent done. The colonel authorized the mining," finished the officer. There was a hint of smugness in his voice.

Mike had missed that call in his monitoring; he was surprised at the announcement. "He authorized Jericho?"

"Well, I told him we were mining the building."

"But not how?"

"He said use your initiative."

Mike laughed at the irony. "That's a first. Okay, we might be covered." He was to regret the choice of words.

Mike's experienced and helpful AID, Michelle, flashed a complex schematic of the engineering platoon's progress in a virtual hologram floating at eye height. The completed areas were in green, the areas that should be completed by the time the Posleen arrived were in yellow and the areas that would not be completed were in red. Mike touched an area near Charlie in Qualtren.

"Concentrate over here, if you please, kind sir."

"Why certainly, *bon homme*, and with that I bid you *au revoir*."

"Roger, out."

Mike took one more look at the schematic and flicked it off with a gesture. With the colonel now on board his "go-to-hell-plan," even if the battle went straight to hell, the battalion's sector would still be secured. "Good luck, Tom."

"Captain Brandon," Mike said, triggering a burst into a structural member on the second floor of Qualtren.

"Lieutenant O'Neal?"

"Yes, sir. I suspect we'll start the fallback shortly after contact. I would like your assistance in an expansion of the commander's plan. All your guys have to do is fall back on the routes I download to them and destroy a few structures on their way out."

When he reached the ground floor he headed for an ammunition cache. As he scooted he was studying the schematic as the engineers frantically laid charges, and larger and larger areas turned green.

"What's the plan?"

"It's called Jericho, sir." Mike took a few moments to explain.

"That's a hell of an expansion, lieutenant. It'll give us a breather, but..."

"Sir, it'll give us more than a breather, it'll secure this whole sector. Then we can move into support of 7th Cav." When he reached the ammo dump he started loading a grav sled with an M-323 machine gun and ammunition boxes. "Frankly it is what we should have done instead of sending out the mobile forces to get wiped out."

"Mike, this isn't one of your computer games. Just keeping the company from bolting will be hard enough."

"Sir, when we fall back the personnel will lose their sense of direction. I've been lost in a unit before; you'd take directions from the devil himself. This extracts them without exposing them to fire and secures the sector. What more could anyone ask?"

"Uh, limiting collateral damage?" asked the commander rhetorically. "Okay, okay, we'll do it. Make sure the information is available immediately when we fall back."

"The company's AIDs already have the plan. All it took was your okay."

"Good luck, Lieutenant."

"*Vaya con Dios*, Captain, go with God." He paused for a moment to let the channel clear. "Michelle, get me Captain Wright." Then picked up a loaded grav sled and headed back up the ramp, watching the schematic as he went.

> From panic, pride, and terror,
> Revenge that knows no rein,
> Light haste and lawless error,
> Protect us yet again.
> Cloak Thou our undeserving,
> Make firm the shuddering breath,
> In silence and unswerving
> To taste Thy lesser death!
>
> —Kipling

27

Andata Province, Diess IV
2208 GMT May 18th, 2002 AD

"Knock, knock, mind if I join you?" Lieutenant O'Neal used the local circuit. He knew there were troops from Charlie company in the next room, but he didn't know who they were. The AID could tell him, but he'd been too busy to ask. Besides, there were few troopers in Charlie company that he knew personally. And given how keyed up everyone was, letting them know he was coming before barging through the door seemed like a good idea.

"Come ahead," said Sergeant John Reese, looking over his shoulder. Through the double doors came a squat figure towing a grav sled loaded with weapons and ammunition. Among them was another M-300 and a tripod-mounted HVM. Reese recognized him as Lieutenant O'Neal; the silhouette was distinctive. Apparently the lieutenant believed in being prepared. "Can I help you, sir?" Reese jerked his head at the ammo bearer, Private Pat McPherson, to go help with the load.

"Thanks. I figured I'd join the party if you don't mind." Mike's suit flashed a heads-up-display of the names and ranks by the suited figures in the room. It was a heavy weapons team with the heavy weapons squad leader. Their own M-300 heavy grav gun was set up and bins of ammunition were ganged together ready to go. All three of the team were crouched against the outside wall, their force-screens covering the probable axis of approach. The descending F-1's sunset glow had turned a weird violet that mottled the suits like purple haze.

"Hell no, sir. Every little bit helps," said the assistant gunner, Spec-Four Sal Bennett.

"Was that by any chance a short joke, Specialist?" Mike asked with mock sternness.

"Oh, hell, sir. That wasn't what I meant!"

"I know, I know, just a little levity, right? Little levity, get it?"

The squad laughed as Mike started tossing thirty-kilo ammo bins against the wall.

"Michelle, give me an RGB representation of Indowy, Posleen and humans in the nine-block sector."

The AID flashed a three-D representation of the nine megascrapers, then began drawing in Posleen, human and Indowy concentrations in red, green and blue. The green was a solid core in the corners of Qualtren and Qualtrev with scattered others behind. The projected locations of Indowy were a heavy concentration in Saltren and Saltrev and blue flowing downward like an hourglass in Qualtren and Qualtrev; time was running out for the inhabitants of the megascrapers. On Sisalav Boulevard there was a solid band of color flowing out of sensor range, but just out of view, around the Daltren/Daltrev jog, the solid blue band abruptly became red.

"They're almost in sight," said Mike, taking a sip of water as he crouched behind the spurious shelter of the wall and set up the HVM to fire automatically.

"Orders are to wait for a signal from Captain Vero before we open fire. What are you looking at?"

"Michelle, slug hologram to squad view," said Mike as he finished readying the missile launcher. It was set to track his fire and add its own weight offset ten meters. He started to set up the M-300 on the opposite side of the squad's position. It would be set to do the same thing. Thus he would be controlling not only his own light grav gun but two other heavy weapons. It was not a hard technique to train for or to set up. But the battalion, of course, had not prepared for it.

"Huh," Sergeant Reese said after a moment, "I didn't know they could do that."

"Yours can't, not in any detail. Command suits have extra processing and data collection ability." There was a moment of silence, then Mike said in a flat tone, "There they are."

The words came as a surprise and Sergeant Reese popped his head up from hologram and peered down the darkening canyon. "AID," he said, "Mag six, enhance and stabilize." The view leapt forward and brightened.

The way the stabilization system worked, the world moving at a different rate than reality, always made him a little queasy. What Reese saw in his view-screen just made him sick. He broke out in a cold sweat and goose pimples as his sphincter tightened. He wanted badly to piss and his mouth was dry. When Pat started to vomit he was forced to join in. This caused a complete loss of control.

The Posleen had regained control of the front rank and the remorseless abattoir was in full swing. To either side they could see the late-moving Indowy pouring out of the megascrapers, trying to avoid the oncoming horde. It was easier to empathize with these Indowy, having watched movement within and among the megascrapers during their setup. The peaceful little boggles that the Posleen were slaughtering had become like neighbors and seeing them slaughtered was a terror.

They always told you it was okay to be afraid, but surely they didn't mean this stark terror, this abject fear. The briefings had been clear. Although the suits were proof against many things, the Posleen palmate blades had mono-molecular edges; they could chop apart a suit like a housewife with a chicken. All Reese could think of as the Posleen advanced remorselessly on the fleeing Indowy was that those knives were headed for him and the whole world seemed to be filled with flashing steel.

He couldn't understand it. He was one of the brave, the fearless Airborne. For five years he had jumped out of planes over fifty times, enduring the occasional injury, without the first qualm. He enjoyed the thrill that terrified others. He'd laughed, inside, at the guys who were white-faced and shaking, who closed their eyes and headed for the sound of the open door. He loved the sight of the chutes opening out the door, the earth, plane and sky tossed in a chaotic kaleidoscope for those first brief moments after you stepped out. The chute opening was almost a letdown and the landing no hassle, except when something broke. But no fear, ever. Now, he feared. He feared the Posleen and wondered why those white-faced troopers put up with this over and over again.

The cold-blooded rendering of the defenseless Indowy was almost more than Reese could take; with their tiny stature and love of bright colors they seemed almost like children to him. As the Posleen closed the distance he found himself pulling his M-232 tighter into his shoulder and rubbing the breech. "Come on.

Come on." As his eyes flicked to his ammunition level readouts he did not notice the tears running down his cheeks or the stink of an overloaded environmental system. His fear slowly began to be replaced with anger, a white hot rage at the evil yellow dog-men coming towards them. "Come on, you bastards."

Mike drew his magazine again and actually looked at it this time. *Yup, thar's bullets init.* He reseated it and touched the charging button. With an unnoticed whine the first teardrop-shaped bead of depleted uranium was lofted into place. He felt as though he were looking at the scene through deep water. He recognized it as a fear reaction and ignored it; his mind was going faster than it ever had in his life. He had thorough plans for virtually every contingency. He had prepared so hard for this moment that it seemed as though he had lived it before: a lethal déjà vu.

"'It seems to me as though I've been upon this stage before,'" he quietly sang. The AID, correctly surmising that it was a personal moment, did not broadcast it. "'And juggled away the night for the same old crowd...'"

"Charlie company, stand by."

Mike snugged the butt into his shoulder. *Talk about target-rich environment.* "'These harlequins you see with me, they too once held the floor...'"

"Fire!"

Over three hundred rifles and machine guns, the combined firepower of Charlie and Alpha companies, and four terawatt lasers, belched coherent light and metallic lightning at the Posleen horde. As if one animal, the whole phalanx was shocked, its front third vanishing in the silver fire of detonating relativistic projectiles.

Fuckin' A! thought Mike. *It fuckin' works! We're gonna get our asses kicked, 'cause there's too damn many of 'em, but the hardware fuckin' works!* The HVM launcher began to spit kinetic missiles at the area designated as hostile and the M-300 followed.

Then the thousands of remaining Posleen in view raised their weapons at the source of the fire.

"For what we are about to receive..." whispered Mike, shifting fire to the rear body.

In the front phalanx there remained eight thousand normals and twenty God Kings. The combat suits were proof against the majority of the weapons, but there were still fifteen heavy lasers and five multiple HVM launchers with automatic targeting systems, nine hundred 3mm flechette guns and four hundred fifty handheld HVM launchers. As a storm of fire struck the battalion's positions the battle descended into an orgy of mutual annihilation. In the first two minutes following the opening volley six thousand more Posleen died, but over sixty paratroopers died and twenty more were injured. In that moment the battle was lost; there was a finite number of paratroopers, but a steady stream of centaurs replaced Posleen dead. As the output from the battalion reduced the Posleen were able to advance, pouring like a yellow avalanche towards the source of the fire. And as they advanced they were able to search out the sources of fire more effectively.

A heavy laser, targeting on the Charlie company machine gun, scythed into the room housing Mike and the squad. Spec-Four Bennett would never see Trenton, New Jersey again. The laser cut sideways, exploding the wall inward and momentarily blinding the squad with debris. It narrowly missed Sergeant Reese, bubbling the hologram projectors on his helmet, and sliced diagonally across Spec-Four Bennett from left shoulder to below the right nipple unchecked by his force-screen or the immensely refractory armor.

The laser slashed through the front of his armor but was stopped by the combination of his mass and the rear armor from cutting all the way through. The tremendous heat of the coherent beam of light caused his torso to flash into steam and sublimed calcium. The armor held together, however, except a two-inch-wide strip blasted out of it, and Bennett's pureed remains squirted out like cherry soda from a shaken bottle. This ejecta flipped him backwards across the room.

The laser served as an aiming point for the God King's brigade of Posleen normals and a broadside of flechette and missile fire vomited at the hapless machine gun team. The missiles were wildly inaccurate at the seven-hundred-meter range of the current engagement. It would have been the greatest of bad luck to be hit by one, but Madam Chance knows no favorites.

Lieutenant O'Neal and Sergeant Reese were hurled backwards by the weight of metal. For a few moments O'Neal returned fire, riding the wave of rounds as he had practiced, and his heavier prototype armor was proof against the hail of fire. Private McPherson was less lucky. Two 3mm rounds penetrated his abdominal storage, setting off a cache of grenades and popping the blowout panels in a sea of actinic fire, then through his body armor. After that they were unable to exit and began bouncing around inside. McPherson's suit began to hop and flip randomly through the air, arms and legs flailing to keep up as the two hypervelocity flechettes bled off their kinetic energy within the body of his suit. Two seconds later, when it finally, mercifully, stopped, the only evidence of damage were two tiny holes, one above the right hip and one almost centered on the navel. The storm of directed fire had died to a light shower and Sergeant Reese started towards him.

"Forget it," said O'Neal, scanning a map of the area for a new firing position.

"He was having convulsions!" said Reese, surprised and angered to find the lieutenant interfering in first aid.

"He's dead. Check his telemetry. Convulsions don't..." he said as he turned to stop the trooper but it was too late. Sergeant Reese popped the seals on the helmet and a red mass, unpleasantly reminiscent of spaghetti sauce, poured out on the floor. Reese began to dry heave as McPherson's head rolled out of the dead helmet and squished into what remained of his body. The underlayer gel, red tinged, oozed out behind it.

"...flip you backwards for a full gainer and a half twist through the air. Come on, Sergeant, time to scoot." O'Neal popped the power cartridge out of the grav sled, laid a charge on the ammo, picked up two boxes and trotted to the door. "Come on. They're dead, we're not. Let's keep it that way."

The next thirty minutes were forever a blur for Sergeant Reese. He had forgotten his rank, his unit and even his name; all he could do was blindly follow Lieutenant O'Neal, firing when and how he was told. He vaguely remembered, as in a dream, the views from various windows and rapidly firing before moving to another location. He remembered the order from Lieutenant Browning, the XO, voice cracking in terror, to fall back to Saltren. He remembered inexplicable orders from Lieutenant O'Neal to shatter certain beams and arches, placing demolition charges, in low, brightly lit corridors down which he crouched while the shorter lieutenant floated with lethal, catlike grace. He returned to stark reality during their first close encounter with the Posleen.

They were in a subbasement headed he knew not where running down one wall of a mammoth warehouse. The shelves were filled with green drums, like rubber oil barrels. As the lieutenant passed one of the aisles, both their AIDs screamed a belated warning. A group of fifty or so Posleen, accompanied by a God King, opened fire on Lieutenant O'Neal with everything they had.

There were six high-density inertial compensators along the spine of the suit. They had been placed there to prevent severe inertial damage to the most vital portions of the user. Lieutenant O'Neal launched himself into the air and away from the threat, an instinct of hundreds of hours of simulations, while his AID dialed the inertial compensators as low as they would go. This had several effects, good and bad, but the net effect was to make it less likely that the flechettes would penetrate his armor as they had the private's; at this range their penetration ability was vastly improved.

The lack of inertia permitted the suit to move aside or be pushed away as if no more substantial than a hummingbird. Combined with the strength of the armor it successfully shed the first sleet of rounds, but it made him as unstable as a Ping-Pong ball in a hurricane. He was picked up by the impacts, flipped repeatedly end for end, struck the warehouse wall and blown sideways.

Sergeant Reese screamed and fired on the target vector flashing in his display. The Posleen were masked by the barrels, but he figured with the power of the grav rifle he could saw through the barrels quickly and take the Posleen under direct fire.

As it happened, actually hitting the Posleen became unnecessary. The barrels throughout the entire warehouse were filled with an oil processed from algae. It was used by the Indowy in cooking. It was as ubiquitous as corn oil, and the five million Indowy of Qualtren used so much they needed a half-kilometer square warehouse. Like corn oil, it had a fairly high flash point but given certain conditions it could burn, even explode.

The depleted uranium pellets of the grav guns traveled at a noticeable fraction of the speed of light. The designers had carefully balanced maximum kinetic effect against the problem of relativistic ionization and its accompanying radiation. The result was a tiny teardrop that went so fast it defied description. It made any bullet ever made seem to stand still. Far faster than any meteor, rounds that did not impact left the planet's orbit to become a spatial navigation hazard. It punched a hole through the atmosphere so fierce that it stripped the electrons from the atoms of gas and turned them into ions. The energy bled in its travel was so high it created a shock front of electromagnetic pulse. Then, after it passed, the atoms and electrons recombined in a spectacular display of chemistry and physics. Photons of light were discharged, heat was released and free radicals, ozone and Bucky balls were produced. The major by-product was the tunnel of energetic ions indistinguishable from lightning. Just as hot, and just as energetic. A natural spark plug.

In two seconds a thousand of these supremely destructive teardrops punched through fifty drums of fish oil. One pellet was enough to finely distribute a drum of oil over two to three thousand cubic meters of air. The following rounds found only vapor, and these excess pellets, following the immutable laws of physics, set out to find other drums to divide. The oil from thousands of drums suddenly flash blasted into gas then ignited from compression, rather like a diesel piston. The net effect was a fuel-air bomb, the next best thing to a nuclear weapon in Terran technology, and the basement warehouse became a gigantic diesel cylinder. For Sergeant Reese, in an instant the world flashed to fire.

The warehouse was two levels below ground. It had six levels below it and was three hundred fifty meters from Sisalav Boulevard, a hundred fifty meters from Avenue Qual. The fuel-air explosion blasted a two-hundred-meter diameter crater down to bedrock, gutted the building for a kilometer upward and set off all the charges planted for Plan Jericho. The shock wave smashed structural members all the way to Sisalav and Qual and spit many of the remaining troopers on the ground floor out of the building like watermelon seeds. It killed every unarmored being in the mile cube structure: three hundred twenty-six thousand Indowy and eight thousand particularly quick and greedy Posleen. The Jericho charges worked as planned, shattering a hundred and twenty critical monocrystalline support members. With surprising grace, the mile-high edifice leaned to the northwest and slowly, as if reverently kneeling, fell into Daltrev, blocking Sisalav and Qual and smashing the southeast quadrant of Daltrev. It crushed more Posleen and completely blocked an enemy advance from the massif to Qualtrev.

Following a predetermined plan, when the last shaken but mobile survivors of Alpha and Bravo quit Qualtrev five minutes later, that structure's charges detonated as well. The building

settled across Avenue Anosimo and the rest of Daltrev, blocking Posleen advances through both the battalion's sector and
the primary axis of advance into the 7th Cav sector. With the
Posleen advances blocked, the remnant of the battalion was free
to support the Cav. If it could be reconstituted.

Mike moaned and opened his eyes. At least he thought he
did but the world was as black as before and he suffered from
vertigo. Either there was something wrong with his inner ear, or
he was basically upside down and on his back.

"Lieutenant O'Neal," said his AID in her most soothing voice,
"you're not blind, there just is no light."

"Suit lights," muttered Mike, dazedly.

"First let me tell you where you are. What do you remember?"

"Headache."

The AID correctly interpreted this as a medication request
and chose three items from the pharmacope.

"Whew," said Mike after a minute or two of shutting his eyes
against the soul-drinking darkness, "that's better. Now, where am
I? And turn on the damn helmet."

"What do you remember?" the AID temporized.

"Entering a warehouse in the basement of Qualtren."

"Do you remember what happened in the basement?"

"No."

"Do you remember Sergeant Reese?"

"Yeah. Is he alive?"

"Barely. You encountered some Posleen. In firing on them
Sergeant Reese struck several bladders of oil with kinetic pellets. This caused a fuel-air explosion which in turn detonated
the Jericho charges..."

"I'm under Qualtren," said Mike in sudden horrified realization.

"Yes, sir. You are. You are under approximately one hundred
twenty-six meters of rubble."

28

Ft. Indiantown Gap, PA Sol III
0025 August 5th, 2002 AD

Pappas' eyes were open, his back straight, his arms crossed and a fierce expression was fixed on his face. For all that he was, in reality, asleep.

It was after midnight as the swaying bus ground to a halt at the MP guarded entrance to Fort Indiantown Gap. The bus driver had wondered as they approached about the red glow of flames in the distance, but the greeting from the MPs drove all thought of it out of his head. He leaned out of the window to ask where the recruits and their humorless sergeant were supposed to go, but before he could ask the question the MP answered it for him.

"I don't know where the fuckers are supposed to go, who they are supposed to report to or what the fuck to do with them. Are there any more questions?" the MP private asked in an angry and aggressive tone.

Pappas' eyes flicked open and before he was fully awake he had exited the bus and had the MP dangling by his BDU collar from one hand.

"*What the fuck kind of answer is that you pissant?*" he raged. The MP's companion started awake and clawed at his Berretta.

"*Draw your weapon and you will be splitting rocks in Leavenworth on Thursday, asshole!*" said the infuriated Pappas turning his fulminating gaze on the companion. On top of the difficulties of the trip the attitudes of the MPs had just been too much. The backup quit clawing at his sidearm and popped to attention.

"Now," said Pappas as his fury cooled slightly, "what the fuck is your problem, Private?" He lowered the MP so that his feet contacted the ground without actually releasing him.

The MP had had his share of problems lately and plenty of opportunity to practice hand-to-hand combat. But he had never had anyone manhandle him so quickly or completely and the experience was shattering. The NCO in gray silks, which designated him as one of the nearly untouchable Fleet Strike Force, was a mountain of muscle. The dim lighting and red flickering of distant flames turned him into a surreal figure of almost primeval strength and fury, like a volcano on two trunk-like legs. The private did a quick reevaluation of his environment.

"Sergeant," he was definitely a sergeant, although it was hard to read the Fleet stripes on his shoulder, "we got a lot of problems..."

"I don't want to hear problems, private, I want to hear answers."

"Sergeant, I don't *have* any. I'm sorry." The private's face was screwed into near tears and Pappas suddenly had to reevaluate the situation as well.

"What the fuck is going on?" he asked releasing the private and smoothing the fabric of his BDU collar. He finally turned his head to look at the distant fires. "What the fuck is going on?" he asked again, shaking his head.

"Sarge, Sergeant," the MP corrected quickly, "the fuckin' place is out of control." He stopped and shook his head.

"Sergeant," said the backup, "I'm sorry we were so fucked up on our answer. But we really don't know where to send your troops."

The original MP nodded his head in agreement. "The first thing is last week they had to move a bunch of the units 'cause their barracks got burned out in the riots. Then they lost some of the troops and the rest were shacking up in open barracks. When they tried to move 'em there was riots over that. An' whenever we break up a riot, the rioters tend to fire the trailers when they're runnin' away. So, where youse was supposed to go might not even be there..."

"Holy shit," whispered the former Marine. He could hear the troops getting off the bus behind him and raised his voice. "Get me Stewart, Ampele, Adams and Michaels." The squad leaders. "The rest of you yardbirds get back on the bus!"

While the squad leaders assembled he watched the flickering

flames at a position of parade rest. He gently blew his lips in thought. "You guys getting any help?" he asked.

"Not much, Sergeant," said the MP. "There's about three or four battalions that have their troops under order, but even they have problems. And we can't really use them for riot suppression, 'cause we can't tell the sheep from the goats." The private stopped and shook his head. "It's a real rat-fuck, Sergeant."

"Gunny."

"Okay, it's a real rat-fuck, Gunny." The MP chuckled.

Pappas wheeled on the assembled squad leaders. "This is a fuck-up, folks, but it's one we gotta work with. Apparently the Army has lost control of its units." He turned back to the MP. "How many units are we talkin' about?"

"Two divisions, some attached Corp units and the Fleet Strike battalion. We're havin' most of our problems out of the support units and a couple of the infantry battalions, though. The problem is that most of the senior officers and NCOs haven't got here yet, so all we got is a bunch of fuckin' recruits and castoffs from other units. If we had a full officer and NCO Corp we'd be okay, at least that is what our provost says, but until all the officers and NCOs get here and we start havin' some court-martials it's just gonna continue like this."

Pappas nodded his head and continued. "Here is how we're gonna handle it. First, we ain't takin' the bus into that rat-fuck. So we gotta walk. But we ain't gonna try to find where we're supposed to be loaded down with baggage. So, Ampele, First squad is baggage guard."

"Gunny . . . !" the large private started to protest.

"It's more important than you think. We're gonna unload all the baggage here." He looked around. "Down by the stream." He gestured with his chin. "Hunker down and wait for support. When we find our quarters and unit I'll send back transport and most of the platoon to pick up the baggage. But be aware that you could be attacked." He looked at the MPs and they nodded.

"Yeah," said the now fully awake backup. "We've had groups out here before. If you get hit, we'll back you up," he continued, "but we can't fire without being fired on," he finished sourly.

"So be prepared for anything. I'm leaving you here because you're the one I trust to keep his head and hold onto his people best. Don't bitch about a fuckin' compliment. And you better guard our shit good." Pappas thought for a moment and decided to ask the question. "Umm, have they briefed you guys on something about Fleet Strike being under different rules..."

"Yeah, Gunny," answered the first MP. "You guys are hands off. Fortunately other than fights in the barracks area Fleet Strike hasn't caused a lot of problems." He paused and thought about it for a moment. "Well, for us," he amended. "CID's another story."

"Okay," said Pappas, wondering about the comment. "We're gonna take the other three squads into that," he gestured with his chin, "in movement to contact formation." He puffed his cheeks in thought.

"I'll take three members of first squad as a headquarters group. Move slow, stroll. But keep your eyes open and looking around. Designate one team for primary forward movement and one team for security. Have buddies carry on conversation, don't bunch but don't get scattered. If one squad gets into something they can't handle, the other two pile on. If we get bogged down in someone else's turf we are dog-meat, so kick their ass, don't pee on them, we have to cut through any opposition fast." He took a proffered map from the MP and had a quick conversation.

"Okay," he continued, looking at the map in the subdued light and wishing for a set of Milspecs from the equipment they were going to be issued. "We're probably way over by the old heliport right at the base of the mountains." He glanced into the darkness. "Right by the fires." He shook his head.

"Stewart," he turned to the diminutive private. "Second squad has point. Don't do any looting along the way; it's not only against regulation, we don't have fuckin' time. You understand?"

"Yes, sir," said the young man. He stood at parade rest, his face as serious as a statue.

"You don't call me 'sir' anymore, Stewart," said Pappas, dryly. "It looks like I'm back to working for a living," he sighed deeply. "Well, it can't be worse than Hue, right?" He thought about that for a moment. "Do they have firearms?" he asked the MP, deep in memory.

The private winced. "Not many. We generally take those away as fast as they turn up. That is the one thing that really lets us drop a load of hurt on their head. Lots of clubs and knives though," he warned.

Pappas nodded his head. "Pick up anything that looks like a

weapon as you go. The order of movement will be second, fourth, third. I'll be moving between second and fourth. Third, Adams, keep an eye on our backtrack. If we're being tracked we need to swing around and nutcracker them."

"Right, Gunny," said the former drill corporal.

"Okay, remember, try to look casual as possible, but keep in sight of the other squads. Go get your people briefed." He paused for a moment and shook his head in resignation. The expression on his face was lugubrious. "What a fuckin' nightmare."

"We can handle it," said Stewart, confidently. "We've got the training, we've got the teamwork and we've got the leadership." He smiled at the gunnery sergeant, obviously wondering why he was so shaken by the situation.

Pappas turned calm eyes on the private and smiled cheerfully. Since the situation was totally screwed up, Stewart instantly realized that he had said something the sergeant considered particularly boneheaded.

"Stewart, you are an idiot," he said, gently. The sergeant gestured towards the distant rebel units. "In a year or two we are going to be depending on those fuckers for support. Think of it this way. What would happen if the Posleen landed tomorrow?"

"Oh." The private looked back at the fires and scratched his head. He blew out his cheeks and rocked back and forth at parade rest. "Yeah."

Pappas had not seen Stewart pick up the two lengths of broom handle. But the way he twirled them in both hands bespoke forms of training that surprised the veteran NCO. The aggressive drunk had not even had time to cry out before he was down and being dragged into the darkness by two other members of second squad. That obstacle overcome, the platoon continued its slow movement into the maelstrom.

It seemed as though the world was on fire. Wood and siding ripped from the trailers that made up the majority of the barracks were piled in courtyards and parade grounds burning. The substance of the soldiers' homes was being consumed to warm the autumn night.

Small groups wandered everywhere, some of them bearing bottles, others smoking fragrant substances. From the darkness a squeal told of other pleasures being dispensed. Since it sounded consensual, Pappas ignored it. He frankly was not sure what he would do if it were not consensual. The mission was to find and join up with their unit. Once they were attached things would get easier. Or so he hoped.

He gestured for second squad to stop and the platoon to form a perimeter. The troops dropped into position in the shadowed area, a variety of bludgeons clutched in their hands, as the squad leaders joined him at the center. He pulled the map out of his cargo pocket and gestured for them to look at it in the flickering light of distant fires.

"To get to our initial objective, which is where the MPs think the battalion is at, we have to pass through there." He gestured through the buildings at a parade ground. The point was marked on the map as a former heliport. From where they crouched in the darkness it was obvious that the area was some sort of meeting ground. There was a giant party in full swing with numerous bonfires and large groups were wandering around. There were easily a thousand people, males and females, in the area.

"We might not run into any opposition, but, then again, we might. We could swing around, but it would take us well out of our way and sooner or later we're gonna run out of luck." He gestured to where the drunk was sleeping off his concussion. "I am open to suggestions."

"How 'bout we just run through, like we're doing PT?" asked Michaels. "They're less likely to bother a formation, don't you think, Gunny?"

Stewart snorted. "See anybody doing PT?" he asked.

Adams shook his head. "I gotta go with Stewart on this one, man. I don't think anybody around here does PT. We'd stick out like a sore thumb."

"And if we bunch up, we might look like a threat," pointed out Stewart. He had his eyes narrowed.

"Okay, we'll—" started Pappas.

"Gunny, sorry, can I say something?" the little private asked. A few days before the concept of interrupting his drill instructor would have been unthinkable. But not only did the situation call for ideas, the conditions they were in were a weird form of home to Stewart.

"Okay," said the gunny, "go ahead."

"I think me and the boys could draw some of them off," the private said. His eyes were on the distant party as his brow creased in thought. "We could probably open up a hole, kind of a corridor, and the rest of you could slip through."

"How?" Pappas watched the private thinking. He had already recognized that while he had the recruit beat on experience and knowledge, the private was light-years ahead of him on guile and cunning.

"By joining them," continued Stewart. He seemed oblivious to the sergeant's close regard. "Look, just about all of us in second are from a barrio," continued the little private. "We're all home-boys; this is like, home, for us. We'd be in the middle of that and loving every minute of it," he gestured to the party, "if we didn't have an idea why not." He turned and looked at the NCO with newfound respect in his eyes. "Your speech makes more sense now than ever."

The NCO nodded in understanding. "Go on."

"But we can . . . infiltrate that party. I've got some pretty good attention getters, circus tricks I've learned. I can attract some of them around me and the boys. That will open up the hole you need."

"And if it don't work?" asked Pappas.

"We all run like hell," smiled the private.

Pappas gazed at him thoughtfully. "When will you get to the unit?" he asked. The suspicion was obvious.

Stewart shook his head in reproach. "Gunny, I ain't saying we won't do a little partying. We're gonna have to to blend in. But we'll rejoin the unit, all of us, by dawn. Getting out will be harder than getting in. Drawing off their attention from you will be the easiest part."

Pappas nodded his head and regarded the private sagely. "Uh, huh." He puffed out his cheeks in thought. "You know Stewart, some day I'm going to have to ask you how you got your entire street gang through Fleet Strike's personnel filters and into my basic platoon." He paused. "Intact."

Stewart smiled thinly. "But not tonight," he said determinedly.

"Not tonight," the NCO agreed. "However, I'm not going to trust to your streetwise for everything. Once we pass through the area we'll take up over-watch until I think you're doing okay. Don't hurry, we'll be there as long as we need to."

"I'll be fine, Sergeant," said the private, with quiet confidence.

"Okay, then you won't mind if we watch?" Pappas said with a smile.

Stewart shook his head in resignation. "Whatever, boss."

"Okay," said the NCO, "time to play."

Stewart wiped his hands surreptitiously on his silks then stepped forward and slapped the broad shoulder of the soldier in front of him.

"*Hola, 'migo, ¿dónde 'stá el licor?*" The job was going to require some high-proof spirits.

The big Hispanic soldier turned with a snarl. "*Que chingadero quiere saber, cameron?*"

"Hey, we just got here. I need a drink." A twenty appeared as if by magic in Stewart's hand. The squad behind him had taken on the standard swagger, hands thrust into their belts or in pockets, hips thrust out, looking around. Just a bunch of homeboys looking for a party. Stewart had thrust the two broomsticks into the back of his jacket so that they jutted out the neck. In a pinch they would be in action in an instant.

The big soldier took one look at the gang and rethought his approach. He had his own group of bullies to call on, but the time was not right for a fight against unknown odds. He was pretty sure he could break the shrimp like a twig, but you never knew. He looked awful confident.

"It's hard to find, man," the big soldier said, taking a swallow of the raw tequila. "Maracone over by the bleachers, he usually got some."

"*Gracias,*" said Stewart, the twenty suddenly sprouting from the pocket of the Hispanic soldier.

"*De nada,*" said the trooper and turned back to his buddies.

"Anything?" whispered Wilson.

"Had a shiv," said Stewart quietly, "and some kind of pistol."

"Had," smiled the second in command.

"Had," said Stewart, with a complete lack of humor. He was totally concentrated on the mission. "We're gonna do a deal."

Even at halfway across the field the dealer was obvious, a ratty little private surrounded by heavies and a group of female soldiers with their uniforms cut down to nothing but midriff tops and shorts. They must have been freezing in the cool, moist autumn night.

"Okay," said Wilson, doing an automatic sweep of the area for threats. Then he checked to see that the rest of the squad was in position, looking out. They were and he nodded to himself in satisfaction; everything was rikky-tik as the gunny would say.

"Then I'm gonna do the sword swallower routine," continued Stewart. He was thinking about future plans and tactics while Wilson handled the present and security. They had developed the relationship as a survival necessity in the barrio, never realizing that they had simply reinvented the officer/NCO continuum.

"Got it."

"Here." He slipped the private the small pistol. Using Stewart as a shield, the private quickly checked the .25 caliber automatic. "Cover me."

Stewart stepped toward the dealer. One of the bodyguards stepped in front of him only to be waved aside. It was a pro forma demonstration of power that Stewart noticed no more than the wind. Now that he was inside the perimeter the dealer and at least two guards were dead even without Wilson's backup. *These guys are such fucking amateurs*, he thought.

"*Hola*," he grinned, "whacha got?"

"What you want?" asked the dealer in a bored voice. "We got about everything."

"Need some high-test booze, man. We're just in from basic and got us a powerful thirst!" He grinned maniacally, a stupid little basic trainee way in over his head. Yeah, that's it.

"That's pretty expensive, man," said the dealer. "Booze is hard to get. The fuckin' MPs keep raiding my stash."

"Hey," said Stewart, whipping out a wad of bills, "I got nothin' but money, man. You got some high-proof tequila?"

"Sure," smiled the ratty little soldier. He gestured to one of the girls who reached in a spray-painted ammunition box and pulled out an unmarked bottle. "That's sixty."

"Jesus," said Stewart, shaking his head, "that is steep." He counted out the bills and took the bottle. One sip was all it took to ensure that there was sufficient alcohol in the mix for his plan. "*How!* Time to *Party!*"

"Yeah," the dealer said sourly. "Somewhere's else, I got other customers."

"Sure, man, later." Stewart smiled again and walked back to the squad.

"Sniper on the top of the bleachers," whispered Wilson. "I can't see the rifle, but it's there somewhere."

"Can you take him from the other end?"

"Not with this fuckin' little Astra. Maybe you, but even then not with the first shot. And somebody's already got that end staked out."

"*No problemo.* People are always willing to recognize talent," Stewart smiled.

"You are a fuckin' nut, Manuel."

"My name is James Stewart. Don't ever forget that."

"Sure, and I'm the king of Siam."

"Handkerchiefs," Stewart said without comment, holding out his hand. The squad handed over the items and he tied them on the ends of the broken broom handles. Doused with the two-hundred-proof tequila they were torches waiting for a match.

"Here goes nothing," he said and walked towards the group that had staked out the section of bleachers away from the area's single dealer.

"Hey, folks," he said to the group of white soldiers. They watched him approach suspiciously. He nodded at the obvious leader, a heavyset balding sergeant with rolls of fat on his neck.

"You know what this party needs," Stewart asked in a loud happy voice.

"A fuckin' idiot?" asked the leader. His group laughed at the rough humor.

What an Einstein, thought Stewart. "No, some entertainment!" He hopped up on the bleachers and took a swig of the raw whiskey. With a flick of a lighter he spit it back out in a cloud of fire. The belch of dragon's flame lit the area and there were gasps from the group on the bleachers.

"Ladies and gentlemen," he called out to the surroundings, "welcome to the Greatest Show on Earth! I will shock and amaze you with my powers of prestidigitation and psychic abilities! My powers know no bounds!" As he spoke he whipped out the batons, lit them and began twirling.

"Okay," said Pappas, "that's the signal. Get ready to move."

The wait as Stewart moved into position had been an eternity, but now that the show had started the crowd was, in fact, moving. He decided to move with it.

"Fourth, head towards Stewart, try to get as close as possible. Third, head into the middle of the field. When Fourth is in position, head for the barracks." He shook his head. "Fuckin' everybody and their brother is headed for that little idiot."

It was the largest crowd he had ever performed for; even the dealer and his bodyguards had moved over. These people must be really hard up for entertainment. On the other hand, it had gone well. The mental act always amazed people and the tequila had held out long enough to do both the juggling act and the fire-swallowing.

But he was down to magic tricks and it was about time for the big finale. He gestured at Wilson who rolled up his sleeves. He positioned himself across from Stewart and looked toward the squad. One of the members tossed him a knife and he tossed it to Stewart. Stewart tossed it back and they started a two-man juggle. One of the other members of the squad started to sing a well-known dance tune and they began dancing up and down the bleachers spinning and doing handstands as the squad tossed more and more items into the juggle. After fifteen minutes, Stewart found himself exchanging fourteen items, including the burning torches and two knives, and knew it was time to call it quits. With a nod at Wilson he flipped himself upward one-handed and caught the fountain to complete the act to thunderous applause.

"Gunny," said Adams, working his way into the packed crowd. "We got more problems."

29

The journey of a hundred meters begins with one push, thought O'Neal. The suit lights had banished the enveloping darkness, but the twisted masses of plascrete and rubble they revealed was just as depressing.

"Okay, have you come up with any ideas?" he asked his AID.

"Only one. There is a small open area 3.5 meters away at 123 degrees mark 8. If you can worm your way there, you can work your way towards the nearest exit by blasting small openings with the activator charges on your grav rounds."

"What, you mean use them as explosives? How?"

"If you jam one of them firmly in place then shoot it with your grav pistol, it will fracture the antimatter activator charge, releasing the energy as an explosion."

"That sounds...odd but possible. Okay, all I have to do is make it ten or eleven feet up and to the right. How do I turn over? Never mind...I've got an idea." His right hand was, fortunately, near his grav pistol. The suit's biomechanical musculature made short work of the intervening rubble and he sighed as his gauntlet contacted the familiar grip. He drew it and angled the barrel across his abdominal cuirass, the point that seemed most tightly constricted. Whispering a brief prayer to whatever gods might be watching this dust bowl of a planet, he triggered a single round into the plascrete mass.

The concussion belled unexpectedly loud through the armor, transmitting by contact noise that previously had been comfortably muffled. Despite the muffling underlayer, his ears rang as though someone had put a tin bucket over his head and whacked it sharply with a stick. There was a moment's freedom as he rolled quickly to his left then his right shoulder stuck fast again. If he were out of the suit, he could have flexed his shoulders inward and made the turn. On the other hand, if he was out of the suit he would be dead. The external monitors indicated very low oxygen levels and aerosol toxins, probably a result of all the combusted fish oil and associated burning.

He worked the barrel upwards and carefully turned his head to the side. If the round struck the helmet or any part of his armor dead on he would be pureed as effectively as that poor private in the first contact. Pressing the barrel as much as possible into the slab, he triggered another round. This time it skittered ineffectually along the plascrete and ricocheted off his cuirass. The relativistic teardrop left a deep, glowing trench in the refractory armor that had shed thousands of lower velocity flechettes in the earlier battle and the heat dissipated through the underlayer.

Rattled by the near miss he tried again and on the second attempt cracked the refractory plascrete. He twisted like a cat and found himself on his stomach facing slightly downward. Although there was pressure on several points he could move the rubble after a fashion, courtesy of the tremendous power available from the combat armor. After he twisted back and forth for a bit, the slab piece that had cracked to the left of his shoulder and was now across his right slipped beneath him with a resounding crash and a small area was opened to the upper right. He holstered his pistol and snaked a hand up to a convenient handhold revealed in his suit lights. With a firm grip on a piece of structural ceramet he dragged the rest of his body sharply up and to the right. Since this was the way he wanted to go he braced his feet on the rubble he had extracted himself from and pushed upwards. He was rewarded by sliding sharply backwards.

After a good bit more struggle and twice being forced to use his pistol when vigorous activities were rewarded by large slabs pinning some point of his armor he finally reached the promised open area. Above his head was some indefinable piece of machinery. It was this large something, another indefinable bit of Galactic machinery that created the pocket. He took a sip of water and just sat and scanned his situation for a moment. No rifle, lost sometime during the explosion. Shoulder grenade launchers sheared off clean. Replacement was a simple field repair assuming spares which he ain't got. One hundred twenty-eight thousand remaining rounds of depleted uranium 3mm penetrators with antimatter activator charge, pretty much useless without a rifle. Grav pistol and forty-five hundred rounds. Two hundred eighty-three grenades, hand or launcher useable. A thousand meters of 10,000kg test micro line, universal clamp and winch. C-9, four kilograms. Detonators. Sundry pyrotechnic and specialty demolition supplies. Personal Area Force-screen; useless against kinetic weapons, as he had pointed out, but of some utility otherwise. His suit had air, food and water for at least a month.

Unfortunately, at his current rate of energy consumption he would be out of power in twelve hours; the kinetic damping systems had been forced to work overtime counteracting not only the effects of the fuel air explosion but also the settlement of the rubble. Combine all of those with the unexpected and unprecedented strains involved in extracting through the rubble and it was a recipe for disaster.

Mike took a bite of suit rations. Ah, pork fried rice pulp. The semibiotic liner of the suit absorbed all bodily wastes, skin-borne oxygen and nitrogen, dead skin cells, sweat, urine and, ahem, and converted them back into breathable air, potable water and surprisingly edible food. In fact the food was quite tasty and constantly changing; just now it changed to broccoli. The texture was still paste, but the system pulled a little power and *voilà*. No worries about anything but power, as long as he did not think of where the food was coming from.

Well, if it took twelve hours to work through the rubble, he might as well be dead; by then he would be far behind the lines. If he was alone, he *would* be dead. On the other hand...

"Michelle, how many other members of the battalion are down here and functional?" The GalTech communications network could easily punch through the rubble and determine precise positions of every unit.

"Fifty-eight. The senior is Captain Wright of Alpha company. Captain Vero is also trapped under Qualtrev, but he is severely injured and his AID has administered Hiberzine. There are thirty-two personnel who will survive if they are evacuated to a class one medical facility within one hundred eighty days. All are now in hibernation."

Mike rocked his armor back and forth on the plascrete pile trying to make a more stable spot. "Okay, gimme a three-D map with locations, and note rank with increasing brightness levels. Those out of action in yellow, functional in green."

As he spoke the map formed in front of his eyes. Most of the severely injured were those closest to the fuel-air burst or close to Jericho charges.

"Are any of the others starting to extract themselves?"

"A few. The AIDs are sharing the technique. It was initially hard to start without a pistol, but Sergeant Duncan of Bravo company suggested using grenades. So far, that is working."

"Get me Captain Wright," said Mike, happy to have someone else find a solution.

"Yes, sir." There was a chirp and the sound of muted and futile swearing.

"Ah, sir?"

"Yes! Who is it?" Captain Harold Wright checked his heads-up display. "Oh, O'Neal. Your splendid idea worked like a charm. Congratulations."

"It would have been fine if it weren't for the fuel-air explosion, sir," Mike said with chagrin. A drift of dust dropped out of the ceiling of the rubble pocket.

"That is what contingency plans are for, Lieutenant. As it is the battalion is combat ineffective, not to mention trapped in this damn rubble! Any more brilliant ideas?"

"Work our way to the periphery, gather the survivors and head back to friendly lines?" Mike asked rhetorically.

"And we start how?" asked the captain.

"Your AIDs have the plans, sir. I've moved to an open pocket and am preparing to move to the periphery. Basically, we'll blast our way out."

Hal Wright took a moment to consider the plan mapped out by the AID. "Okay, that might just work. I need to start rounding up the NCOs...."

"Sir, the AIDs can sketch out a TOE based upon who we've got and who can make it out. My AID has significantly more experience than yours. If you wish, it can conference with yours and help it along with some of the rough spots..."

"Like a certain helpful lieutenant?"

"That was not in fact the idea."

"Well, whatever the idea, according to this schematic your helpful AID just supplied, you are the only surviving lieutenant under here. Congratulations, XO," he concluded, wryly.

"I'm not in the chain of command, sir."

"You are now. Also, according to this schematic, we will end up widely separated. You'll have about thirty-five soldiers gathered in your area. When you're concentrated we can try to use these utility tunnels to rendezvous. First, though, we have to actually extricate ourselves. Contact your personnel, they include Sergeant First Class Green, platoon sergeant of my second platoon. Get them sorted out and moving, then get back to me."

"Watch your energy level, sir," Mike warned, checking his own decreasing waterfall display. "Mine is well down already. We can scavenge power if we find sources, but in the meantime..."

"Right. Make sure you emphasize that. Get moving, XO."

"Airborne, sir."

For the next few hours soldiers and NCOs were contacted and units worked out. Personnel who were mobile were sent to free thoroughly trapped comrades. The grenade idea worked well except in the case of one unfortunate private who discovered after arming the grenade that he could not retract his arm. Fortunately GalTech medical technology could regenerate the missing hand if they ever got back to friendly lines. Given that the pain was quite brief, the suit sealed the breach and pain-blocked the damage almost instantly, it caused a certain amount of black humor at his expense. It only got worse when he told them his last words were, "This is gonna huurt."

Despite the occasional setback, by seven hours after the detonation all the personnel who were going to be recovered had reached the utilities tunnels. This did not, unfortunately, include Captain Wright or three other personnel from Alpha company. They were trapped within a tremendous pile of heavy machinery. In spite of repeated attempts to reach him, troops had been unable to make a significant penetration of the machinery. After all the other personnel were withdrawn Captain Wright ordered the remaining trapped troopers to activate their hibernation systems and then, placing command in the hands of Lieutenant O'Neal, he activated his own.

O'Neal surveyed the group of dispirited soldiers gathered in the water main. The end of the two-meter-tall oblate tube was shattered and dangled over a manmade cavern the troops had hollowed out over the last few hours. One of the squad leaders had gone up the tunnel and stated that it was sealed at the other end. Cross that path when they came to it.

"Sergeant Green."

"Yes, sir?"

"Get the men fed and do a weapons and systems check. Cross load ammo. All the usual post-battle chores. By then I should have a handle on the environment and I'll give an operations order."

"Yes, sir."

Okay, one problem down. Just take them one at a time and everything would be fine. "Michelle, who is left in the command structure?" Mike tapped the configurable controls on his left forearm and pulled up a colorful schematic of the troop's energy levels. He took one look and winced. *Charge or die*, he thought with grim humor. *The Energizer Bunny we're not.*

"Major Pauley is currently in command of the remainder of the battalion."

"Okay, get me in contact. Where are they?"

"The unit has retreated approximately six kilometers in a direct line towards the MLR."

"What? Where is the cav?"

"The American cavalry units are engaged in a general retreat towards the MLR. They are at less than thirty percent of their nominal strength. In any other conditions they would be considered combat ineffective."

"Show me." The local schematic drew back until it showed a mass of red, broken directly above, but otherwise nearly continuous, in contact with a thin line of green. There were breaks up and down the green line but the landward portion was entirely open with a large gap to the rear and another small portion of green well separated from the remainder. The gap was opening and it was obvious that the red of the Posleen would shortly flank or encircle the beleaguered green armor units.

"He's still pulling back," said Mike, watching the ACS unit make another bound towards the dubious safety of the MLR.

"Yes."

"Is he in contact with higher authority?" the lieutenant wondered aloud.

"I am not at liberty to discuss communications with higher headquarters," said the AID primly.

"Great. Connect me."

"He is currently in communication. I will connect when he is available."

"Okay." Mike studied the schematic again, flexing his hand idly. The AID automatically adjusted the resistance of the glove to that of the torsional device he normally used. "Is that solid mass of red accurate or are there any clear areas?"

"The information is based upon a survey of visual and auditory sensors thoughout the affected areas. It is fairly accurate. I would recommend drawing further away from the edge of the battle area before emerging on the surface." The AID highlighted probable areas of low Posleen presence on the map.

"Well, where is the nearest sewage main?" Mike asked. "We need a way out of here." He stopped for a moment then did a double take. "Hey, how the hell did you find that out now but didn't know it before the assault?" he asked angrily.

"What do you mean?" queried the AID.

"When we were waiting for the Posleen assault the only information we could get was bits and pieces from the Indowy and the Himmit."

"You refer to the battalion intelligence briefing," said the AID.

"Yes," replied Mike, hotly.

"You never asked *me*," said the AID. Mike could almost hear the sniff.

Mike thought about the statement and had a sudden urge to just quit. It was moments like this that made him hate suits. If he was not in a thousand pounds of ceramet and plasteel with a three-inch-thick helmet he could do such things as slap his forehead, bang his head on the wall or, at least, shake it from side to side. As it was he just had to stand still as a statue as the adrenaline released by feeling like such an utter *fool* coursed through his system. He took a deep breath. Blowing it out created a tiny amount of back pressure in the small open area in front of his mouth. It was as close as he would come to tactile feedback.

"Michelle, are you filing continuous reports?" he asked tiredly.

"No, the unit is under emission control, local transmissions only." The suit local transmission system used directional pulses of monoperiodic subspace transmissions. The transmissions were traded in a distributed network from one suit that was in sight to another, shuttling through the group in the same manner as a data packet in the internet. Since the transmission simply jumped from one suit to the next, the power was a trickle and the likelihood of detection or interception was next to nothing. If a Posleen could detect the transmission, it meant they were already in the perimeter.

"Okay," sometimes the Posleen seemed to use direction finding, so it made sense. "Well, the first time we get in touch with higher, which will be soon, I want you to file a full report for me. Include that little tidbit. Now about the sewer lines?"

"There are no major sewer lines. There are toxic chemical dumping lines, but I discommend using them; over time they could damage your armor."

"Well then, how are we getting out?" asked O'Neal, puzzled. Michelle had clearly indicated that she had a plan.

"Through the water mains," said the AID.

"The system is sealed. If we break the seal we squirt out like grapes and getting back in will be a pain. Can we shut the water down?" he asked. Mike studied the schematic of the water system. The water flowed in from the ocean through processing plants along the shore. There plankton and minerals were separated from the water to be refined for further use and the purified water was pumped to the megalopolis. Although most of the products necessary for life were recycled within the megalopolis, significant quantities of water were lost in direct evaporation, thus the need for a tremendous resupply system. The tunnels flowed throughout the megalopolis, crossing and cross connecting into a continuous network.

"We cannot shut down the flow," answered the AID, taking the questions back to front. "The Posleen have gained control of the majority of the pumping systems between here and the sea and are in the process of installing their own hardware and software controls. In addition, even if we shut down the pumping stations, we would be faced with reverse flows from the various megascrapers."

"So how do we get through the obstacle?"

"I don't currently have a plan," admitted the AID, chastened.

"Well, neither do I. Cross that bridge when we come to it."

Duncan rubbed the sides of his helmet. The external oxygen monitor indicated that there was just enough O_2 for humans in the tunnel, but the platoon or so of troops would use it up rapidly if they took off their helmets. Which sucked, cause he really wanted a Marlboro.

"Gimme Sergeant Green," he said to his AID and looked at the new lieutenant. O'Neal looked like a fucking spastic, his fingers flicking in front of his armor. It was the same guy from Division; he had been around the battalion in the last month or so as they suddenly went into frantic training overdrive. It was stupid. There was no way the battalion was going to get ready in less than two months after pissing away all that other time on the ship; it was just window dressing. On the other hand, the training that Wiznowski had been bootlegging had really helped. He wished that someone had forced the colonel to listen to him; Wiz really knew his shit.

"What's O'Neal lookin' at?" he asked. He had found that all the AIDs were linked and sometimes he could peek in on what someone was doing with their system.

"I cannot access his system," the AID answered.

"What about Sergeant Green?" asked Duncan, kicking some of the rubble on the floor, the plasteel chips skittering away in the suit lights to flip off the jagged end of the tunnel.

"He is in conversation with Sergeant Wiznowski."

"Try to break in." He felt confident that they would let him in. During the trip his had been one of the first squads to be included in Wiznowski's secret training sessions and they had developed a good rapport.

"Yes, Duncan," Green asked, tiredly. The NCO's attitude had come around, but he was still an occasional pain in the ass.

"We got any word?" he asked. He could see the two NCOs at the other end of the tunnel. They were examining the blockage there, a trickle of water shining silver at their feet in the suit lights.

"Some, I was just talking to Wiznowski about that. The lieutenant says we're gonna get out of here through the water main. We need to break the troops down into squads. I want you to take seven, Bittan and Sanborn from your squad, and an engineer. I'm gonna give Brecker his own squad."

The names of the troops flashed up and the suits of the troopers scattered through the tunnel were highlighted. Duncan tapped one of the names and data began to cascade across his vision.

"Okay, can do. I got one question: does that fucker," he flipped a laser designator at the lieutenant, "have any idea what the hell to do, or are we gonna have to frag his ass?" The last was meant jokingly but came out harsh as the reality of the situation hit again. They were trapped under a hundred meters of fucking rubble and the surface was a hell of Posleen. Basically, they were fucked. And the officer appointed over them was a total unknown to everyone in the battalion.

O'Neal had stopped flicking his fingers and now stood like a gray statue. The light seemed be drunk by the camouflage skin of his suit. He suddenly shimmered out of sight then shimmered back in. The officer's suit was apparently performing diagnostics. Green turned his body toward Wiznowski and apparently carried on a side conversation for a moment. After a moment The Wizard raised his hands palms up, as if in resignation.

"Duncan," said Wiznowski in an unusually cold voice, "if you give that dwarf bastard the slightest problem he will frag *you* so fast it will flat amaze you. Briefly. Where the *hell* do you think I got my amazing level of training about everything in the world to do with suits?" The other NCO's snort carried clearly over the circuit.

"Oh," said Duncan. That amazing repertoire had been the subject of several discussions. It was assumed that he just had a better rapprochement with his AID. In every case of a question raised during the training it turned out that the AIDs had the information all the time. "How the hell did ... ?" he trailed off.

"Whenever we were training, O'Neal would sit in his cabin controlling the whole thing like a puppetmaster. Hell, half the time when 'Wiznowski' would answer the question it was O'Neal or his AID." The smile in Wiznowski's voice was evident. "He was even present plenty of times. All he had to do was tell your AIDs to not 'see' him."

"Damn."

"So," answered Sergeant Green, "yeah, the LT has his shit together. Now, why don't you pay attention to your fuckin' job instead of his, squad leader?" The NCO could be ascerbic when he wanted to be.

"Okay, just one more thing."

"What?" asked Sergeant Green.

"I figured out a way to get out of here, if the LT asks."

"Okay, I'll pass that on. Just out of curiosity, what is it?"

"Well, we could set up our personal protection fields behind us and pop that plug," he said gesturing at the pile of rubble blocking the tube. "That would flood this area like an air lock."

"Okay," said Sergeant Green with another look at the pile. "I'll pass that on. Now get your squad together."

"Roger, dodger," said Duncan, pushing himself off the wall. "I just hope the lieutenant knows what to do after that," he ended.

Sergeant Green walked to where Lieutenant O'Neal was standing. The featureless command suit shifted slightly, indicating that the lieutenant had noticed him coming.

"Sir," he said on a discreet channel, "can we talk?"

"Sure, Sergeant. I guess I oughta call you Top. But somehow I don't feel like the Old Man." The voice was precise with an enforced note of humor, but there was fatigue whispering in the background.

"I think we're both out of our depth, Lieutenant," said the NCO.

"Yeah, but we gotta keep treading water, Sergeant. That's why we get paid the big bucks," the officer said in an encouraging tone. Green was something of an enigma to O'Neal. He was not one of the NCOs involved in Wiznowski's training program so Mike had not been able to closely study his methods. He seemed, however, to be a very sturdy and capable NCO. He had better be.

"Confirm, sir. Okay, that's the trouble. The men know we're in deep shit, sir and I don't know a way out. There has been one suggestion but I think it is frankly flaky." Green told him Duncan's suggestion.

Mike nodded his head and briefly communed with his AID. "Yeah," he said, "I think that will work. Tell Duncan thanks, that's two I owe him.

"Get with him and have him experiment with it. We need to be sure before we put all our eggs in that basket. If it is gonna work, we'll start to move out as soon as I contact higher."

"Can you reach higher through all this rock, Lieutenant?" Green was happy to have the lieutenant in charge. He apparently not only knew his stuff, but was willing to use good suggestions. He had started talking to Wiznowski in the first place because Wiz was the official battalion expert. When Wiz told him where the expertise came from the lieutenant had gone up several notches in the NCO's eyes. He wondered how many of the company commanders had been in on the deception?

"Sure," said Mike easily, "these communicators aren't affected by line of sight. They're just stepping on the frequency."

"Yes, sir." The instant answer was another encouraging sign of the officer's expertise. "Okay, how soon on the mechanics, sir?"

"Soon. Do you think it would be better to move out, or to rest up then move?" Mike flashed the schematic of the proposed route up so that they could both view it.

"Is there anywhere down the line we could stop, sir?" asked the platoon sergeant, trying to decipher the three-dimensional representation. He should have been much more familiar with the symbology, but the lack of training with the systems was hampering him still.

"Probably." Mike flashed several possible stopping places.

"Then I'd suggest moving out as soon as possible, sir. The troops are on the ragged edge in here; if we don't get them somewhere more open they'll start to crack. And then there's the other problem."

"Roger that, Sar'nt, the weapons and energy." *Three hundred miles, hah! Seventy-two hours, hah! I told them to use antimatter!*

"Yes, sir, or the lack of weapons. Most of us don't even have a pistol."

"Well, right now we don't need them and later on we'll find some, don't you worry. What about the other group? Where are they?"

"Sergeant Brecker has eighteen men with him, sir, including two of the engineers. They were about two hundred yards away in another tunnel. They're mining their way here right now."

"When they get here we'll start work on the next phase. I need those engineers, but everybody will help."

"Lieutenant O'Neal?" his AID broke in.

"Yes?"

"Major Pauley is about to be available."

"Right, connect me. Sergeant, get the troops who aren't working on getting out of here mining towards Sergeant Brecker and his men. I have to talk to battalion."

"Yes, sir." The relief in the sergeant's voice was evident. He got started on cross mining to the other group, comfortable now that there was a clear mission.

✧　　✧　　✧

The chirp of connection cued him. "Major Pauley, it's Lieutenant O'Neal."

"O'Neal? What the hell do you want?"

"Sir, I am currently in command of the survivors gathered under Qualtren. I was looking for orders, sir." Mike watched the NCO leading a group across the scattered rubble. The first suit to reach the far side grabbed a piece of rubble and pulled it out. There was a prompt slide into its place and a section of ceiling fell out, momentarily trapping one of the other troops. With some hand motions and swearing on a side channel Green got the group to move more circumspectly.

"Who the hell put you in command?" demanded the distant officer.

"Captain Wright, sir," answered O'Neal. He was expecting some resistance but the harshness of Pauley's voice made him instantly wary.

"And where the hell is Wright?"

"Can I deliver my report, sir?"

"No, dangit, I don't want your dang report. I asked you where Captain Wright was." The panting of the officer over the circuit was eerie, like an obscene phone call.

"Captain Wright is irretrievable with what we have available, Major. He put me in command of the mobile survivors and put himself into hibernation."

"Well, the hell if any trumped up sergeant is going to lead *my* troops," said the major, his voice cracking and ending on a high wavery note. "Where the hell are the rest of the officers?"

"I am the only remaining officer, Major," O'Neal said reasonably. "There are one sergeant first class, three staff sergeants and five sergeants, sir. I am the only officer on site."

"I do not have time for this," spit the commander, "put me through to another officer."

"Sir, I just said that there are no other officers."

"Dangit, Lieutenant, get me Captain Wright and get him *now* or I'll have you *court-martialed*!"

"Sir," Mike choked. He began to realize that Major Pauley was not tracking well. The position of the retreating ACS battalion should have prepared him somewhat, but nothing could have fully prepared him. "Sir..." he started again.

"Dangit, Lieutenant, get those troops back here *now*! I need all the forces I can get! I don't have time to eff around with this. Get me through to Captain Wright!"

"Yes, sir," Mike did not know what to do, but ending this conversation would be a start. "I'll get the troops to your location as fast as I can and get Captain Wright to contact you as soon as possible."

"That's better. And put him back in command, dang you. How dare you usurp command, you young puppy! I'll have you court-martialed for this! Put yourself on report!"

"Yes, sir, right away, sir. Out here. Michelle, cut transmission." He thought for a moment. "Michelle, who is next in this rat-fuck chain of command?"

"Brigadier General Marlatt is MIA. That makes it General Houseman."

"Okay, who is left in the battalion chain."

"Major Norton and Captain Brandon are still in action and collocated with the battalion."

"Put me through to Captain Brandon."

"Left, left! Bravo team, move back!" Captain Brandon was maneuvering the remaining troops in contact on an open channel, usually used for platoon maneuver. Since from the map Mike was scanning Brandon was in command of fewer than forty troopers, it fit the condition.

"Captain Brandon."

"AID, partial privacy," said the captain quickly. "O'Neal? Is that you? I figured you were dead under your pyramid.

"Thanks for the cover," Brandon continued sarcastically, "unfortunately most of my damn company didn't quite make it out of the building!"

"That explosion was not the demolition charges, although they were detonated sympathetically," Mike began, lamely.

"Fine, now come up with some miracle to get us out of this nightmare! Or give me my damn company back!" the captain ended angrily.

"I have some of your troops down here, sir. We're going to start E and Eing out of here as soon as the rest link up. But, I just tried to report to Major Pauley, and, well, he was..."

"Babbling," Brandon said, flatly.

"Yes, sir."

"We know, thank you. Anything else?"

"Well,...", *go ahead*, he thought, *say it*. "What the hell do I do, sir? I'm... I'm just..." he bit back what he was about to say, "... not sure what course to follow, sir."

"I don't have time to hold your hand, O'Neal. Do whatever you think will do the most damage to the enemy until you can get back in contact. Take that as an order, if it helps."

"Yes, sir." Deep breath. "Airborne, sir."

"O'Neal."

"Sir?"

There was a short pause. "Fuck that shit about being a jumped up NCO, you saved our asses by dropping the buildings. Sorry about jumping your ass, it wasn't right. So, good hunting. Pile 'em up like cordwood, Lieutenant. That's an order." The officer's voice was firm and unwavering.

"Yes, sir," said Mike, unfelt conviction in every syllable. "Air-fucking-borne." *Vaya con Dios*, Captain.

"Now get off my damn freq; I got a war to run here. Alpha team! Position Five! Follow the ball! Move!"

30

Andata Province, Diess IV
0626 GMT May 19th, 2002 AD

As Mike whipped in the current, dangling like a lure on a trolling line, he really wished he had either been smarter, and had come up with a better plan, or stupider and had not thought of this one.

Once the improvised air lock was in place and area flooded, the next problem was how to move through the water mains. Between ongoing use in unconquered areas and unsealed breaches, the flow rate was high. An unencumbered person who is a good swimmer can only swim against three to four knots of current. The water was flowing past their location at what Mike judged to be about seven knots.

Mike had trained under water in battle armor, but never with a current. When he checked the flow going past at the first "T" intersection he experienced a sinking suspicion that his armor would not handle worth a damn, especially since the lack of power meant he could not "fly" the suit under impellers. He was still unsure what the mission plan would be, other than "to stack 'em up like cordwood" but he fully intended to see Diess' fluorescent light again, and soon. That meant getting out from under the zone of total destruction and the only way out from under the buildings was through the water mains, current or no current. Since swimming the armor was out, that left "rappeling" down the current. He worked out a route that flowed with the currents and would come out under a building three blocks away from Qualtren. Since the first principle of leadership was that you never asked someone to do something you would not do, Mike elected, over the protests of his platoon sergeant, to scout the first bound.

A line would be secured at the starting point by universal clamp and paid out with the scout, in this case O'Neal, dangling from it like a spider in the current. Waypoints had been determined, areas where there should be lower currents, and there personnel could be marshaled for the next bound. After the first bound, it had been agreed, other troops would take over the scouting duties. Once the line was emplaced the following troops would clip to the line and rappel to the waypoint.

The winch and line were built-in features of the suits. The winch was a bulge the size of a pack of cigarettes on the back of the suit and the line was thinner than a pencil lead. Designed for microgravity work they were rated to reel in a fully loaded suit against three gravities. On the other hand although the reel system and the universal clamp, a "magnet" that acted on a proton-sharing technology, had been extensively tested for full immersion, neither had been tested under heavy strain *while* fully immersed.

That lack of testing, since he had been the test pilot, was a personal indignity of the highest order. If there was any failure Mike had precisely *no one* else to blame. As he went bouncing off into the darkness he would be forced to curse only himself: designer, test pilot, user. Idiot.

For it was inky darkness his suit lights barely penetrated. Silt from breaks swirled through the tube and as he twisted wildly in the raging current the light swung randomly, illuminating for a moment then being swallowed by the turbidity. A moment's flash of wall, empty water, wall, opening, broken bits of plascrete from the shattered infrastructure, what was once an Indowy. The feeling of helplessness, swirling movement and flashing lights induced massive vertigo. He abruptly vomited, the ejecta captured and efficiently scavenged by the helmet systems.

"Down," he continued. "How much farther?" He would have looked, but he had to close his eyes for a moment. That made it worse so he opened them again and glued his eyes to the suit systems, checking the schematic just as the suit slammed into the wall. The heavy impact was more than absorbed by the suit systems and Mike hardly noticed.

"Two hundred seventy-five meters to waypoint one," answered the AID.

"Increase rate of descent to five meters per second."

As the descent rate increased, the swirling lessened, the suit moving at approximately the rate of the current. He started stabilizing himself, fending himself away the next time he swung toward the wall.

"Michelle, adjust the winch to maintain a tension of ten pounds regardless of rate of descent, up rate of descent to ten meters per second."

"Lieutenant O'Neal, if you strike a serious obstacle at ten meters per second, it could cause serious damage. Regulation maximum uncontrolled movement is seven meters per second."

"Michelle, I wrote that spec, and it's a good spec, I like it. But there are times when you have to push the specifications a little. Let me put it this way, what was the maximum gravities sustained by a mobile survivor of the fuel-air explosion under Qualtren?"

"Private Slattery sustained sixty-five gravities for five microseconds and over twenty for three seconds," answered the AID.

"Then I think I can take hitting concrete at an itty-bitty thirty or forty feet per second," Mike answered with a smile.

"Nonetheless, his suit systems indicate some internal bleeding," protested the AID.

"Is he still functioning?"

"Barely."

"'Nuff said."

Her silence was as good as a sniff of derision to Mike after so much time in the suit. He had amassed over three thousand hours before this little adventure and he, the suit and the AID were now a smoothly running team. This was again proven when Michelle started flashing an unprompted warning as the waypoint appeared. Restrained by her programming, she could not override his rate setting but she could communicate the need to start slowing down quite pointedly. He sometimes wondered where she had picked up so much personality. Most of the other AIDs he dealt with tended to be flat. He decided to tweak her nose a bit and let the rate setting ride until the last moment. Playing chicken with an AID, what would he do next?

As the waypoint loomed up through the haze he thumbed

the manual winch control. The descent braked to a stop just as Michelle intoned "Ahhh, Mike?"

"Gotcha," he laughed. Again the lack of response was pointed. The braking maneuver immediately started him spinning near the far side of the three-meter tube. He let out a few more feet and tried to "fly" over to the opening by twisting his body into a position used in skydiving called a "delta track." Essentially it forms the body into a self-directed arrow. Unfortunately, the external design of the suit did not lend itself to the maneuver and although he swung briefly toward the opening he just as swiftly swung back. He grasped the line and tried to swing toward the opening again, but the current and the geometry of the movement defeated him.

He finally stopped the spin by the simple expedient of switching on his boot clamps, universal binders again, locking his feet onto the far wall, and studied the problem. He had to cross three meters of water with every bit of physics working against him. Wait, which way was gravity? Well, it was perpendicular to the direction of movement, so that was no help. He slowly paid out the line until he was perpendicular to the wall on which he stood facing into the current. He deliberately stopped thinking about gravity again, and stretched his arms as far as they would go. No way to reach, he was way too short. What to do, what to do?

Suit boots. Damn. He released his right boot, stepped a foot sideways and reclamped it. Then the left boot. Step. Clamp.

"Lieutenant O'Neal?" sounded a concerned Sergeant Green a few minutes later.

"Yeah?" Mike puffed.

"You okay, sir?"

"Yeah," Mike grunted, fighting the physics of the situation was like carrying a boulder up a hill and the suit almost made it worse; the pseudomusculature had never been designed to side step against current. *My fault again.* "I'm almost to the first waypoint," he gasped. "Get the first team ready."

"Yes, sir."

Now he was climbing up the side of the slippery tunnel. The boots refused to slide, a tribute to the Indowy makers he decided, not the idiot designer, but getting them to clamp was noticeably harder. Finally he got a boot over the sill and with his right hand he clamped a binder onto the waypoint wall. Switching grips on the binder he rolled into the still waters of the side tunnel with a final grunt.

"No rest for the wicked," he rasped, sucking in oxygen and pulling himself up the wall. "Michelle, increase the O_2 percentage, please, before I panic."

"Say again sir?"

"Nothing Sergeant," Mike said, fighting a desire to tear off the armor and get a really deep breath. Of water. The increased O_2 level started to help the oxygen starvation. "I'm down. Recheck those binders and I'll clamp off on this end."

"Yes, sir."

"Send the next suck…ah, volunteer for the bound down first." Mike said as he clamped the end of the line to the ceiling. He let out a few feet of slack and then clamped his line to the wall, belaying himself into the tunnel. "I definitely need to brief him. This is not as easy as I thought it would be."

"Yes, sir," said Sergeant Green, with a chuckle. "I will tell you that you just made me fifty bucks. The betting was five to one that you wouldn't make it at all."

"Beg pardon. I designed these systems. I, at least, had total confidence in them." *In a pig's eye.* "It's just the last part that's hard."

"Ah, airborne, sir, whatever you say."

The rest of the move out of the zone of destruction was time consuming, but not dangerous. As the move progressed the line men discovered myriad techniques to overcome the flow. Notably, stopping before the occasional turn and walking through. After three more hours they reached a pump room four kilometers beyond Qualtren in the subbasement of another megascraper.

Ensuring that there were no Posleen in the area, Mike put the AIDs on guard and ordered the troops to get some rest. He, on the other hand, had to keep going. His problem was that although he had fifty some odd troops who, as soon as they got some rest, would be ready to murder anything with more that two legs, they were effectively weaponless. Their external weapons had been swept away in the explosion and only the few gunners with sidearms still had projectile weapons. On the other hand they each were carrying several thousand rounds of ammunition that used antimatter as a power source so there had to be something they could do. First he had to catch up on "the big picture."

Mike felt too drained to use the voice systems so he called up a virtual desktop. His first query reported the current overall battlefield. The schematic was far worse. There was now a second green line in contact with the Posleen mass. The primary defensive line the mobile units were supposed to hold the Posleen back from for twenty-four hours had been reached at twelve.

The mobile units, what was left of them, had been pushed to the sea and were encircled with their backs to it. Mike ran another query and watched as the perimeter withdrew, flickered and died. Eight hours. The same operational projection called for the primary defense line to break in eighteen to twenty-four.

Next he located the remainder of the 325th in reserve of the primary defensive line. The ACS unit had been the only mobile unit able to retreat fast enough to avoid being encircled. He did not bother to determine his new chain of command, he assumed that Major Pauley was no longer in command and that would make the new commander Major Norton. That was no improvement from his point of view. It looked on the map like the American unit had been grouped with, possibly under, the German unit.

The encircled perimeter of armor units consisted mainly of French, German and English units. The 17th Cav, farthest from the sea and with its right flank left vulnerable by the retreat of the 325th must have been rapidly eliminated. Shades of Little Bighorn. *It didn't have to happen this way.* The primary Posleen assault through the sector had been decisively crushed, literally, by the demolition of Qualtren and Qualtrev. With the reinforcement of the battalion, 7th Cav could have survived. If the oil had not detonated, shattering the battalion's morale and killing Colonel Youngman. It would have worked.... *And it could work again,* he thought. No weapons, but lots of explosives. We could break that encirclement. He started sketching out a battleplan.

"Michelle, see if you can get either General Houseman or General Bridges. I think we can pull this rabbit out of the hat, yet."

"Sir, First Lieutenant O'Neal, from the ACS unit is on the horn. He insists on talking to you."

Lucius Houseman was in no mood to talk to Lieutenant O'Neal at the moment. He could read maps just as well as the lieutenant and if he could not he had any number of staff officers ready to tell him what the morrow would bring. Once the mobile units trapped against the sea were finished off, the Posleen there would come after the primary defensive line in a serious way. It would be poorly defended without the support of the cavalry divisions destroyed by the retreat. He now had to agree with the lieutenant that the ACS unit had not been ready for combat, not that as a cavalryman he had ever had the liveliest faith in the damn airborne. But he also did not want to listen to O'Neal say "I told you so!" in any way shape or form.

He also had heard some rumor that the destruction of the battalion before the combat was even fully joined was because of some cockamamie plan on the part of the "expert" he had been saddled with. He considered for a full minute whether to take the call. His thinking, after twenty hours of watching his forces being destroyed piecemeal, was getting sluggish. He took a sip of tepid water from a canteen and considered his options. *I guess that is what I get for splitting my forces in the face of the enemy. We could go nuclear,* he thought, *it would give us a breather, push them back for a space.* Finally he nodded and the aide handed him the receiver.

"What do you want, O'Neal?" he snapped shortly.

"I can pull this out, sir."

"What?"

"We can still win this one, sir. I'm behind the lines with a half company of troops. We don't have any weapons but we have antimatter out the ying-yang." O'Neal was talking fast because he knew what he was about to suggest was not the way America played the game. But he also knew that if General Houseman thought about it he would see the truth of the battleplan.

"We can move to the area of the encirclement and drop the megascrapers right on the Posleen. All it requires is taking out about thirty critical supports and these buildings will fall. We can drop them on the Posleen and at the same time clear the way for the MLR. Probably we could cut a swath to the primary line and break the cav out, but at the least we could protect the cav units until they can be withdrawn by sea."

"You want to blow up *more* of these buildings? The Darhel are already screaming about Qualtren and Qualtrev!"

"Sir, with all due respect, two items, three really. One, the buildings are going to be lost anyway unless we go nuclear. Then it will be centuries before they can use the real estate. Two, it is not a political decision, it is an operational one. The Darhel have already agreed that we decide how to wage war. And, whereas I know that the United States Army prefers to limit collateral damage, sometimes it's time to just get down and do the dance, sir, hang the consequences. Any friendlies in there are dead anyway."

"Give me a few minutes to consider it, Lieutenant. How long to get from your present location to there?"

"About an hour, sir, the way I'm going to go."

"All right. I'll be back in no more than five minutes. Would the support of the ACS units in the reserve be useful, critical, or unnecessary?"

"I need weapons more than troops, sir. If you can get me weapons and detonators, I don't need more than another fifty troops."

General Houseman felt energy moving back into him, the crushing depression of the defeat evaporating. Whether he went with the option or not, whether they won or not, the Posleen were going to end up knowing they had been kissed, or his name wasn't Lucius Clay Houseman.

Three minutes and forty seconds later General Houseman was back on the line.

"I concur with your plan, Lieutenant. Your mission is to move with your unit into the area of the Dantren encirclement and to begin demolition of megascrapers in and around the encirclement with the primary purpose of reducing the pressure on the encircled units and secondary purpose of creating a window for the encircled units to withdraw to friendly lines.

"You may use any method and any level of force up to and including the use of significant quantities of antimatter. You are specifically charged to break the encirclement at any cost. I will call for volunteers from the ACS units in the reserve and will detach thirty-six troops in nine combat shuttles to attempt to make up a forlorn hope resupply run. I cannot at this time offer more personnel or equipment support than that."

"Thank you, sir," said O'Neal, his voice firm. "We'll move out as soon as I wake my troops up and give a frag order."

"Good luck, son, good hunting."

"Gary Owen, sir."

"Why you damn wind dummy! Only cavalrymen get to say that!"

"I can run faster than an M-1 and shoot an Apache out of the sky," said the lieutenant, quietly. "I am not infantry or cavalry, neither fish, nor fowl, nor good red meat, sir."

"What are you then?" asked the general humorously.

"I'm just the damn MI, sir."

"Well then, 'Footsack, you damn MI.'"

"Yes, sir. Out here. Michelle, platoon freq. Sergeant Green, start wakin' 'em up."

"Ah, Jesus, sir. We just stopped!" the sergeant complained.

"Sometimes you eat the bear, Sergeant, and sometimes..." He squeezed gritty eyes together and sipped stale suit water. They had been up since before dawn, fought a "murthering great battle," been blown up by a catastrophic explosion, tunneled out of hell, swum the Stygian depths and now had to go on after a ten minute stop. Well, that was what technology was for. "Michelle, order all the AIDs to administer Provigil-C."

The drug was a combination of a Terran antinarcolepsy drug and a Galactic stimulant. The Terran drug prevented sleep from forming. However it was believed that the stresses of combat were such that more than an antinarcotic was necessary.

When the powerful and persistent Galactic stimulant started coursing through their veins, the troops started to move. Some of them popped their visors to wipe gritty eyes and sniff uncanned air, but they were mildly surprised to find that the storeroom they had occupied was black as night. The AIDs had automatically been enhancing ambient light or using the ultraviolet suit lights for so long the troops had lost all sense of light or dark outside their private environments. The few troops who had sustained noncritical injuries, including the luckless trooper with only one hand and Private Slattery, now forever immortalized in combat suit statistics, were visited by the medic, more for human reassurance than because he could do anything the suits could not do.

Meanwhile Mike gathered the NCOs around and sketched out an initial order of movement. The engineers suddenly became critical to the success of the mission. Withal they could move nearly as fast as the infantry they supported, their armor was so bulged with storage they looked like walking grapes. Most of the storage was detonators and triggering devices. When it came down to it, there were lots of things that one could convince to explode, if one had a detonator and, although there were a number of ways to convince a detonator to explode, the best ways involved being far away at the time. So, rather than load up on explosives and light on detonators, they went the other way. They did carry twenty kilos of C-9, reduced somewhat from the tunneling, but it was a minor chunk of their storage.

The armor was circled with storage compartments, each designed precisely for explosives storage. The store points had blow-out panels and two of them had blown out on one of the engineers during the explosion under Qualtren; it gave him a lopsided look. Now they opened the compartments and started distributing their packages of good cheer. Every troop took fifty detonators and triggering devices. The triggering devices were fairly intelligent receivers that could be set to detonate by time or on receipt of a signal. In addition, the platoon redistributed their own C-9 so that each of them had at least a half kilo; that would be enough for their purposes.

The trickiest part was that they needed to move on the surface to the encirclement. There was not enough time to use the water mains. If they went that way the units would be dead and digested by the time they reached the area. Mike had a plan and he would have to overcome vocal and severe objections when he told them about it. His stock, however, had gone up since the first bound in the tunnels and especially when he led them to relative safety. Now they had to go back into the fire, but like troopers immemorial they faced that each as he needed to and got up and danced.

31

"Sergeant," said Pappas patiently, "I have had a long goddamn day. And I am not in the best fuckin' mood to handle bullshit. I have got a platoon spread to hell and gone and I need somewhere to put them up. I need transportation and quarters. What I don't need is bullshit from you."

He was actually glad to see that the company was maintaining a Charge of Quarters. The NCO in question was half out of uniform, had obviously been asleep when Adams found him and was being a pain in the ass, but it was still good to find. Now if he could only get the CQ to enter some vague condition of reality.

"I'm sorry, Sergeant," said the overweight NCO, mulishly. He waved the copy of their orders that Pappas had handed him. "This is not sufficient authority for me to allow your troops into the barracks. For all I know they might be forged." He looked at the gathered squads standing in the darkness.

The discussion was being held under the pool of radiance from a yellow bug light on the porch of a trailer, one of many in the area. Each of the trailers held a platoon. They were gathered into five trailers to a company. There were, in turn, five company areas gathered in a battalion area with a battalion headquarters at one end and trailers for senior NCOs at the other. The battalions were separated from each other by a street on one side and a parade ground on the other. The lack of lighting turned the whole mass into just another maze of buildings.

Pappas turned purple and started to throttle the stupid jerk

269

but stopped himself with difficulty. "You do realize, I hope," he said with a dangerously quiet voice, "that you are dealing with your new first sergeant?" The naked threat dropped to the floor like an anvil.

"Well," said the NCO in a priggish voice, "we'll just have to see what First Sergeant Morales says about that."

Pappas looked momentarily nonplussed. "You have another E-8 in the company?" he asked. It was not the information he had been given, but none of the conditions at Indiantown Gap matched any briefing he had received.

"Well," said the CQ with a slightly flustered expression, "Sergeant Morales is a Sergeant First Class," he admitted. "But he *is* the first sergeant of this company," he ended confidently.

Pappas simply looked at the sergeant for a moment. Then he put his hand over his eyes. *What did they do, dump a loony bin in here or something?* he thought. He leaned into the NCO's face then turned to the side. "I want you to look right here," he snarled, pointing at his upper arm. "I want you to count these rockers! How many do you count?"

"Three," whispered the NCO, all confidence fled.

"And how many does Morales have?"

"Two."

"Do you know what that means, you fuckin' pissant?" snarled Pappas, turning and putting his face right in that of the other NCO.

The sergeant's mouth turned into a wide rubbery frown and his eyes started to tear up.

Pappas' eyes widened. "Are you starting to *cry*?" he asked, incredulously.

A tear started to roll down the CQ's face and he gave a sob.

Pappas stepped back and looked heavenward. "God in heaven, why me?" he asked. "Where the fuck is the SDNCO?" he snapped.

"I don't know what that is," said the chubby sergeant.

"How the hell could a sergeant not know what the battalion Staff Duty NCO is?" asked Pappas. Then a thought struck him. "How long have you been a sergeant?" he asked.

"A month." The sergeant continued to snuffle, but the tears had stopped.

Pappas shook his head and continued the interrogation. "Is this the first unit you've been in?"

The sergeant nodded mutely.

"And how long have you been here?"

"Since April."

"*April!* You've been in the fuckin' Fleet six months and you made *sergeant*?!"

"Special circumstances, Top," said a voice from the darkness. A tall soldier stepped into the puddle of yellow light.

"You'd better stay out of this, Lewis," hissed the CQ. "Or you know what'll happen."

"Shut up," said Pappas conversationally. "If I want any more shit out of you I'll squeeze your head 'til it pops." He examined the soldier in the yellow light. His gray silks were neat and trim and he had a fresh haircut. He wore the rank of a specialist, but there was clear indication that another rank, probably the chevrons of a sergeant, had been in place recently.

"What special circumstances?" he asked. He glanced at the roly-poly NCO. "I mean...?" He gestured at the example.

"The company is a little short on NCOs right now," the specialist answered wryly. "Shit, the only thing we're not short on is trouble."

"I've got a load of new troops for the company," said Pappas, turning his attention fully away from the useless CQ. "I need quarters."

"You can't bring them in here," said the CQ, nastily.

Pappas finally lost it. He reached out with one hand and picked the overweight sergeant up by his collar. Without looking he slammed him into the door of the trailer then pulled him up until they were eye to eye. "I will tell you this one more time," he said icily. "If I hear one more word out of you that is not an answer to a direct question, I will personally frag your ass. Do-you-under-stand-me?"

The quivering NCO began blubbering but nodded his head in agreement. When Pappas let go of him he collapsed into a heap.

"I can take you to someone who can help," said Lewis, calmly. "It's not far."

Pappas regarded him thoughtfully for a moment then nodded. "Okay, let's go."

Lewis gestured with his chin at the quivering sergeant by the door. "Um, we might want to take him along." He paused and considered what he was going to say carefully. "Let's just say that there are people we don't want him calling," he concluded.

Pappas nodded at the logic. It was obvious that the situation in the company was substandard; surprising this Sergeant First Class Morales might be for the best. He did not even look around. "Adams. Handle it."

As he led the platoon off into the maze of trailers he shook his head in disgust. "Lewis, or whatever your name is," he said calmly, "maybe you could explain what the fuck is going on around here?" *Does anybody in the Fleet have a clue?* he wondered.

32

"First thing we do," said Mike on the platoon push, "we kill all the lawyers. But shortly after that, we gotta power-up."

"And we do that how, sir?" said Sergeant Green, immune by now to the vagaries of his abruptly imposed commander. It was bound to be harebrained, but on the other hand "it just might work!"

"Set the suits to search for power supplies in general; we'll scavenge as we go. As we move upwards keep an eye out for mobile equipment. They all use the same energy sources, they're usually on the righthand side in a green painted compartment and they look like large green gems. When they're fully powered up they glow brightly then fade as the power falls off. They'll fit in that secondary power receptacle on the rear right of your suit. When we find them, they get distributed to those with the lowest power levels.

"Also, look for very heavy machinery, like the stuff Captain Wright was trapped under. The power receptacles for those can be jury-rigged to bleed off to the suits. The problem is that the suits will recharge with a heavier draw than all but the heaviest machinery. Now, give the pistols and their ammo to the scouts. Put them on point and we'll move out.

"If we can't avoid a group of Posleen, charge 'em, concentrating on the ones with the heavy railguns. The light guns can't penetrate our armor so don't bother with them. After we take down the ones with the heavy weapons, we can finish off the rest like killing fish in a barrel. If we can, we want to completely avoid them, though, so move fast but quiet. Once we power-up, crank up your compensators, it'll cut down on that elephantlike thumping. We gotta be swift, silent and deadly. Okay, that pretty much covers it. Scouts out, follow the bouncing ball."

The four remaining scouts caught the grav pistols tossed to them and moved out of the door to the room, following a heads-up projection of a green will-o'-the-wisp ball, bouncing ten feet in front of them. The ball would lead them on without their having to constantly refer to a map. It was dim enough to not impair their target line and, of course, invisible to the enemy since it was a projection in their helmets. Wiznowski stopped just before exiting the maintenance area beyond their sanctum and tossed a small sensor ball into the next room. Satisfied by the take from the sensor he motioned the first scout through the door. Moving out of the maintenance area the scouts spread out through the manufacturing section beyond. Gigantic looms rose on either side, metallic forests of industry.

Mike tapped one trooper on the arm and gestured to a general-purpose lifter abandoned in the midst of a repair project. The trooper found a faintly glowing gem which he waved around triumphantly. It was passed to a third squad trooper with an energy readout blinking in distress. When the gem had been drained by the power receptacle his energy reading was still blinking, albeit slower, and the gem was dark and cold. Mike gestured and the trooper tossed him the discharged gem. If they ever found an opportunity the gem could be recharged.

Sergeant Green made a hand gesture at the looming machinery to either side but Mike shook his head and made a wide gesture indicating that it had to be much bigger. As they progressed towards the building core they twice stopped to let randomly looting groups of Posleen pass.

Although the platoon was hardly silent in its movement, between the suit systems and Michelle's tap on the security systems, they were able to detect the Posleen well in advance. When they neared the power plant, Mike called a halt. The scouts fell back as the platoon dropped into a perimeter. It was time for a council of war.

"All right, I want some opinions," Mike said on the platoon push. They were in a large open area, another storeroom, this time for some type of large parts. The shelving loomed three stories above them, and rank on rank of structures marched away into the distance. Mike tapped a command and all the enhancements changed to Posleen Normal. The light level dropped to nearly nothing. There was a distant illumination near one end of the warehouse, probably an office or entryway. Another command bypassed the ventilation system and adjusted the hearing to normal. The ring of suits around him was totally silent, the gray camouflage skins fading into the darkness making it nearly impossible to see them. There was a faint smell of organic solvents and ozone. There was no indication of any activity in the area but it never hurt to check with normal senses. He turned his sensor suite and ventilators back on and continued.

"I won't say that I'll take the advice but I will listen to it," he continued. "We are about five minutes away from this building's power station. We can get all the power we want there, but there are Posleen there taking it apart. It is still fully functional for our purposes but to take it means we'll have to fight and we may attract attention.

"Inter-Posleen communication is not fully understood nor is Posleen territorial activity in the immediate post-battle period. What that means is we may have two billion Posleen around us at the first shot. Or we may not see any.

"There are multiple exits and we can probably cut our way out but we may use more power than we gain. On the other hand, there may be no response, especially if we hit hard and quiet. Now, I want the opinion of the NCOs, most junior first. Sergeant Brecker?"

The young third-squad leader raised his hands palm upward. "I'm down to about two hours normal use, sir. And one of my troops is lower. We haven't scavenged enough to matter. As far as I'm concerned there's no choice."

"Sergeant Kerr?" First squad.

"Can we, like, redistribute the power, sir?"

"No, the suits can scavenge but not share, that's why I was distributing it on the basis of lowest power first. It's a subject there was a lot of technical debate about; ask me about it if we both survive. Basically, if you have an open power output, it can be tapped under certain circumstances. On the other hand, whether we live or die the technical report on this will go to

Earth and I'm sure this will tip the debate some other way. Too late to help us, however. So. What's it gonna be?" he asked.

"Attack, sir, no choice."

"Noted. Sergeant Duncan?" Second squad.

"Why not just go where there is heavy machinery, Lieutenant?" Duncan asked with a note of interest.

"It would take us about an hour, at our present rate of movement. Too far out of our way." Mike noted his tone. The council of war had more than one purpose, it was the first time he had conducted a two-way communication with his NCOs. He was learning a lot from their responses. "What's your vote?"

"Attack." The response was clipped but almost enthusiastic.

"Sergeant Wiznowski?" he asked.

"Kill 'em all, sir," said the Wizard with uncharacteristic savagery. "I don't think there's a choice and I wanna kick some butt."

At that there was a muted growl on the platoon net.

"Sergeant Green?"

"Go for it, sir."

"Right, I'm glad to have your opinions. We go for the power. Now, by squads, who has real experience in knife fighting, wrestling or serious martial arts? Oh, yeah, if you've *won* more than your share of bar fights. I want somebody to back you up, not just your word for it. Squad leaders, get that information on the squad push. Three minutes."

He watched in amusement as the squads broke up into gesticulating groups. He could tell by the arm movements that several of the troops were defending their personal brawling skills but when he switched on the exterior sound systems the only noise was the occasional foot stomp until one of the arguing troops banged a fist into his palm with a resounding clang.

"Second squad! Quiet!" snapped Sergeant Green, before O'Neal could say anything.

"Sorry about that, Sergeant," said Sergeant Duncan. It was only then that Mike realized it was Duncan who had made the noise. With a command to Michelle the name of each trooper was blazoned on them momentarily as Mike looked at them. Fifty-eight human beings depending on him to make the right decisions and he knew maybe six or seven of their names. Two minutes left, enough time to contact higher.

"Michelle, try to access General Houseman."

"I've got headquarters," she said after a moment. "General Houseman is on the way."

"Okay, thanks."

"You're welcome."

"O'Neal, what's your progress?" the general asked tersely.

"We're nearly out of power, General. We have to take a short detour to scavenge. It will push our ETA back by about an hour. On the other hand, we'll be able to move faster once we power-up."

"All right, it'll have to do. How are you going to get to the pocket?"

Mike told him.

"You're fucking crazy, O'Neal," the officer chuckled grimly. "Will it work?"

"No reason it shouldn't, sir. I can't analyze the likelihood of Posleen resistance, but we should be able to outrun organized resistance. The only thing I'm worried about is resupply. Any chance?"

"I'll punch out the shuttles whenever you're ready for rendezvous. I will tell you, there's gonna be casualties; those shuttles are sitting ducks for the God King vehicle weapons."

"I need the weapons more than I need the troops, sir. Keep the troops with you."

"I'd hoped you'd say that," said the distant general with a relieved tone. "I'm not sure I was going to renege, but the more I thought about it the less I liked it."

"Just load each of the shuttles down with ammo, rifles, grenade launchers and power packs and let us do the rest, sir. Send them on remote, for that matter."

"That's how we'll do it. Call me again when you have a rendezvous."

"Yes, sir."

"Out."

"'Kay, troops," Mike continued, Michelle automatically switching him back, "who's the lucky winners in the Diess Fantasy Lottery Drawing? Second squad?"

"Just me, sir," said Sergeant Duncan.

"I think I have a vague memory of you having some capability in this arena," Mike said with a chuckle. "Actually, thinking back about ten years I remember you having a punch like a mule. Glad to have you. Next, First squad?"

"Lyle, Knudsen and Moore, sir," said Sergeant Kerr.

"Sounds like a Minneapolis law firm."

"Yes, sir," chuckled Sergeant Kerr. "Well, Lyle and Knudsen both do kung-fu. I went to a couple of their tournaments, back when. They're okay. And Moore..." He gestured at an exceptionally large suit of armor standing next to him that the AID dutifully highlighted with "SP4 Moore, Adumapaya."

"...was obviously the biggest one in his class," finished O'Neal.

"Ah played some ball too, sah. Ah kin hold mah own," said the velvety bass.

"Righto, third?"

"Well, sir," said Sergeant Brecker, "none of us really fit the criteria, but I am coming. I wrestled in high school and I'm sure I can hold my own."

"I won't deny you, your squad needs to be represented. Scouts?"

"I'll go, sir," said Sergeant Wiznowski. "Just try to stop me."

Mike scanned the team's power levels and approved; all of them were in the yellow, but none of them were approaching failure. "Okay, here's the plan," Mike said, casting a map to each of the platoon members. "Scouts lead to the room second layer away from the power room," he said, highlighting it.

"Between it and the power room is a hallway, right turn, ten meters to the power room on the left. We check the hallway then the team moves to the door to the power room while the rest of the platoon stays in that location. Order of movement is Wiz, Moore, myself, Lyle, Knudsen, Duncan, Brecker.

"Wiz, down corridor security. The door reads as sealed on the building sensors. Moore, take the door, then down. I'll take out anything moving on immediate entry then Lyle, Knudsen and Duncan move past. I move. Wiz pull back and past. Moore move. Brecker, hold the door. I'm downloading the vectors of movement to your systems.

"The Posleen have removed or destroyed some of the sensors in the room so we don't have perfect intelligence on where they are. If one of you is rendered ineffective the vectors will automatically update. We'll move the rest of the platoon in on my command. At that time I will designate corridor security. Questions?"

"How many Posleen in the whole power-room area?" asked Duncan.

"About thirty," Mike said.

"Thirty?" Duncan choked, "and only seven of us?"

"Yes," Mike said, "magnificent isn't it?"

"Sir..."

"Can it, Sergeant. There is not time for debate. You may decline to be on the entry team at any time. It is totally voluntary," Mike waited for the response.

"Never mind," said Duncan after a few moments' thought. "I don't think it can be done, though, Lieutenant."

"Noted. Any other questions?" There were not.

"Scouts out."

The movement to the corridor outside the power room was successful, but when they reached the last corner there was a snag.

"There's a sentry," Sergeant Wiznowski whispered.

"That cans it," whispered Duncan.

"They can hardly hear us through the armor, Sergeant Wiz. And it hardly 'cans it,' Sergeant Duncan. I considered this. Okay, the rest of you hunker down and quiet. Quietly, team, line up." Mike dialed up his compensators and moved to the door. Fortunately there was a certain amount of masking noise from the roar of the fusion reactor in the far room. He studied the door for a moment to ensure it would open easily and popped his belly armor. He drew out the discharged power gem the soldier had given him and tossed it to get a good grip.

"Michelle, throw aiming grid. Left arm on automatic, visual targeting." He whipped open the door, stepped into the corridor and looked at the Posleen normal guarding the power room. "Fire." The pseudomuscles of the armor swiveled the left arm of the suit to vertical and delivered the one-kilo gem at two hundred meters per hour to the forehead of the Posleen. The centauroid dropped like the rock that hit him.

"Move." Wiznowski ghosted past him down the corridor and he fell in behind Moore. When Moore reached the door, Mike checked that everyone was in place, stooped, drew the dead Posleen sentry's palmate blade with his left hand and said, "Do it."

Moore took a half step back and threw himself through the door and down; his charge carried him several feet into the room. Mike was suddenly happy they had not charged in guns blazing as he realized he was looking at the primary cooling system of the fusion reactor.

"No grenades," he snarled as he picked out Posleen in view.

As each one came into view his AID popped a round out of his ready storage bin eject under the left arm and threw it with a Frisbee motion. The rounds were three-millimeter needles of depleted uranium. They arrived at the target at over one hundred meters per second with deadly precision.

There were seven Posleen in the room ranged neatly side to side with the exception of one almost directly in front of him that was masked. The five across the room from him were worrying over the primary coolant controls while the one to the left had just entered the area and the one directly in front was moving right to left. The moving one was targeted first. The teardrop of depleted uranium only weighed two ounces, but it was traveling at the speed of a .45 caliber round and struck dot accurate.

The teardrop entered the Posleen's crocodilian head at the juncture of the chin. It continued upward, passing through the cranial/spinal juncture and lodged in the rear of the skull. The neck of the Posleen squirted yellow blood as it began to fall, dead as a pithed frog. The three at the coolant controls were eliminated just as efficiently, dead before the first target had hit the ground. But the Posleen entering the room was a senior normal with improved reactions and weapons.

Mike grunted as a three-millimeter round passed entirely through his left leg, and flipped a round off-hand at the aggressive Posleen. It avoided his fire by diving for cover behind the secondary controls. Mike took out the last standard Posleen and bounced left while drawing his pistol. He did a gunslinger's toss, switching pistol and sword, still hoping to keep the noise and energetics down. He was not sure if there was a point; the hypersonic "crack" of the railgun rounds must have been heard throughout the building.

Suddenly the Posleen popped back up several feet from where he had gone to cover and three-millimeter railgun rounds caromed off Mike's heavier cuirass, smashing him backwards. Mike spun on his left foot, the impact of the rounds turning him around in a controlled spin, and released the blade. The three foot, mono-molecular blade whistled through the air and into the chest of the Posleen with the sound of an air lock closing. The Posleen stuttered for a moment, dropped the railgun and settled to all four knees, coughing yellow blood.

Mike yanked the knife out, kicked the rifle aside and took

off the Posleen's head to make sure. He checked the room but all the Posleen were down and his entry team had already spread out. The only thing left to do was set out on his vector.

Mike's self-appointed mission was to secure the outer flank of the sweep. He suspected that if there were an organized counterattack it would be from this direction and he preferred to handle it himself.

He started off with a limp, but his suit's biomechanical repair processes were already underway. The armor's auto-doc administered a local stun and jetted the area with quick-heal, antibiotics and oxygen. The inner skin of the armor sealed the area, reducing blood loss and pumping the leakage away to be recycled into rations and air. At the same time, nano-repair systems began the task of replacing the outer "hard" armor one molecular-sized patch at a time. Given enough time, energy and materials, the self-repair systems would completely heal even major damage.

As he got a better grasp on the size of the complex, O'Neal ordered the platoon to move to the cooling room, relieving Sergeant Brecker to begin a sweep. Three more times he ran into Posleen, but never more than one at a time and none of them with heavy weapons. The normals would fight gamely but with ultimate futility, their one-millimeter rounds from railguns and shotguns bouncing off of the suits with the sound of raindrops on a tin roof. There had been only one other enhanced normal and he had been finished off by Sergeants Wiznowski and Duncan. There were no casualties.

By the end of the sweep Mike was becoming exhausted by the strain of hours of combat. He stumbled back to the coolant room, where the engineers were happily plugging troopers into the power circuits. He joined the line and finally collapsed into one of the undersized Indowy chairs.

"What's the status, Sergeant Green?" he rasped. Why the hell he was so whipped under Provigil-C he had no idea. He had participated in the field trials and they were harder and longer than the tribulations so far. During the trials he had participated in seventy-two hours of virtual-reality combat and was fresh as a daisy at the end. It was like the Provigil part was entirely missing. They would have been better off taking a simple amphetamine.

"Only three more from the entry team to power-up." The sergeant's speech was slurred with fatigue also. "We found a store of energy gems and everyone's got at least one. We're twelve minutes behind schedule, even the updated one. No casualties in the entry team or elsewhere, and we picked up all the Posleen weapons. But, sir, the troops are scared and tired as hell, Wake-the-Deads or no. We have to rest sometime."

"This is the last break, Sergeant," O'Neal stated. His eyes started to close and he took a deep breath. *That damn Wake-the-Dead was supposed to be good for ten hours!* he thought. "We've got a mission to complete. When the last troop is recharged we're moving out."

"Sir, I think you should talk to higher about that. These troops are gone. I mean look at 'em," he gestured around at the suits collapsed against the walls. "You want to take these guys into battle? They need at least an hour's sleep. When you asked back under the building if we should rest there or later you implied there would be a later."

"There aren't a few hours, Sergeant, and there isn't any time to argue. Get the men moving."

"I don't think they can, sir."

"You mean you don't think they will."

"Yes, sir."

"Any suggestions?"

"No, sir, I don't know what to do about it."

"Will you go on?"

"I . . . yes, sir, I will, but I'm a career NCO. I'll charge hell with a bucket of water, just 'cause it's orders. These troops have just seen their whole battalion destroyed and their morale is shot. I don't think they will. I think they're beyond motivation."

"O, ye of little faith. Platoon push. Troops, listen up, here's the deal. Show schematic . . ." Michelle flashed the schematic on all the visors except the entry team members still hot-footing it back to the coolant control room.

"This is a map of the area," said Mike, highlighting some of the landmarks the troops might recognize. "You see that pocket of blue? Michelle, highlight—that's the remainder of the NATO armored forces and they're surrounded. We are going to relieve them." There was an audible groan of disbelief.

"They don't have a lot of time, so we have to get there fast. The way we are going to do that is unconventional. Did you notice up top that these buildings are close together? And all the roofs are at the same level? Well, they're all identical and close enough together for a trooper in armor to jump from one roof to the other. And that is just what we're going to do.

"We are going to go up to the roof and double-time from here to the pocket, jumping the gaps as we come to them. Then we are going to mine all the damn buildings around it and drop them right on the Posleen. Along the way I have been promised resupply of weapons and ammo," he continued into a sullen silence, "and we are going to make that rendezvous. It is as simple as that. Am I understood?" Sergeant Wiznowski, the last back, was sitting down to power-up as Mike's power-levels topped off. Silence.

"I said, Am I understood?"

"Yeah." "Sure." "Yes, sir."

Mike looked around at the gathered suits. The slumped postures clearly bespoke fatigue and resentment. "I asked if I was understood?"

"Yes, sir," the platoon responded tiredly.

"I'm sorry, my AID must be acting up," he said, twisting one finger against the side of his helmet, as if cleaning out an ear. Michelle helpfully transmitted a squeaking sound effect. "I can't HE-ar you."

"*Yessir!*" The general tone was angry for a change, which beat tired or mulish from Mike's point of view. Now to redirect the anger.

"Up until this moment we have been taking it in the ass," he stated. "I do not care for that, no offense to any of our sexually open-minded politicians. And whatever your orientation, I don't think anyone in this room cares for taking it in the ass either.

"Now, I personally promise you something," he said, his voice dropping to a malevolent whisper, "and in case you haven't noticed, I may be an asshole, but I get things done. And I keep my promises.

"This is what I promise, nothing more. We are going to stick this operation up the Posleen's ass, sideways. I guaran-fuckin'-tee that. I don't guarantee that any of us will be around to see it. That is not part of the bargain," he hissed.

"So, to do that, we are going to get up on our damn feet and go out and dance with the devil. We may lead, or we may follow. But we are gonna do the damn dance, am I understood?" he whispered.

"Yes, sir."

"God dammit, quit sounding off like a bunch of fuckin' hairdressers!" he shouted.

"*Yessir!*"

"*What are we gonna do?*"

"Fight?" "Get our asses kicked?" "Kick some butt?"

"We're gonna dance, sir," said Wiznowski, disconnecting from the power system.

"We are gonna *dance*. Now, what are we gonna do?"

"We're gonna dance, sir."

"Dammit..."

"WE'RE GONNA DANCE, SIR!" they sounded off.

"WHO'RE WE GONNA DANCE WITH?"

"THE DEVIL!"

"WE GONNA LEAD OR FOLLOW?"

"WE'RE GONNA LEAD!"

"DAMN STRAIGHT! SCOUTS OUT!"

33

Ft. Indiantown Gap, PA Sol III
0305 August 5th, 2002 AD

The officer and NCO accommodations were at the end of the battalion area opposite the battalion headquarters. The trailers were no different from those of the troopers, they just had fewer people in them. NCOs who were E-6 and under, staff sergeants and sergeant squad leaders, were quartered with the troops. Platoon sergeants, battalion staff NCOs and first sergeants, the senior noncommissioned officers, had quarters on one side of the area and the platoon leaders, company commanders and battalion staff had quarters on the other. The two groups were separated by a small quadrangle. The battalion commander had his own fancier trailer on one side of the quadrangle at the very end.

The intent of the setup was that the battalion commander and his staff would be forced to travel through the battalion area on their way to the headquarters, thereby forcing a daily cursory inspection of their battalion.

Unfortunately there was no battalion commander and very little in the way of staff. And, from the looks of things, most of the quarters were empty. Trash littered the area and most of the trailers showed some signs of damage; one of the trailers in the NCO section was completely off its foundations.

Lewis led them across the quadrangle and into a maze of trailers on the far side. As they entered the maze, Pappas noticed furtive movement on the edge of the area. Immediately afterwards a group of five or six looters burst out of one of the trailers and ran off into the night. The whole base seemed to be a mass of scavengers picking at the body of the beast.

Lewis finally came to a trailer indistinguishable from the others. He stepped up on the rickety stairs to the trailer, knocked on the door and stepped back. A moment later there was a shuffling sound from in the building. A window blind flickered as someone checked to see who the visitors were, then the yellow porch light clicked on.

The man who opened the door, .45 caliber pistol in hand, was tall and prematurely balding. He looked at Pappas then at Lewis and the CQ between two burly privates and raised an eyebrow.

"Yes?" he queried dryly.

Pappas saluted. "Lieutenant Arnold?"

The officer looked Pappas up and down, then cast his eyes over the squad following him before responding. "Yes." He returned the salute, permitting Pappas to drop his.

"I'm your new first sergeant, sir. Gun—Master Sergeant Ernest Pappas, reporting with a group of forty enlisted." Pappas was unsure what it was about the solemn figure in the doorway that was so unsettling. Although he was neither formidable in appearance nor even particularly fit, there was an aura of depth to him. He was older than the standard first lieutenant and had not received regen; that was part of it. But there was an immediate impression of humorful wisdom and caring in his light brown eyes. Considering the obviously screwed up condition of the company, it was hard to believe this officer was the acting company commander.

The officer regarded him for a moment longer then a broad smile split his face. "Samoan?" he asked. There was a slight note of glee in his voice.

It was the last thing Pappas had expected out of his mouth so he simply nodded.

"Are you trying to tell me," the officer said with the beginnings of a chuckle, "that the Fairy Godmother Department," he continued, obviously having a hard time controlling his laughter, "has seen fit—" he broke off to choke on a deep laugh.

"*To send me a marine! Samoan! First sergeant?!*" he finished with a shout of joy.

"So that's the situation Top," said the lieutenant, watching his new first sergeant for a reaction.

They were in the kitchen of the Bachelor Officers' Quarters for Bravo Company 1st Battalion 555th Infantry. The "Quarters" was a sixty-six-foot trailer subdivided into four single rooms with a shared kitchen, living area and bathroom. The rooms were the approximate size of a walk-in closet and the sole light fixture in the kitchen was an overhead outlet that had arrived sans cover.

The acting company commander was sharing these munificent quarters with the company's sole additional officer, the leader of first platoon. That worthy along with Michaels and fourth squad had been harried off into the night with the almost impossible task of securing transportation for the first squad and baggage at the front gate.

Arnold tried to read the mind of the veteran NCO, his face an expressionless mask in the yellow light of the exposed bulb.

Pappas, meanwhile, was trying to figure out how to get his ass out of a cleft stick. Everything would be fine if he had the backing of the commander, but if Arnold played it light things would get sticky.

"Let me see if I've got this straight, sir," he said carefully. "You just got here five days ago. The other El-Tee, Richards?"

"Rogers."

"...Rogers got here two weeks ago. Until then the company was being run by this Sergeant Morales?"

"Yup."

"And, might I ask your personal evaluation of the ability of this Sergeant First Class Morales?" Pappas asked carefully.

"Well, Gunny," said the officer with a note of precision in his voice, "I try not to have personal evaluations. I prefer everything to be aboveboard and out in the open. Might I add that thus far Sergeant Morales has managed to avoid turning over to me document one on the state of personnel training, counseling, leadership skills or, for that matter, the company's inventory. Every time I ask him about it there is another set of papers to shuffle that are much more important."

"Oh," said the NCO and blew out his cheeks. That settled that hash. There were to be no "unofficial" actions taken in regards to the House That Morales Built. "But," he paused. Saying the next thing could very well get him into trouble. But there were loose ends to tie up. "Well, sir, why haven't you already called him to heel?"

"And then what, Sergeant? Sergeant Morales has had six months to sew this company up. All of 'his' people are in the key positions. Anyone who disagreed with him during those six months, such as

Lewis, has been stripped of rank or rotated out to another unit. The door to his office is locked, deadbolted, and he is apparently the only one who has a key. And he has numerous meetings that he has simply *had* to attend over the last week." The frustrated lieutenant paused and ran his hand over his buzz-cut hair.

"And then there was the whole problem of what to do about it," he continued, meeting the eye of the somber NCO. "Let us say that I got up on my high horse and insisted that he hand over the documents forthwith. And let us say that he did. And let us imagine that, between the drying lines of newly set ink," he said, with a wry grin, "that I found clear evidence of missing inventory, falsified administrative punishments, what have you. What then, Top?"

Pappas had never been down this precise path before but he knew the general regulations. He pulled a Skillcraft pen from his breast pocket and started to scratch his head with it. "I guess you would call the battalion commander, sir, maybe the IG, for a full investigation. If there's major evidence of a crime or crimes, maybe call the MPs or the CID."

Arnold smiled tiredly and glanced at his watch. "Well, I think we don't have a lot of time to discuss this, since you, or I now rather, have a platoon scattered to hell and gone and some housecleaning to do. So I'll keep it brief. There is no battalion commander."

Pappas stared at him in perplexity. "Sir, even with missing officers and NCOs there is still a chain of command," he said definitively. It was a Rock of Gibraltar to the military. There is always a chain of command.

"The battalion commander is also the Charlie company commander. For all practical purposes that is all he is. Captain Wolf is hard at work keeping his company together. There is no 'brigade' commander because although we are a separate combat regiment, we are effectively three separate battalions; there is no regimental commander or even regimental staff. The next actual commander in the chain of command of this company, after Captain Wolf, is General Left at Titan Base."

"Oh, shit," whispered Pappas.

"You think perhaps I should call him? 'Excuse me, General Left, this is Lieutenant Arnold. My first sergeant is being mean to me and I don't know what to do.'" The officer smiled again.

"There is *one*, count 'em, *one*, field grade Fleet officer on the east coast, Major Marlowe, the S-3 and acting battalion commander of Second Batt down at Fort Jackson. I called him day before yesterday. He stated that he understood I had a problem, that he had so many he couldn't begin to count them, and that I was on my own until my own battalion staff started to show up. The 'Triple Nickle' is the last ACS unit to be formed from American units. It is last in line for equipment, it is last in line for training and, especially, it is last in line for personnel."

Pappas was shaking his head. Not in disbelief, but rather in horror. "I didn't know we were that fucked up."

"Believe it, Sergeant. I can't believe you got rejuvenated. You are definitely one of the lucky ones. Over four million enlisted personnel have been recruited and trained in the last year. But," he smiled and threw up his hands, "because the Galactics ran out of rejuvenation drugs, only five percent of the positions designated for majors, lieutenant colonels and full bird colonels have been filled.

"There was an article in the *Army Times*," he continued, "on the filling of unit positions. Only three percent of the combat arms and combat support brigade and lower positions are filled."

"Ouch!"

"The same thing goes for the equivalent enlisted ranks. Congratulations by the way, you are the acting battalion command sergeant major." He paused and ran his hand over his hair again.

"So, Smaj, where should I go? Oh, the CID and MPs. In case you didn't notice, there is something very like a war going on out there," he gestured with a thumb out into the darkness. "The MPs patrol in squads. At night they stay in their armed Humvees and the Humvees stay in reaction range of each other. A cantonment of this size would normally have an MP battalion. We have a company. We should have a platoon of CID, possibly a company. We have three personnel. Less than a squad.

"So," Lieutenant Arnold smiled with grim humor, "as I said before, goddamn am I glad you showed the fuck up."

"What would you have done if I hadn't?" asked Pappas.

"Braced him, probably tomorrow or the day after."

"And then what?"

"I'd probably have been dead by morning," the officer answered with complete seriousness. "Four personnel in this company who were sergeants and above are officially carried on the roster as deserters. I overheard one of the men say that they did not want to end up like Sergeant Rutherford," he smiled grimly once again.

"I think I was supposed to overhear it. One of the first pieces of paperwork the operations NCO gave me was the record of desertions. Losing a staff sergeant with eight years in the Army Airborne and a chest full of medals stands out."

Pappas shook his head. "Fuck, sir. It's the seventies all over again."

The officer wrinkled his brow. "What?"

Pappas shook his head again and took another scratch. He dusted the resulting dandruff off the table. "Never mind, sir. Way before your time." He thought for a moment and glanced at his own watch. "When does Morales usually show up?" he asked.

"He usually manages to roll in by nine," the lieutenant said with a chuckle. "Officially he does 'solo PT.' The one remaining staff sergeant handles the formations. Sergeant Ryerson is probably all right, he's just learned to keep his head down and his eyes shut. I don't know about the CQ, though, he might have tried to contact Morales."

"Well, sir," Pappas said glancing at his own watch, "in that case maybe you could come on over to the barracks with me. I need you to verify the fact that I am now in the chain of responsibility. After that you can just sit back and watch. Sir."

"Oh, with pleasure, Gunny," said the acting company commander with a tight smile. "And I think we will make a stop by the Arms vault," he continued, the smile going quite feral. "It only responds to properly coded individuals. Morales was never coded for it and he has been asking me for my codes for the last week."

"Weapons, sir?!"

"We don't have suits yet, but we've already received our full supply of weapons. M-200 grav rifles, M-300 grav guns, terawatt lasers, mortars, grenade launchers and a basic load-out came in one package including the vault." The lieutenant smiled tightly again. "If I had to brace him this week, I was preparing a coup de main with certain elements of the company. As it is I'm glad to have you aboard; it would have gotten messy. We need to hurry. I doubt he knows you are here yet, so do you think we can do this without a full Operations Order?" he finished with a wry grin. His eyes were somber as he slipped his silks top on over the holstered .45.

"Aye aye, sir," said the gunnery sergeant grimly, standing up and heading for the door. "Semper fuckin' Fi. *Adams! Front and center!*"

34

Andata Province, Diess IV
0821 GMT May 19th, 2002 AD

I think I should have waited to motivate them until now, Mike thought. Diess' rising primary cast a fierce green fluorescence over the tableau on the roof. Fifty-eight sets of combat armor were planted at various distances from the edge of the roof, some of them slightly crouched as if trying not to face something. One was parked right on the edge. The roofs could be seen stretching in a continuous checkerboard from the inland mesas to the far green sea. In the extreme distance to the west Mike noticed some breaks and of course there was the missing set against the mesa, the fallen Qualtren and Qualtrev. Almost the length of a football field away was another megascraper roof at the same level.

"How far away is that megascraper, Sergeant Wiznowski?"

The NCO focused his range-finder crosshairs on the far wall and confirmed his rough guess. "Seventy-two and a hair meters, sir," he answered, reading off his Heads-Up-Display.

"And do you happen to know the maximum jump range of a Warrior Combat Suit?"

"No, sir, sorry, sir."

"Right, well it just so happens that the maximum jump range in the specifications we called for was one hundred meters for warriors, one twenty for scouts and one fifty for command." Mike crouched and whispered an order. His suit rolled backward over the mile high drop and sprang outward. In apparent defiance of gravity it shot out and over in a back flip and landed neatly on the far roof. He then sprang back, landing with a thump in their midst.

"Sergeant Wiznowski, I want you to take a running jump to the other roof..."

"Uh, Mike, sir..."

"You can do it, Wiz. If I can, you can. Back up a couple of hops, take a running jump at it and as you jump, tell your suit to jump. Do it." His visor faced that of the NCO, two blank surfaces, armor unreadable. He wondered what was going through the mind of the scout at that moment. Wiznowski had always been the consummate airborne NCO, brave to the point of suicide. Now he apparently was facing a challenge he was not fully prepared for. "Do you want me to jump again?"

"No sir, I'll do it." The tall suit backed up from the group and ran at the edge. There was total silence on the net as he reached the edge and whispered, "Jump." Again, the suit soared upward in defiance of gravity and common sense. This time with his additional speed, far greater than an unarmored man, he soared far onto the roof, almost a hundred meters from the edge.

"That was a little excessive, Wiz. I said we spec'ed them for one hundred and twenty meters; it turned out to be a bit better than that." Mike bounded farther into the roof to get a running start. He said, "Michelle, command run and maximum jump, execute."

The legs of the suit began to blur. In the hundred meters from his position to the roof's edge it accelerated to over one hundred kilometers per hour in a series of ground-devouring bounds. As the boots of the suit came in contact with the roof, a grappling field would engage to prevent slippage, therefore maximum energy was applied to each thrust. When he reached the roof's edge the suit's AID automatically launched him into the air. Under the combination of forward momentum, his inertial compensators' contragravity function, and thrust from the inertialess thrusters built into the suit, he was carried over two hundred meters onto the far roof. With a return series of bounds he reached the edge of the roof and bounced effortlessly back to the platoon.

"Of course, this is a prototype command suit, not an issue one. Quite the thing, actually. But a suit can take a gap like this without breaking a sweat as you should all know. Powered suit drills is what your jobs are all about now; if you goons had ever been given proper training we wouldn't be having this conversation.

"We will move out in an extended watch formation, twenty meters between personnel, thirty meters between squads, scouts forward leaning left. *If* somebody misses the jump, the team falls out and recovers them using their winch system. If you miss the jump, don't worry, your suit will automatically hit the anti-grav and your momentum will carry you to the face of the building. Use the universal clamp in your palm pad, clamp to the wall and wait for your buddies to recover you, or climb up hand over hand for that matter. The first rally point is the resupply rendezvous and we don't need everybody there at first so if somebody misses, that troop's team drops and only that team drops, everybody else drives the fuck on, is that clear?"

"Clear, sir."

"If we take any fire from Posleen, those with weapons take them under fire. Kick their ass, don't pee on 'em. Lay down all the fire you can and blow the fuckers away. We do not want to get held up on these rooftops without weapons.

"Now, just to get the feel for things, we'll drop back and start moving forward across the roof as a platoon, not a cluster fuck, right?"

"Yes, sir!"

"Sergeant Green!"

"Yes, sir."

"I want to take this at a long slow lope."

"Yes, sir."

"All-righty then, move out." The platoon moved back, slowly, and the NCOs got it sorted out. With the men in position, Mike got his headquarters' squad, effectively Sergeant Green and the engineers, in place, right rear, and hollered, "Move 'em out!"

The scout team started forward in long bounding strides and the platoon, spread over nearly a half kilometer, perforce bounded out behind them. As they neared the edge Mike consulted with Michelle.

All of the scouts took the jump without a hitch and when several of the regular troops, naturally, balked, the suits overrode them and jumped anyway. As they crossed the next building, still without opposition or even harassing fire, the troops began to get into the rhythm of the run. Runners all, as any soldier had to be in the modern airborne, the comforting rhythm of a light run was an anodyne to their nerves and the speed and distance involved a boost to their ego. Mike gave it a few more minutes then cranked on the tunes. Suddenly, from each troop's AID, the

Pat Benatar song "Legend of Billy Jean" started to play. "Benefits of not having to be tactical," he commented to Sergeant Green.

> *"We can't afford to be innocent,*
> *Stand up and face the enemy*
> *It's a do or die situation*
> *We will be Invincible.*
> *And with the power of conviction*
> *There is no sacrifice*
> *It's a do or die situation*
> *We will be Invincible."*

As the kilometers passed with no Posleen in sight, the songs continued. Seventies rock, alternative, raker rock, turn fusion, heavy metal. Many of the songs emphasized the ephemeral nature of life and the importance of honor and courage, or at least resignation, in the face of inevitability. If the troops objected to the playlist there was no evidence, just a susurrant hush of breathing, each troop lost in his own thoughts. As they neared the rendezvous, a megascraper about three "blocks" or six kilometers from the encirclement, Mike cut onto the platoon push, breaking into a live version of "Don't Fear the Reaper."

"Okay, hold it up in the middle of this next building, cigar perimeter, personnel with weapons on the outside," he said, looking around the empty rooftop. "We're supposed to be meeting our resupply here."

"Mike," said a puzzled Wiznowski on a side frequency, "what's that?"

In the east, towards the distant line of human resistance, a fireworks display had suddenly erupted. "Michelle, enhance."

Lines of fire were blasting upward from the break between two buildings. Hypervelocity missiles and other kinetic energy weapons along with lasers and lines of plasma reached up to the heavens. Suddenly the broken body of a combat shuttle, gloriously aflame, burst into sight above the intervening buildings. It was followed by six more, one twisting off, crippled, just as the shuttles reached the dubious safety of the air over the megascrapers. One crested too high and a plasma bolt that would do credit to a space cruiser slapped it out of the air. The fire penetrated its antimatter containment field and it exploded with the sun-bright flash of nuclear detonation, destroying the upper portions of the buildings to either side and forcing one of the other shuttles off course into a roof.

The platoon's visual sensors automatically screened the optical overload. "Damn! There goes half our ammunition," cursed Sergeant Green as the debris of the buildings crashed down all around.

"More likely a third," contradicted Mike just as a half dozen Posleen God Kings in their saucer-shaped craft swooped upwards in pursuit of the shuttles. His mind slipped into razor sharp fugue, every detail diamond clear. "*Platoon, down! Activate deception systems!*"

As the suit careted the Posleen, Mike's pistol locked onto them automatically. The God Kings were concentrating on the undefended shuttles and Mike's first silvery burst swept two of them out of the sky from three kilometers away, one of the vehicles disappearing in actinic fire as the relativistic teardrops searched out its power supply. He hopped sideways and dropped as the remaining vehicles' targeting systems slewed the God Kings' weapons onto his location. A hurricane of fire swept his former position, but he took out another from his kneeling position. Two of the remaining Posleen went back to attacking the shuttles as one swept towards the platoon's position.

The suits were doing a good job of mimicking the top of a building in every frequency so the Posleen thought there was a sole human to deal with. Mike missed the rapidly dodging craft with his next two shots and, in a series of wild jumps and somersaults, dodged three bursts of plasma, one of which cooked the external sensors on his right side. The Posleen was moving in at over three hundred kilometers per hour swerving crazily from side to side. Michelle tossed the suit to the side under thrusters as another burst of plasma passed through the space he had just occupied. Mike tumbled over onto his back and was trying to fire upward, an awkward position in a suit, when he was suddenly covered with the flaming wreckage of a God King's saucer.

"Sucker figured he had you bagged, sir," said Duncan, holstering the pistol borrowed for the sweep, "so he finally stopped flying all over the sky."

"Thanks, Duncan," said Mike, rolling to his feet. "Little too close, that one."

"Just a little walk in the mornin', sir."

"Airborne. Anybody see where the other God Kings or our shuttles went?"

"Negatory, sir," said Sergeant Green. "Nothin' in sight."

Two remaining shuttles suddenly popped up to the west, still relentlessly pursued by the God Kings. The personnel with pistols or captured Posleen weapons, having recovered from the shock of the attack, opened up on them. One more shuttle crashed after taking plasma fire but the God Kings were both dead moments later. The last shuttle banked towards the platoon's location and nosed up to a landing in the center of their perimeter. Its back door dropped immediately.

"Okay, first squad, inside, grab what you need and then back out! Move it! Sergeant Green, handle the distribution, the shuttle should have an inventory."

"Roger, sir," the NCO headed for the drop-door as the first squad lined up for weapons.

"Posleen!" called one of the troopers on the perimeter. Sun bright nicks of ricochets began skipping off the shuttle's armored skin. Mike looked seaward towards the source of the fire. A group of Posleen normals had gotten up onto the roof of the far building and were firing toward the shuttle and the platoon grouped around it.

"Spread it out!" He noted that first squad had hardly ducked getting to the shuttle. "Fire dammit!" He slapped a fresh magazine into his pistol and demonstrated, tumbling several of the distant horse-figures. The personnel with captured Posleen weapons began firing.

"I'm hit!" screamed one of the troops, followed by a bemused, "I thought I was hit." He sat on the roof looking at his thigh. "Am I hit?"

"You're hit," said Mike, belatedly falling to a prone position. "Everybody get down, dammit. Don't sweat it, your suit will take care of it."

"Second squad!" bellowed Sergeant Green.

"Fire from the west!"

"God Kings from inland!"

"Expedite this, Sergeant Green! First squad, concentrate on the God Kings!" Suddenly one of the second squad suits headed towards the shuttle began doing its death dance. As the suit tumbled it knocked aside others in the squad. They started to try to catch the suit, but it suddenly stopped and was still.

As they began to open the suit, Mike snapped, "*Do not pop his suit!* In case some of you have never seen that, Private Laski is *not* recoverable. Sergeant Green?!" Mike opened fire on the approaching God Kings.

"Third squad!" Sergeant Green bellowed, by way of answer.

Wiznowski suddenly bounded out of the shuttle and off to the west; Mike had hardly noticed him fall back to it. The lighter and faster scout began firing at the approaching God Kings with an HVM launcher. He moved around the rooftop like a hyperactive flea. The fire of the four new God Kings angled in on him as he ran, stopped, jumped and dodged to avoid it. From time to time he would stop just long enough to fire off a hypervelocity missile.

"Wiz! Dammit, quit trying to be a hero!" Mike shouted, triggering another burst while bounding forward in support. "Get your ass back here!"

"If you wanna dance, sir..." the scout panted and was washed away by a God King HVM.

"Wizzz!" Mike screamed and leaped to his feet.

"*Fuckers!*" He reloaded and started running towards the God Kings. "Michelle, evade pattern Gamma, maximum run, broken field automatic, execute!" Now all he had to do was reload and fire and he slammed in magazine after magazine as he closed on first four and then three and then two saucers. The God Kings' fire flailed around him uselessly as they closed the distance.

The suit dodged in a random zigzag pattern as he maintained constant positive traction through the suit boots, the occasional hit by a railgun round shedding like water. A hundred meters out a laser briefly washed his suit, but with the exception of frying a set of sensors, it was not in contact long enough to do more than raise his temperature.

He closed the final distance to the last God Kings at an oblique as their saucers slewed, trying to track the frenetically dodging combat suit. Like a weasel Mike leapt on the offside saucer and, taking the God King's head in his gauntlet while planting his boot on its shoulder, ripped the sauroid head off clean. At that the other God King swung his saucer around to run but Mike flipped the palmate blade off his back and hurled it entirely through its thorax with all the rage in the world.

Then he bounced over and whacked the other God King's head off. He stepped down off the faltering saucer and collected both heads. Tossing them a distance away, he drew his pistol.

A burst of fire into the energy pack of the nearest saucer devoured the vehicle in a shattering explosion. He rode out the explosion as if it were an epiphany, staring into the fire like a soul in hell. There was no danger; the suits could shrug off any explosion short of the sort of cataclysm that struck Qualtren. And even then they could give it a run for its money.

He next turned his scorched pistol on the far God King's vehicle, devouring it as well. Then he kicked the vehicles over one by one, pulling all the pieces of the God Kings he could find out of the wreckage. He made a pile, hopped up and down on it until it was flat, piled it back up and put an antimatter grenade in the resulting mass.

He set the timer, stepped back and watched the last remnants of the two God Kings blown sky high. Then he picked up the nearest saucer and hammered it into the roof until the roof was massively holed and the saucer was junk. His rage sated, he picked up the two heads by their crests and flew his suit back to the platoon.

By the time he returned the other fire had slackened. Those had been the only God Kings so far in contact and the normals were ineffective except in overwhelming numbers. He thrust the fresh heads at the first trooper he encountered.

"Go put these on Sergeant Wiznowski's smear," Mike snarled. The paratrooper hurried to obey.

"I swear before all the gods," he said to himself, but Michelle faithfully broadcast it, "that samadh will grow beyond all measure."

He stared off toward the ocean, without thoughts, avoiding recent memories. Immured in his armor, he had killed soldiers under his command in numbers beyond count, but every one of those was a mere electronic chimera. For the first time he had lost actual human beings, living breathing entities with whom he had established a bond.

The sudden intrusion of reality into his highly developed notional world of bloodless combat was momentarily stupefying. He shuddered in his armor, conscious for perhaps the first time that these were not shadows on the wall of some electronic cave, but people who had hopes and dreams. These were people whose mothers carried them for nine long months, the trail of their lives leading to a barren rooftop under a sun not their own.

As the platoon consolidated and checked equipment, he stared off into the distance in a moment snatched from eternity, infinite and finite. Unnoticed, one of the engineers connected new auto-grenade launchers and filled his magazines. Finally Sergeant Green broke into his reverie.

"Sir?"

"Yes, Sergeant Green."

"We're ready to move out."

"Thank you." Duncan handed him a rifle. Mike checked the magazine then checked that his store was still in place. He noticed he was still staring off into the distance. He was loath to move.

"Sir?"

"Yes, Sergeant Duncan."

"We *need* to move out."

"Yes, I suppose we do." He still hesitated. Something vital was missing, the drive that usually carried him through the tough times. If they hit a tough spot without it, it might mean all their lives down the toilet. He hunted around for it, but the house in his soul where it lived seemed to be empty. That particular mask was in hiding.

"Michelle," he said wearily, "download coordinates of all destruction points.

"Platoon, mission order." O'Neal's voice was an emotionless monotone. The team might have been taking their commands from a non-AID computer. "Consolidated platoon, second battalion three twenty-fifth infantry battalion will perform a covert insertion of the megascrapers Daltren, Arten, and Artal. The platoon will separate into designated two- and three-man teams. Each team has a series of points that they either will directly destroy or lay charges upon.

"Once all the charges are laid and all the primary points are destroyed, the unit will pull out of the buildings then destroy them." As he spoke the troopers drew in around him. The action was tactically unsound: one lucky burst by a God King laser could have gotten them all. But the platoon was reacting to the deaths of their fellows much as Mike was and each of the soldiers felt a need to feel part of a group, a need for touch and feeling. The suits created a strong emotion of alienation through their control of every sense. Moments like this were a slice of humanity bitten on the run.

"Subject megascrapers should drop in an L shape leading from the ocean and curving around the trapped units. That will leave those units free to concentrate on pushing out of the encirclement towards the friendly lines. This is the good part, people: the major mass of Posleen on this whole damn continent is in the group trying to pry the *Deuxième* and the Lancers out of those buildings, so when we drop those buildings on them the war is half done." He paused and there was a tired but heartfelt "Hoo-wah" to that. The clustering of the platoon was sounding a warning to him, but he was beyond caring. The flip side was that the same clustering was beginning to act upon him, beginning to bring him out of his fugue. Even with all his time in suits, he was as susceptible as the troopers to the sense of alienation.

"We are going to be operating in two-man teams. If you run into any Posleen you can't handle, break contact and call for support. Headquarters will support third squad and the engineers in the 'L' building. The engineers will work on that building 'cause it needs a lighter touch. One team from each squad will stay in support and as the other teams get finished they will go into a support role and be tasked as needed." He looked over at the gathered scouts and felt a stab of grief at the lack of a tall lanky suit in their midst.

"Scouts, your job is to emplace some charges, but mainly I want you to launch flicker-eyes across the unmined buildings. You should be above the line of fire but if the Posleen notice you you'll be in for a hot time tonight. After the charges are all laid, head towards the ocean-side processing plants through the water lines."

He paused in his flat monotone delivery and looked around, the slight twitches of his neck muscles swinging the viewpoint from side to side. The suits were featureless as always; the platoon might have been a set of poorly cast plasteel statues. A sudden question intruded upon his narrowed reality as he wondered how many would be alive on the morrow.

"Because of all the damage the lines are mostly empty; if yours isn't, blow out the walls and drain it; according to my data, none of the water plants are functional in this area.

"We're about to start moving over to our respective buildings.

We don't have time to dick around so we're going down the outside on compensators. Your AIDs have the drop programs loaded. Fall fast then punch up the compensators and hit hard. It'll be just like a jump except we'll fall faster and won't disperse. When we hit the ground, split up and do the mission." He looked around the rooftop then back at the gathered platoon.

He was not sure what to say. It seemed a moment for a motivational speech but he was damned if there was one in him. "A quick prayer," he said finally and bowed his head. He paused for a moment longer, running through the short list of prayers he could remember. None of them seemed appropriate. Then, suddenly, a fragment of verse from an unknown poem came to mind. He thought about it and found it highly appropriate. He took a deep breath.

> *"Ah, Mary pierced with sorrow,*
> *Remember, reach and save,*
> *The soul that comes to-morrow*
> *Before the God that gave!*
> *Since each was born of woman,*
> *For each at utter need—*
> *True comrade and true foeman—*
> *Madonna, intercede!"*

"Sergeant Green!"

"Sir?"

"Move 'em out."

"Yes, sir. Scouts, Second, First, Fourth, Third, Headquarters, Fifth. Move it!"

When they reached the first building to be mined, the squads broke up and moved to their buildings. Third squad, tasked to this building, waited lined along the roof with headquarters for the other squads to get into position. When the other squads were in position, the platoon stepped over the edge. The suits dropped under an artificially induced two positive gravities to within one hundred meters of the ground then began to slow. They hit the bottom still traveling at nearly six meters per second, but the suits absorbed this with bent knees. There were a few Posleen milling aimlessly on the boulevards.

"Squads, put a covering team behind you and head to the

demolition points. Third, Sergeant Green and I will cover. Do it, people." Mike hefted his grav-rifle and followed the red priority carets. Michelle could analyze all the Posleen in line of sight or range of sensors and determine the highest priorities of fire. Take out the ones with heavy weapons first, moving outward from nearest to farthest, unless ones farther out were targeting Mike and nearer ones were not. Mike followed the flashing carets listlessly; the moment of rage at Sergeant Wiznowski's death had destroyed something important for him and he could feel depression lingering around the corner.

Posleen fell relentlessly, but Mike was becoming more distant. It felt as if he was watching the world through TV and the actions in the beyond were unreal shadows.

He and Sergeant Green covered the entry of Third squad and moved into the building.

"How are we gonna support from here?" asked Sergeant Green standing in one of the giant vehicle bays on the ground floor.

"Poorly. We'll move toward the central shaft and down." Mike and Sergeant Green headed inward, mopping up the occasional Posleen along the way. When they did not notice the Posleen, the Posleen nonetheless attacked them. Mike finally determined that most of the Posleen in the building were ones that had been released by the death of a God King. Mike considered the briefings he had, a million years ago back in The World.

Normal Posleen were barely sentient. Most of them were below moron level on a human scale. There were a few that were of slightly higher intelligence that the God Kings used as foremen or NCOs. But all of the normal Posleen "normals" and "superior normals" were bonded in a very real sense to an individual God King. They would not even flinch from death if the God King ordered them to die.

But if the God King died, their bonds were released. If this occurred with another God King around, the other God King could try to rebond them. Rebond them "in the heat" as it was called. However, if they were not rebonded in the short period after the death of their lord and master, they were impossible to bond for some time thereafter, up to two weeks. Then they would begin looking for another God King. He mentioned that to Sergeant Green.

"Must make things interesting for a couple of weeks after the battle, sir."

"Why?" Mike asked in a disinterested tone.

"Well, sir," said Sergeant Green, hoping to reawaken the lieutenant's interest in the proceedings, "these things have always attacked us on sight, and I've noticed a bunch of them that are recently dead."

"Yeah, I noticed that too."

"I think they attack their own kind, too, sir. So the area behind a battlefield has to be littered with these things, all looking for a fight, for a couple of weeks. Makes it hard to consolidate, yah know?"

"No secure rear," said Mike, with the beginnings of interest. The lethargic depression from losing Wiznowski was still around the corner, but his basic instinct to continue the battle was beginning to fight it off.

"Yes, sir. Not if there's been a battle, one where a bunch of God Kings got killed. Those God Kings that took off after the shuttles, what do you want to bet their group mutinied, or whatever, after they left?"

"Except for the ones that got rebonded in the heat," Mike pointed out.

"Yes, sir, but look at all the ones around here. They must miss a lot."

"How do we use that?" Mike mused.

"Beats me, sir, but it's got to work for us. They have to move supplies, 'an army travels on its stomach' right? So, it's got to affect their logistics."

"Not really, most of their logistics is pickup." About then they were called to help out a team that had run into a group under the leadership of a God King. After a hairy few minutes with no casualties to the humans they were back in their conversation.

"What did you mean about their logistics, sir?"

"You mean pickup?"

"Yes, sir."

"Well, they survive much the same way an army has survived throughout history, by gleaning. Until fairly recently in history what we now call looting and punish people for was the accepted way that troops fed and paid themselves. Have you noticed anything about these Posleen?"

"Besides the fact that they're shooting at us, sir?" joked the sergeant.

"I meant the stuff on their harnesses," Mike answered with a slight smile.

Sergeant Green studied the nearest Posleen corpse.

"They've got bits stuck all over them, sir."

"Yeah, shiny bits. If you dug through the ruck you'd find a few with silver or gold. More high-quality stuff on the God Kings. In their pouches are going to be bits of Indowy and other plant and animal matter. Some of the Indowy is moved back to the landers, ammunition presumably moves forward. The indigenous population and supplies are their food and they gather semivaluable and valuable materials for their bosses. In the consolidation period following conquest they build sort of temple palaces to the God Kings and fill them with the loot they gathered. I guess they're like a lot of soldiers. You know what Kipling says: 'It's loot, loot, loot that makes the boys get up and shoot.' But that can't be their only motivation." *Can it?*

35

Ft. Indiantown Gap, PA Sol III
0523 August 5th, 2002 AD

"Whoooee!" said Stewart, as he entered the company headquarters. "What a fuckin' party!" Behind him the sky was just beginning to lighten, but it was still impossible to tell a black thread from a white. A very technical "before dawn."

At the tableau at the CQ desk he stopped dead.

The room was not particularly large, what would have been a living room in a single-wide house trailer. The floor was cheap linoleum, the overhead bulbs shielded with simple plastic covers. On the far wall was a desk made from unfinished plywood with a phone on it. Above the desk was a sign welcoming the entrant to Bravo Company 1st Battalion 555th Infantry, "The REAL Black Panthers." There was a door on the right with the sign "Day Room" over it and a corridor led off to the left.

Beside the desk, taped to a folding chair with wrap upon wrap of duct tape, was a chubby sergeant unknown to Stewart, his eyes wide over the gag. Behind the desk, butt firmly planted in a swivel chair and feet propped up, was Drill Corporal Adams, eyes closed. A massive gray machine gun of some sort was lying on the desk, the oversized barrel covering the door. His hand rested lightly on the pistol grip. By the door to the day room were three of his squad, similarly armed, machine guns slung on shoulder straps. All three had evil grins on their faces.

"What the fuck?" asked Stewart and stepped forward for his squad to enter behind him. At the first glimpse of the tableau the squad began to spread out, some of them taking up positions to look out windows while others fanned out through the room. Wilson simply spun around to cover Stewart's back.

Adams rolled his head up and cracked one eyelid.

"Top wants to see you in his office," rasped the drill corporal. "Now." He jerked his head towards the corridor and closed his eyes again.

Stewart took one more look then headed down the corridor. The corridor followed the far wall of the barracks to another open area. In the open area was another desk that had Ampele sprawled across it, mouth open wide and snoring. An MP private was sitting in the chair of the desk, cleaning a 9mm on the oblivious private's broad chest.

Along the left-hand wall of the corridor were three doorways. The first door had a hand-carved plaque that read "The Swamp." The second had a piece of cardboard with the word "Latrine" scrawled on it in black magic marker. The last doorway was open. Its door was leaning against the wall a few feet to the side.

The door had a brass plaque on it engraved with the words "First Sergeant Morales." The brass plaque was set in an expensive mahogany frame. On the hinge side of the door was a large bootprint. Stewart contemplated it for a moment by the light drifting from either end of the corridor. He picked up his own boot and compared the tread pattern. Then he held his boot up next to the mark. He shook his head and looked down the corridor. Ampele's boots were in view. He peered at them, looked at the door, Ampele, door. He shook his head again and gingerly knocked on the shattered doorframe. The noise evoked a snort from Ampele. Then the snores started again.

"Come in!" said Pappas' rumbling voice from within.

Stewart stepped through the doorway into opulence. The room was very small but almost overwhelmed with expensive objects. The desk was mahogany, hand finished and recently buffed. On it was a top-line twenty-two-inch flat-screen monitor. The carpets were Persian, turned in the lofty wool style of Isfahan. Prints of various quality were on all the walls and the light shone from reworked nineteenth-century oil lamps. They gave the room a warm yellow glow that complimented the deep garnet wood.

The first sergeant was bent over in front of a large antique safe turning the knob. He glanced over his shoulder then stood up, fury in his eyes.

"Stewart!" Pappas growled. "Where the hell have you been!"

Stewart knew better than to give the flippant reply he had rehearsed on the way from the parade ground to the barracks. If nothing else the bootprint made him very circumspect.

He assumed a position of parade rest. "Sorry, First Sergeant. If we thought you were having problems we would have been here sooner. I admit I pushed the 'by sun-up' thing. No excuse."

Pappas shook his head. "Forget it. I knew you'd push it, but I didn't feel like I could send a runner for you in there," he admitted, gesturing with his chin towards the parade ground. "But we do have problems. I need this safe opened," he continued, "and this computer cracked." He gestured at the workstation on the desk.

Stewart didn't even bother to protest. "Wilson," he said in a raised voice, "get Minnet." He walked over to the safe. Taking a small black device with an LED readout from his blouse pocket, he placed it on the face of the safe. Pappas took one look, shook his head and stepped out of the way.

"Yeah, boss?" asked Minnet, slipping through the door. Even smaller than Stewart, the elfin private was rapier quick in his movements. He stopped and looked around. "Jesus!" He picked up a small figurine of a ballerina and checked the bottom. "Damn, this is real Dresden! It's worth a mint!"

"Put it back," rumbled Pappas, without even looking to see if it disappeared. "It's evidence."

Stewart nodded his head and the figurine made its way back onto the shelf.

"And put back the lighter," said Pappas, flipping through files in an unlocked cabinet.

Minnet looked surprised but slipped the solid-gold lighter out of his sleeve and set it back on the desk.

Stewart shook his head. "Minnet, take this thing apart," he said, gesturing at the workstation.

The private nodded his head and got to work.

Stewart spun the wheel of the safe several times foward then back. After a few moments he nodded his head and began spinning the dial back and forth. In a moment the safe was unlocked.

"Don't open it," snapped Pappas. "We need the old man here." He headed for the door then stopped. "And *don't*."

"We won't," said Stewart.

"Okay," he said and headed out the door.

"Don't what?" asked Minnet, contemplating the readout on the black box he had produced out of his breast pocket. He frowned at the readings and touched a control. Apparently satisfied he smiled again.

"Don't take nothin'," said Stewart, "don't move nothin', don't touch nothin' you don't have to."

"Oh." The private punched a button and shook his head. "People think they're so fuckin' smart," he murmured. He inserted a floppy disk into the computer and started it up. When the password screen came up he punched the button on the black box. The computer looked over the entry, decided that it liked it and let him in. "That's what happens when you change the password for the CMOS.

"What are we looking for?" he asked a moment later.

"Take a look around," said Pappas, coming in the door followed by Lieutenant Arnold and the MP private who was holstering his sidearm. "Take it from me, this is not normal décor for a first sergeant's office."

Stewart, overcome by curiosity, swung open the safe door and whistled. "Whewww," he exclaimed. "Let me see. Stacks of bills, a case of vials of something called Tolemiratine and some green crystals." He picked one up and examined it. "They're not emeralds," he continued, expertly. "What are they?"

"Well, I got a file that's called 'Company Expenditures,'" said Minnet, not to be outdone. "And it's encrypted."

"Make it decrypted," said Lieutenant Arnold, coldly.

The private glanced up, got one good look at the acting company commander's face and began frantically tapping keys.

"Sergeant First Class Tomas Morales?" said the MP lieutenant. His nose wrinkled at the smell of alcohol and pheromones wafting from the Annville apartment. The half-dressed male in his thirties stopped trying to pull on his silks blouse. The lieutenant could see a female form behind him. Unless he was much mistaken the bleached blonde on the bed could not have been of legal age of consent. The ACS sergeant had Coke-bottle-thick glasses and a head that cocked off to one side. His prominent Adam's apple bobbed as he nodded agreement.

"You are under arrest," said the lieutenant as the NCO with him stepped forward and secured the former acting first sergeant. "The charge is peculation and black marketeering of restricted Galactic Technology. You have the right to remain silent..."

36

Andata Province, Diess IV
0947 GMT May 19th, 2002 AD

Organized resistance or a counterattack stubbornly refused to
appear and Mike and Sergeant Green were left to ponder that
in the darkness of the megascraper's bowels.

The two were in a small alcove off a main corridor. The
bitter fighting around the perimeter of the entrapped divisions
had caused massive damage to this portion of the megascraper.
The lighting in the area was dim, the Eterna lights popping and
sputtering from damage. The blue-green light was more countered
than reinforced by the flickering light of fires. The area was given
over to the light industry that permeated the Indowy megascrapers; this region seemed to be devoted to chemical processes. The
ubiquitous Indowy paintings were dim and colorless under suit
enhancement, defaced by the scars of railgun needles, the copper
nicks of rifle ricochets and fire. The fractional distillers that filled
many of the surrounding rooms had burnt like torches under the
hammer of the guns.

In the past thirty minutes, Mike had begun to realize that the
waiting really was the hardest part of a battle. Unable to properly
fidget because of the suit, he kicked a bit of detritus on the floor
at his feet then recognized it as the barrel and barrel shroud of
an M-16A2. He looked around the alcove but could see no sign
of the weapon's owner. A murmur to Michelle fixed the location
for later possible retrieval, assuming they could find it after they
dropped the building. Then he went back to waiting.

"We've had a hundred and twenty-three encounters among

our forty-five personnel," he said after another ten minutes of studying figures and screens, "and only three encounters have involved disciplined parties of Posleen."

"Their rear area seems fairly soft, sir," said Sergeant Green. The NCO appeared to have the patience of a saint.

"Yeah, concur Sergeant. The only problem is getting through the rind. And, I'm sure, if the frontline troops had any idea we were here they'd be descending like locusts."

"How are the troops in the encirclement doing?"

Mike checked the schematic and studied the notations. "It looks like they're holding temporarily. The line hasn't reduced noticeably."

"Think the shuttles distracted the threat, sir?"

"Not for this long. And I don't think that the loss of ten or so God Kings could disrupt them that badly. I think the survivors of the armored divisions are just some bad motherfuckers." Mike snorted at the thought. It was always that way, the first battle often decided who would live or die for the rest of the war. It was one reason that veteran units were so dangerous in battle; they had a core of bitterly capable survivors.

"I guess the Posleen aren't too happy about how things are going, huh, LT?" asked the sergeant. Perhaps the waiting was getting to him as well.

"No, I suspect not," he said. There was a brief pause. "And," he continued, a note of animation in his voice, "they're about to have a worse surprise. The last team is complete!"

"Time to rock and roll!"

"Fuckin' A. Platoon," O'Neal called, the AID automatically switching him to broadcast mode. "All personnel, retreat through the tunnels following the assigned vectors. You have fifteen minutes to reach minimum safe distance! Good luck and see you at the processing plant!

"Let's move out, Sar'nt."

They headed to the nearest lock along with a fire team following the same path. Mike checked the locations of all the teams and breathed a sigh of relief. The plan had invited defeat in detail: a gut-wrenching terror that was now off his back. It was a central military axiom that you never divide your forces in the heat of battle, but the intelligence conferred by the suits as well as the disorganization of the Posleen rear area permitted enormous missions to be accomplished in record times. Without a doubt, if a practical method could be found for passing through Posleen lines, the deep strike was the premium method for battling the Posleen. Outside their hordes they were as dangerous to a man in a suit as so many mosquitoes, painful but hardly life threatening. The difficulties would be finding a way to attack the Posleen rear area and viable methods of disruption. The fate of the shuttles was graphic proof that the traditional techniques of deep strike would be impossible.

The teams slid through the tunnels as slickly as so many ferrets, noting and designating the location of the occasional human body. In most cases the personnel would stop to remove a dog tag or other identification if there was time. The platoon rally point was in the basement of a processing plant and fifteen minutes was plenty of time to get there.

The building was technically in Posleen hands, but the formed units of Posleen were fully involved trying to dislodge the battered survivors of the 10th Panzer Grenadiers in the nearest megascraper and the only Posleen in the basements were unbonded stragglers.

Mike triggered a fatal burst at a Posleen that wandered into the processing floor, and popped off his helmet. The basement smelled of seaweed and smoke, but not of rotting organics; the hygiene was surprising under the circumstances. The troops around him starting popping their helmets as well and before long there was a cluster of alert soldiers scanning the scattered machinery of the basement. The molecular seals of their headwear were bright circles in the dimness.

"All right troops," Mike said, for the first time seeing the faces of the soldiers he had been leading for almost twenty-four hours. The troopers in turn studied the diminutive officer who had carried them through hell. They were so far beyond any human reaction that Mike was unable to decide what was in their expressions. They faced him like so many sharks, eyes dead and uncaring in their carnage. He shivered for a moment, showing it no more than the troops around him.

He had seen many of these soldiers only two days before suiting up in preparation for the battle to come. Most had been frightened, covering it with bravado. Some had been so brainwashed with the airborne mentality that they were awaiting the moment of contact with eagerness. Some had been openly fearful, but ready to do their duty. Now they were one and all automatons. He had taken them from childhood to some region beyond and at this moment he feared the Frankenstein monster he had created. But the professional dies hard and he carried right on.

"In a minute and a half the remaining charges will blow," he continued in a soft but carrying voice. There was distant gun and cannon fire, felt more than heard, and a drip-drip of water from broken pipes. "When they do we'll watch on our helmet systems. That was why the scouts planted the flicker-eyes, that and to see if there was any concerted response to our little incursion." He felt himself drifting with fatigue and wondered what would happen if he wavered. The way they were looking at him he half expected them to turn on him in some sort of feeding frenzy at the slightest sign of weakness.

"When the buildings drop, the armor units should be able to break out to the MLR. After they pass through the lines we'll sneak back to the MLR ourselves and hopefully get a well-earned rest." He smiled tiredly at the half-hearted cheer. "Now, helmets on, unless you want to miss the show." He ducked back under his helmet like a turtle. The eyes were on him still there but at least he could no longer see them.

"Michelle, get me General Houseman."

"Okay, Mike." The circuit crackled with static; General Houseman had to be away from his command post, using a shunt through a regular Army frequency.

"O'Neal? What's the hold-up?" the general asked impatiently. Mike could hear the freight-train roar of artillery in the background and a nearby jackhammer sound of a heavy machine gun.

"The charges are laid and about to blow, sir," he said, glancing at the countdown clock. "We ran into a few snags."

"Yeah, we saw what they did to the shuttles through the monitors. Was that you leaving your position?"

"Yes, sir."

"Don't get carried away, son, this is gonna be a long war."

"Yes, sir." Mike could not begin to explain over this open circuit the red tower of rage that had overrun him at that moment.

"When do they blow?"

"In . . . twenty-five seconds," Mike answered. He split the screen to give him an overview of the trapped divisions. The numbers were not looking good.

"Very well, the armor forces really need the help. Good luck, son, and carry on."

"Roger that, sir, Airborne."

"Out here."

Mike shunted the view from the remote sensors into the platoon's helmets, each squad overlooking its own building. In the upper quadrant was a count-down timer. Precisely at zero there was a gout of dust, fire and less definable things out of the lower floors of the buildings. Slowly they began to topple, gaining speed and finally crashing to the ground in a shower of rubble.

There was cheering on the platoon net with the troops laughing and swearing in relief. Until that moment Mike had not realized their level of disbelief. Only a couple of them had thought that the buildings would really fall. He shook his head in wonder that they had not simply evaporated to the rear.

He put the thought aside and ordered the NCOs to assemble for move out. As the platoon started towards the locks he updated the schematic of the encirclement. Then he had to ask Michelle if it was accurate.

There were too many breaks in the chain. The fighters in the encircled building were a hodgepodge of units from five different countries. Although there was a clear road out, the infiltrated Posleen and broken communications meant that none of the units could reinforce the panzer grenadiers on the open side.

In that brief glance at his monitors Lieutenant O'Neal saw the end of his life and the lives of those around him. He considered for a moment ignoring the results. He and the troopers from the 2/325th had done their share and more. But, it is not enough for a soldier to simply do his best. A soldier has to continue the mission until the mission is completed or he is no more. The mission of the Armored Combat Suit units was to break the encirclement and relieve the armored units. The fact that the conventional units' inability to maintain communication created the situation was beside the point; the mission was incomplete.

"Hold it." Mike called up a keyboard and began running scenarios. As he did the troopers held their collective breaths, not knowing what dark angel had dropped into their midst but gut certain that the promised haven was retreating.

"They're still pinned," Mike said into the silence. The troopers shuffled their feet and began checking their virtually unused weapons. Feed tubes just so, grenades in place, swivel launcher. Mike tapped a command and a clear route out of the basement to the sea was displayed. The large seawater intakes would be more than adequate to the task.

"The panzer grenadiers can't dislodge the Posleen straight on. Look." He threw the image outward where the red and blue icons floated in the darkness like an evil kiss. Sip of water, check ammo levels.

"The Posleen are the ones with their backs to the wall now, but they have enough forces to hold in both directions and there isn't a good way to break that stalemate, not in time for it to matter." Mike threw up a schematic of forces driving into the Posleen from either side.

"Something has to hit them in the flank, preferably from the sea, and drive them inland to open a corridor to the walls." The landward arrow disappeared and the seaward arrow drove in, pushing the Posleen out of position. The lines of friendlies drove forward in support and the Posleen symbols were gone.

"And it looks like that's gotta be us," he concluded. He took a sip of the chilled suit water and smiled ferally. Dropping buildings on the bastards was just numbers; he could call up the estimates if he cared. But this was going to be one on one, at ground level. Point-blank slaughter. It was time and past time to build the samadh. Pile it high.

"Why us?" asked one plaintive voice. "What about the Germans?"

"Their ACS is shoring up the MLR inland," Mike answered, checking that status of that unit. He was careful to keep the low snarl out of his voice. "And it's nearly as beat up as our battalion. We are it, people."

"Fuck that, fuck, fuck, fuck, fuck!"

"Shiiit!"

"At the fuck ease!" snarled Sergeant Green. "The LT was talkin'."

"Hell, Sarn't," Mike laughed. The sound was just a bit on the high side. "I agree. But like the man said, 'ours is not to question why.' On your feet, troopers. It's time to follow the bouncing ball."

Mike wondered when one of them would get the idea to frag him, but so far so good. He suddenly felt a wave of energy enter him and his fatigue fell away like a cloak. He feared it was because he saw the future of glorious battle this morn'.

His sudden desire to close with the enemy frightened him. He had no purpose leading troops into battle if he could not control his hatred. But he also could not see any alternative. The German ACS unit was well and truly engaged and could not be redeployed. An ACS unit was the only effective unit under the circumstances and his platoon was the only remaining mobile ACS unit. So, time for some payback.

"Okay, here is how we are gonna skin this cat," he said as the platoon filed into the lock. "We are going to go out to sea through the intakes and come up on the beach. The *Schwerpunkt*, the point of emphasis, is the Boulevard Alisterand which is being traded back and forth. We will deploy in close formation and move forward taking the Posleen under marching fire.

"There is no way to do this except brutally. I've got a couple of tricks up my sleeve. They might keep us undetected even after we fire.

"When we deploy it will be no place for scouts, your lighter armor'll be useless. Stay under water until we open fire, then lift up under AG and enter the buildings. Go up a few stories and move to sniper positions. When you reach them start snipering the God Kings. I can't believe their targeting is going to detect directed fire in the heat of battle, but I'll take the first targeted shot at them just to be sure. Oh, yeah," he chuckled for a moment, "no grenades without my call." Some of the troops laughed grimly. "We're here to pull the Germans out, not kill 'em all." The platoon had hit sea level and ducked into the still, black water, their inertial compensators flying them through the muck towards the intake.

The water was packed with siphonophores feeding on the detritus of the plant's backwash. When the pumps failed, the water that had been in process flowed backwards and stirred up thousands of microscopic fungi that lined the walls. The jet-propelled siphonophores had rushed in to partake of the unexpected bounty, and the water was a mass of darting jelly creatures, each intent on getting its share of the feast. As they fed they vibrated internal organs that pulsed low-pitch sonar through the waves. Much of the sound was in the audible spectrum, a caressing wave of soprano cries.

Slashing through their midst were the oversized carnivorous polychaetan worms. As the suits brushed the jellies they gave off multihued luminescence and little distress cries so that the platoon seemed to be flying through singing fire. The flash of a jelly's death as it disappeared into the maw of a worm was a contrapunctuation to the symphony.

The unalloyed beauty of the moment was lost on the platoon. They had entered the narrow straits between normal life and battle and in that chastened realm there was no room for distraction.

"Now, when we were fighting our way over here," Mike continued, "I saw God Kings break and run twice, so they can be routed. I want to scare the shit out of these bastards as we come out of the water. They just lost hundreds of thousands of troops and God Kings under those buildings and when we come out I want it to be the last fuckin' straw.

"We are going to maintain camouflage until we are on the beach, using holograms of the waves. Once we are fully emerged I'll kick in a special hologram program for camouflage during the battle. Remember to let your barrels drain for just a moment before you open fire. At that point we will give them the whole can of kick-ass. Clear?" He finished the brief operations order just as the platoon reached the intake. The light beyond dimmed the flashes of light from the dying siphonophores and the water transmitted thunder of battle overwhelmed the delicate creatures' subtle cries of distress.

"Clear, sir," they sounded off as they flew through the shallow water to deploy parallel to the shore.

"Engineers, we're gonna use a shit-load of energy here," O'Neal continued. "Once we secure a beachhead, go into the building with B team Third squad and get to the reactor. Run us a heavy-duty line out to refuel us." He paused and tapped a control.

"And that my bonny boyos is the fuckin' plan. Are you with me?" he asked, wondering at the precision of the moment. He hefted his grav rifle as his boots settled in the muck, the water only a meter over his head.

"Yes, sir!" Whatever their individual doubts, as a unit they could say nothing more. Pride and unit-integrity, sin and savior, drove the soldier as always.

"So, what are we gonna *do*?" he asked as he took the first step forward.

"We're gonna dance, sir!" they responded, following.

"WHO WE GONNA DANCE WITH?" His helmet crept out of the water and the fury of the battle beyond was shocking. Tank cannons jutted from the ground floor windows exchanging point blank fire with God King saucers while Posleen normals grappled hand to hand with the gray uniformed grenadiers. The thin line of beach was a charnel pit, impassable from the bunkers of bodies gathered from building to waterfront, the grenadiers and Posleen grappled even in death, their blood mixing in stagnant pools to flow to the cleansing sea. A volley of grenades opened a hole in the Posleen mass then it surged forward over the ruck of bodies. A tank gouted fire and threw its turret into the air as a plasma gun searched its vitals. The white curtain of fire incinerated the packed grenadiers and Posleen alike.

"THE DEVIL!" screamed the troopers, the powered grav guns dipped to drain in awful synchronicity. A blast of fire from a God King's heavy railgun sawed through lead Posleen and grappling grenadiers, their red and yellow blood flashing up in a fountain of gore. The fire from the God King saucer was abruptly silenced by a German sniper.

"WE GONNA LEAD OR WE GONNA FOLLOW?" shouted Mike as he cycled his rifle and charged his grenade launchers.

"WE'RE GONNA LEAD!" they shouted as the guns raised in unison. Barrels shifted slightly as individual Posleen were targeted. In the midst of the battle one of the God King saucers rose up and leapt across the battleline, diving on a panzer grenadier holding only a knife. Mike, and several troopers drawn to the movement, tracked in on the Posleen saucer.

"Michelle, engage program Tiamat." His command suit began to rise into the air under its antigravity system, the energy level indicator dropping like a waterfall. The air in front of their suits shimmered for a moment and then cleared. "PLATOON, OPEN FIRE!"

37

Andata Province, Diess IV
1004 GMT May 19th, 2002 AD

Tulo'stenaloor, First Order Battlemaster of the Sten Po'oslena'ar, considered himself a connoisseur of war. He had studied the three disciplines and all the history available to his rank. Not for him the te'aalan battle madness that he had seen destroy his nest mates. But never in all his study, in all the time upon this conquest and other conquests, during his rise from scoutmaster to his current rank, had he ever faced ferocity such as the gray-clad demons his oolt'ondai now faced. The enemies' ill-favored red fluid stained the walls in the fury of the combat, and still they resisted the might of the Sten Po'oslena'ar.

"Tele'sten," he shouted over his communicator, "take your oolt to the left to support Alllllntt's, and prepare to receive his oolt'os."

"Your wish," chimed the communicator. The nearby eson'antai was panting with exertion. He had dropped from his tenar to aid another kessentai, wounded by the thrice-damned thresh-kreen. Such selflessness was rare among the Po'oslena'ar, almost unheard of. Possibly even immoral. The young kessentai leapt back to his tenar, the mission successful. "You believe he will fail upon the path?"

"As sure as the sun rises," said Tulo'stenaloor. He looked up at the ill-favored green sun of this blasted world. He should have stayed on cloud-shrouded Atthanaleen. It might be well on its way to ordonath, but at least there was rain! And none of these fistnal gray thresh!

"Those thrice-damned demons infest the upper stories no

matter how we flail them. Note how he moves his tenar in a regular pattern, soon one of their simple chemical rifles will remove him from the path. Learn from his mistakes, eson'antai!"

"Your wish my edas'antai."

"Tulo'stenaloor!" His communicator boomed at him in turn, "get your tel'enalanaa oolt'os into that building or I'll pass through you!"

Al'al'anar, his fellow battlemaster, had been heard from.

"I wish you would, Al'al'anar. Then *you* could lose oolt after oolt on these threshkreen."

"You always have been too soft! Move or lose the path, a'a'dan!" snarled his fellow battalion commander.

"*You want the path!*" shouted Tulo'stenaloor, sudden rage turning his vision yellow. "*Take the fistnal path!*" He had lost half his oolt'ondai so far and was in no mood to listen to this puppy's complaints.

"Tulo'stenaloor! Al'al'anar!"

"Your wish," said Tulo'stenaloor, the rage still rippling in his voice. He clacked his teeth and fluttered his crest in a battle to regain control.

"My edas'antai," chimed Al'al'anar.

"Tulo'stenaloor will take the path," ordered the higher commander from the distant dodecahedral landing circle. "Al'al'anar will wait and learn wisdom."

And I will lose my whole oolt'ondai because he is your eson'antai. "Your wish, aad'nal'sa'an. However, soon I will be without oolt to progress."

"I discern this. Al'al'anar, pass behind Tulo'stenaloor's position and prepare to attack from the seaward flank again. I discern a weakness there; there are less of those tel'enalanaa tenar."

"Your wish!" exulted Al'al'anar.

"Your wisdom," said Tulo'stenaloor. *Thus I lose status,* he thought. *Now, to make the best of it as that thrice-damned puppy bungles a simple movement.*

Again and again Al'al'anar had failed to effectively support other oolt'ondai, instead succumbing to battle madness and chasing the defenseless green thresh like a wild oolt'os. Without the influence of his gene derivative he would be a scoutmaster at best, or more likely dead. Such is the battle of the Path.

Alllllntt's saucer suddenly spun out of control as the God

King's head burst like a melon; a German G-4 had successfully targeted him after he raised his tenar for a better angle on the front line. The oolt'os of his company flailed the upper stories of the building for a moment in a berserk rage, then began clawing their way to the rear. As they did, the panzer grenadiers pressed in a hard local counterattack and retook their secondary positions.

"Tele'sten! Get your oolt in there now!"

"Yes, aad'nal'sa'an, your wish." The young God King, only recently promoted from scoutmaster, was attempting for the first time in his life to rebind the normals of a deceased God King in the heat of battle. At the same time he was trying to retake the lost positions. Since each normal had to be physically touched, there were, for a moment, simply too many demands on his time and he paused in his random shuffling. A single 7.62mm round ended the path for the young company commander.

"Tel'enaa, fuscirto uut!" cursed Tulo'stenaloor at the death of his son. "Alld'nt! Drive the oolt'os of Tele'sten and Alllllntt into the gray demons and be damned with them!" *Tele'sten, my eson'antai, how many times did I tell you: Never stop moving.*

"Major Steuben, we have retaken the secondary positions!"

"Wonderful Lieutenant. Hold them hard! I am trying to get some help here but I am now confident we can hold this position until relieved!"

"Yes, sir, the Tenth Panzer Grenadiers will never surrender!"

"Good job, Lieutenant Mellethin. I have to go now. Hold like steel!"

"Like steel, sir."

Like steel, indeed, thought Major Joachim Steuben, *even the steel is burning.*

From his position on the lower floor of the megascraper he could clearly see the tanks of his depleted division burning, charnel pits for their dead crews. Worse than the sight was the smell, strong even at this distance, of burning pork and rubber. The remnant of the 10th Panzer Grenadiers could not make a decent reinforced battalion and they were out of contact with the majority of the supporting divisions of French, British and Americans elsewhere in the megascraper. If something didn't happen, and soon, they were all finished.

He had just said as much to high command and they had

responded with their usual platitudes. Help would come, the American Armored Combat Suit battalion was still mobile and was on the way. What they could do when they arrived he had no idea. The officers of the 10th Panzer had spent the division as frugally as a miser, as frugally as any officer corps in Germany's illustrious history. But it had been to no avail.

Early on they discovered that in the heat of battle the God Kings' targeting systems could not spot sniper fire and Steuben's late battalion commander had pressed that to great advantage. By targeting God Kings and relentlessly counterattacking in the confusion immediately following their deaths they long delayed the inevitable. But now it was simple mathematics. They were surrounded by overwhelming force and the best they could do was spend their lives as carefully as possible.

"Major," said the one of the few remaining communication technicians, holding out a microphone, "Corp Command."

"Major?" barked the voice of the American Corp commander.

"Yes, *Herr General Leutnant*," he replied tiredly.

"You are about to receive a pleasant shock. It will not take the pressure off you, but it will allow the other units to reinforce you. The megascrapers to your east and north are about to fall over, hopefully missing yours."

"Ex . . . excuse me, sir? Could you say that again?" As the startled major stuttered into the microphone, the ground began to shake. *"Mein Gott! Was ist so heute los, hier?"*

Around him the sturdy panzer grenadiers were screaming in supernatural terror as the ground surged beneath their feet. The communications tech, with the consummate discipline so characteristic of the panzer grenadier, hurled himself into their last remaining long-range transmitter just before it crashed to the floor.

"Major!" screamed an operations NCO from the landward side, "the other buildings!"

The street to the east was suddenly filled with dust and rubble as the building to their northwest scattered its upper stories along the boulevard. Rubble crushed the front rank Posleen and a few of their remaining Leopards were covered until they huffed and grunted out from under the debris. However, most of that front was covered by the French and English, with the remnants of the American 3rd Armored and 7th Cav on the north. Now if he only had viable contact with those units he could call on them for aid to break out toward the lines. He suddenly realized he had a Lieutenant General on hold.

"*Herr General?*" said the major, coughing on the cloud of dust that blasted through the headquarters.

"I take it worked?"

"Yah, all *ist so heute los* at the moment but we'll soon be over it. This may give us a chance, *Herr General!*"

"That's the idea. Now order those other armored units over to your position, we're out of communication with them, and break out as fast as you can."

"I would, *Herr General*," said the major, apologetically, "but I regret to inform you that we have been out of communication with those units as well, for over two hours."

"Damn! Well, send runners."

"I have, sir, and radios, but none have returned. We have Posleen infiltrated into the building in company strength at this point. My flank is in contact with a French unit but I am out of communication with that flank and I cannot get to the other NATO units without detaching all of my reserve." He paused and considered the situation. "I have had to use it too many times to be willing to do that, sir, without a direct order. For all practical purposes I am only in control of the troops in my immediate vision."

"No, you're absolutely correct. Major, this *is* a direct order. If you can get your unit out without the support of those units, do so. Do not hold that position in the hopes they will turn up, we can't take that sort of gamble at this point; for all we know they could already be gone."

"*Jawohl, Herr General.*"

"Good luck, Major."

"*Danke schön, Herr General.* Good luck as well."

"Yes, we all need a dose of luck at this point."

"Major!" shouted an NCO, listening to a radio. "The seaward flank!"

Would the a'a'lonaldal battle demons of this world never quit? What new surprise would await them? Tulo'stenaloor had heard of the great fall near the mesa, but that had been put down as battle damage by most observers or perhaps poor construction.

This was clearly an action designed to deny the area from the oolt'ondai to the north and west. Here on the south, they would soon face the full wrath of the combined or'nallath in the building.

The only good note was that Al'al'anar's oolt'ondai had completed its move to reinforce his seaward flank and had started a te'naal charge the likes of which he had rarely seen. He might not like Al'al'anar but he had to hand it to him, he could motivate his oolt'os. The oolt'ondai had descended on the gray demons as they tried to recover from the disaster to the west and had been pressed home hard. It was taking tremendous damage but they were down to hand to hand at which the Po'oslena'ar excelled. The fistnal or'nallath would soon be cleared to the seaward side and they could press forward here in the center.

The 10th Panzer Grenadier command post was completely abandoned. Major Steuben hurled the entire reserve and every clerk and walking wounded he could find into the seaward flank but the new Posleen battalion pushed them steadily backwards into the building. The grenadiers were down to hand to hand and as he reached the line he saw the turret of one of the remaining Leopards leap into the air in a catastrophic kill. The sheet of fire from the exploding ammunition cooked the grenadiers and Posleen packed around the tank into one continuous bubbling mass.

Seeing there was nothing else to be done, he grabbed a G-3 from a dead trooper and raced into the battle, determined at the end to at least get an honor guard in Valhalla. Overcome with emotions, all the anger and frustration of the day welling up out of control, he leapt to the top of a pile of rubble, fully exposing himself to fire, and searched for the enemy commanders.

Al'al'anar of the Alan Po'oslena'ar, battlemaster and warrior, was in his element. The ill-favored blood of his enemies anointed his head and he searched for honorable single combat. His oolt'os and oolt commanders knew their jobs, leaving him free to engage himself as he would. He drove his tenar forward, driving down oolt'os that failed to leap clear and striking down the gray-clad thresh like so much wheat. He saw, on the far side of the battle line, a thresh brandishing its puny chemical weapon. It met his eyes and contemptuously tossed the weapon aside, drawing an even more puny knife. Al'al'anar drew his blade, raised his saucer on anti-grav and pounced on the thresh with a bitter laugh.

The Posleen saucer swept across the battle with blinding speed. Major Steuben's Gerber combat knife was contemptuously sliced off three inches from the tang by the God King's monomolecular blade and the saucer banked around for another run. Steuben spun around, determined to go to his end like a man, on his feet and facing the enemy. As he turned to meet his fate he stopped, arrested by a form rising from the sea. A multiheaded red dragon the size of a building was humping itself up out of the green waves. Dozens of heads were snaking low out of the water, while one central head was raising itself to full extension with a broad fringe ruffling and puffing around the purple-lined maw.

As the battle-maddened and oblivious God King lined up for another charge, the dragon heads opened their mouths and began to breathe silver lightning.

With the first silvery breath a ringing scream, so loud that it was for a moment a physical thing, burst forth from the beast. At that first scream of rage and raw emotion Major Joachim Steuben, oblivious and uncaring of the closing death, sank to his knees and burst into un-Teutonic tears. Then the drum riffs of Led Zeppelin's "Immigrant Song," at the maximum volume available to the sophisticated sound systems of the Armored Combat Suits, brought every action to a momentary stop.

Mike's first action was to destroy the Posleen God King attacking the lone soldier on the mound of rubble. Since three other troopers had the same target, the God King and his saucer disintegrated under the concentrated fire of the grav guns. The slap of explosion as its energy bottle let go killed hundreds of the packed Posleen normals. Since the God King had been lined up almost across the boulevard from the soldier, the effect on the panzers was negligible.

Next Mike targeted God Kings elsewhere in the battle. When the platoon had been consolidating he had taken a few moments to consider the first contact battle. That battle had been fraught with mistakes. Deploying the battalion without any fixed fortifications, without mines, barbed wire or bunkers, meant that the Posleen had been able to use their full mass and fury against the troopers without any distractions. Furthermore, deploying the battalion vertically, while it permitted fire into the rear ranks of the enemy, had opened the unit up to fire by tens of thousands of Posleen instead of hundreds.

By contrast this style of battle was what the suits had been designed for. At ground level with both flanks secured, there were only so many Posleen that could fire at the troopers at one time. And the pile of Posleen and human bodies acted as a breastwork over which the platoon could fire.

The one item that would have helped the battle of Qualtren, no one had thought of until afterwards. The battalion had been ordered to open fire at the mass of the Posleen. However, deployed vertically as they were, hundreds of God Kings had been in sight. If the battalion had been ordered to concentrate on the God Kings, the mass of Posleen normals would have been left bereft and leaderless. The deadly mass that destroyed the battalion in minutes would instead have been as insignificant as the loner rogues they had been destroying for the last day. Mike intended to rectify the situation if possible.

As he potted God Kings, the main body of the troopers began concentrated and continuous fire into the Posleen mass. There was nothing elegant about the conflict, no charges or feints, it was simple, brutal slaughter. Most of the Posleen by the beach had allowed themselves to get so packed in their rush to reach the panzer grenadier positions that they could not even deploy their weapons. Since they completely filled the boulevard, it was first necessary to move them out of the way and the only way to move them was to mow them down. For the first few minutes of the battle hardly any fire was returned toward the main body of troops as they fired continuously and without contest into the mass of Posleen.

The hypervelocity grav-gun rounds caused an energy wave front to build up in front of them. As the stream of rounds hit an individual Posleen, the effect was catastrophic; the hydrostatic wave front advanced away from the rounds at a fraction of the speed of light. Despite the relatively small size of the teardrops, the explosive force on the first Posleen hit was equivalent to packing a hundred pounds of TNT into its body cavity and detonating it, splattering yellow finely distributed muck over the landscape. And then the teardrops, hardly degraded in form or velocity, would seek out the next Posleen in line, and the next and the next. Most of the fire drove six or seven layers into the mass, cleaving them like a nuclear weedeater.

Rather than stacking them like cordwood, they piled them like hay, from a lawn left uncut too long in the summer. Heaps and mounds of yellow leaking corpses and unrecognizable bits built up on the ramp to the beach. The blood began to pour in a yellow river to the sea as the Posleen heaved and bucked under the explosive fire of the kinetic energy rounds.

At the same time, cloaked by their holographic technology, the scouts flew unnoticed to the nearest windows, gossamer soap bubbles floating through the green-tinged air, and rushed to find sniper positions.

The statement that the Posleen could not retreat was disproved in those hideous few minutes. Faced with a being from myth, the semisentient normals shattered like glass. Mike could see the rear ranks peeling away in fear of the unknown. Many of the normals were returning fire and he was taking some hits but the hologram around him distorted his true location. The only accurate targeting point was the barrel of his rifle as it spat dot-accurate streams of fire each of which removed one more link in the enemy's morale.

He was suddenly struck by a wave of fire and Michelle careted a distant God King surrounded by the disciplined forces that had him targeted. He fired at the God King, but it had slickly moved aside. Mike fired four more rapid and accurate bursts but each missed by the skinniest of margins, destroying dozens of normals in the wake. Whoever that God King was it handled its saucer like a master and was too hard to bother with. Instead, Mike auto-targeted his grenade launchers on the normals around the dexterous God King and forgot about it.

"Thral nah toll. Demons of the sky and fire, *what is that*?" Whatever it was, thought Tulo'stenaloor, it favored the gray-clad demons. He took a precious moment to consider as his oolt'os broke around him, the bindings fraying under the primal fear of a beast both larger and more dangerous than they.

"Tel'enalanaa," he whispered after a moment. "It is illusion!" he shouted. "Alld'nt! Look you! There are simple soldiers in the midst of the beast! Target the breath! There! The lifted head! Target and fire!"

The oolt'os, faced with positive orders and a clear and defined action, opened fire with all their will. The railguns spat their slender needles downrange and disappeared into the dragon's head without apparent effect. Hypervelocity missiles passed through without detonating.

"There! No blood! It is a trick! False demon! Somewhere in it is the kessentai! Fire at the head! Target and fire!" He manually swiveled his heavy laser and began cutting at the dragon. In return it roared and swiveled towards him. His talons tapped controls and the tenar danced aside as the dragon's breath came near enough that the heat seared its covering. He tapped the controls again and the dragon missed once more. Two more times and the beast seemed to lose interest. But then, even as it spat fire at a distant third-level battlemaster, tremendous explosions began falling all around him. As his oolt'ondai fell to the terrific explosions he decided that enough was enough. For now the enemy would take the field; the People always triumphed in the end.

"Lo'oswand!" he ordered, gesturing to the rear. "Oolt'ondai, lo'oswand! Together we retreat fighting!"

As the scouts reached their positions and began to peck away at the God Kings, Mike felt it acceptable to return to the ground. He had also used up over thirty percent of his available power, mostly hovering, and needed to return to ground mode.

As he hit the ground the squads started their first bound forward. By odd squads they leapt over the wall of Posleen bodies into a less cluttered area beyond. The suits automatically compensated for the treacherous footing and the squads opened fire again. They were taking far more fire now, but on the ground at such close quarters the only Posleen that could target them were those in direct contact so it was effectively a one-on-one battle. The massive pressure of Posleen was funneled to the troopers whose only realistic fear was that the ammunition would run out.

Mike landed just as the second group prepared to bound and he bounded with them. In the air he checked the status of the platoon. Very few losses and the majority of the troops were at over seventy percent power. Ammunition levels were dropping, but the heavy-duty fire would reduce soon. When they landed he checked the battlefield schematic and decided that the Posleen were nicely bunched.

"*Platoon! Volley fire grenades, program: single line deep, fifty percent overlap, close support FPF softies to the left! Ready...Fire!*" There was a rapid series of thuds around him. "*Check grenade fire!*" He did not want the troops to randomly fire their grenade launchers given that they were in close contact with friendly forces.

The grenades were antimatter charges wrapped with osmium self-forging projectiles. Each had the explosive power of a 120mm mortar. They had a hard kill radius, a zone of total destruction, of fifteen meters and a soft kill radius of nearly thirty-five meters. Using them all with the *Panzergrenadiere* in close contact was dangerous. However, since they did not have as much shrapnel as a 120mm, they were slightly less effective at distance; the "soft-kill" zone had less than a fifteen percent likelihood of a kill against human targets in the open.

The programmed fire shot a double line of grenades down the 75-meter-wide boulevard, the grenades landing 15 meters from the Posleen-held building and 20 meters apart. Thus the total destruction zone stretched outward 50 meters from the Posleen-held megascraper with a further "soft kill" distance of 25 meters. The line stretched from thirty meters in front of the combat suit line for nearly a kilometer. The soft kill radius stretched to the *Panzergrenadiere* lines but most if not all of the grenadiers had sought cover by this time and those who had not would have to take their chances.

The explosions started rippling down the boulevard and Tulo'stenaloor could see what was coming. The white fire seemed to expand from side to side of the avenue, each pair of enormous explosions coming a fractional second apart. There was no escape through the south building; most of the entrances had been destroyed in the fighting and those that remained were choked with the most fleet of foot or saucer.

As the barrage progressed towards his retreating battalion, the battlemaster found himself cringing at each drawn out pause between crashes. All of the grenades were fired at the same time but some had farther to travel. So each hellish interval got longer and longer as the rounds neared them.

He knew he could flee, leave his oolt'os and take the other kessentai and escape on their tenars. But to lose his oolt'ondai that he had built so carefully over the years of only the finest genetic material; no, it would be better to die than to start over. Like Lot, he turned his face away and led his flock to safety as the doom came nearer and nearer.

As they reached the far intersection the latest pause drew out and out. Tulo'stenaloor finally took heart to look back.

From the ocean inward half the length of the building was a carpet of Po'oslena'ar dead, oolt'os and kessentai intermingled, in death their difference reduced to a fraction in size. No living Po'os moved in all that vast abattoir, no living thing. The energy of the explosions caused superheating of the immediate surroundings. The smell of cooked Posleen filled the air, a soft steam arising from the baked flesh, and smoke rose from the shattered tenar as well.

As his oolt'ondai turned south into the cross street he looked back once more and saw the sea demon ripple and dissolve into a grouping of thresh in hulking metallic space armor. This then for their sea demon. As he watched they finished off the few scattered oolt'os with their terrible silver lightning and began to advance implacably down the boulevard in ground-devouring bounds. He had seen and would remember; these thresh'akrenallai were tricky, tricky.

38

Andata Province, Diess IV
1009 GMT May 19th, 2002 AD

Major Steuben pulled himself up on a block of masonry and wiped the blood from his mouth. The ringing in his ears seemed permanent but he was alive, something on which he would not have taken odds at any point in the last twenty-four hours. Total hearing loss seemed at the moment a small price to pay. He tried to stand but a wave of dizziness overcame him and he sat back down. It was then that he saw the first squad of MI bounce forward and spit silver fire downrange. The crash of the kinetic energy weapons was a dull ringing in his ears, but it was the first sound he had heard since the explosions.

He remembered the flame from the illusory dragon wiping the attacking God King out of the air like swatting a fly. That sight was a bucket of cold water to his sanity and he dove off the masonry mound, scooping up the G-3 in passing, and headed to one of the hasty bunkers the grenadiers had cobbled together. He needed to get to communications now that it seemed the unit might miraculously survive. Before he could reach it he was blocked by a Leopard panzer snuffling forward, scenting Posleen blood in the water. The blast from its main gun was an assault on his ears and he despaired for a moment of regaining any control in this mad and chaotic world.

He ducked behind a shattered wall support and poked his rifle around the corner. The scene beyond was shocking even given the horror of the past few days. He was slightly elevated so he could see the holographic dragon heads pouring fire into the massed

Posleen on the division's seaward flank. The Posleen were unable to maneuver or flee, trapped by the inertia of bodies, and they were now being blasted apart like a clay cliff before a fire hose; bits and pieces flew into the air under the concentrated hammer of the dragon's breath. When the pile had grown so large as to be an impediment, the lower heads leapt up and forward over the mound of bodies, first half the heads, then the other half, the streams of fire never stopping, even in midair. As the second set of heads landed the single lifted head dropped to the ground and a group of small, round objects flew upward and outward from them.

It took a moment to think about what those might be. Major Steuben had been briefed, a thousand years ago on Earth, about the capabilities of the Fleet armored combat suits. He watched the harmless looking, relatively tiny little balls drift lazily upward then begin to drift down. He suddenly turned sheet white, screamed "INCOMING!" and dove backwards with his hands over his ears.

Now he pulled himself to his feet again, determined to force his recalcitrant body to bend to his will, and stumbled out into the street. As the second group of MI bounded forward he lurched directly in front of one of the flankers, an NCO by the stripes on his shoulder. Steuben hoped the sergeant would be able to see him. There was no apparent visor, the front of the helmet was blank, sloped gray plasteel.

"Officer!" he shouted at the trooper, pointing at his collar tabs. "I need to talk to your commander!"

The trooper's weapon never wavered from the targets downrange and continued to hammer at them. Major Steuben swatted the trooper's arm; it was as useful as punching an I-beam and nearly broke his hand. He felt he was talking to some insensate robot and wondered for a moment if there was a human in the suit.

"*Eine Minute, bitte Herr Major. Der Leutnant ist hierher unterwegs,*" the trooper said in accentless Hochdeutsch.

"*Was? Was? Ich bin ein wenig taub.*" Louder!

"*Eine Minute bitte, Herr Major. Der Leutnant ist hierher unterwegs,*" the suit boomed again.

"*Sind Sie Deutscher?*" shouted Major Steuben, surprised; he could see the red-white-and-blue patch on the suit's shoulder clearly, despite the gouges it had taken in the day's battle.

"*Nein, Herr Major, Amerikaner. Die Rüstung hat einen Über-setzer. Bitte, Herr Major, ich muss gehen.*" (No, Major, American.

The suit has a translator. Excuse me, Major, I have to go.) The platoon bounded off leaving a short set of combat armor behind. It stumped over to the major and saluted with a clang of gauntlet to helm.

"*Leutnant Michael O'Neal, Mein Herr,*" the suit boomed loudly. "*Tut uns leid dass es so lang gedauert hat. Wir hatten unterwegs eine Störung.*" (Sorry we took so long. We had a spot of bother along the way.)

"Better late than never, Lieutenant. Do you need to move out with your unit? Where is your commander?"

"I'm it, sir. The rest of the battalion is either dead, buried under Qualtren or in the MLR." O'Neal suddenly had a pistol in his hand. The weapon spat a stream of fire into the darkness of the far building's lower story. There was a dwindling scream and by the time the major looked back the pistol was in its holster again. The whole action happened in less time than Steuben could have pulled a trigger.

"Well," Steuben said, shakily. "You are looking at the last of the 10th Panzer Grenadiers as well. We don't even have enough left to bury our own dead, if we could find them."

"Yes, sir," said the suit of armor, stoically. "We'll all face the reaper someday but just too damn many met him today."

"*Ja.* What are your orders?" asked the major. He began to blink with fatigue as the adrenaline rush of the last few minutes wore off. He felt a sudden urge to vomit, barely suppressed.

"I have verbal orders from General Houseman to relieve the units in this building and expedite getting them to the MLR, sir."

"Well, we are fairly relieved and I think that the fallen buildings will be a relief to the British, French and Americans as well," said the major, sitting down abruptly on a convenient pile of rubble. "But we are completely out of contact with them. We can't even tell them that the way out is clear."

"Well, technically it isn't, sir. We will have to fight our way to the MLR."

"Yes, but we can, now that the main bulk of Posleen have been pushed out of position. Anyway we can if we leave before they counterattack in force and that I cannot guarantee. The avenue to the west is open and we have three more buildings and two avenues to contend with on the way."

"Hold on a moment, sir. I gotta do some handling." The

combat suit was immobile and featureless but something about
the set of it told the major that this young, he thought young,
lieutenant was as tired as he.

"We've secured the intersection, Major," Mike continued after
a moment, "and are in contact with your units there. I submit
that we should move up there, at least I should. We need to get
this wagon train a-rollin', sir."

"*Ja, verstehe.*" Steuben's head swiveled around and spotted
the Leopard that had blocked his retreat. The commander and
driver were now up out of their hatches, as the battle moved
out of their sector, surveying the piles of Posleen dead. The tank
commander was a lieutenant from Third Brigade with whom he
was only distantly familiar. No matter. He stood up, walked over
and grasped the handhold. He swayed for a moment from a head
rush then planted his foot and on the second try managed to
boost himself onto the front deck. He took a deep breath.

"Lieutenant," he barked, "we are going to a mobile phase.
I need transportation and this sector needs to be secured, the
wounded dealt with and the personnel prepared to pull out. I am
taking your tank and you are taking command of this sector."

The lieutenant gulped and prepared to protest but swallowed it
manfully. "*Jawohl, Herr Major.* I understand." With that he hopped
out of the TC's seat, unbuckled his helmet, traded with the major
and hopped off the panzer to begin organizing the survivors.

Major Steuben slumped into the comfortable seat gratefully as
the armored womb of the Leopard enfolded him. He had come
up through panzers and loved the days he had spent as a TC.
He wished that was all he were now, with only the responsibility
of his tank and survival. But no, greater and greater responsibility was a drug to him, something to be sought not shirked. He
must face this moment as so many others had in history, as a
German, and a Steuben. Head up, shoulders back and thinking.

"Driver, head up to the intersection, *schnell.*"

When Mike reached the intersection the situation was well in
hand. The street to the north was entirely blocked by the fallen
megascraper to the east. The few remaining panzers with dozer
blades had shoved debris into a line, and a hasty barricade of
masonry now blocked access to the road east. The wall was shored
with structural membranes ripped from the buildings by the MI

troopers and was lined with *Panzergrenadiere* mingled with a squad of MI. The Posleen were in evidence in the distance, over a kilometer away, but those groups seemed to be in full retreat. Mike wished he had the forces to harry them but he could not even think about that now.

The street to the south was also blocked but a large sally opening had been left. Here the Posleen were still in evidence, as the groups between the intersection and the MLR were firing heavily in both directions. Most of the remaining platoon was here, exchanging long range fire with the Posleen. Most of the HVM fired by the Posleen were detonating in the barricade, requiring constant reinforcement but again the situation for the time being was well in hand. The MI were maintaining fire like the veterans they now were and scouts even now entering the flanking buildings were beginning to pick off the God Kings, ruining the force's command and control. Mingled with them were the snipers of the *Panzergrenadiere*, nearly as effective with their scope-mounted G-3 rifles.

"Sergeant Green," Mike called and the platoon sergeant moved back from the southern barricade.

"What's the breakage, Sergeant?"

"We lost Featherly and Simms, Meadows is badly injured but his suit took him under and he's stable."

"Not bad considering what we did." Still, Mike now knew that each loss would ache at him in the depths of the night. His casual approach to combat was as gone as Wiznowski. From here on out each counter on the screen was a real person and he would not forget it.

"We need to reestablish contact with the other units in the building. The Germans are out of contact with them and they say that Corp is too. Send Duncan's squad with two scouts into the building and have them find those units. We will hold here until I order us to retreat. As each unit exits the building it will temporarily reinforce the lines to cover the retreat of the other units."

"Yes, sir."

"I'll get with this Kraut major to make sure they'll hold here until we can pull the other units out. Then we'll skeedaddle, daddy-o."

"Yes, sir, good luck." Sergeant Green headed over to the barricade to pull out second squad calling for two scouts on the platoon push.

As he left a Leopard snuffled forward, its main gun questing to the east. With a crash and a burst of flame a distant saucer flipped into the air. Mike noted that the TC was the German major and hopped onto the turret. He checked his energy levels but he was still at over twenty-five percent.

"Sergeant Green, call for a general energy and ammo check. Redistribute ammunition and check on the engineers' progress. See if you can raise higher for some evac for wounded—they can come in from out to sea through the secure vector. Push some troops into the building to the south and make sure this avenue remains secure."

He tried to think if there was anything he was missing, but he was so tired. He felt his eyes start to close as he stood on the tank and knew it was time for another stim.

"Michelle, another Wake-the-Dead and then get me General Houseman."

"You are about to exceed your maximum prescribed dosage."

"Just do it," Mike snapped, driven far beyond courtesy to a machine. "Order them throughout the platoon, we're not out of the woods yet."

"Yes, sir, General Houseman is on the line."

"O'Neal? What's the situation? We've lost contact with the Tenth." The general sounded upset.

"We have relieved them at this time, sir," said Mike, tapping a command to upload the data. "And have cleared their positions of Posleen. The other flanks are covered by the fallen scrapers. We have secured the intersection and created hasty barricades with the Tenth's support. We've, we've . . . retaken the position and are attempting to contact the other units at this time. We have sustained affordable casualties in the movement and engagement. What are your orders, sir?"

"Lieutenant," the general started and then stopped to clear his throat, "you just hold on there for a bit while some of those units get out of the buildings and then come on home. Now that you're in line of fire of the MLR you can call for limited artillery support. As you retreat we'll cover the road behind you in fire. Just hold there for a bit. Can you do that?"

"Airborne, General, we'll hold on here until ordered to retreat. Could we get some evac on the wounded, sir? Aircraft should have a clear zone out to sea and they can come into the boulevard for pickup. I've got one trooper in a bad way and the grenadiers are up to their necks in wounded."

"Hell yes, son, hold on." As Mike waited he noticed that the wall of the building seemed to be pulsing in time to his heartbeat. *What an odd sight,* he thought. He looked up through the deep clear water at the sky above him and took a breath of the cold, dry air from the regulator. The reef around him was alive with vibrant shades of yellow and red, unusual for such a depth. But the rapture of the dive enfolded him and he ceased to analyze the situation, just let the time flow over him, spending each second as if it were eternity. Lieutenant, dustoff is on the way. O'Neal? Specialist is this radio working? Yes, sir, we've got his carrier wave, I think he's there, sir just not answering. Okay, *O'Neal! Wake up!*

"O'Neal! Answer me!"

"Yes, sir, sorry sir!" Mike snapped back to the bitter reality with a shock.

"Are you okay?"

"Fine, sir, couldn't be better. I'm just fine, sir. Just fine." Mike's head swiveled from side to side, trying to reacquaint himself with the situation. The lack of normal input, the feel of a breeze or the smell of the battle, made the situation even more unreal. He felt that he was sinking into an electronic simulation and tried to remember which one it was. The German major was staring at him with a blank expression.

"O'Neal!" snapped the general, sensing that the lieutenant was drifting again. "Don't you crack on me now. Get those units back here then I'll give you a break, but don't lose it in the middle of a battle. Can you get some rest?"

"I'll be fine, sir, really. All of us are a little tired. And I think I overdid the stimulants."

"You can't crack, son. If one of your troops loses it it's one thing but if the commander cracks all hell's out for noon, you of all people should realize that. Get some shut-eye if you can, even a few minutes would help."

"Yes, sir. I'll try," said Mike, taking a deep breath. The wall started pulsing again.

"Now get to work."

"Yes, sir. Work. Right. Out here, sir."

✧   ✧   ✧

Mike knew that part of the problem was the suit, so he popped
the helmet. The overwhelming stench of Posleen dead assaulted
his senses and he gagged for a moment.

"*Er ist eine Geruch, nicht wahr?*" said the German major.

"*Ja, er sind.* Sorry, but without the suit closed it's hard to
keep up with the translation and I don't speak much German.
Do you know English?"

"Yah, I was assigned to an American Armor unit as a junior
officer," the major answered with a distinct English accent. "Major
Joachim Steuben, by the way, pleased to make your acquaintance."

"Likewise, sir. I was just talking to General Houseman. If I
may suggest a course of action?"

"Certainly, *Leutnant.*"

"If you could hold here until we start getting the other units
extracted. Then as units come on line we could replace your unit
with the relieving unit. My platoon will cover the rear as we
retreat along the boulevard. General Houseman stated that we
could be covered by artillery as we pulled back to the MLR, so
my platoon should be enough."

"Sounds like a good plan, *Leutnant.* But how are we going
to fight through to the MLR?"

"Hmm, well when the first unit comes up of sufficient size,
one or the other, yours or theirs, could, with my platoon, push
the line through to the MLR, placing blocking forces at the intersections and patrolling the building fronts. My platoon would, I
submit, remain in a mobile supporting role. Once all the units
were out we would pull back with the last unit."

"I agree with this plan, *Leutnant.* Now, can I make a recom-
mendation?"

"Of course, sir."

"Get some sleep. You look like death warmed over. I have told
off my unit to get some rest as possible. You should do as well."

"If the major will permit the liberty," Mike chuckled, "the
major doesn't seem so hot his own self."

After obviously struggling for a moment with the idiom, Major
Steuben laughed. "Well, I'm going to sit in this comfortable seat
for a bit and if I happen to drift off I'm not going to feel remiss.
After I ensure everything is secure."

"Yes, sir, well I'm going to go make a quick check of my positions and then, if I am still for an unusually long time you can

draw your own conclusions." Mike flipped the major a sketchy salute, resquelched his helmet and bounced over to the barricade.

"So, Sergeant, what's the word?" he asked Sergeant Green as the latter leaned against the rubble wall, rifle pointed downrange. The only fire was a distant hammering from inland on the MLR. It was as quiet as Mike had heard it since the first moment of contact.

"The Posleen don't seem to want to come right back, sir," answered the NCO. "They're retreating along both boulevards now and infiltrating to the east and north. They may be pulling back from the MLR as well; those units are reporting less activity. They seem to be backing far off from us; I guess we really scared the shit out of 'em.

"The engineers will be here in about five according to their last ETA. They ran into a couple of Posleen, but nothing the team couldn't take care of. Second squad is in contact with the Frogs and they're moving back. There's a French general still in command but the unit apparently is down to about a brigade. I passed on the plan for them to relieve the Germans and they're okay with that.

"Duncan is trying to find a senior officer of the British right now. He reports that the Brits are pretty much trashed. They're having to clear out a lot of Posleen in the Brit sector that got through. Still no word on the American unit, Williams is out looking for them."

"By himself?"

"Yes, sir. He should be fine, he's slick as a cat. When he finds the Americans he'll contact us. He thinks maybe they're in better shape than the Brits 'cause there's less Posleen in the area."

"Right, well, fine then. Do you put a medal on him or court-martial 'im? Fine, great, fine, let him write his own damn letter."

"Sir?"

"What?"

"You're babbling," said the sergeant. "Can I make a suggestion?" he continued, diffidently.

"I know, get some rest. That's what everybody is saying. The general, the major, the sergeant. Before you know it the fuckin' privates are gonna be coming up. 'Lieutenant O'Neal, you need to get some rest,'" he concluded in an annoying little kid's voice.

"Yes, sir, we should be able to get you up in time if anything happens. Let's go siddown over by the wall, sir." The platoon sergeant turned the lieutenant with a tactful hand on his shoulder and led him to a block of masonry along the wall. There he pushed him to a sitting position and patted him on the shoulder. "Just catch a quick nap, sir."

He had long experience of the stresses of leadership. A private just has to do his duty, follow the flow. He can often rest standing up or walking, his senses on alert but otherwise checked out. The leaders have to constantly be thinking, feeling, paying attention. They have to be running around and motivating. It eats them up and the higher on the chain the harder it is. But junior leaders rarely conserve themselves and burn out faster. Eventually they learn. Or they don't and find an easier profession.

"Okay, Sar'nt, okay. Oh, put the platoon on thirty percent stand down and, and, umm..." Mike trailed off. He knew he had forgotten something but it just wouldn't come.

"Yes, sir, we'll take care of it." Sergeant Green stood by the officer until he was sure he had gone to sleep, the depletion of the constant strain of command as sure as any drug. "AID, is he asleep?"

"Yes, Sergeant."

"Okay, leadership push. Squad leaders, put your troops on thirty percent stand down, one third on guard, the other two out, and I want you O-U-T, asleep, not playing fuckin' spades! Sorry second, we'll let you get some sleep when you get back. Scouts, divvy it up between you. First and third squad leaders, turn it over to your Alpha team leader and rest dammit! AIDs, administer Wake-the-Dead antidote and if the sleepers don't, report it to me. And tell your people to continue to prepare these positions, this can't last. Thirty minutes rest only then rotate. Any questions?"

"When do we get to pull out?" asked Sergeant Brecker.

"When the LT says so, anything else?" There were no further questions. Sergeant Green looked around trying, like his commander, to decide if there was anything undone. He considered telling the Kraut major what the situation was but the officer in question was oblivious, head cradled on the TC hatch and asleep. There were no Posleen in view on either boulevard, the occasional straggler marked by the hammer of a machine gun or grav gun, depending on whose reflexes were faster. He shrugged his shoulders and decided to take a walk around the perimeter.

Shortly after that the engineers got back, full of stories of their adventures and set up a charging station. Sergeant Green took the precedence of rank and then had the scouts come in one by one and recharge. There were four charging stations so he figured they would be able to fully recharge in about an hour. He ordered the engineers to set up a shunt and start charging the suits of the personnel who were asleep. Starting with the lieutenant.

As the first turnover of rest groups was occurring an FX-25 French Main Battle tank nosed out of the rubble of the human-occupied building, turned and sped to the intersection, grinding the Posleen pulp on the street to a finer slurry. Sergeant Green bounced over to it and waved for it to stop. A bare-headed captain occupied the TC hatch of the vehicle which had a long deep scar runneled down the left side. The captain bore a large bandage on the same side of his face. Sergeant Green thought there was probably a good story there. He saluted.

"Sergeant First Class Alonisus Green, 82nd Airborne Division, *Monsieur Kapitan*. I take it you're the first French unit?"

"Captain Francis Alloins, Sergeant, *Deuxième Division Blindèe*," · the captain responded and saluted with panache. "*Enchantè*. Yes, we're the first. We have many wounded, do we have to fight them out?"

"Well, sir—" Green's AID overrode the conversation with an incoming transmission.

"ACS 325th, ACS 325th, this is Medevac Flight 481, we need to know where to land."

"Medevac is inbound, sir," said the sergeant, gratefully. "You can take your wounded down to the water. If you could detach a unit to handle the medevac I'd appreciate it, we're really short-handed." Sergeant Green switched from external to the medevac frequency and started coaching in the birds.

"*Certainement*," agreed the captain, unaware that he had already been effectively dismissed by the NCO. "*Pardon*." He picked up his radio and barked rapid orders into the handset. As he did more FX-25s poked out onto the street, followed by APCs and support vehicles. A cavalry scout vehicle pounded down the boulevard and slid to a stop opposite the tank.

A tall and gangling general in camouflage descended from the scout vehicle, looked around and hitched his belt into a better position. He was immediately followed by a squad of heavily armed infantry who spread out to cover him. The captain jerked to attention and threw a parade ground salute. Sergeant Green, nettled, clanged a gauntlet into his helmet and left it at that.

"*Bonjour, Sergeant, bonjour!* I must say that I am extremely pleased to make your acquaintance," the general said, returning the salutes and then taking the sergeant's gauntlet into his hand and pumping it strenuously. "There were any number of times I was sure that I would not. And good day, Captain Alloins! Fancy meeting you here! How was the ride?"

"Simple enough, with the flanks secured for once, *mon General*," the captain said with a smile. He gestured grandly towards the suit of armor. "General Jean-Phillipe Crenaus, may I introduce to you Sergeant Alonisus Green of Confederation Fleet Strike."

"Yes, yes, I have already been apprised of Sergeant Green," said the general. "And where is the indomitable Lieutenant O'Neal?"

Sergeant Green wrinkled his eyebrows, an expression impossible to see beyond the blank mask of his helmet. Where had the general heard of Lieutenant O'Neal? "He's taking a nap, sir. He's wiped out."

"I'm sorry to hear that," the general boomed. "Sergeant Duncan assured me that he was made solely of steel and good quality rubber! It seems beyond the pale that he could require such a mundane thing as rest!"

Sergeant Green was beginning to realize that the general was one of those people that could only talk in exclamation points. Then he noticed the solemnity of his eyes and remembered that this was the general who had preserved his unit far more than any other in the battle. That spoke volumes for his ability. "Well, sir, sorry. But the LT is as human as you or I. Did Sergeant Duncan pass on the battle plan? And do you approve?"

"Yes," said the general. He looked around at the windrows of bodies with a mildly pleased expression then kicked a Posleen forearm out from under foot.

"I agree with one exception. I believe that I have the largest cohesive unit left. I insist that *Deuxième Blindée* should hold the intersection until the other units are past, although I agree that your ACS unit should maintain the final retreat. It is uniquely suited for it since it can, in extremis, exit through the buildings or for that matter over them." He smiled again at his little joke.

"Major?" asked the sergeant, tiredly, wrinkling his brow again.

"Fine by me," said the panzer major, "we're down to a short battalion after that last push by the Posleen."

"Excellent!" exclaimed the general, rubbing his hands together. Sergeant Green could not believe he had so much energy. "We can begin the relief within fifteen minutes. My unit will form up on the boulevard. We will continue to send the wounded to the seaward side to be evacuated by air. Sergeant, since you are the only one with effective communications, please ask your personnel to pass on the word to the other units to move the wounded forward as fast as possible."

Sergeant Green passed on the word and watched in bemusement as the intersection was rapidly and effectively invested by the French forces. The perimeter was pushed farther out and the rubble walls reinforced.

The exhausted ACS and panzers thankfully turned over their positions and dropped back to assembly areas. Soon, a continuous stream of medical choppers was shuttling to the seaside ramp, now cleared of Posleen by the simple expedient of dozering them into the sea. Sergeant Green told off first and fourth squads to help the Germans drive to the MLR.

The French general had decided he had enough troops to hold the intersections as well, so all the Germans had to do was reach safety. Sergeant Green monitored the nets as the reduced division organized itself and moved out. Within forty minutes after the first French XF-25 had appeared, all the Germans in the perimeter, the wounded, the hale and the dead were gone, by tank, truck, foot or helicopter and Sergeant Green decided it was time to trade places with his commander.

39

Andata Province, Diess IV
1037 GMT May 19th, 2002 AD

Az'al'endai, First Order Lord of the Po'oslena'ar, clenched his fists and gnashed his teeth as he fought a rising tide of te'aalan. His finest genetic product dead and his oolt'ondai, including that thrice-damned puppy Tulo'stenaloor, in full retreat! If these threshkreen thought to triumph they were sorely mistaken!

"All security oolt'ondai to the command ship," he barked into the communications grid as the oolt'os of his bodyguard looked on with adoring eyes. "The command ship lifts in five tar!" Let them try to face his just wrath as he swooped upon them in his oolt' Posleen. He stewed as the scattered battalions and their vehicles, including the Posleen tanks used for ship security, were reloaded into the vast dodecahedron. Thousands of normals and their God Kings filed into the cavernous holds packed with cold sleep capsules and all the machinery necessary to set up a Posleen civilization.

"I shall have the get of my enemies as thresh!" he snarled, switching from screen to hateful screen. "And the structures of my enemies shall burn beneath my claws. I shall reap the blood and sear the bone. They will burn and burn until the burning sends word to the demons of the sky that none shall oppose the A'al Po'oslena'ar!" The scattered lampreys, trapezoidal craft that attached to the facets of the command craft in space flight, were left with their own small security detachments as the vast ship lifted under anti-grav and ponderously thundered towards the fragile human lines.

Something painful was waiting beyond the veil that surrounded him and Michael O'Neal refused to face it. It waited with hungry

345

mouths to devour him and he fled down endless brightly colored metal corridors ahead of it. Wherever he turned it was there and it called to him with a seductive voice. Michael, wake up. Lieutenant O'Neal, wake up. Wake up, wake up, wake up. I'm sorry Sergeant, I can't get him to wake up.... All right. A sudden searing pain jerked him into wakefulness and was as quickly gone.

"What the hell was that?" he mumbled blearily.

"I applied direct pain stimulation to your nervous system," the AID answered nervously.

"Well, next time try shaking the suit or something, okay? That hurt like hell." He checked the time and shook his head. It would just have to do.

"Yes, sir."

He tried to rub his face and was balked by the suit. He almost popped the helmet and then thought better of it. The last time he had the helmet off the smell had hit him like a blowtorch. He could only imagine what it would be like after an hour in the hot Diess sun. He took a sip of liquid and Michelle substituted coffee. Unfortunately, it was the one thing the suits absolutely could not get right. It tasted like coffee-laced mud.

"Thanks," he muttered and sipped his mud; the caffeine was less strenuous to the system than the wake-ups would be. He did not want another hallucinatory experience right now. He stared around bemusedly at the scene of normal human activity. "You've been busy, Sergeant."

"Well, sir," said Sergeant Green with upraised palms, "that Froggie general is a real pistol. He just rolled in and organized. I can see now why his troops think he walks on water. He wants to see you ASAP, sir."

"Okay, get me up to date then rack out." Mike took another sip of mud and had Michelle replay all the sensor data since the battle at ten times speed. He was afraid he had missed stuff during his hallucinatory period. As the unit counters flickered on his screen he listened to Sergeant Green with half an ear.

"First and fourth are up helping the Krauts through to the MLR, sir. They're not having much difficulty, they're using some good deception techniques and the scouts are flanking them through the buildings and taking out the God Kings ahead of them as we go. We lost Creyton, though. I think the God Kings' targeting systems are learning about snipers. I told them to shoot and scoot since that.

"The Frogs are securing the boulevard as they move and the MLR is going to sortie and hold the last intersection. The German ACS unit inserted a company behind the Posleen in their sector, using the tunnels, and are tearing them up on that end of the MLR. Generally, the Posleen assault is in disarray but Corp doesn't expect that to last much longer."

He replayed some of the details at slower speed and confirmed a hunch. When he tagged the Posleen unit that had killed Specialist Creyton and ran it back, it was the Posleen battalion that just made it out of the nutcracker.

"Nice briefing," said Mike, following the movements of the particular battalion until all intelligence units lost contact with it.

"Thank you, sir," said Sergeant Green, pleased.

"Where'd you get that information?" Mike raised his eyebrow at his energy levels then nodded at the reason. He then noticed the engineers were still ministering to the sleepers, but they had also started a sleep rotation.

"Hey, I've been watching you for the last two days, sir. I told my AID to learn from yours and when I asked it for a briefing it told me most of it."

"Okay," said O'Neal with an unseen smile. "On to the French general."

"General Crenaus. Organized as hell, real friendly bastard but don't let his personality fool you, he's a pistol. And apparently Sergeant Duncan played you up to him real big. The general wondered that you had to sleep; he said he'd heard you were made of steel and rubber."

"Hah! Right now I feel like I'm made out of Jell-O and that stuff you find between your toes." Mike finally popped his helmet and took a whiff. The stink of Posleen was noticeably faded. Sergeant Green noticed his expression.

"When the engineers showed the Frogs how to get water, the general put some of his troops to work washing the Posleen out to sea, sir. For a while there it was getting pretty whiff out of the suits," the NCO admitted.

"*Formidablè.*"

"Huh? Sorry. Huh, sir?"

"Formidable."

"Yes, sir," the staff sergeant admitted. "That's General Crenaus in a word."

"And last but certainly not least, speaking of Sergeant Duncan?" Mike punched up Duncan's location and frowned.

"The Brits are just now reaching the Frog perimeter, sir. They're just going to be shuttled through to the MLR."

"And the American unit?" asked Mike, scanning back and forth for eagle icons. They were damned few and far between and all represented small units.

"There ain't an American unit, sir," said the sergeant, somberly.

"What?"

"Williams is reporting scattered survivors, quite a few of them, and they apparently were putting up a hell of a fight, but it's a mishmash of platoon- and company-size units, none of them the original force. There are even a few senior officers, but they're in command of companies and platoons made up of clerks. It's really confused, sir."

"Bit of a dog's breakfast. Okay, I'll send in the rest of the squad in two-man teams to roust out as many of the survivors as possible. When they get back, we'll pull out."

"Roger that, sir."

"Hit the rack. What's the schedule on the rest?"

"Umm, when first and fourth get back, they take up the defense and third and fifth rest, sir"

"Right, get some sleep."

"Yes, sir." The NCO's speech was starting to slur. He slumped on the block the lieutenant had vacated and was instantly asleep.

Mike contacted second squad and told them they had thirty minutes to round up all the stragglers and get them moving back to the intersection. Then he went to find the "*formidablè*" French general.

He found him in the former German command post, talking to Corp on the panzer's transmitter. Mike stood aside as aides scurried in and out with reports and orders. Surrounded by the babble of a functioning command post he felt out of place in his smoke-stained battle armor. Despite the rigors of their combat most of the officers and men of the command post were well turned out in neat if not crisp fatigues. Next to them his armor seemed rather shabby.

Yeah, but they'd be nestling fodder by now if it wasn't for us.

The general looked up and fixed him with a glance, "Lieutenant O'Neal?" he asked.

"Yes, sir. Sergeant Green said you wanted to see me."

"We've reports that the Posleen are massing. What's the ETA on those other units?"

"I told second squad thirty minutes then start falling back. As long after that as it takes, I suppose, sir." Mike's shrug went unnoticed inside the armor.

"And your estimate is?"

"One hour, total, sir. The American unit is shattered fragments. My men are going to have to go through with loudspeakers, effectively."

"Won't that make them a target?" interjected one French staff officer.

Mike flicked a switch and a hologram of a snarling panther's head was superimposed on the helmet. "One less Posleen more or less is what that'll mean, sir," he said.

General Crenaus laughed, "So, a product exactly as marketed! You are as fierce as your sergeant suggested, yes! Well, we need such in this hour! Come, let us talk." He gestured for Mike to precede him deeper into the building.

He stopped at a short distance from the command post. The area was near the deepest penetration of the Posleen in the panzer's sector. The walls were bullet pocked and torched, large holes blasted through them by 120mm cannon and hypervelocity missiles. Mike's feet ground drifts of shell casings under his thousand-pound armor. The general looked up at a gutted Marder AFV then turned and tapped Mike's chest.

"In here beats the heart of a warrior, Lieutenant O'Neal," he said seriously. "But warrior and soldier are not always the same thing. Do you have the discipline of a soldier or only the fierceness of a warrior?"

"I can take and give orders, sir," said O'Neal after a moment's consideration. "I consider myself a soldier. The aspect of the warrior is one that the current service tends to suppress, incorrectly in my opinion. Only a warrior can carry through when all around him are dead. There are many soldiers in the world, but battles hinge on the warriors."

"Then listen to this with your soldierly aspect, Lieutenant," the general said with a grim expression. "If the Posleen come back in strength, we are going to pull out, whether the American unit is here or not."

It was much what he had expected but less than he hoped.

"Did you talk to General Houseman about that?" asked the lieutenant, carefully.

"It was his order. One that I fully concur with by the way. The main line needs my troops relatively intact. When the Posleen come back they will be here to stay; they won't be frightened off again. The Corp needs my division in support of the line. We cannot stay here and sacrifice ourselves on the altar of courage. Do you understand?" The general looked at the blank face of the armor and wondered what the face inside was expressing.

"Yes, sir. I understand." Mike paused and tapped controls on his forearm. After a moment he continued. "Sir, I and my platoon will remain here until I feel the position is untenable."

"Very well, I concur. I hope that the situation never comes to pass."

"*Mon General!*" one of the French staff officers shouted, gesturing with a radio microphone.

General Crenaus walked back to the command post, trailed by Mike.

"General, there is a transmission from one of the Medevac helicopters. They report a large vessel of some sort coming towards us over the city."

"Give it to me," said the general, snatching the microphone from the staffer. "This is General Crenaus, who is this?"

CWO4 Charles Walker liked nothing better than flat out, low-level flying. Crank a Blackhawk or OH-58 and take it down to the deck on maximum overdrive. Pissed the hell out of maintenance personnel and commanders were never really happy about it, but when you came down to cases, it was the best place to be in combat. As the current situation proved.

There was a small gap in the coverage by the Posleen and it was on the deck in a twisting course into the landing slot the ground-pounders had cleared out. There was insufficient room to turn around and go back out to sea, so to land the helicopter was required to spool up to the top of the building and swivel around and drop sharply down to a landing. Then the broken bodies of the armored cav troopers would be loaded and you went back out on the deck. There were over a hundred helicopters from the different contingents operating and the miracle was that no crashes had occurred. As Walker made the last low-level bank and turned into the climb up to the roof his right seat, a CWO1 he had never met before today, let out a gasp.

"What the hell is that?" he asked gesturing with his chin.

Warrant Officer Walker looked up and to the left. In the distance, it was hard to determine how far because the perspective was distorted, a gigantic multisided ship was rising. It echoed a tantalizing memory for a moment then it came to him. In his younger days he had watched a Dungeons and Dragons game going on in one of the junior officers' rooms; the vessel raising itself up in the distance looked identical to one of the game's oddly shaped dice. Black and pitted by... weapons. Oh, shit.

"Get the Frogs on the horn," he snapped. "I think they're about to have company." He poured power to the engines fighting into the climb as fast as he could. As his engine temperature started to increase he could only hope that his chopper would be too insignificant a target to matter.

His right seater was gabbling in the radio as he decided not to take the chance. He jinked hard right then left. In the back, the crew chief was preparing to open the troop doors. The sudden bank threw him across the cargo area and into the far door with a "whuff" of expelled air. He grabbed his tether line and started to hand over hand to a seat. Walker continued a hard swerving, sliding climb toward the top of the building.

Suddenly there was a wash of heat as a bolt of plasma passed through the space the helicopter had just occupied. Walker jerked the collective up and over and the Blackhawk was suddenly inverted and headed for the deck. His copilot yelled and tried to grab the controls as the abused crew chief in the back let out a scream but Walker flattened the bird back out practically on the deck. They had descended over a thousand feet in a pair of seconds.

"Call the French," shouted the concentrating warrant officer. "I am didee-mao! We can't crest that building and live. And if we can't crest the building we can't pull the wounded out. Therefore we are outta here!"

He felt like a shit to be leaving all those wounded behind but there was no way he would face whatever that was. He saw the other helicopters banking into the land, running for the cover of the seaside buildings, even if they had occupying Posleen. Better that than the battleship headed this way. In the distance those too far out to sea started to flare and die.

He cursed fate but there was nothing he could do. Even if he was riding a slick there was nothing he could do; there was nothing in the armory that could attack that thing and live. But finesse it? He thought about the caverns between the buildings, he thought about good times he'd had, he thought about stupid pride and arrogance and he pulled the bird into a hard bank.

"What the hell are you doing now?" asked his right seater. In the back the crew chief let out another "chuff" as he was swung on his line and slammed into a seat. This time he got a grip on it, climbed in and strapped down.

"We can extract down the secured boulevard to the MLR. We'll take fire briefly at the intersections but if we firewall it we might make it."

"*Might* is not a good answer!" shouted the copilot.

"There are wounded and we are going in for them, Mister. That is all there is to it."

"Fuck."

"That's 'Fuck, sir!'"

"Fuck, sir."

"You know the Coast Guard motto, boy?" asked the warrant officer after a moment.

"'*Semper Paratus*'?" the right-seater asked, confused.

"Not that one, the unofficial one. 'We gotta go out, we don't have to come back.'"

"Oh. Yeah." The junior warrant nodded his head with a resigned expression. "Roger that, sir."

"Excuse me, sirs?" said the crew chief on the intercom.

"Yes?"

"Just what the hell was that?"

"That's a command ship," said Mike, into the silence after the transmission, "what's called a C-Dec, a command dodecahedron. Holds about 1,200 of a Posleen brigade's best troops, most of the brigade's armor, heavy space weapons, interstellar drive, thrusters, foot-thick armor, the works." He paused and looked around at the Gallic staff. "That, gentlemen, is what we Americans call the whole shootin' match, meaning that the battle is effectively over. When it comes overhead we don't have a thing to stop it."

The building shuddered as a plasma cannon struck its roof and a shower of massive debris fell in the street. A French trooper was crushed under a section of plascrete as the vehicles in the street were covered. In the distance Mike heard the flutter of a suicidally brave medevac pilot coming into the landing zone. Mike figured his chances of making the turn at the intersection alive to be about one in ten. If he wasn't hit by debris he would be hit by the C-Dec's guns as it came overhead.

"I think this counts as overwhelming strength," Mike said with a whimsical smile. "Start pulling out, General. We'll help the Americans go to ground. We might make it for a while on the E and E. We'll get by."

"*Oui . . . Merde!* Well, as they say: '*Aucun plan de bataille ne survit contact avec l'ennemi.*'"

Mike laughed grimly to hear the quote coming from a French general. "And that is in the original Klingon, right?"

"*C'est qui?*" asked a puzzled aide as the general laughed as well. The moment of levity was brief.

"Second squad!" Mike said into his transmitter. "Sergeant Duncan!"

"Yes, sir, we've gathered the survivors we can find. What the hell was that?"

"That was the end of the world." Mike looked around and snatched up a French backpack. Ignoring the protests of the owner he started dumping the contents out as he headed for the building entrance. He stopped by the entrance to the operations center and relieved a French guard of a piece of equipment. At the first angry protest, the general waved the guard to silence. Mike never even noticed.

"Start taking the survivors downstairs. Get as deep as you can. We have a serious problem here, ask your AID about it, I don't have time. Sergeant Green?"

"Yes, sir," came the sleep-slurred voice, "I'm up."

"We've got company."

"Yes, sir. What are we gonna do about it. And what is it?"

"It's a command ship, a C-Dec. You're gonna take the platoon up on the roofs and play laser tag with it. Hopefully you can keep it off the MLR for a little while. Leave me one HVM launcher, no . . ." He thought for a moment. "What did we do with that combat shuttle?"

"It's still there as far as I know," said the sergeant in a puzzled voice.

"Okay, get moving. Take two squads and head for the roofs.

Spread out and move away from the MLR and away from the shuttle. Take the C-Dec under fire and shoot and scoot. Keep dodging. When you have lost twenty-five percent of the platoon, or the C-Dec is ignoring you, retreat. Although if we can't stop it I don't know what will."

"What about a nuke, sir?"

"It's able to destroy virtually any delivery system we have available," said the officer as he stepped outside.

"Okay. What are you gonna do?"

"I'm headed for that shuttle," said Mike as he engaged his antigrav and shot straight upward.

"What's there, sir?" asked Sergeant Green as he organized the platoon into two teams.

"A world of hurt."

Mike leapt across the roofs at full speed with his deception systems on maximum. Besides the camouflage hologram, now carefully mimicking the color and texture of the rooftop, a modification of the personal protection field warped radar and subspace detectors around him while a tiny subspace field reduced movement turbulence and sonic signature. The host of deceptions appeared to work like a charm; the C-Dec was content to concentrate its fire on the human-occupied building.

The roof of the Dantren megascraper was now a twisted mass of slagged metal and plascrete while the fallen buildings to either side looked like a Salvador Dali painting. The beams of plasma were now blasting at the MLR and the retreating French unit. Mike saw the suicidally brave Dustoff blasted from the sky trying to make the turn at the intersection and he decided not to look back after that.

The C-Dec had totally ignored the shuttle and when he reached it Mike found out why; the Posleen had been there and the interior was wrecked. The remaining weapons and ammunition were scattered or destroyed, craters in the building roof showing where the Posleen had detonated ammunition in their haste.

Mike ignored the weapons and headed for the drive section. Lifting a deck plate he keyed in a code on an inconspicuous pad. A drawer opened with a susurrant whoosh and Mike lifted out the heavy canister within. He put it in the French backpack and started adding grenades from his suit, its cavernous ammunition storage disgorged two hundred and eighty-five. To this he added all of his magazines and all the ammo on the shuttle that was handy. He carefully duct-taped his last grenade to the outside. In the end he had one hundred kilos total weight, at least .005 percent of which was pure antimatter.

When he exited the shuttle he checked on the C-Dec. It had, indeed, reversed course and was pursuing the platoon, dropping lower for better targeting. Following orders, the platoon was heading away from the MLR with the squads widely spread. They were moving, uncamouflaged, across the surface of the roofs as fast as they could and keeping up good fire. The lines of silver lightning drifted across the face of the black cube and fire erupted behind them. All of their fire was scoring and he could see two weapons positions that were damaged. They looked like flies leading a horse with their stings. Mike checked for Sergeant Green's beacon but it was gone. Next he checked the casualty graph and noted that the squads had already exceeded twenty-five percent loss, but they seemed content to continue to picador their massive bull. This was a win/lose proposition, the damage from a space weapon would rarely be wounding. *C'est la guerre*: you join the Army to die and it will send you where you can die.

Mike checked his own energy levels, shrugged his shoulders and began chasing after the retreating C-Dec, backpack over his shoulder.

He turned on the run adjustment and his legs began to blur. The massive cube filled the sky above him as he approached. With three final strides he bounded into the air and floated up under anti-grav. The weapons and detectors of the Posleen ship were designed to fight space weapons. There were lasers that could pick a hypervelocity missile out of the air. There were plasma cannons that could slag mountains. There were detection systems that could spot enemy ships at a light-hour. None of them were designed to spot a single armored combat suit.

The cloaking holograms and subspace suppressors, the radar and lidar deceptors, carried him inside the space-designed defenses and to the very skin of the space cruiser. He clamped his gauntlet to the skin of the ship high on one facet and hand over handed upward to the nearest large weapon position.

"Michelle, all-frequency override broadcast," he said softly. He clamped the backpack to the skin and then double-clamped it for security. "Maximum priority. Nuclear detonation, thirty seconds. Slug current coordinates."

"Yes, sir."

He swung outward on his clamp and hooked his finger through the pin of the old-fashioned grenade he had "borrowed" from the French guard. He was completely out of timers or, for that matter, detonators.

"Michelle."

"Yes, Lieutenant."

"It's been nice working with you," he said, watching the timer creep downward.

"Thank you, sir."

"Put that letter to my wife on the net, dump your guts to command, and please tell the platoon to seek shelter. Its work here is done."

"Already done, sir. Nuke warning protocols specify an immediate data dump. It has been nice working for you. May the Alldenata keep you."

"Thanks." Suddenly he felt a series of detonations through the skin of the ship as a line of flechette ricochets moved towards him. His armor slammed into the skin of the ship and rattled like a pea in a pod. He felt the inertial damping system fail.

"*Michelle?*" he shouted as the suit systems cut out without warning. Only a viselike grip prevented the metallic gauntlet on his right hand from slipping off the clamp handle. The ship began to drop sharply, turning the face he was attached to towards a mass of Posleen pouring onto the roofs below.

"*Warning, warning!*" said a slurred metallic voice, faintly familiar, the suit entity, his own gestalt, "*Suit failure imminent! Suit failure imminent! AI-D damage: one hundred percent, Environmental damage: one hundred percent, Power systems: Emergency backup. Power system failure twenty seconds!*" Posleen rounds continued to erupt around him and he felt a tearing sensation in his abdomen as an HVM smashed into the ship only yards away. He knew it was now or never.

"I love you, hon," he said and let go of the clamp; the grenade pin went with him. As he swung out and down he manually overrode the suit systems and set the suit to maximum inertial protection. It was a long shot but what the hell.

Az'al'endai pounded the console and hooted in triumph.

"These threshkreen burn beneath my talons!" he shouted, looking around toward Arttanalath, his castellaine. The diffident kessentai shook his sauroid head from side to side as the view-screens filled the room with the light of the descending primary.

"You drive them too hard, Kenellai. These thresh are tricky as the Alld'nt."

"Nonsense," snorted the brigade commander in derision. He fluttered his crest and shook his head. "You are an old toothless fool." He triggered another blast from the plasma primaries at the dodging suits. It was like fighting fleas with a blowtorch, but it got two of them.

"Look how these metal-clad thresh burn! They are like stars in the night sky!" Most of the stations in the control room were empty but that was normal; the ships were designed to be run by no more than a single God King. The fact that the battle depended almost entirely on the decisions of quirkily programmed computers never crossed the mind of the kessentai. How the ship ran was how it ran. They no more understood it than a chimpanzee understands television. It works, I can change the channel. *Voilà*.

"Az'al'endai!" came the cry from a side channel. It was that thrice-damned puppy, Tulo'stenaloor.

"What do you want?" raged the commander. "First you kill my eson'antai, then you destroy my oolton', then you flee, then you—"

"Az'al'endai, shut up!" roared the impatient battalion commander. "You have a metal threshkreen on the side of the oolt' Posleen! He must be up to no good. We are firing at him now!"

"What?" shouted the suddenly confused ship commander. "Uut Fuscirto! Where are those detectors?" He hunted the panel in front of him, then realized that the control was at one of the other positions. But which one?

"Cursed Alld'nt equipment!" he shouted, hurrying from position to position. At the third he recognized the symbols he sought and slammed his talons into the appropriate buttons. The readouts made him gasp. He slapped the communicator button at the detector station.

"Tulo'stenaloor! Fire! Kill it! It has an antimatter bomb!"

He ran back over to the primary controls, pushing the babbling castellaine aside, and began to turn the oolt' Posleen toward Tulo'stenaloor's oolt'ondai. As he did so another beacon began to squawk and at its cry of doom he slammed the course downward in a panicked reach for safety.

✧　　✧　　✧

Lieutenant O'Neal's suit was buffeted aside by the descending ship, the massive structure descending faster than the acceleration of Diess' light gravity. The buffet was the last thing Mike felt, as the fragmentation grenade went off in near simultaneity.

The grenade initially caused massive failures on the part of the grav-gun ammunition and the suit grenades. The rifle ammunition used a dollop of antimatter as its propellant charge. Under normal use a small energy field, similar in design to the personal protection field, would reach out and shatter the miniature stabilization field that prevented the antimatter from contacting regular matter. Another field held the antimatter away from the breech of the weapon so that it only contacted the depleted uranium teardrop. When the antimatter touched the uranium, the two types of matter were instantly converted into a massive outpouring of energy.

This energy was captured in a very efficient manner and used to accelerate the uranium round down the barrel of the grav-gun.

When the conventional French grenade went off, it shattered a large number of the antimatter stabilization fields immediately around it. Each of these fields contained an antimatter charge equivalent to two hundred pounds of TNT. There were several hundred in the backpack.

The rupturing of the rifle ammunition in turn smashed the antimatter grenades. The grenades actually held a smaller charge than the rifle rounds, but the casing provided much more in the way of shrapnel and that proved providential.

The canister from the shuttle also contained antimatter. Quite a bit of it.

The ubiquitous substance was the primary energy source for all high-energy systems in the Galactic Federation. In the case of the combat shuttles it was the source of choice because of its high mass-to-energy ratio. The shuttles not only had to have an energy source that could carry them for short interplanetary hops, but also one that could fuel their terawatt lasers.

The canister, however, unlike the grenades and ammunition, was heavily shielded against damage. The possibility of penetrating damage that reached the bottle was anticipated by the designers. The bottle was not only made of a heavy plasteel similar to the armored combat suits, but also had a heavy-duty energy shield around it.

When the first ammunition detonated, the rapid explosions, effectively one expanding nuclear fireball, were shrugged off. Likewise the initial explosions of the grenades; the explosive force simply was too weak to destroy the integrity of the well-designed antimatter containment system.

However, the grenades were detonating practically in contact with the bottle, and their iridium casings were accelerating at nearly half the speed of light.

The first few bits of molten forged iridium shrapnel plastered themselves to the outside and sublimated under the expanding fireball. But by a few microseconds after the explosion of the conventional grenade thousands of forged particles were bombarding the outside of the canister. Under the assault, first the outer shielding, then the plasteel armor, and finally the inner shielding failed.

At which point nearly a quarter kilogram of antimatter detonated, with an explosion to rival the Big Bang.

The buffet of the suit occurred as the God King commander performed his last panicked course change. The course change placed Mike's suit slightly around the corner from the antimatter limpet mine and above it when it detonated.

The first few microseconds as the rifle ammunition and grenades detonated saw a number of occurrences. The ship was rocked backwards and up, slamming into the suit again. The wash of the initial explosion destroyed the plasma cannon that had been firing at the rapidly retreating suits permitting the last few survivors of the platoon to make good their escape. And the buffet of the explosion slapped the ship commander into the controls, taking him out of play.

The second impact also slapped Mike into unconsciousness. At that action the biotic-gestalt reacted and injected him with Hiberzine; once the user was out of play the gestalt could make its *own* tactical judgments. It analyzed the situation:

1. A nuclear weapon was detonating in close proximity to its ProtoPlasmic Intelligence System.
2. The likelihood of the survival of its PPIS was low.
3. Termination of the PPIS would result in the termination of the gestalt.

This analysis was suboptimal. Immediate remedies for the analysis were in order.

Thus, when the initial wash of energy swirled around the edge of the cruiser, it struck a set of armor that was rapidly becoming as insubstantial as a feather. The suit was nearly thirty meters away from the ship, nearly inertialess, being flooded with oxygen, and outward bound at high acceleration when the main packet detonated. Under the circumstances, it was the best the gestalt could do.

The explosion tore the space cruiser in half, vaporizing the facet against which the material had been placed and blasting two separated pieces of ship away from each other. One was blasted sideways into the nearest megascraper, which was already coming apart from the nuclear wave front. It slammed into the top of the mile-cube building and smashed half of it to the ground, taking out two more buildings as well before it finally ground to a halt.

The other section of the massive ship was blasted nearly straight up. It rose on the edge of the mushroom cloud, a black spot of malignance on the edge of the beautiful fireball, and finally curved back downward to smash into another Posleen-held megascraper.

Mike's suit was near the former section of ship. Initially shielded by the downward hurtling half of the space cruiser, it was soon caught on the edge of the main nuclear fireball and rapidly accelerated to over four thousand miles per hour. The suit skipped across two megascraper roofs, where the legs were scraped off, and finally *through* a seaside megascraper, where it lost one arm. The remnant cuirass and helmet came out of the megascraper on the back side of the wave front and skipped several times on the roiled ocean. Finally the bit of detritus slowed enough to enter the water and settled beneath the waves in two hundred feet of water.

An armored combat suit cost nearly as much as a combat shuttle, and even the most damaged suit held some residual value. When the suit was settled in its watery grave, the final salvage beacon, installed at the absolute insistence of the Darhel bean counters, began its plaintive bleat.

Either the bureaucrats were prescient or they were idiots. The SEALs attached to the expeditionary force had yet to decide which. When they were ordered to Diess, at the last possible moment, no one could tell them why. Since SEALs are used for a variety of purposes besides covert strikes, it could have to do with virtually anything. They could be there for explosive ordnance disposal. They could be there for cross training foreign forces. They could be there to investigate the Posleen rear area by seaborne insertion.

As it turned out, they were doing a booming business in salvage.

The nuclear explosion the week before had blasted all sorts of things out to sea. Besides various bits of reusable Indowy equipment, the armored combat suits were the most ubiquitous, their beacons calling for pickup in a most depressing way. Of the fourteen that had been recovered, only four had survivors.

This one was a sure write-off. The plasteel looked *cooked,* portions of the metal had turned blue from the nuclear blast. One arm and the legs were missing and a worm was struggling to fight its way past the biotic seal over a protruding bit of burnt brown flesh. About the only part that looked intact was the head, torso and abdomen.

"Man," said the team leader over the underwater communicator, "this guy got hammered. Check 'im out, Spock." He brushed a questing siphonophore off his wet-skin, the delicate creature disappearing in a luminous cloud.

The PO tech kicked over to the head of the suit and attached a lead. The hastily cobbled together device sent a pulse for update to the suit's final distress center. The readout came back slowly.

"This is that lieutenant they've been lookin' for, sir," said the petty officer to the background of bubbling air. He patiently waited for a condition update. "The AID is cooked, and most of the environmental. I don't think they're gonna get much ... *Holy shit!"*

40

Andata Province, Diess IV
1324 GMT June 24th, 2002 AD

Mike swallowed, "A month?"

"Yep," said General Houseman, "you've been in the body and fender shop over a month and you'll be here for a while yet. It took them two weeks to do a proper number on the radiation damage alone."

"What's happened to the expeditionary force? On Diess?" *My platoon?* he wanted to say.

"Well, the C-Dec blew up quite spectacularly and did a number on a large section of the city. We sortied in the aftermath. The Posleen weren't able to move through Ground Zero and we used that terrain obstacle to our advantage. Then, holding those positions, we got the Indowy to build us an abattoir," he smiled grimly. "Then we slaughtered those sorry bastards."

"Would you care to be more specific?"

"Do you know what murder holes are?" asked the general, holding a cup of water with a straw up for the lieutenant to drink from. His newly grown arm was still weak.

"Like in castles? Holes to pour oil in the entrances?"

"Burning oil and stick spears through, yes. Towards the end of the castle period and into the twentieth century they used a different technique.

"Just inside the main gates would be a field for sorties to form on. Occasionally the enemy got through the first gates. The walls on either side of the sortie field would be gun ports, hundreds of them. The enemy would pack onto this field and it would become a killing field; the origin of the term, by the way.

363

"A First Division officer managed to develop a relationship with a high-ranking Indowy. With this Indowy's help we converted the boulevards behind the MLR into killing fields, two buildings deep. Then we pulled back into them.

"The Posleen came down the boulevards in their normal swarm and the Corp opened up from either side. The boulevards were plugged by ACS in concrete bunkers and there were thirty-foot-high walls on either side. Snipers with fifty calibers along the fifth story just to engage the God Kings. It was hell.

"Hardly any of the Posleen made it to the ACS positions. We set up two boulevards that way and had all the others blocked and supported. The Posleen just kept coming and coming until there were hardly any left and those few leftovers turned tail. We sortied again and pushed them back to their landers where they boarded and left—those that survived the rout. We recovered over seven thousand landers, Lampreys and C-Decs that were left behind."

"You mean we won?"

"Yep," said the general, sadly. "As the poet said, it was a famous victory; we only lost the better part of seven divisions to achieve it," he concluded, shaking his head angrily.

"But, there is general agreement that the turning point was the extraction of the armored divisions and the destruction of the C-Dec. You have a few 'colored pieces of ribbon' coming your way." He slid a blue box across the covers. "That's the first to be approved, besides the purple hearts; it's a theater decoration at my discretion. Congratulations, your first Silver Star, wear it in good health.

"That's just for rallying the survivors of the battalion; I can imagine what they're going to come up with for the other stuff. By the way, the rest of the personnel under Qualtren have been recovered—which was quite a job—and Captain Wright says, 'Hello.'"

Mike solemnly picked up the box. "Wiznowski?" he said and looked up.

The general nodded his head. "I'll take care of him and Sergeant Green."

"Thank you, sir. Can I have another AID? And is Michelle's personality center available for download?"

"There's a new AID issue in your drawer." The general paused and looked slightly awkward. "The data dumps when the nuke warning went out meant that a lot of data was lost. I'm afraid that most of...well, the Darhel say that the personality programs couldn't be saved."

Mike looked stunned. "I told her to back up," he insisted.

The general had been briefed about this by a psychiatrist that he thought was frankly quackers. As it turned out the shrink was right; the officer who had sustained the word that he lost most of his platoon and three limbs in the battle was misting up over a goddamn computer program. Were all these Fleet Strike johnnies nuts, or what?

"The Darhel liaison told me that there was just too much lost in the scramble to back everything up. 'Non-vital' data was the last to be saved. By the time they got to backing up all the AID personalities the damage was already done." The general paused. By the shattered look on the lieutenant's face, something else needed to be said. "The Darhel worked for nearly a week before they gave up. I'm sorry."

The officer visibly pulled himself together. "It's okay, sir. Heck, it was just a program, right?" The officer squeezed his eyes shut and took a deep breath. "Is that all, sir?"

"Oh, a couple of points. You remember that memorable period where you checked out on me on the radio?"

"Yes, sir," answered O'Neal with a sheepish expression. It was the closest to a smile the general had seen on him yet.

"Well, we checked that lovely little pharmacy in your suits after it happened. You know that the 'Wake-the-Deads' are loaded into the suit, not produced by it, right?"

"Yes, sir," said Mike, wondering where he was going.

"Well, there was a little problem with the batch in your suit. And in most of the rest of the battalion's as well. The damn pharmacy company that produced it forgot to put in the Provigil, the 'anti-sleep' drug. All that was in it was the GalTech stimulant."

"Oh, God," groaned Mike. The Galactic pharmaceutical was ten times as powerful as methamphetamine. It was no wonder he had felt like a tomcat in a room full of mechanical presses. He was surprised his head had not rocketed through the top of the helmet.

"And, since they apparently loaded it by volume, you were getting a triple dose."

Mike put his hand over his eyes and shook his head. He finally grinned: "Well, sir, I guess that gets me off the hook anyway."

"Yep. Sergeant Duncan is up for a pretty fair award as well. He was leading the Americans back to the lines, after the detonation, when the first Posleen counterattack came in. We weren't ready for them and it would have been hairy, but he and a major from Eleventh Cav rallied the cav survivors and hit the Posleen on the flank. When those nuclear grenades of Duncan's started landing it broke them like a twig. It gave us a breather we really needed and it put some spine back in the cavalry."

"He's a damn good NCO," said Mike. "From what I heard he just never seemed to get a fair shake. He ought to get a promotion as well."

"I'll take care of it," the general concluded, with a nod of agreement to the lieutenant. "You're scheduled for a casualty lift day after tomorrow. Thanks for coming along, Lieutenant, it was a hell of a ride." The general leaned forward to shake the lieutenant's hand. "Good luck and Godspeed."

"I have been to the speed of God, sir," Mike intoned solemnly, "and I discommend it."

General Houseman patted him on his shoulder with a tiny smile and silently left the room.

Mike opened the box that so many had paid for and regarded his first medal for valor with an iron face. He was afraid there would be more.

> "Heroes occur because someone makes a mistake.
> We don't want any heroes today."
> —United States Army Battalion Commander,
> "Somewhere in Eastern Saudi Arabia,"
> February 15, 1991.

EPILOGUE

2118 GMT July 4th, 2002 AD
Orbit, Diess IV

Tulo'stenaloor gazed back at the receding planet and calculated all he had lost—better than half his oolt'ondai on the bloody retreat as the threshkreen pressed them hard, his oolt' posol, and his eson'antai. His net-granted fiefs were back in the hands of the green thresh; he had even lost his castellaine, who had followed him for over fifty years. He limped away in this claptrap oolt' posol, fit only for a scout, and if he could not find a oolt' Posleen to bind to he would be left in the system to be hunted down like an abat.

All in all if he never saw another gray-clad thresh or, gods forefend, a metal one, it would be far too soon. He caught a transmission from a wandering oolt' Posleen searching for oolt' pos. It spoke of a distant world, far from these hated thresh and the asa' endai seem reasonable. Whatever, a ride was a ride and the farther from this misbegotten star the better.

1428 GMT March 13th, 2002 AD
Ttckpt Province, Barwhon V

Mosovich raised his eyes and nose above the muck and peered around the clearing. The first rendezvous had been a bust, the AO covered with hunting Posleen. He had been holding position for two days awaiting pickup at the second and last rendezvous point and was about to give up. Twice Posleen patrols had swept

367

the area. He knew that the Himmit were about as courageous as mice; if they had a sniff of a hot LZ they were didee-mao and so much for Momma Mosovich's youngest.

His protein converter was gone along with his communicator. Already looking like a death camp survivor from malnutrition and vitamin deficiencies, there was absolutely no way he was going to survive another year until the AEF arrived. If the Himmit waved off he might as well just blow his brains out and get it over with. He dipped back down and began to breathe off a snorkel again.

Precisely on time he felt the muted rumble of a Himmit stealth ship transmitted through the muck. As he cautiously raised his head above the scummy surface, he sensed movement through the violet Barwhon mists.

Crap. That close. *If the fuckin' mules had held off two fuckin' minutes,* he raged to himself. *Maybe if I snuff 'em quick enough the Himmit will land anyway,* he mused doubtfully.

He raised the misbalanced Posleen shotgun to his shoulder and waited for a target. The rumble of the stealth ship continued to build and he felt amazement.

If he heard Posleen, the supernaturally effective detectors of the Himmit surely had acquired them. *Maybe Rigas is having a brave fit,* he chuckled grimly.

He raised the shot cannon out of the swamp and took up slack just as the scout shimmered into sight. The ramp dropped and two camouflage-covered figures darted out of the violet cover and pounded through the swamp towards it. Mosovich did not let shock slow him as he threw the shotgun over one shoulder and the cached bag holding a single surviving nestling over the other.

Mueller stopped long enough to take the bag and Ersin threw one arm under his shoulder as the three survivors lurched into the scout ship. It lifted out with a barely noticeable hum, the holographic distorters reengaged. All three sprawled to the floor in an untidy heap of mud and soldiery.

"Ironic, idn't it," Mueller gasped, spread eagle on the plasteel, violet mud and eel-leeches cascading to the floor. "Sometimes the diversion is the best place to be."

Ft. Indiantown Gap, PA Sol III
2242 November 15th, 2002 AD

Ft. Indiantown Gap, Pennsylvania was seeing a rebirth unlike any since World War II. Beyond the MP's shack Mike could see work crews in fatigues and civilian clothes erecting temporary quarters on Utility Road. He handed his orders to the MP along with his ID and waited blank faced as the VW muttered. The scars were nearly invisible now but he could still feel weakness even with the time in the ship gym and in numerous gyms since landing. He longed to get back into a suit and do some serious cranking, to hop on a motorcycle and just open it up.

It was taking the MP an awfully long time and he waved several cars past as Mike waited. O'Neal could see him talking animatedly on the phone and wondered what was up. No more receptions, please, no more hand shaking. No more banquets or speeches. *Just give me back a suit.*

Since his triumphant return, he had been showered with awards. When he complained that he just wanted to get back to preparing for the next battle, the PAO shit-head major who had been put in charge of him told him that the public needed a hero. He was the best available, so shut up and soldier.

The campaign on Barwhon dragged on, and the factors that made Barwhon a tough nut to crack—relative lack of relief, and high levels of resources for the Posleen to draw on—were magnified on Earth. The victory on Diess, the victory that required thousands of the Earth's finest soldiers, was being spun as the work of one man. No matter how he protested, no matter how he stressed the importance of teamwork, he knew better than to mention the problems of training; in his speeches, it always came out as "O'Neal, O'Neal, O'Neal."

And, in the "briefings" to senior officers—actually dog and pony shows for brass hats who wanted a good war story—when he pointed out the mistakes in training and doctrine they stopped being so friendly. He had yet to meet one senior officer on Earth that could find his ass with both hands. And now this.

He did not even know what unit he was reporting to. His orders just directed him to report to 555th Fleet Strike Infantry for duty. "The Triple-Nickle" was a separate regiment, ACS and even Fleet Strike, but it was the last one to be formed before the invasion. Last on the list for equipment and personnel, last on the list for duty. A crap regiment handed crap duties in World War II and inactive ever since. No regimental honors, no decent history, unsupported by other ACS.

And now receiving a lieutenant, battered and more than a little shocky, for duty. Duty, training and preparation. The next time he would be ready and so would the men he commanded. He swore that on the souls of his dead.

He had taken the time in the hospital, immediately after the general left, to start on the letters to the families. The information was sketchy on who exactly had been in the platoon. Sergeant Green and he had the only complete rosters. Sergeant Green had bought the farm and Mike never memorized his, depending upon the "late" Michelle to remember it for him.

He remembered the total well, fifty-eight. But the total that the survivors could remember only came up to fifty-five and he had never been able to reconstruct who those other three were. It ate at him. Three of his men, MIA and unknown soldiers. Was there anyone he should have written letters to?

Letters to mothers and fathers, letters to wives, letters to sweethearts. Who had come up with that masochistic custom? *Tell me that the Mongols personally told the wife that her husband would not be coming home? Well, yes, probably and then married them to keep them from poverty.* Probably the British, it was a properly masochistic tradition; their style if anyone's. Or maybe an early American officer, knowing that the congressman would be writing a letter to ask anyway and then the tradition started...

"Dear Mr. and Mrs. Creyton, I was your son's commanding officer when he lost his life and I wanted to tell you what a fine and honorable young man he was. He was covering the retreat of the German Panzer Grenadier...etc." Thirty-two letters. He was saved from writing three because they listed no next of kin. One of them was Wiznowski. *Well, I remember you, Wiz. Drink one for me in Valhalla. I'll be there shortly.*

"Sorry about that, Captain," said the MP, breaking Mike out of his daze. His expression was different. Mike saw the now-to-be-expected hero-worship, but there was something else. Mischief?

"We have to call in all the officers coming in under orders, to find out where they go. The units keep moving and we don't have the central processing facility set up yet. Anyway, Captain, the problem was that your orders had changed and they had to find the new ones."

"It's Lieutenant, Sergeant, and where do I get the new ones?"

"I wrote them down, Captain." He cleared his throat. "So much of paragraph 13587-01: 'O'Neal, Michael L., First Lieutenant USAR to report to the 555th Mobile Infantry, Fort Indiantown Gap, Pennsylvania, for duty.' Now to read 'Captain O'Neal, Michael L., Federation Fleet Strike assigned Bravo Company, 1st Battalion 555th Mobile Infantry, Fort Indiantown Gap, Pennsylvania, for purposes of assuming command.'"

"Damn!"

"Congratulations, sir!"

"Uh, thanks."

"Are you who I think you are, sir?"

"Yeah, probably," Mike shrugged.

"Is it as bad as they say, sir?" asked the MP, his voice lowered.

"Worse, Sergeant, worse," said Captain O'Neal, shaking his head. "It's dancin' with the Devil, Sergeant. An' the Devil's leading."

> E'en now the vanguard gathers,
> E'en now we face the fray—
> As thou didst help our fathers,
> Help Thou our host today.
> Fulfilled of signs and wonders,
> In Life and Death made clear—
> Jehovah of the Thunders,
> Lord God of battles, Hear!
>   —Kipling